SEPANG LOCA & OTHERS

Amelia Lapeña-Bonifacio

Sepang Loca
& Others

UNIVERSITY OF THE PHILIPPINES PRESS

DILIMAN • QUEZON CITY • 1981

PHILIPPINE WRITERS SERIES
LIKHAAN: Sentro ng Makathaing Pagsulat
U.P. Creative Writing Center

ISBN 0-8248-0768-5

Distributed outside the Philippines by the
University Press of Hawaii

BOOK DESIGN BY THE AUTHOR

First Printing
PRINTED IN THE PHILIPPINES
BY THE UNIVERSITY OF THE PHILIPPINES PRESS

To MANUEL, for the shared years

If that were to happen, if the enterprise should fail, you would be comforted by the thought that you had done everything in your power. In any case something would have been gained. The corner-stone would have been laid, the seed would have been sown. After the tempest some grain might perhaps sprout, survive the catastrophe, save the species from annihilation, and serve as grain seed for the children of the perished sower. The example of others can encourage those who only fear to begin.

Pilosopong Tasyo to Ibarra
in Jose Rizal's *Noli Me Tangere*

Acknowledgment

ACKNOWLEDGMENT is here made to the following magazines and publishers in which some of the literary pieces in this volume first appeared: The *Sunday Times Magazine, This Week Sunday Chronicle Magazine, The Literary Apprentice,* The *Panorama,* The *Philippine Collegian Literary Review,* The *International Magazine,* Row, Peterson & Company and The University of the Philippines Press.

The photographs reprinted here were taken by Mr. Kirby Brumfield for SEPANG LOCA; De Longe Studio in Madison, Wisconsin for ROOMS; Mr. Rodolfo San Diego for WALKING CANES AND FANS; and Mr. Raul Uyenco for THE SHORT, SHORT LIFE OF CITIZEN JUAN.

The three etchings *(Amihan, Mga Bulaklak, Prosisyon)* which appear in this volume were made by the author in an Art Workshop at the Museum of Philadelphia in 1970 and are reproduced in their actual sizes: 4 x 6 inches.

Preface

IT IS WITH SOME DEGREE of trepidation, nay reluctance, that I go back to the finished work which constitute this volume. As the playwright Lillian Hellman once wrote, "communion with what was ended is unhealthy for if you returned too often to what you had already done, you might come to like it and yourself too well or dislike it and yourself too much." I also agree with her that work of many years ago are as far away as childhood and that your chance was ahead and not behind.

Yet, time and again, to go back seems inevitable and the need to put together some of your work of many years back, a necessity. It appears that to pause for this task, vexing as it is, is an obligation a writer must face up to, just as he must pose for a photographer sent on an assignment or sit down to answer questions in an interview from a young writer in whom he sees his own beginnings. Possibly also, not to stand still so that one can be measured properly is to neglect what I am tempted to call, a periodic writer's checkup, an accounting to which a writer must submit himself, of his own free will, at least once in his lifetime. It is to provide the measuring rod in his early and flawed work against which his later maturing productions, if given time to flower, can be correctly assessed.

Actually, the more pressing reason is simply this, a time comes when a writer runs out of copies of his work to lend out to students who must be told, gently, that there are borrowing desks in libraries over which a yellowing periodical, dated so and so, if properly requested for, can be had for an hour or more or that with the convenience of a xeroxing machine, a facsimile of the work can be bought. The practicality of making available in a single volume some selected work then is the state devoutly to be wished. The choice which is the writer's may also say something of how he regards his own work besides making it easier for those who find the need to read them for a term paper (they are always a pleasant surprise to me) or for enjoyment (they delight me no end!). While some of my artist friends regard their having accomplished a work as a reward in itself, I feel rewarded only at the first sign of reaction to my work. I suppose that is the reason why I am partial to drama where this interaction is vital and direct. How long it will last is a question a writer would rather not ask, for if at least this interaction is kept alive during his lifetime, it is the one blessing he cannot be thankful for, enough.

The short stories, plays and others which are gathered for this first definitive volume of my work in English, were written within a span of two decades from 1951 to 1970. If anything, it represents quite a substantial period of commitment to a line of work, time enough for growth into womanhood, time enough to prove that one had willingly and consistently stuck to an activity which, as most of our critics have pointed out, is replaced by the business of making a living when the Filipino writer reaches age 30 or so. The first two short stories written in a fiction class under NVM Gonzalez as well as the eight others which are included in this collection are what I call fledgling stories. And I call them thus not only because of their subject matter but because the characters, themes and plots are part of my fledgling years in a difficult but highly creative and highly rewarding period of apprenticeship.

Between designing stage sets, book covers, posters, programs and invitations in the University of the Philippines and painting with the *Primitives,* I started writing in the short story form, with some promise I was told. I was described by one critic as the writer with "the greatest sensitivity" among the U.P. writers of the fifties. During that time, a course in fiction writing was offered for the first time at the University of the Philippines. The professor chosen to teach it was NVM Gonzalez. It was a fairly sizeable and very lively class where we learned about point of view, how to strengthen the plot, the hard task of rewriting, eliminating clichés, how to break into a good opening or a strong ending, etc. All that time, we were getting noticed by critics Francisco Arcellana, Armando Manalo and literary editor Johnny Gatbonton, these last two of the Sunday Magazine of the defunct *Manila Chronicle.* During that lively, friendly, competitive period of learning, we were being featured in Francisco Arcellana's essays, Manalo's literary column and being published in Gatbonton's section for fiction and poetry. "Death of a Baby" was the first short story I wrote for that fiction class. It was published even before the semester ended because NVM Gonzalez told me to polish it for Johnny. That was really quite something, being published and being paid a professional fee when you were only a sophomore in college, writing your first short story!

I wrote "The Bird and the Boy" for the same class and it promptly won the First Prize in the *Philippine Collegian* Literary Competition in 1952. It was also published by Johnny who liked the simple tale of a talking bird and a servant boy. (I am sure all of us young writers then would remember Johnny with some fondness be-cause he respected the fictionist and poet so well, never mixing their work with ads and giving them a generous spread of illustration.) After that Fiction Writing class came several other stories published in literary journals like *The Literary Apprentice* and The *Panorama,* etc. The last three short stories in this collection were written abroad, "The First Confession" published in the Sunday Magazine of the defunct *Manila Times,* was written in Madison, Wisconsin and "The Stairs" and "When the Innocent is Found Guilty, Part of the Native Land is Exiled" were written in Philadelphia. The last two are among manuscripts in my *To Be Published* files.

The middle section of this volume subtitled, "Tributes and Poems" consists of selected short essays beginning with "Sepang Loca" which I wrote in 1953 for a column, "From the Subsoil, Upward" as Literary Editor of the U.P. *Philippine Collegian.* I was twenty-two and full of self-righteous indignation and staggering idealism. It be-came the foundation for the play, predating it by about four years. Rereading these short essays now, I was struck by the one unifying theme of farewell in them, the heavy pall of death even, which is, I suppose, a morbid preoccupation of most young writers raised in the shadows of World War II. The tribute to my father was written just two months before he passed away suddenly but as one professor had commented then it seemed as if I knew he was going to die within that same year. The tribute to Professor Gabriel Adriano Bernardo although written in 1977 is included as the last essay in this section because he meant a great deal in my development as a writer.

The poems were snatches composed on pieces of paper, realities captured which marked by clumsy progress as a beginning wife and mother. They intruded during the times I washed countless dishes and pans, scrubbed the kitchen floor and bathroom tiles, sweated over the cooking, trembled when the baby had high fever, watched TV or read while my husband pored through piles of books for his doctoral examinations. They are on various subjects including my trips to museums, theaters, etc. I was surprised that they got some very enthusiastic applause during a poetry reading program at the U.P. but it could be that its reader who had since brought them to Northwestern University for her Oral Reading entrance examination is an excellent reciter of poems.

The plays included here are the only five plays I have written in English. "Sepang Loca" (1957) is my first play and "White Holocaust or A Pacific Playright's Protest against the Bomb" (1969-70) is the fifth. However, it was during the premiere performance of *The Short, Short Life of Citizen Juan* (1968-70), published by the University of the Philippines Press in 1971, that I resolved to write my plays in Pilipino.

It may be pertinent to mention that I was out of the country through several years when so many social, political and economic upheavals were taking place and could write *Citizen Juan* only from the rumblings which echoed from letters, news clippings, newspapers and magazines which our joint families mailed to us faithfully. The play had an excellent production but somehow having projected a very relevant, compelling national malaise, I felt the embarrassment of having forced an alien tongue on my own people whose grief can be expressed most privately, most compellingly in the language they were born with. Since then, I have sorted out my own feelings: that drama, being the most national of all literary arts, demands nationality, craves nationality, connects instantaneously to nationality and thrives in nationality. I think what I mean is the identification of realities of language, traditions, aspirations and national purpose.

What propelled me to write "Sepang Loca" as a play was a playwriting competition at the University of Wisconsin at Madison during my first year as a Fulbrigth Smith-Mundt scholar there studying Theatre Design. I entered it in the contest where it competed with some forty or so entries submitted anonymously by graduate and undergraduate writers. I was interested in getting a play staged on the horseshoe stage of the experimental U.W. PLAY CIRCLE which was part of the prize aside from the prize money, because I was trying to learn stage designing and I thought I would learn more if

I tried writing for the theatre too. *Sepang Loca* could have won First Place. Professor F. G. Cassidy of the Department of English at University of Wisconsin and one of the final judges, wrote of it:

> This play has real character as a play (drama) and as a show (spectacle). It rings true in its overall depiction of simple folk; their language and action seem real and are sympathetic. The emotional situation both of the community together and of the Son, the Father and Mother, and of the figure of Sepang Loca; and the basic dedication to life and submission to death; all are genuine and moving. Technically, the story is handled with skill. The exotic scene; the 'frame' of the new road sweeping the past away; the lights, the bodies, the plangent antiphony of the dancing women would all go well on the stage. This is to me clearly the best of the group of eight (finalist) plays. It has real skill, and a good deal more originality and freshness than its only competitor, *Night of Mourning*.

However, the playwright Ronald Mitchell, a professor of drama voted it NO RANK which propelled it from its 1st position to 3rd place. On his judgment sheet, he commented, "18 characters and 3 scene changes, this playwright should be taught economy!" I was so upset with his view that I asked to design the sets on their "shoestring" budget (I used strings for the sets) to show it could be done. My greatest triumph was to have Prof. Mitchell apologize to me after the premiere performance, for having made a mistake in judging the play. But then of course it was too late.

After my experience in *Sepang Loca,* I decided to meet my American competitors on their own home ground. *Rooms* which I wrote as some kind of a challenge, is an American play. I remember Prof. Mitchell sending me a note to say he was "delightfully surprised" to find out that I wrote *Rooms*. He judged it First Place with the following comments:

> *Rooms* is an expert and touching play, carrying a strong impact and very theatrically conceived. (There are) dance motions, contrapuntal sequences, sophisticated knowingness and youthful tragedy starkly juxtaposed, and characters that jump out in primary colors with no intervening mud of gray dialogue.
>
> This author thinks and feels in dramatic terms. *Rooms* is an intensely feminine play, yet with masculine vigor; an eagerly youthful play, and yet with a painful maturity—as if the author, like one of the characters had grown up too soon; and the ending is grimly effective. The playwright knows in a very keen and knifelike way what she is doing. I think it is a she, I would be very surprised if it isn't.

Professor Mitchell's note said that he knew I had a play in the competition but that *Rooms* was the last play he thought I would write. Which meant it succeeded as an American play. Which meant also that the many hours I spent listening to telephone conversations from across the hall of our graduate house were not for naught. About its prize (again!), I remember I got a phone call from the then secretary (?) of the Wisconsin Players telling me if I didn't mind getting 2nd Place because my *Rooms* and a Mr. Mason's play were very close competitors for the 1st Place. I was quite irritated as I recall, getting a phone call like that but ever the gracious foreign exchange scholar, I said of course I would not mind if it is *the* place it deserved. When I got the judgment sheets and started adding up the scores, I discovered that three judges out of five voted it First! An American friend told me then that I should forget it but that experience has remained with me through these years. But I did bring up the matter to the attention of two of my professors. That was shortly before I left for home at the termination of my Fulbright grant. I don't know exactly what measures they took; however, the following years, the UW Playwriting competition eliminated the positions, declaring three equal winners and letting the audiences judge which should be First, Second and Third Places. Suffice it to say that *Rooms* got the applause Mason's play did not get after every performance, got the Critic's vote in a published front page review which said that clearly it should have been judged *First* and got published by Row, Peterson and Company. Those should be justice enough.

Walking Canes and Fans (1961), premiered in 1962, is a play set against the Philippine Revolution of 1898. I was engaged in a research on Philippine zarzuela and the play, beginning with the traditional expository opening scene of the *comico* and the *comica* as well as the comic interact involving these two characters, became my experiment on the zarzuela form without music. In directing it, Behn Cervantes added music from the period hence partially giving it its rightful flavor as a zarzuela. Someday, I hope to be able to write some lyrics for it, find a composer and make it the zarzuela it deserves to be.

The Short, Short Life of Citizen Juan (1968-70) was simultaneously launched as a book and premiered as a play under the sponsorship of the Sigma Delta Phi and the U.P. President's Committee on Culture, November 25-27, 1971 at the Abelardo Hall in connection with the Third World Theater Festival. I started the play in Philadelphia in 1968 and completed it in the summer of 1970 at the Eugene O'Neill Playwriting Center in Waterford, Connecticut. There I sat under the sun, watched the boats down the bay and sketched on a square piece of paper the set for the play and the three divisions or acts and the scenes under each. In the mornings, I would race with two or three playwrights for the only typewriter up the attic and type out the dialogue until by the end of my brief stay there, I had a whole sheaf of pages of my almost completed play. When I submitted it to Pacifico Aprieto who was then Director of the U.P. Press, I was told that he spoke so strongly for it that it got approved for publication almost right there. In a matter of months, it was ready for launching because I insisted on the easily finished and cheaper paperback edition. In a unique reception of this play, three reviewers, Joseph A. Galdon, S.J., Paul A. Dumol and Royce S. Reyes wrote a total of eight pages of reviews which appeared simultaneously in the Book Review section of the 3rd Quarter, 1972 issue of *Philippine Studies*.

"White Holocaust or A Pacific Playright's Protest against the Bomb" (1969-70) was written in a time of riots, demonstrations and assassinations. There was then a great uncertainty about banning the bomb and news about mass killings were almost daily fare in the newspapers in the U.S. The idea of the facelessness behind the mask came from a suggestion from Manuel who discussed at one time how many masks each of us wear and what if after tearing off the very last mask, we should find there is no face underneath? I remember that I was struck then by how that could be a very stunning image of annihilation, of death. And that is how his suggestion was used in the play.

So here it is, this collection representing two decades. I wish to thank quite a number of people who had helped bring it to fruition. For this book is my way of saying thank you to the following administrators and friends from the University: to my late mentors and friends, Secretary Nathaniel Tablante, Professors Gabriel A. Bernardo and Natividad Verzosa: to the following chairmen of the English Department, the late Professor Cristino Jamias, Drs. Alfredo Morales, Dionisia Rola, Elmer Ordoñez, Damiana Eugenio and Josefina Mariano; to Professor Consuelo Fonacier, former chairman of the Department of Speech and Drama; to the following deans of the College of Arts and Sciences: Drs. Tomas S. Fonacier, Francisco Nemenzo, Sr., Melecio Magno, Cesar Majul, Augusto Tenmatay, Dominador Salita and Francisco Nemenzo, Jr.; Associate Dean Pacita G. Fernandez; to the following University Presidents, Drs. Vidal Tan, Vicente Sinco, Carlos P. Romulo, S. P. Lopez and O. D. Corpuz. I single out the least "literary" among them, Dr. Vicente Sinco, who provided me financial help for the staging of my play, "Rooms" and who visited me in the library soon after in order to talk about drama and to offer me the use of U.P. VS Pampano in order to bring my plays to some of the islands, an offer, which regrettably, I failed to take up.

This volume then is proof of the support which administrators give, knowingly or unknowingly, to the writer whose greatest and most urgent need is TIME. This is of course being realized through the AIR program which has done so much to generate a climate of creativity on campus since I proposed its institution some three years ago. Putting this book together in its present form was made possible under this program.

Also, there must be some value in going back—the Fifties was an important period in Philippine Literature because just when our writers were successful in grappling with the twin horns of technique and language, the reverse occurred the following decade—writing back in our national language, from the Sixties. It might be pertinent to point out that I belong to those who found out that it is not too late to switch.

Lastly, there must be some value in sharing these short stories, plays and others with friends and readers who were generous in their appreciation of them. I only hope that in going over them again, they will be as generous as they were so many years back.

I cannot end this Preface without mentioning the constant support of my family, particularly my husband, Manuel and without saying that the reluctance I felt when I started this task has turned to unexplainable joy—the joy of a brickmaker recalling the whole mystifying process of how clay and straw hardened into bright red bricks.

AMELIA LAPEÑA-BONIFACIO

21 July 1978
FC 1056
Department of English
College of Arts and Sciences
University of the Philippines

An Afterthought

I F IT HAS TAKEN SO LONG for this book to be published, after its approval for publication in 1975, it is largely my fault. I have lingered too long over the manuscript, made excuses by delaying my choices of the photographs, labored too much over the program notes, fidgeted over the book design, did not write the introduction until the middle of 1978, debated over the book cover designs, etcetera. During the time, about half a dozen literary books got published ahead by the U.P. Press, including NVM Gonzalez's collection of short stories. One thing though that gladdens me is that this book is now second in the U.P. CREATIVE WRITING CENTER book series.

For their encouragement in printing of this book, I wish to thank Director Francisco Arcellana of the Creative Writing Center and the following members of the staff: Professors Alejandrino G. Hufana, Rogelio Sikat and Alberto Florentino.

For their valuable assistance in the publication of this book by the U.P. Press, I wish to thank Ms. Nelia Lopez-Gahol and Ms. Maribel P. Lasala, editorial assistants; Mr. Herman Palma for typesetting; Mr. Ven Caguimbal for composing; Mr. Renato L. Correa, chief of the Editorial Section and Prof. Luis D. Beltran, acting director of the U.P. Press, although not necessarily in that order.

Having delayed its publication, so many things have happened that need to be mentioned. First, my case in *Sepang Loca vs. Tinimbang Ka Ngunit Kulang* is now drawing to a close after six years of court hearings. The voluminous court proceedings deserve publication just as the witnesses deserve thanks, but alas, too late for this book. Second, *Walking Canes and Fans* is now undergoing its transition into a full-fledged zarzuela, the songs are almost finished and Maestro Lucio San Pedro has promised to write the music for it. And third, having been engaged in Children's Theatre and successfully establishing my own children's theatre troupe, TEATRONG MU-LAT NG PILIPINAS, and getting support for it through the University President Emanuel V. Soriano, I have now left adult theatre and the types of plays published in this volume. Since 1973, I have entered the magical world of Children's Theatre and have travelled much indeed, and I don't mean geographical mileage only.

So since I can't find any more reasons not to release the book, I now bring the manuscript, black and blue with corrections and additions, still with much hesitation, to the printer.

A.L.B.

September 7, 1980
LIKHAAN: Sentro ng Makathaing Pagsulat

Contents

THE PLAYS

Short Stories

Death of a Baby

ROSIE TOOK QUICK STEPS through the dark dining room past Uncle Julio's mosquito net, and through the sala where her sisters were sleeping on the wide buri mat on the floor. In front of Kuya Gideon's room, she paused to regain her breath. The door was locked.

"Kuya," she called, knocking lightly.

"Coming." Kuya Gideon's voice sounded muffled.

It took quite a long time for Kuya to reach the door. Rosie heard the noise of his leather slippers on the floor. She waited impatiently. When the lock clicked open, Rosie pushed the door.

The room was dark except for the corner where Kuya Gideon's reading table stood. The table lamp with its slightly tilted shade threw a circle of light on the open book on the table. The top of the shade cast an angular beam across the neatly stacked medical books above on the built-in shelves.

Kuya was pulling the covers from his bed. "Yes, Rosie," he said without turning to her.

"Mother wants you to go to Beling tonight. She said Beling and the baby might need you."

"Yes. I'll go. Tell Mother."

"She wants me to go there too, Kuya."

"You must be in bed at this hour, Rosie. Growing girls need lots and lots of sleep."

He went to his reading table and placed a slip of paper on the open book.

"Mother wants me to—" Kuya just stood there fingering the slip of paper on the open book. She finished her sentence hastily. "Mother wants me to help a little."

There was a frown on his face. He closed the book. "Well, we shall go there together then."

"I'll wait for you, Kuya."

"Yes, Rosie. I'll be there."

Quietly, Rosie closed the door. Her sisters were still asleep. Under the thin net, she traced the vague outline of their silent forms and her own empty pillow beside them. She walked slowly back to the dining room. Mother asked her to go. What could she tell her three other sisters about Beling and the baby in the morning? Beling had given birth to the baby the morning before. Such a handsome boy. The whole family, from her white-haired Lola to her wide-eyed niece Raquel, liked the newcomer instantly, even before he gave out a loud shriek while they all watched and held their breath as Kuya Gideon dipped the tiny bluish body alternately into two basins, one of ice and the other of hot water. Kuya Gideon's gloved hands were very deft. His right palm hollowed to support the moist head and his left hand that kept a firm clasp at the feet of the baby were very steady. How quietly confident he seemed that he could call the boy back to life again. He stood straight and tall inside the circle of expectant faces, swinging the body of the baby from one basin to another. Watching him then, Rosie felt very proud: this young god was her brother.

Back in the kitchen, Mother poured two cups of coffee. She scooped two teaspoonfuls of sugar from the old brown jar on the table and stirred each of the teaspoonfuls into the cups. She picked up the red-labelled can of evaporated milk near the brown sugar jar, brought it near her ear and shook it. "You'll have to drink your coffee black tonight, Child," she said throwing the milk can into the tall refuse box near the stove.

Rosie reached for the cup and began stirring the hot liquid slowly.

"What did your brother say, Rosie?"

"He said he'll go. He asked me to wait for him here."

Rosie dipped her little finger into the cup. The coffee was not so hot any more. It was bitter but good. She felt warm all over.

She was putting her cup down on the table when Kuya came. He had his thick flannel jacket on. He drank the other cup hurriedly and handed the empty cup to Mother. "Come along, Rosie," he said.

Mother placed the empty cup on the stove and reached for the handle of the steaming coffee pot. She went to Rosie near the door. "Find out if they need anything else besides, Rosie," she said handing over the pot.

Rosie took the pot carefully. "I will, Mother," she said.

"Tell them I'll come later."

"Yes, Mother."

"And Child, tell Lola to come home and get some rest. She hasn't come home since the baby's arrival this morning."

Outside the night was cold. Rosie placed the pot on the stone walk and pulled her collar close to her. She shuddered when she heard Mother fastening the latch of the narrow kitchen door, closing the comfort and darkness of the house after them. She stooped for the pot. Across the backyard, through the thick foliage of the tamarind trees, she caught sight of the lighted windows of her sister Beling's house.

Kuya Gideon's voice sounded impatient when he called out from where he stood several paces ahead of her.

"Come on, Rosie, we haven't got all night."

She straightened quickly and followed him, picking her way on the well-used path under the tamarind trees, and wondering all the while what was going on behind the lighted windows.

"What will happen to the baby, Kuya?"

Kuya stopped and steadied himself upon a sharply-cut stone under his foot. "I can't tell exactly, Rosie," he said slowly. "The boy came a month ahead of its time. It is difficult to say what will happen to a premature baby."

"Do pre—premature babies have to fight hard to live?"

"They all have to. Why do you ask?"

"Beling's baby will live, Kuya?"

"Sure he will. There are many babies born before their time but they live. At least most of them do, anyway." He slowed down his walk and dug both of his hands into his pockets.

The flat stones half-sunken on the walk drew a dim line to Beling's house. Rosie stared quite hard at the lighted windows framed by the dark unpainted boards. Beling. God, she hoped nothing sad would happen to Beling again. Two years back it had been a still-birth. A beautiful girl, but Beling never had a chance to see her. This time it was different. This morning, right after the baby was bathed, Kuya lay him down beside Beling. Beling regarded the pink face above the pillow covers for a long time. Then she drew the boy close to her breast. She beamed at all of them gathered around the bed. Closing and opening her large brown hand over the tiny hand of the boy, she announced proudly, "My boy's fingers are long and tapering like an artist's. He shall be a pianist—no, a violinist! My boy shall be a violinist then, my boy shall be a violinist—"

The stone path stopped in front of the steep stairs. Rosie climbed the narrow steps slowly, afraid to spill the hot coffee over her bare legs. Kuya found the door unlatched. He pushed it quietly and held it open for her.

Rosie entered into the lighted room. The glare of the flourescent lamp on the low ceiling pained her eyes. She blinked them hard once or twice until the blurred figures before her took form. Beling was facing the wall on the green iron bed that occupied almost half of the room. The boy lay beside her, rosy and quiet. Her anxiety vanished. Perhaps everything would turn out right yet.

She turned to her brother-in-law, Maneng. His crumpled pajamas, unkempt hair and tired eyes made him look older than he really was. He was seated beside the open window, looking past her at Kuya Gideon who had moved toward the bed. Kuya bent over the baby.

"Mother asked me to bring some coffee," Rosie said swinging the pot carefully over her left hand.

Maneng smiled. "Good," he said, "I'll go and get the cups."

Rosie approached the lone table at the head of the bed whose green coat of paint shone against the glare of the fluorescent. The table was covered with a clean white towel. Kuya Gideon's instruments spread over it shone very white. She piled them on the side of the table and covered them with a free end of the towel. She placed the pot on the cleared portion. It was heavy and her fingers felt numb.

Kuya pulled a chair near the bed. Rosie stood behind him and watched the baby. The boy was awake; never closed his eyes since that morning. Never cried too, except for that first shriek when his tiny bluish body touched the basin of hot water for the third time. He looked small against the pillows and strange the way he kept staring unsteadily at the ceiling. Perhaps all babies born before their time behave this way, she thought.

Rosie walked to the foot of the bed to get a better view of the baby. She leaned against the bed post and rested her chin on the brass ball on top of the post. Lola Lisa was sitting on the floor, well hidden from view by the bed. Her back was resting on the wall, white head bent over her black rosary that shone bluish against her long calico skirt. Rosie smiled. Lola never seems more happy than when she is praying, she mused.

The boy's gasping came to her distinctly. It came softly at first, then rose and fell in unison with her Lola Lisa's prayers.

Kuya Gideon stood up and he looked at the baby closely. "Call Maneng," he whispered.

Rosie nodded quietly and turned to go. A thin crash broke the quiet of the room. She stopped suddenly. Maneng was at the door, his lips were white. On the floor near his feet were the broken cups.

Maneng smiled at them uncertainly. He combed his unsteady fingers through his hair and brushed the broken pieces of china with his foot.

Beling turned from the wall with a cry. She looked at Kuya Gideon. There was alarm in her red swollen eyes. Kuya drew his eyes to the floor, to the table, and into his breast pocket. Silently they all watched him pull a long rubber tube from his breast pocket. He dipped the tube into a bottle of alcohol.

"There is nothing wrong really," he began very slowly, wiping the wet tube with a cotton ball. "If we can help him get rid of the mucus, he can breathe nicely again."

His voice was quiet and unquivering like an old doctor's. Rosie felt it warm her all over, making her hopeful once more. She only hoped Beling and Maneng felt that way too.

Kuya Gideon inserted one end of the tube into the boy's nostril. He covered the other end with a piece of gauze. Maneng bent stiffly when Kuya Gideon handed the covered end of the tube to him. His face was rigid. Only the slight quiver in his lips betrayed his feelings. But he steadied them by pressing them firmly over the tube. Then he began sucking noisily until the gasps died down and the boy's breathing sounded free again.

Outside the window, the motionless branches of the tamarind trees in the backyard were heavy with the cries of night crickets. Somewhere deep in the dark neighborhood, a dog howled plaintively.

The brown Big Ben sounded midnight. Kuya Gideon sat back and drew a deep puff at his cigarette. "I am afraid the chances of saving the baby are very slight now." His voice was scarcely above a whisper; he was looking at Beling, whose shoulders move heavily with her noisy breathing.

Maneng paled at his words. "If there is anything that can be done—perhaps, an injection or a serum," he suggested weakly.

Kuya gave Maneng a long look. He crushed his cigarette fiercely on the ash tray. He got up and patted Maneng on the shoulder, saying lightly, "Okay, old boy. We can try."

Maneng stood up with Kuya. He placed a hand on Kuya Gideon's arm. "Beling won't ever understand if anything happens to her boy, Gideon."

"We must learn to accept many things," Kuya said to him quietly.

"Beling has made so many plans for our son," Maneng continued as though he didn't hear Kuya, "and he's such a lovely boy."

Kuya Gideon stooped for his satchel under the night table without answering him. He placed the satchel on the bed and opened it.

"Beling will make a good mother for him, eh, Gideon?"

"Sure, sure. She'll make a good mother," he answered taking a big nickel-plated syringe case from the open mouth of his satchel. He fished out a bottle of merthiolate, a bottle of alcohol, and a roll of cotton wrapper in blue paper. He deposited all of them on the table. He snapped his satchel close and returned it under the bed. He pulled the stopper from the alcohol bottle and poured a generous amount of the colorless liquid into his palm. Then he began rubbing his hands together, washing his bare arms with the fluid vigorously. The smell of alcohol, strong and acrid, rose and engulfed all of them standing in the silent room.

"First time Beling heard her own baby cry was this morning."

Rosie sensed Maneng was bent on being talkative, she turned and nodded her head at him encouragingly.

"Quite a yell the boy gave too. After waiting for it for so long, I felt a sudden twisting inside of me."

There was a catch in his voice that betrayed how much he was suffering. Rosie wanted to reach out and touch him and say everything would be all right. Only, she wouldn't know how to say the words to him properly. She turned to Kuya Gideon guiltily. He was too busy sucking the liquid with the syringe needle stuck into the rubber cap of a bottle marked Parenteral Fluid which he held high with his left hand to notice how flushed she was.

Kuya handed her the bottle and asked her to tape the cap. She got it eagerly and started pulling adhesive tape, thankful she found a good reason to turn away from Maneng. Kuya commenced rubbing the baby's leg with a cotton ball wet with merthiolate. The antiseptic marked a vivid circle of red on the light skin.

He called out to Maneng who was watching him. "Rub the boy's thigh this way," he instructed, stroking the thigh of the baby. "With this," giving him a cotton ball soaked with alcohol.

The 50-cc. syringe was fatter than the baby's leg. When Kuya stuck the needle into the thin mass of flesh that was the baby's leg, Rosie held to the bed post for support. She felt sick at the pit of her stomach and so weak at her knees, she was afraid she would fall. The colorless liquid pushed the skin of the thin leg into a mold. She broke out into a cold sweat. The growing mold reminded her of the cellophane bags she used to fill with water when she was a child. The only difference was, she used to puncture those swollen bags in order to watch the thin strands of water squirting from the tiny holes. Kuya Gideon sealed the puncture with a wisp of cotton soaked in collodion. Maneng was having a difficult time pushing the accumulated fluid in the mold upward to the boy's thigh. Rosie closed her eyes. She felt faint.

Back on the chairs with Maneng slumped exhausted near her, Rosie watched Kuya Gideon with a mixed feeling of hope and impatience. Kuya Gideon crossed his legs and folded his hands over his knee. He stared stonily at the baby, watching the color gradually fading from the boy's cheeks, the skin slowly pulling the flesh skulltight. She leaned forward from her seat and waited for him to leave his chair and walk to the bed and stand straight and tall above the baby. But Kuya merely tightened his locked fingers over his knee, his knuckles showing white. She pulled her eyes away from him and directed them to the floor. She felt hurt and bewildered.

She looked up when Kuya got up from his seat. He snatched the baby from the pillow, held it over the basin of cold water and sprinkled water over its forehead. Beling protested in horror. Maneng, his voice quiet and quivering, tried to calm her; "He's just trying to even up the boy's temperature, dear. Everything will be all right afterward."

Then Lola Lisa's voice, shrill: "I have told her many times, even after her first baby that she must not be over-fond of saints. But she's stubborn, goes to church every evening. She goes to stare at the replicas of saints. 'Ave Maria Purisima'... I told her Jesus takes the beautiful children from their mothers. Makes them His angels. I told her—"

Rosie slipped away from the room and went down the stairs quietly. She stepped slowly from one stone to another under the tamarind trees, feeling very tired. She passed a moist hand over her tired eyes. How she wished forgetting were as simple as closing a door. Just slamming it tight and leaving everything behind—as she closed

The Bird and the Boy

IT WAS A GREEN BIRD. It was as big as a man's balled fist. Gleaming bluish-green under the pale yellow of the lamp chained from the darkly-varnished ceiling, its feathered body swayed heavily from side to side as its claws perched and unperched themselves on the elaborately carved crown of the wine-red narra china-cabinet.

"Thief! Thief!" Its voice was shrill inside the big kitchen.

The boy swallowed noisily. He placed the fried drumstick on the plate and peered at the bird above him. It was still swaying excitedly, the black bead-like eyes set above the vivid dash of orange beak were fixed on him.

"Thief!"

The boy walked to the icebox. He opened it and placed the plate inside the meat compartment. He shivered as he inserted his hand into the biting cold of the frozen box. He wiped his mouth and fingers with the loose hem of his shirt, went back to the sink and turned the tap on a glass. He gurgled, spat water through his gritted teeth and then began to drink solemnly.

The green bird flew down to the table beside the sink. Its claws clattered on the hard board as it moved restlessly, its green body swaying heavily from side to side.

"Tell Charito! Tell Charito! Thief!"

The boy put down his glass and regarded the bird quietly. Tell Charito! He never thought of that. As soon as his señora comes home from the city, the bird would tell. The bird would do it. The bird could do almost anything.

Every afternoon at two, the old lady—his señora would let it out of the house. It would fly over the tall adobe wall draped with *cadena-de-amor,* over the mowed lawns and the tall *acacias* and flowering *banabas.* It would perch from one window sill to another, calling out: "Canasta! Canasta! Canasta!"

Then the bird would fly back to the single room on the third floor where the old lady would be waiting for it beside the balustrade. It would fly past the old lady into the open french window and alight on the canasta table at the center of the ash-blue room. It would walk around the squat glasses of cold beer, flapping its wings and crying shrilly, "Canasta! Charito. Canasta!"

And the old lady would take it in her arms and coo to it softly.

He had often wondered if the old lady was not too lonely. There were the regular afternoon canasta with the white-haired ladies who spoke like chirping birds. Gundo, the blind gardener had told him they were españolas like his old señora. There were the servants of course. And the bird. But the house was big and quiet except for the rustling of the purple drapes flowing into graceful lines when the clear-glass shutters were pushed back to let in the soft wind blowing endlessly through the lawn and the profusion of *banabas* and *acacias* below and with it the occasional sound of tooting horns when the family cars of those living in the quiet neighborhood returned at about the end of the day.

Three months ago, when he was led into the hushed drawing room by Sendang, the cook who pulled the wanted-a-houseboy sign at the door after he went in, he saw the old lady half-buried in an armchair that looked fat and soft. The old lady drew the drapes with the dull yellow quilts on the edges and regarded him. Sendang left them. Her brown feet, fat and slipperless, were muted by the thick carpet covering the floor.

The señora was old, it was true. But he observed after looking at her brown eyes that formed pleasant wrinkles at their slants when she smiled that she was a very handsome woman. Her white hair with little curls falling over her temples was combed back loosely into two soft buns at her nape. Her shoulder was wrapped with a gray shawl, the two pointed ends held on her lap by a straw basket wherein lay a confused assortment of balls of colored wool thread. Her feet were resting on a cushioned footstool.

She was asking him if he wanted to take the job when a shrill voice from above the head of the old lady said, "*Bobo, Charito, Bobo!*"

He felt a stinging warmness close around his ears. He looked up and saw the portrait of a man who must be a sea captain because he wore a blue suit, his stern face was tanned and a big steering wheel shone golden behind him. It was of course foolish even to think that the man on the portrait spoke. Then he saw the green bird perched on a cluster of flowers carved out of the wide narra frame.

At first he thought the bird was a part of the glossy frame. But it flew to the carpet near the legs of the footstool. It faced him, its glassy eyes piercing in their intentness. He almost ran away when it spoke again, its sharp voice, half-mocking and half-tart. *"Bobo! Bobo! Bobo!"*

Tell Charito! Why, the green bird could do that very easily. The old lady would listen and look at him gravely, very gravely. Perhaps she would not say it but her eyes would: "Thief!" And all the time, I thought he was different from the rest—she would scold him. Send him out of the house perhaps. Like Tino, the chauffeur who stole a few auto spare parts and was discovered by the green bird. And where would he go then? To the big city with the tall buildings that looked beautiful and frightening through the glass windows of the third floor whenever he cleared the soap suds and scrubbed them hard until they shone? He would get lost in its nameless streets and alleys. Get crushed under the wheels of automobiles and buses that whish through its wide avenues. Send him away. No!

He looked up at the white kitchen clock embedded at the center of the big wooden flower on the crown of the narra cabinet. Its little hand was pointed at five and the long one at twelve. In two or three hours, his señora and Sendang would return from the city.

He went to the icebox, opened it and scanned the wire divisions. There were the porcelain pots of clear yellow butter and chunks of cheese, a tray of eggs, stacked heads of cabbage, celery, apples, oranges. The brown bottles of beer and the flat water bottles and the covered jars of thick jelly lined the lowest rung. He got an apple and went back to the sink.

He peeled the apple awkwardly, half-hopeful for the green bird was flapping its wings and edging near him excitedly. He offered the apple to the bird. The bird eyed the fruit, then the boy suspiciously. The boy placed the apple on the hard board. The green bird walked around the apple several times. It raised one of its claws and pinned the naked fruit down. It began to dig its beak into the white meat and turned the juicy bits in its bill with its thick pink tongue. Looking at the boy intently, the green bird sucked the apple meat and threw the pulp on the hard board.

The boy stood watching the green bird for a long time. It was toying with the exposed seeds of the half-finished apple. The hard board around it was littered with bits of whitish pulp.

He walked to the door, a feeling of relief sweeping over him like tiny drops of nice cool rain.

He was at the door when the shrill voice called, "Thief!" The boy slowly turned and looked at the green bird. It was still pecking playfully at the half-finished apple but its beadlike eyes were now turned full on him, strangely menacing.

The boy bit his lip fiercely. He walked back to the table. He looked at the bird helplessly. The green feathered chest was heaving excitedly as the shrill voice taunted him, "Thief! Thief! Thief!"

He felt anger rising inside him and pricking his eyes with big hot tears. Blindly, he grabbed the green bird on the hard board. The bird began to bite his hands—sharp painful bites into his soft flesh. It squirmed out of his grasp, its glossy feathered body suddenly slippery against his clammy palms. It inched out of his hands and flapped its wings furiously but the boy held its scaly legs hard.

He ran into the drawing room, his short quick footfalls muted by the thick carpet, the bird tightly imprisoned in his hands.

Except for the cries of night crickets, the garden was quiet and white under the early risen moon. The garden was very still. The leaves of the *acacias* above him were closed. The low branches of the *banabas* and the long untrimmed stems of the *gumamelas* lining the path to the driveway drooped as though tiredly protesting the heavy whiteness of the moonlight. Not a leaf moved. Even the bermuda under his feet was cold and very still.

He slackened his pace when he came to the cemented driveway. The hot throbbings in his temples had partly abated. The warm body of the green bird in his hand had ceased to struggle as though it had finally realized that it was futile to fight.

The boy continued walking close to the patches of geranium growing beside the cemented barrier bar that kept the garden soil from eroding into the driveway whenever the rains came and with it the small floods.

The drone of night crickets broke and the uncertain twanging of a guitar rose.

The boy stepped over the patches of geranium and crouched close to the thick growth of *gumamelas*.

A song came up and joined the uncertain notes of the guitar.

The boy crawled around the *gumamela* bush and peered at the bend of the driveway from where the raspy voice came. The voice was familiar, although he could not understand the words of the melancholy song.

He continued crawling on the cold bermuda until he reached the bend of the driveway. Then he sat still and watched the man who was plucking a guitar. It was Gundo, the gardener. The man's face was turned to the moon, his sightless eyes were unflinching. All about the blind man lay the whiteness of the moonlight, splattered here and there with black patterns of the leaves of *banabas* and the tall *acacias*.

The boy sat and listened. Gundo was plucking his guitar, sending quick notes into the night air. The man was rasping a sad love song about a faithless maiden who went away, far away over the blue seas.

The boy stood up and tip-toed past the gardener.

Gundo stopped plucking his guitar.

"Who's there!" he said sharply.

"It's only me Cardo, the little houseboy," the boy said.

"Ahoy, Cardo. And what do you wish to have from me?" The blind man lay his guitar on his lap and turned to the boy.

The green bird squirmed in the boy's hold and it began to squawk. The boy held the orange bill close.

"I am going to give Tilda her bath. The señora told me. I forgot to do it this afternoon," the boy said.

Gundo took up his guitar and plucked the tense strings absently. Then he began to sing under his raspy voice.

"The body must love the bath
'Twill make it clean and fat,
Tra-la-la-la
Tra-la-la-la..."

The boy walked past the blind gardener to the dark garage at the end of the driveway.

With one free hand, he lifted the bolt of the unpainted door of the garage. He was pushing the heavy doors when he heard Gundo stop his singing. A horn tooted at the gate.

The green bird in his hand began to struggle fiercely. He looked at it. The bead-like eyes were staring at him sullenly.

He stiffened as the squeaking of the small wheel of the steel gate against the semi-circular rail at the fan-like mouth of the driveway rose sharply behind him.

He ran into the dark garage. The green bird shook its beak free from his fingers. It bit his hands, sharp tiny bites that knifed his flesh. It even clawed his arms, the hooked nails digging into his arms and cutting thin raw lines through it.

Outside he heard the car engine purr then draw near.

The boy stifling a cry, his fingers smarting from the pain of the tiny bites sought the bird's throat and found the little life beating furiously under the green feathers.

His fingers closed over the active little spot and pressed it hard. The claws gave a few angry spurns. The wings, a few hard flaps. Once or twice he felt the green body convulse, then lie limp in his hand. It felt heavy and suddenly cold against the livid lashes and lacerations in his arms and hands that were all tender and sore and deeply hurting.

(1951) First published in *The Philippine Collegian New Review*, Commencement Issue, April 1952.

The Old Woman

I GOT OFF AT BLUMENTRITT MARKET. It was cooler inside the low-roofed market. The cemented place was moist and cool under my feet and the fruit vendors and rice dealers who called out, Anything, Miss? looked friendly. I began to feel light and happy.

The steel gate leading to the row of unpainted apartments should be somewhere behind the stalls at the back of the market. I had been to the place twice. Once, when Sukhdev took me there on her birthday. We had a gay party with plenty of sandwiches, ice cream, cokes, chatting and laughter. There was no dancing, although the small portable radio-phono on Sukhdev's study desk filled the room with sweet music. Besides, the place was small and only girls were invited.

The last time I went there was when I visited Sukhdev who wrote me that she could not come for our hiking date because she was ill. I found her in bed with fever and a severe chill. I sat with her, holding her cold hand in mine and listening to her heavy breathing, until the small room grew dark around us. Then I slipped out of the room. At the door, I met her brother Diwan and two men carrying a canvas stretcher. I leaned against the door and waited for the men to come down. They were very noisy as they descended the narrow stairs. Sukhdev was on the stretcher. She was wrapped up in a white sheet. Only her face showed. Her lips were pressed tight. I wanted to call out to her but her eyes were closed, her long lashes thick and shadowy against the pallor of her skin.

A week later, I received a letter from Sukhdev. It was postmarked Quezon City. She wrote of the big white ward, of the friendly people in it, and of Diwan who sailed for Spain to take up a postgraduate course in thoracic surgery because he said he loved her very much. The letter was written with a kind of warmth and simpleness that touched my heart.

I found the steel gate after passing through the many stalls that line the market place. Except for the shed leaning on the closed leaf of the steel gate and under which two elderly women were cooking and selling *pansit,* the place had not changed.

Many children were shouting boisterously and running after one another on the cemented walk between the row of unpainted apartments and the long adobe wall.

The last apartment close to the blank stone corner where the long adobe wall ended was Sukhdev's place. I tucked the package under my arm and knocked on the door.

It was Sukhdev's mother who opened the door. She greeted me with a smile. She gathered the folds of her loose house dress under a stiff brown girdle, passed her hand quite confusedly over her white hair, and then invited me in.

It was dark inside the house. Sukhdev's mother took my hand and guided me to the narrow stairs leading to the small receiving room above.

She pulled two rattan chairs from the huddle of furniture covered with a large and dusty sackcloth and asked me to sit down. I sat in the dark and tore off the brown paper covering the package wrapped in pink on my lap. It was an English translation of the *Ramayana* and the *Mahabharata.* Once, Sukhdev showed me a copy of the two epics written in strange-looking and thick Hindu characters. She spoke proudly of the book. I had come across the English translation by Romesh C. Dutt while browsing in a bookstore, and had bought two copies—one for Sukhdev and another for myself.

Sukhdev's mother walked to the windows and began pushing the shutters which lifted the warmth inside the room. Then she vanished behind the brown post near the window and switched on the lights. The flourescent lamp above my head gave a few uncertain flashes, then caught and flooded the small room with relucent light.

The old woman sat down. I started to talk of the heavy work in school, the examinations and term papers. I spoke slowly, watching the deep eyes looking at me. The old woman nodded her head as though to assure me that she understood what I was talking about.

"I couldn't visit you and Sukhdev often. Too much school work," I said.

"I understand," she began, then stopped to stare at the pink package on my lap.

I took it and held it out to her.

"It's a little late," I said. Sukhdev's birthday was five days ago.

"Is for my Minnder?" she asked twisting and untwisting her handkerchief.

"Yes, where's Sukhdev?" I asked.

She continued to stare at the pink package I was holding out to her, twisting and untwisting her handkerchief and showing not the slightest intention of taking the package. I placed the package back on my lap. Sukhdev must have gone out. To a movie or party perhaps. In the last letter she wrote me, Ward B was gay, and she sounded very much like her old self. She described the fun she had at the Wednesday night movies in the ward, the chats with friendly nurses and patients. She closed her letter by saying she was already well. I must not insist on going there, she wrote, because it would be dangerous. But she would spend her birthday in their old apartment in Blumentritt and I might visit her there.

I sent her a thin book—*Looking For a Bluebird.* On its cover, I wrote briefly, "Have faith. You'll soon find your bluebird."

I did not receive any answer.

The old woman continued to remain silent. Her eyes, deep and dark like Sukhdev's, were as inscrutable as the empty holes punctuating her ear lobes and left nostril.

"Sukhdev go away," she said quietly.

"Oh, that's bad," I said. "I was hoping I would see her today. Where did she go?"

"Last month, Minnder died," the old woman said in the same quiet tone, her eyes still lowered on the pink package.

I sat back limply and stared hard at the old woman. There was a tightness in my throat.

The old woman looked up and met my eyes. She did not say anything for a long time. Then, she pulled her chair to me and reached out for my hand. The deep eyes set above the prominent freckled cheekbones were bland and soothing. She smelled clean like bleached clothes and the hand that clasped mine was warm and steady.

"Write, I no know," she said, "Diwan, so far, far away," she said, sweeping her brown hairy arm to the window.

"Minnder died quiet," she continued when I did not speak. "She was praying. She says to me, Bebe, join. I no know," her voice trailed off. She stared over my shoulder at the blank wall.

The tightness in my throat was gone. But it felt dry and very coarse. I cleared my throat noisily.

The old woman took her eyes away from the wall and looked at me intently as though seeing me for the first time.

I cleared my throat again, feeling very uneasy under the intent gaze of the deep eyes.

The old woman smiled absently. She took her hands away from mine and began twisting and untwisting her handkerchief again.

"Minnder embroiders good na, Minnder's hand good," she said, showing her brown bony hand as she passed thumb and forefinger over each of the knotted fingers.

In the sewing cubicle at school, Sukhdev had sat beside me, talking endlessly while her thin brown hand passed a needle through a cloth drawn taut over a hoop. Then on the cloth, she had embroidered brilliantly-hued leaves, petals and birds.

"Minnder sew white dress for birthday na. Then she say to me, Bebe, put this dress on me when I die. I say to her, Minnder, is bad to talk of death. Minnder point to stairs, like this," she pointed her bony forefinger at the stairs. "Bebe, a man is there. I see no man na. I say to her, I see no man there. But Minnder has gone—died away. You understand me yes, no?"

I nodded.

"I wash Minnder clean. I put the dress on Minnder like she say to me, Bebe, put this dress on me when I die. Then I call to the neighbors, Sukhdev has gone—died away, I say to them."

Outside, the late afternoon sky had turned black. The sound of the market place and the jammed street a little beyond the low-roofed market had quieted down. Only an occasional blunt tooting of horns and a shrill whistle rose, but they all sounded faint and far away.

"Where is she buried?" I asked.

"San Lazaro crem...cremto..."

"Crematory," I said.

"Yes, yes," she said nodding her head vigorously.

"And the ashes?"

"I ask Minnder's father, let me keep the box, I say to him. He take it away." Her voice sounded flat and crisp.

"Away. Where?" I asked.

"To—what you call that, the place many, many people swim?"

I looked at the old woman. She was gesticulating, working her thin brown arms in an awkward breast stroke.

"A beach," I said.

"Yes, beach. Pasay beach."

"Into the sea?"

"Into the sea," she echoed.

The bright line of the sea rose in my mind, a box rising and falling with the waves. Then suddenly I remembered a poem I had read of a king who had come to his people as a bundled infant on a raft. When he died, his people placed his corpse on a raft they had made near the sea, and piled near his body grains of gold and many-colored stones that shone under the setting sun. Then they pushed the raft into the water and watched it as it slowly drifted away.

The old woman walked to Sukhdev's study desk and opened its drawers.

"You like these," she said as she returned with some books in her arms.

I stood up and took the books from her. I placed them on my seat. On top of the pile I saw the thin book. I opened it and saw my big handwriting staring back at me. The ink had faded but the writing was still discernible—"Have faith. You'll soon find your blue-bird."

I closed the cover abruptly.

"I can't take them," I said.

"I no need them," she said.

"But you can keep them for her."

"Keep?" she said looking quiescently at the pile of books as though the idea of keeping them fascinated her. "I no need them," she said very quietly.

At the landing of the narrow stairs, I laid the books on the floor and waited for her to come down. She was taking each step very slowly. I waited for her and held her elbow the rest of the way down.

"When you no busy, you come, please," she said placing an arm around my shoulder. Her voice sounded unsteady.

Under the yellow gleam of the small bulb above the landing, I glanced at her. She smiled briefly and then bit her lower lip.

I stood with her for a long time not knowing what to say. I thought of Sukhdev who had gone away and of Diwan who was in Spain taking a postgraduate course in thoracic surgery because he said he loved Sukhdev very much.

"Diwan will come back. He'll get married and give you many grandchildren," I said.

The old eyes shone and the hand tightened over my shoulder. We stood looking at the dark adobe wall outside. She lifted her hand from my shoulder. "You come back, huh?"

I stooped for the books and gathered them in my arms. Then, I walked out of the house, looking back once when I reached the steel gate. The old woman was standing at the end of the cemented walk, her back against the blank corner of the adobe wall. She waved her hand when she saw me turn.

I wanted to wave back but the books were heavy in my arms.

(1952) First published in *The Literary Apprentice*, 1952, pp. 84-89.

A Christmas Story

W HEN HIS BIG WET NOSE SHONE through the thickets and his soft wheenee greeted me, I knew it was Kordel and so I made a hole through the tangle of leaves and twigs to reach his side. He met me joyfully, passed his rough nose over my face and ears and nudged my sides with his spiral horns. He smelled of hay and earth where his heavy long coat hung pasted into points of thick dried mud. There's a meadow full of fresh young grass over there, I heard him whisper.

I stretched my neck out to kiss him full on the mouth. He pulled his face away from me and said with quiet dignity. Pshews—pksst, no time to lose. The meadow waits for us. He turned his thick rump on me and started to walk away.

I followed Kordel through the field careful in maintaining a respectful distance between us until I could no longer bear the night cold that kept creeping into my short coat and the sounds of many strange cries from thickets and trees, I ran to him and stayed close to his side. His thick coat warmed my body and I felt safe and happy again. Without breaking his even pace nor turning his face to me, he said, It isn't very far now.

The field shone white under the stars where the land rose in big round bumps. Far down to the edge of the wide fields were the dark big mountains that hid the hem of the sky and behind us, beautiful with the many quiet blinking lights, was the little hometown. I remembered the master and the others whom I have left behind and suddenly I wanted to go back. Kordel stopped and waited for me as I lagged behind. Hurry up, he said. The meadow is only a few paces ahead. He sounded excited and his voice held promise of fresh young grass. How tender the young blades crush and how sweet and juicy, his voice seem to say. I scampered after him forgetting the master and the others on the field.

We trudged a stretch of land that climbs into a hill and when we reached the top, Kordel cleared away the thick growth of grass with his horns and asked me to come near him. On the other side of the hill where the land dropped to a low wide bed, was the meadow! I leaped past Kordel and let my body slip and roll on the slant of the hill until I fell on the low bed of fresh young grass. It felt wet under my coat and I sprang up and skipped about wildly. Kordel followed my prancing with amused eyes and then went to a thick patch not far away and began pulling and chewing with great earnestness. I kept rolling and skipping and jumping over the grass until I felt warm around my face and body. I lay still on the grass and panted. Above, the stars were so low they seemed to dangle from the clear night sky. Stars, stars, stars down to where the blackness arch over the dark big mountains. There was a big bright star over the peak of one of the dark mountains. It blinked at me gaily and for a moment, I forgot all about the low bed and the fresh grass on it and Kordel.

When I stood up, Kordel was about through with a thick patch; all around where he was, it showed bare and yellow. I went beside him and heard his noisy nibbling. At the first pull, I felt the young blades crush all together crispy tender betweeen my teeth, its sweet thick juice trickling down and cooling my tongue and throat. I kept my teeth down on the young shoots and pulled away at them with frantic haste. Kordel paused from his patch to look up at me and say: Easy, kiddo. There's enough to last both of us the whole year. I felt blood rush hotly to my cold nose and I raised my teeth from the green shoots and started to chew the cud in my cheeks. Kordel gave a low laugh and went back to his patch.

The night grew colder and colder as we kept pulling and chewing. The field grown white under the stars was alive with many strange night cries. Kordel's body had grown round under his long coat and I too felt heavy. I moved away from Kordel and climbed the hill where I could rest and watch Kordel eat at the same time. I was lying near the thick growth of grass when I heard the call: Here, kiddie whee-nee, here kiddie whee-nee-ee. I knew it was the master. I called out at Kordel but he did not seem to hear me at all. I heard the master's footfall come trump, trump, trump on the ground to where I was. Before I could move, I felt a large hand reaching out for me and lifting me off the ground on my belly. It was the master, all right. But his dirty face did not seem angry at all. His faded eyes shone under the bushy white brows and he kept cooing low: Naughty kiddie, naughty kiddie, here, here and kept patting me on the head. I snuggled closer to him and licked his cold wrinkled face.

He walked down the hill with me clasped tightly to his breast. Halfway down the hill, he shouted I found him to the group that stood waiting below. Some from the group shouted back, Now we can all go, brother Carl. Yes, we can all go, the rest chorused. And the master held me closer to him and he went down the hill faster.

It was a small group that met us at the foot of the hill: men with their long wooden staffs, the women in their loose dresses and shawls and little boys with coarse cloth tied around their loins and wound about their shoulders. Their faces shone ruddy in the night cold and they kept close together for warmth. Behind them were a few of the others and the little boys picked up the little ones among them who kept bleating they were cold.

We walked across the fields, the little boys pointing up at the sky where the bright star was. The women were excited and kept talking about the angels who came singing to them from across the night sky. Surely, It is the Child, they chirped. It is the Child. I could only half-understand what they talked about, the trip made me sleepy. When we entered the hometown, the houses were all dark and the doors were all barred. The men trod softly over the cobbled streets and all the women hushed their chatter. Still a few windows would light up suddenly and capped heads would stick out of them to ask, What is it? And the women would answer back, The Child, the Child has come! A few had slammed their windows with a naughty Pshaw; a few came down and joined us.

It was over a stable that the star stood still and the master and the group entered the place. It was damp and dark inside and from a dim lamp hanging from one of the low beams, the moist stone floor shone where it showed under the scattered haystraws. The master bent low to avoid the low beams and once or twice, he clapped aside the dusty webs before his face. When we neared the end of the stable, the women fell on their knees, the old men bowed their heads against their staffs and the others hushed their bleating and sat on the hay with the little boys. I felt the master's heart beat hard against my side; he had covered me with his rough coat and was rubbing my body with it until my short coat fairly shone and my skin tingled with warmth under. Then he lifted me up and approached the lovely lady who was bending over the new-born infant. The master put me out to them and the bearded man who stood behind the lovely lady smiled at us. The child from out of his swaddlings reached out for me.

I put out a hoof uncertainly and the child touched it with his little hand.

The little boys came forward with the little ones and offered them to the little child who touched each of them on the head. They placed us on a thick bed of hay under the open wooden box where the child who had touched us was. The little ones looked at me with their big round eyes and blurted among themselves how the child had touched me first before any of them. I curled my body over the hoof the little child had touched and I closed my eyes. I thought of Kordel alone in the meadow and I wished strongly that he would leave the bed of fresh young grass and come to where we were.

I must have fallen asleep for when I woke up, the little ones were talking excitedly among themselves. Did you see their gowns? Of pure gold they are! Surely they must be the richest men in the whole world. My mother has told me about kings but this is the first time I ever saw one! I opened my eyes wider and saw the three tall men robed in gowns of glossy velvet whose hems trailed behind them heavy with embroidered gold and silver flowers. How their stone-studded crowns sparkled blue and green and red and yellow and white and violet. They came solemnly to where we were, their hands loaded with gifts. The little ones talked noisily and ogled the three rich men who came nearer and nearer the child. I felt sad although I could not tell why. I looked at the master and the old men and the women and the little boys who were still grouped under the shadows and turned to the little ones beside me. I looked at my shining coat and then looked up again at the three men who had reached the box above us and who were laying their gifts at the feet of the child. Then I knew. I slumped over the hay and wished that the master never found me anymore. When I looked up again, the three rich men were gathered around the box, rapt admiration on their faces. On the edge of the box, the rich gifts shone neglected. Suddenly I remembered how the child touched each of us on the head and I curled over the hoof he had touched, feeling very happy and light inside.

(1952) First published in *The Philippine Collegian*, January 3, 1953, pp. i; xxiv.

Empty Room across the Hall

E VERY NIGHT IS LIKE THIS NIGHT. You wake up to find yourself
alone. Suddenly alone. Utterly alone. You stand up from the
narrow bed in the corner. You hear the rusty springs say the familiar
squeak, squeak as you shift your weight while feeling the cold floor
for your slippers. The dresser near the window has a misty oval face
mirror. It has a small crack in it. You push the gingham curtain
stringed across the window to let into the room the flood of light
from the many flourescent signs across the street. Over the roofs of
the many hamburger stands with the big flourescent signs blinking
loudly over them is the bay. Now the bay looks much the same every
night. You do not expect it to change its looks, anyway. Dark and
big and beautiful with many dots, tiny dots of light blinking endlessly
over the dark quiet waters. You like it that way. Although the tiny
dots of light have their way of reminding you of pearls on mud. That
was how long ago. You tore savagely at a gift pearly necklace you
were wearing and watched the milky grains fly in all directions then
scatter themselves in a pool of mud. That was when you discovered
the necklace was fake. Little circles of paste stringed together and
sold at some small downtown store ten centavos apiece. The big
phoney. Smooth talker. But that was nothing. Nothing at all. Ah, the
sea has a quieting effect. You rest your forehead against the cold
glasspane of the overhanging shutter and let the seawind blow your
hair, your face, your tired body. Same as any night. It feels cool. It
smells good.

You sit in front of the dresser and start to comb your hair.
Same as any night. The only difference is, tonight a loose white sheet
flutters under the blue jar of pomade. You place the comb down and
reach for the paper. You pull the sheet. Oops, there goes a dark bill
whish on the floor near your feet. You stoop for it and hold it against
the bright window. Twenty pesos, it says. You fold it carefully and

slip it into the low neckhole of your tight bodice. You take up the white sheet. On it is scrawled: many thanks. You crumple that up: crackle. That's nothing. You throw it outside the window. There.

Some guy, eh. Your hair is a mess. Kind of tender sort of fellow. The others just hand you some crumpled bills, leave the room with haste, not bothering to look up at you straight in the eyes nor back at the room. Everything is forgotten. Just like that. With them. How many others were there. How far back. Do they forget? Do they really? Really. Because: you don't. You just can't forget things like these. There was a sick little boy and bills were pouring in. Enough to drive one crazy with fear. A little boy is about to die. Oh, where will the money to pay the food, the medicine, the oh so many things come from? There is a war going on. You don't have to tell me: I know. God, why doesn't Jess write any more. Cold and trembling and wet with perspiration, you toss in half-sleep deep in the night. Jess' body dangling in the mid-air. How mangled and brightly crimson it was. You shudder and clutch at the little boy. How warm and thin he feels. How his eyes grow big and bright with fever. The druggist was a friendly, jolly fellow. He had many friends. . . . The little boy dies even when there is money to pay for the bills. Alone in the room, long after, there would always be the thin face of the little boy whose eyes would grow bigger and brighter on the walls, against the ceiling, on the floor, on the chairs, on the blue bedspread—everywhere— until the lonely room seems to burst blindingly bright, unbearably bright. And the dark strange rooms, compared to that lonely room, would be comforting, sheltering, no longer as revolting as before. . . You have to have some hairpins. That fellow. He bothered to scrawl a note. That's something. Boy, that's wonderful. Only you can never tell if you would meet the guy again. Now isn't that just too bad: tsk, tsk, tsk. Better use some pomade to comb that hair down. You feel tired. And the night has just begun. Think of that. The night has just begun. Makes you feel sick just to think about that: the night has just begun. As always, there are the aspirins.

You stand from the stool and regard the vague reflection on the misty oval face mirror with a small crack on it. You pass your hands flat over the skirt that hugs your full hips flaring down over your thigh and iron out carefully the little creases. You lean across the dresser. The face on the mirror becomes distinct. You wet your forefingertip and pass it over the archs of your eyebrows. Now every- thing is all right, the face on the mirror says. You smile. So many things are hidden by a smile. You smile and then arch your eyebrows

as though you were the movie star you once saw at the Ideal. The
girl was blonde and she said: Try and do it if you can. Then she
walked away, her heels clicking smartly. How she walked. You tip the
bottle of aspirins and let one, two aspirins roll into your cupped palm.
You throw the two white tablets into the far end of your tongue and
swallow them with one big gulp. Now that ought to take care of the
pain in your head that goes throb, throb, throb, and the tiredness
you feel.

The door of the dark room opens into the long dark hall with
the many identical doors facing each other with mute indifference.
The hall is deserted and the many rooms behind the identical doors,
quiet. When you were new in the place, you used to get lost. Betty,
the plump gossip who was there before you, said they ought to put
up numbers. Her surefire method, she had confided, is to walk one,
two, threeing the doors until she stops at her own. Rose, who always
complains about her oily skin, drew a big apple on her door with
one fast stroke with her lipstick; she used to barge into the wrong
rooms. After that, she never got lost. The apple was red and big and
uneven like the apples the little boy drew with crayon sticks: green
apples, red apples, yellow apples, blue apples, black apples all over
the paper. The little boy would start with one bold line from a point
going circular and dipping back into the same point they looked like
exercises on an O with a cleft. On the narrow stairs, you walk slowly,
passing your palm over the cold bronze line of the snaking banister.
Music floats to you, same as any night, slow-timed and sweet and
soft from the floor below.

The floor must be full. Usually is by this time. There would be
the young fellows, the middle-aged fellows with impressive middles,
the old men with dyed hair, mostly men in uniforms: navy-blue,
white, olive-green, sea-gray—eager, interested, sober, boisterous, skep-
tical, strange men all tired from the war and wishing to forget. So
many people wishing to forget.

Now look. The shiny tile floor gleams under the strings of red,
green and blue bulbs swinging from the ceiling with the many long
ribbons of colored crepe. There is the muted shick-shock, shick-shock
of heels joining the soft, slow-timed music. On the floor, the vague
shadows of the couples in tight embrace move like ghosts under the
bluish flood of light now clouded by smoke from cigars and cigarettes.
Same as any night. Nothing new. You get used to it.

You stop at the foot of the stairs idly fingering the bronze ball
that marks the end of the snaking banister. The long blue counter

at your right, the long blue counter closeting the blue glass panels of tall bottles of red, brown, yellow, green and white liquid and the many trays of clear tall glasses is half-full of gaily chatting American sailors and army men and painted women. The small orchestra lost in the shadowy nook, close to the bar has not ceased playing sweet, soft, slow timed music. The couples on the dully-gleaming floor are still moving as if in a trance as the music wraps all of them with its soft wailing strain. Once, a couple walked toward you. They stopped, the man in khaki, very familiar to you, bent to whisper something to the girl. The young girl tossed her pretty head and a long high-pitched laughter spilled from her white throat. They walked past the foot of the stairs where you were standing death-still and climbed the long stairs, the young girl still chuckling, the man not looking in your direction even once. It was a dream. The black mid-air. The dangling body mangled and brightly crimson.

You turn to the tall indian jars of giant ferns and slip to the side door, a hand clapped tightly over your trembling mouth. What if you had shouted all of a sudden as you stood there death-still and he came oh, so near you could touch his arm. If you had shouted before you reached the walk as you shout now like one gone mad. He would have looked at you and said, Fe! Or looked at you and not know you at all, perhaps. And the manager. He would have seen you then. What would he say to you had he seen you slipping away under the shadows. You should have waited around until a fellow comes up to you and asks for a dance or two. Or you should have walked slowly to the bar to join the people chatting gaily in front of the blue counter. Take a drink. Let the golden liquid bubbling from the clear tall glass slowly warm you inside and make you feel again that strange exciting tongue of fire cruising deep down into your very blood. Like you do every night. As if nothing has happened at all.

The sea breeze will do you some good, you say. Sure, it will. A little walk will do you some good.

You walk to the deserted walk outside steadily like that. As though nothing has happened at all. You pass between the many shiny cars parked side by side in front of the club and cross the wide boulevard. A few cars move slowly in the night cutting the dark wide span of the boulevard with their headlights. You stop and wait for them to pass—these people, happy and sure in the peace of their cars driving home, perhaps taking sniffs of the evening breeze before they drive home. Knowing the quiet of a home waits for them. What would have happened had he come to you when the little boy was still alive? You catch a glimpse of a girl who was gazing idly at the bay while her back rested softly on the deep shadowy upholstery of the back seat of a car. What could the girl be thinking about? A jeep toots its horn at you and you step aside to let it pass. The front seat held, beside the man who was driving, a young woman holding the head of a sleeping child on her lap. They could have been from a movie or from the circus. Oh, for the child's sake. For the little boy's sake. If only he came before the going became so unbearably rough!

That tree there would be just fine, you think. There are quite a number of people in the park tonight. You spread your scarf under the tree and sit on it. There. The sea breeze sure feels good, doesn't it. You can sit here forever. You hear the sea lapping the rocks on the shore and the sea breeze fanning the leaves. Except for these sounds, everything is quiet. Makes you feel quiet inside too. Makes you want to cry because you feel too quiet inside. This is nice, isn't it? The air is clear and good to smell. And there are only the people talking in quiet tones and walking easily around. There were many summer evenings you walked with him here. When the low accessoria became too warm and noisy to afford decent sleep. You came with him here before he went away to fight. You walked around not saying anything, the little boy toddling between the two of you, one little hand clasped in yours and the other lost in his big brown hand.

Say, this is too quiet for you. Take a walk. Yeah, why not take a walk. That's what you used to do every night with the other girls, especially when the floor was not full and the manager sent you and the girls out for a stroll. So okay tonight you are going to take it easy. Take a walk just the same. The pain is gone, you say. The grass is wet and is nice to walk on. Nice to walk on. Wet grass.

Hey, your scarf. There. Now, isn't it nice to feel the grass under your feet. There! Look out for that kid. Whew, you caught her just in time, just in time. She would have fallen on the stone jutting from the grassy mound if you had not caught her in time. You wonder why the kid was running away so hard, her little curls laughing with her in the wind while she ran. She is still gasping for her breath even now while you hold her close to your breast.

–Here, kid, that lady is calling for you.

–Baby, come back here.

–Nice kid.

–Baby, let go the lady's skirt. It's getting dirty.

–The kid's a honey.

–She's messing you up ma'am.

–I can always change clothes. You're lucky to have this kid.

–I'm her nurse ma'am.

–Her nurse, did you say?

–Yes, ma'am.

–Nurse! If the kid were mine, I won't give her to no nurse. I'd walk around with the kid and let her curl her little soft fingers around my thumb. Like this now.

–Let's go, baby. She's got enough air to last her the night. She couldn't sleep in her little room, so we came.

–Well, it's late for a kid to be out.

–Glad you saw it that way.

–The draft might get her.

–Yes, sure thing.

–I hate to see the kid go. Here, goodbye, honey. Could I buy her a bottle of pop or something?

–No, ma'am. She wouldn't be able to sleep with a bottle of pop in her stomach.

–Popcorn then. Here, here.

–No, please, that will be bad for her stomach, ma'am.

–Or ice cream. Now she'll love that! That isn't bad for her stomach at all.

–We go. The girl's sleepy ma'am.

–Aw, okay. I hate to see the kid go.

–Say goodnight to the pretty lady, baby. Come on, be my good girl.

–Goodnight, kid.

–Goodnight, ma'am. Say goodnight, baby.

–Aw, that's all right. She's shy.

–She's three almost. Say goodnight like a good baby.

–She's smiling. She's cute.

–Say goodnight like I tell you.

–A smile is better than a goodnight to me. The kid's shy, I tell you.

–Maybe, you're right.

–Say, take care when you cross the street. Never can tell about those drivers you know.

–Yes, ma'am. Goodbye, ma'am.

–A whole careless bunch of drivers. Take care, I tell you.

You watched the two figures cross the grassy ground, the boulevard, the pavement across the boulevard. The two figures grow smaller and smaller and they disappear behind the corner of a tall apartment building. You turn to the bay and look at the white wavelets lapping the rocks below. A little boy with a *kaing* slung over his young shoulder goes near you. You do not turn to look at him; thin face shows too well under the frequent flare of headlights from the passing cars from the boulevard.

Balut Ateng, you hear the boy offer.

No, son, you say without turning.

They're still warm *Ateng,* you hear the boy begin and you know the sales talk would go on and on unless you stop it.

No, I don't want any, you say emphatically. You feel you must be left alone.

What's the matter, *Ateng,* your lover's not here to buy you some? You turn, shocked at the very unexpected retort, to glare at the *balut* boy. You take in his shirt that is dirty and tattered at the shoulder under the strap that holds the *kaing.* The thin face lights up and smiles at you knowingly. You look away and try your best to ignore the young boy. This young *balut* boy. Under your sheer silk blouse, you feel the loud throbbings of your heart. A few people have turned their heads to look at you and the young boy who is still looking up at you with that knowing gleam lighting up his whole thin face. Somebody asked: Is the boy bothering you ma'am? No, you say aloud, too loud. As though you wanted to believe it yourself, no! You walk away from the boy slowly at first, then quickening your pace when you feel the hard surface of the boulevard under your heels. Your lover's not here to buy you some? Not here to buy you some? Not here to buy you some? Not here? Not here? Is the boy bothering you ma'am? No! Not here? Bothering you? Not here? Bothering you? Not here? Bothering you? Not here? Bothering you? No, of course not! Your heels on the hard boulevard beat a defiant click, clock, click, clock, click.

There are quite a number of cars parked in front of the club by the time you reach the sidewalk. You look around furtively to make sure the boy has not followed you. Under the glittering neons of the clubhouse, there are only the shiny cars, couples coming out of them, slamming doors and heading for the daily lighted entrance of the club which is screened by a thick growth of palmettoes. You breathe deeply and walk to the side door of the club. You chuckle to yourself softly. It was silly to be afraid of a little boy. It was foolish to run away from him so.

The floor is crowded now and it seems dimmer by the heavy smoke from cigar and cigarettes. The spotlight focused on the pianist running his fingers over the keys in the orchestral nook is the only bright spot on the floor, all the rest seem to recede into the shadows.

You catch a glimpse of the manager who seems to be headed your way. You feel a sudden desire to escape from him, from the place, hide under the shadows or run somewhere, somewhere he wouldn't find you. You hope, feeling your heart quicken with that sudden thought that he did not really see you. But the sheepish grin hanging on the corners of the tobacco-stained mouth has widened into a lazy smile and your heart seems to sink with the realization that he saw you; that he is coming to you as surely as you stand motionless and waiting near the tall indian jars of giant ferns. You smile back.

The manager is motioning to someone who stands close to the shadows of the jars of giant ferns, the sheepish grin on his tobacco-stained mouth growing wider.

You look. Well, what do you know! A young man. The young man looks at you. His mouth twists into a slow uncertain smile. You smile at him, and then catch your lower lip with your teeth, bite hard at it to keep it from trembling. They all look alike, don't they. Under the bluish flood of light, they all look alike. This young man looks pale. It is because of the lights here, you say. Then you look again and see the dull uncertain smile curling the pale line of the young man's lips. You wonder if that has been caused by the lights too.

You smile in parting at the manager, who bows at you and then walks lazily to the bar. You climb the narrow stairs. Sure, just like that—swaying your hips like the older girls taught you. The fellow with his dull smile will follow you close enough. They all do.

Every night would be like this night. Like tonight until the last night comes. When, you can never tell. Dotty, the girl in the room opposite yours went away last week. A young girl, just a child, who laughs nervously in front of the men, took Dotty's room. The manager with his easy sheepish grin patted Dotty on the shoulder and said genially that she must take a vacation. Dotty was afraid to go. She told you so before she went, remember. While she was packing her things, she told you. And you sat on her bed and listened to her gravely, not knowing what to say. You did not say anything because you did not know what to say to her. In front of the club, the manager patted Dotty on the shoulder again, assured her that he would take her back as soon as she put on more weight and color, laughing as he said so and then hailed a passing taxicab. He opened the door of the cab, shoved Dotty's trunk inside and held Dotty's elbow while she climbed into the back seat near her lonely trunk. You saw the manager push a small roll of bills into Dotty's colorless palm as soon as she was seated inside the cab. You thought it was mighty decent of the manager.

Then briefly, Dotty thrust her peaked face out of the window and under the glittering neons as you raised your hand in goodbye, you saw her smile. And you thought, shuddering inwardly, it was the bravest smile you ever saw in your whole life.

Nervous laughter rings from behind one of the identical doors and pierces the quiet of the long hall. Where could Jess be now. Behind one of these doors. It's funny: just to think about this. Here you are walking with a man. And Jess is somewhere behind these identical doors. What if he would come out of that door, whatever door it is, and meet you here walking steadily like one who has walked this lonely hall every night of her life. Jess would tear himself from the young girl and face you perhaps, perhaps. There would be words. Angry words. Sad words. Maybe there would be nothing said between you at all. As if you two never knew each other at all.

There is your door before you now. You remember the man with the dull smile. He is watching you. You beckon to him and twist the cold knob of the door before you. The kid. What could she be doing now. How lucky her mother is, only she seems not to know it. Not to know it. Her nurse is tucking her in bed, no doubt. You would give your thumb for the kid to hold on to any time. Any time. You grow aware of the man with a dull smile standing near you. You do not look up at him. The door to the empty room stands open. You enter it quietly.

(1952) First published in *The Sunday Chronicle This Week Magazine,* January 11, 1953, pp. 16-17.

Walled City

THROUGH THE HALF-MOON on the rain-mistied glass shield, she saw the thick wall of Intramuros. Against the gray wet sky, its embattlement showed hoary growth that whipped in fury under the gusts of rain. It was a black monster, furious hair in defiance of the wind and rain; a proud and unrelentingly strong monster standing tight against the angry elements, stubborn arm spread around the old city. Somehow the sight held her heart and she shuddered under its tense grip. It frightened her and strangely too, she had to admit, it fascinated her. Home where the Quezon City hills drew a blue background in clear mornings was never so dear to her and never so, so far. She looked up at Dan; he had not noticed her (Was it in anticipation of home?), his eyes were bright, he was stepping on the gas; the car skidded under the heavy arch of the gate, past the wall and suddenly, the old city sprang around her; the sheltered comfortable, ancient city. She felt herself caught, she felt it—inevitably caught inside its darkly beautiful moss-choked walls.

She was alive to the black dripping things the car passed by; the ancient streets on which rivulets marked patterns on the flat cobbles and washed into the canals alongside the narrow sidewalks, the tiny closed shops with clouded square peep windows, the dim houses which wore their huge tile roofs like oversized hats and once, briefly blazed in full by the headlights, the tall immensely quiet Cathedral, half-hidden from view by the waving heads of the rain heavy *acacias*. Snuggled to him, her head nestling on his shoulder, she could still feel the cold outside, alerted to the tiniest sound on the streets, afraid lest out of the dripping things around them, a hand would shoot out to take them both.

Then it was before them, the old iron gate; Dan had turned the car from the road to face it. At three short beeps, after a pause, the gate creaked open and Dan drove over the driveway; after the wet palmettoes shone the high, white-latticed veranda. He stopped the car under the veranda where the foot of the blue-tiled stairway sat among the ferns. She could not see much of the old house. Dan had told her it was old, falling in some parts but the old woman refused to have it retouched. Where it showed in parts through the rain-soaked trees, it looked grayish.

She was half-aware of the man in a torn raincoat until he opened the car and flung open a big black umbrella for her. Dan had alighted and walking to her side of the car said, I'll take it, Mang Desto, take care of the luggage instead.

She came out of the car to him and smiled when introduced to Mang Desto, who according to Dan, was the old family gardener. The old man had smiled brightly murmuring, Welcome, Misses and to Dan, She's pretty, Danilo, at which Dan chuckled and placed an arm over her shoulder whispering as the old man turned to open the back of the car, We're home, hon. Then, he added as if to reassure her, You'll love her, hon, she's a most remarkable woman.

Dan ran half-way the stairs when he saw Candida. He ran to her like a little eager boy, hugged her tightly until on Candida's flushed wrinkled cheeks tears rolled. Dan still held her when he turned saying Didi, this is Editha. Hon, this is Candida. I call Didi my milkmother.

Editha gave her hand to Candida and got a warm embrace instead. So this is my Danny's wife, the old woman said looking at her closely. Editha flushed warmly and the old woman smacking her lips said, My, but you are a lovely child!

Dan's mother was old, about sixty. She had told Editha waving her hand, Sixty or more, what does it matter? She was wearing a blue kimono, fine strokes of bright brown bamboo leaves and orange-beaked white herons racing across the hem. The study where Candida led them after she and Dan have changed their clothes fitted Dan's mother, closed over her like some familiar perfume. It was old, cluttered with so many glossy, sheeny, breakable objects. Dark figurines. Empty vases. Ebony, now reddish statuettes. Porcelain lamps on slender-legged sidetables with prisms that tinkled and glowed blindingly against the light. And near the corner, before the tall screened window, an armchair worn on the back and arms and a footstool; beside it stood a shining stand curved to an "S" with an empty brass bird cage quivering at its hook at the slightest blowing of the wind between the screen slats. The objects sprang from their dead corners at her, each fragile and glowing as empty pink eggshells. And photographs, she never saw so many in a single room all her life. They were faded and showed white spot on the sepia. Set in all sorts of black-varnished frames, square, oblong, rectangular frames, they hang against the old yellowing walls in confusing disarray, without regard to size and shape, all of them commanding attention to their stiff poses, Spanish in feature most and bewilderingly formal and sharp-eyed.

Dan walked to his mother and stooped to kiss her on the forehead. The old woman clung to his collar and purred with misty eyes, "My little boy, you're back, you're back."

Editha stood before them. For a moment she felt like stealing out of the room where she was, it seemed plain, an intruder. But Dan turned before she could make a move and taking her by hand led her to where the old woman sat.

She was sure she heard him say: "This is Editha, Moma." And she bowed not quite knowing what to do, caught the woman's faint lilac smell as she did. When she raised hers it was to look into a pair of the clearest gray eyes she ever saw. And such soft wrinkled face, pink lights seemed to flick from each tiny shellpale fold down to where they flowed to the point of the chin and got lost into the silken collar at the throat. The old woman had Dan's thin nose and flared nostrils and an almost straight line for a mouth.

"And now," the old woman said as though she suddenly remembered a task set before her, "the woman my boy married." She curled her hand over the silver head of the cane leaning between her knees and regarded her as she might, Editha thought, look over a curio piece for her room. The curled hand on the silver cane head gleamed yellow around the old nails and knuckles, it looked like some varnished finely grained pine shiny with years of polishing.

It was inevitable, long as waiting is always long, Editha looked at the floor, her face getting hot all over and when the old woman said at last, "Well, I must say he has disposition..." she raised her head as though shot.

Dan roared with pleasure, patted see-didn't-I-tell-you-she's-okay on her shoulder and walked off to the armchair still chuckling.

Editha turned to the old woman and found the gray eyes still levelled at her." You are," she was startled at the sound of her own voice, "you are better? Dan—I mean, your son told me you are not well."

"Ah, yes, an old trouble," the old woman said laying the faded hand on her silken collar, "my old heart."

"I understand," she said suddenly feeling sincerely sorrow for the old woman and felt she must console her somehow, "Really, it was a small, small wedding."

"Yes, Dan told me you wanted it to be quiet."

"I told Dan," she said picking her words, "we could start saving that way."

"Small weddings are unthinkable," the old woman said with firmness.

"I told Mama and—Dan, I rather would have it quiet. I'm never used to big gatherings. Dan knows how I avoid them. In the colegio, they used to laugh at me."

The wind gushed through the slats, with quick flashes, there was a clap of thunder, the empty brass cage, set trembling from its stand, burned a bright yellow.

For a moment they watched the rain through the slats and the burning empty brass cage. Editha pulled her collars and shivered distinctly.

When she turned the old cheeks were flaring.

"But still weddings must be big. Big! After ten years," the old woman said grasping tightly on the silver head of her cane and getting on her feet, "Mamas on wedding arrangements never fail to reminisce with a sigh on the day they sat under spires of Benguet lilies and bridal sprays in Malate Cathedral for my wedding. Ay, after thirty years even," she said waddling to the old yellowing wall and motioning with her cane to Editha, "Let me see—here, here," she paused before an oblong frame and announced with a ring in her voice, "My wedding!"

Editha looked closely at the faded photograph and tried to discern the old face in the young girl who smiled beneath a crown of tiny blossoms, there was her young man, in a tight suit, and big buttonaire on his lapel, seated on the arm of her chair and leaning softly towards her and behind them, suspended in the black background, as fireworks caught in full burst against a night sky, a bouquet mistily trailed by tulle and lace. Editha caught her breath and gasped, "I never saw anything so lovely in my life."

Editha took her eyes from the picture on the wall. The old woman was silently tracing the floor with the end of her cane, brows knitted. She raised her gray eyes to Editha and said suddenly, "Dan told me you agreed to stay."

So it was what bothered her all the time, Editha thought. She must be lonely and was afraid of being alone. Loneliness is never good. It is killing. One gets old; age is inevitable. But to be alone, whether one is old or young, it must be like dying. Loneliness spreads like some poison and death creeps slowly close behind it.

"I—I wanted to have a little place of our own," she said slowly, she had dreamed of a house near the sea, "a little place—an apartment even. Dan said you must not be alone."

The old woman smiled but she kept her eyes to the floor where she followed the end of her cane. "Dan and I," she said slowly as though the cane was one great pencil and she was taking down every word she said, "have always been together—when his father died—as far as I can remember." The cane halted and the old woman straightened visibly, "Of course, I can get used to being without him if I have to."

The words stung her cheeks like prickly pins and brought blood to their surface. She bit at her lips hard. "Dan told me you are sick— we must not leave you," she said trying to keep her voice down. "As you see," she said seriously, quite shyly, "we cut our plan for Baguio."

"The house is old, but it is big," the old woman said. "And," she added her voice becoming tremulous, "I'll not be in the way."

"Oh, but how you talk!" she cried grasping the old woman by the arm and shaking her, "When we are both your children now."

The old woman held to her almost in tears. "Come," she said smiling, "and I shall show you Dan when he was a little boy."

Editha sighed and passed a hand over her eyes. She felt tired but she must be bright while all these lasted.

"Dan," she said following close to the old woman, "have been telling me how it was when he was young."

"He has?" the old woman said looking at the other frames.

"Yes, he has," she said.

"But how he looked," the old woman said without taking her eyes from the frames on the wall. "Here, they are—I took them all— all—with my camera."

"Aw, Moma," Dan said from behind a newspaper. "Not tonight," he said putting the papers down and winking at the old woman. Editha felt blood creeping to the tips of her ears. The old woman frowned at Dan and he put up the papers before his face again.

"Except this one which the studio took for their annual," the old woman had turned to the frames, "here when he wore his gown." Dan looked thin and strange under a heavy black block cap.

Dan folded the newspaper on his knee and threw it on the table. "There will be time enough for that, Moma," he said.

"—but see this one when he was six months old—I took this one in the porch early in the morning when there was plenty of sunshine." The old woman was fingering the old frames and was smiling to herself. "You know," she said quite intimately, "I always lay him on his belly for sunshine and he would look so cute when he clapped his little hand to catch the sunshine on the floor."

"Editha is tired, Moma," Dan said.

"—and his first suit!" the old woman said as though she didn't hear Dan, "he used to run to me every time, you know. He would shout, Look, look Moma, what I found for you in the garden. See. Moma, how high I can jump."

"It's late, Moma," Dan said almost behind them.

But there was no stopping her "—his pretty butterfly collection, he caught them for weeks, and treated them in the evenings and dried them in the sun, then, he framed them and gave them to me with a bold inscription. "To the best Moma in the world." The old voice tore off even and triumphant.

Dan placed an arm on Editha's shoulder never suspecting tears, and whispered against her cheeks, "Let's go, hon, you must be tired." To his mother as he kissed her on the forehead, he said, "Goodnight, Moma."

The old woman walked away from the wall without saying a word. The light had gone from the grey eyes and they suddenly looked old, very old and dejected.

"We'll go, Mama," Editha said trying to sound light.

"Yes, of course," the old woman said walking slowly away from the frames and marking the floor with her cane. She walked between Editha and Dan. She stopped in front of her chair and declared, gathering the skirt of her loose kimono, "I'm not sleepy. I'll sit up."

Editha took Dan's elbow and heaved a sigh. Everything would be all right, she thought, she was tired, the old woman was tired. Dan was tired. All of them were tired and being tired made them strangers; sprang walls between them. But everything would be all right. She and Dan will be together again. Together they will pull down the wall that have sprung. By the morning, whatever walls there were would be dust under their feet.

"Dan, *hijo.*"

They stopped at the door and Dan turned, "Yes, Moma?"

"The—lights, *hijo,*" the woman said raising one of her slender faded hand over her eyes, "they bother me."

"Turn them off for you, Moma?"

"Please, *hijo.*"

Dan walked back to the tables and begun turning off the lamps until only the porcelain one with prisms sat bright on the side table near the old woman and bathed her with yellow light.

"Moma," it was Dan, "sleep well, we'll see you in the morning."

The old woman waved a hand at him but did not say anything. The rest of the room lay very dark and only the flashes between the slats marked the many dark, dark objects inside the room, once the empty brass cage swayed at the gust of wind. The rain had stopped.

Dan walked back to her at the door and placed an arm over her shoulder. They walked out of the room without looking back. Editha looked up at Dan; he smiled down at her. Yes, she thought everything would be all right.

They were almost at the door when they heard the old woman shriek. They ran back and saw her as she sank to the floor, the faded hem of her blue silk kimono flying about her outstretched legs, her faded hand clutching hard at her left breast.

Dan ran to her, supporting her head and half-carrying her to the empty armchair. "My heart, *hijo mio*," she gasped. Editha held the cushion ready but the old woman tightened her hold on Dan's head and would not let him go.

"Take me to Doctor Ira," she cried her whole body trembling, "tonight or I die!"

Dan looked at her over the old woman's head. He looked pale and there was a pleading look in his eyes.

Quietly, she looked down at the old woman but the old face was hidden completely against Dan's arm. Only an earlobe showed, under the wisps of white hair where it was pierced with a phosphorescent blue eyes of a diamond that winked at her steadily.

Candida came running into the room, almost stumbling at the door. "The señora," she cried, "what happened?"

Editha dropped the cushion and it fell limply on the armchair. "I'll ask the chauffeur to get ready," she said turning away.

(1954) First published in *The Literary Apprentice*, 1954, pp. 62-69.

Tia Purificacion

THE FIRST INCIDENT THE MORNING of Friday Mother and I brought Tia Purificacion to the clinic happened when Tia Purificacion halted before the long narrow mirror hung just before the swinging frozen glass door, passed both of her hands on her sagging cheeks and declared somewhat forlornly "I'm old."

It was a compelling and strange announcement: people do not go around publicly saying they are old aloud and sadly even if they actually were. My uncle's clientele on the white benches in the hall lifted their dull heads to fix their gaze on the creature that was my Tia Purificacion, shifted their feet on the polished red cement, their noses delicately raised, with flared interest in this atmosphere of menthol and antiseptic until they all appeared like wary well-disciplined pointers. A child clutching the limp arm of a rag teddy bear ran wide-eyed into the wedge of its father's legs. Nearby, a man rasped the phlegm in his throat, caught our eye as he stared keenly behind the stunted palmettoes springing from a huge clay pot.

Mother, of us three, jerked first from our held position, looked upon our spectators somewhat unkindly and pulled her sister by the arm into the clinic; Tia Purificacion tripped from the jolt, almost headlong but for Mother's firm hold on her. The girl with the rag teddy bear had started to cry, her father gathered her clumsily on his knees, patted her on the thighs, humming tunelessly. Mister Crutches knocked on the floor, one good leg making way toward the bench in great clap-clapping steps.

The pen of the nurse at the desk halted on the card; our shadows fell over her desk blotter and shaded her writing: she seemed displeased. She tapped the slender tip of her penholder on the blotter. "You have not been called in yet," she told Mother, her wide pupils floating above the half moons of her rimless double-vision.

"We should like to wait here if we may," Mother's voice was apologetic.

"The benches are outside, Dr. Fernando has implicit orders," the nurse said the tip of her penholder still tapping the blotter.

"It is all right," Mother opened her fan with one crisp gesture, "Dr. Fernando is my brother."

The nurse dropped her pen, snapped her card file and leaned on the lid while she got up from her desk. She arranged some chairs for us, shielding her eyes from Mother; the iron legs clanked on the floor, you could see that she was uneasy, but poor woman, she had Uncle's interests and his orders above her heart. Besides, she was new. The former nurse with a limp, Mrs. Reyes, knew us; the sight of Mother enough to send her limping across the place, rag in hand aflutter to dust the dustless seats.

"I'll be back," this new nurse said as she backed to the white taut screen partitioning the room. "There are some magazines under the table," she called out to me.

The magazines were grimy, sad-looking copies of *Life* and *Collier's*. I thumbed through the pages for the coloured photographs and illustrations. Mother was still fanning herself; Tia Sion sat close by sucking at her soggy thumb. *Life* featured four pages on a pajama game, a long question and answer article on cancer, complete with graphs and x-ray pictures and six full spreads on Japanese gardens. A short foreword spoke of the quiet intuitive sense for beauty of the Japanese. The photographs were in brilliant colors. The yellows of chrysanthemums, the greens of bushes and the bright browns of Japanese bridges actually sang from the grimy pages.

Yesterday I discovered gardening to be the only activity that could hold Tia Purificacion. Somewhere in the folds of her brain must still lurk a woman's natural liking for flowers. Yesterday, Mother went to the movies. Tia Purificacion on my hands, not quite certain on what to do to keep her occupied, I had led her to Mother's rose pots. All other activities seemed to flicker before her dull gaze. Naturally, I was dubious as to what her reaction to the idea would be. But she seemed to brighten at the prospect of performing a task she had always watched Inay attend to each morning. Smiling her assent, she had extended her hand to me as if to say: "Lead me to them."

On reaching the wood stands where the mossy rose pots lined, Tia Purificacion pushed up her sleeves and almost at once was pinching worms from the roses and washing the rose leaves with lime water. For the first time in weeks, her cheeks flushed, her hands worked light and quick as butterflies. I fell into the task beside her, the old garden wall cast a wide shade over us and for a while neither of us talked. The soil needed turning, I looked for spades and found instead a dull knife and a pick. I released them from the piece of rattan that clumsily bound them together, handed the dull knife to Tia Purificacion. To stir the soil with, I said, and just as quickly realized my mistake. Tia Purificacion's hands were arrested sharply in mid-air; a sudden breathtaking pause; defined, quiet, alarming.

Her hand tore from the air to snatch the knife from me. She stuck it to the hilt into the wet soil in the pot before her. Veins stood out fat and blue on her knuckle in the effort. She turned her small face from me. She said, "Whenever I see a knife, *iha,* I always think that I should kill myself."

Tia Purificacion, Tia Sion, we call her, had been with us for three weeks. She was Mother's eldest sister, sixty years of age, six years older than Mother. She was tall, slender, acutely thin-boned. She comes under those rare women whose bone formation seem to have barely enough flesh to cover their structure, their figures infalliably striking up a singular sense of delicate frailty and strong angular fineness. Her features were markedly sensitive, a prominent mouth, a small haughty touch of a nose, pointed cheekbones, all: whirling to the whorl which were the eyes (remarkably intense expressive centre), it ran through the whole family, deep smoke-gray eyes shaded by bushy eyebrows slightly curled at points.

Three weeks in the house. Tia Sion could well be a shadow. She barely moved about and took care to keep out of our way. She followed Mother about though, like a toddler grasping at its parent's skirt tails. Once, she sulked when she woke from her afternoon nap and found Mother had gone to visit some friends without the least consulting her. We would only have her with us at the table, even then she had to be coaxed to join, and at it, she would pick her food slowly and disinterestedly. If a dish were pressed on her, she would only shake her head and push the plate away. Mother had always tried to be gay with her, kidding her a lot, prattling endlessly about their childhood days now dead and gone, gossiping about the neighbors, mimicking this and that housewife and sighing gratefully at the faintest hint that the deep eyes shone and were a little bright again. The last few days, Mother made it a point to have Tia Sion with us; set within our group when we had our evening discussions, kept within our circle of laughter. Mother would be there, knitting or darning (her needle marking her mental therapeutic notes?), and without being obstrusive, with tact and naturalness once in a while, she would raise her head and peer through her glasses, prying Tia Sion in the sofa with, "You were there weren't you, Sion, the day Eding got married? She has three boys now, all fast growing. The *bandidos*. Eding, you should see her. A skinny chicken if ever there is one. Poor, dear girl. Well, Lorenzo who got suspended from his classes is Eding's eldest. Fine boy. Taller than his father." Or, "But of course, you remember Esperanza? Tell them how smug Esperanza looked the day her husband ran away."

It was always remember this or that and tell them, Sion, tell them. Thus goaded to talk, Tia Sion would prattle endlessly, closing her evening's performance with a dissertation on her secret fears, fanning them in size; all diseases afflicted her, all sins heaped on her until it would seem that she had complete and absolute monopoly of all the evils in the world. Our laughter would die off and our spirits dampened for the rest of the evening, we would retire to our beds blinking quite foolishly at being so flippant and gay in the face of this miserable, wretched creature.

She got on our nerves with her constant complaints about the night crickets and the grass frogs, of how she was not able to sleep because out in the fields, the vacant lots across the street, these night creatures "bickered too much," her mouth shaped the words, repeated them. Mother laughed it off swearing to us that Tia Purificacion snored the whole night! They slept together, Mother and Tia Purificacion, I had to move out of the huge bed where I had been sleeping with Mother since Father died. Not that I was the bravest. The first week, I suffered nights, whole nights, curled up and awake because each time I straightened, I imagined my toes tracing the shape of my Father's leg.

But Tia Purificacion would say No! It was foolish of Consuelo to say she snored the whole night. She was awake, she counted the clock chimes through the night and towards morning. Doesn't she have shadows around her eyes to prove it? Aren't her hands unsteady? It was because she was unable to sleep. Sleep. Oh, at every free chance, Tia Purificacion would confront us: Tia Purificacion, her deep eyes undilatingly focused on our faces. How does she look? Was she getting old? How were her eyes? Wasn't she very thin? Haggard? Pale? God, God, she was sick! Wasn't she sick? She looked pretty sick, doesn't she? Was she pretty, pretty yet? Was she pretty yet, really?

Beauty and age rarely mix, Tia Purificacion's allusion to her age, before the mirror outside (it has become, as a matter of fact, a piteous chant with her), can be better understood if one knew that she was quite a beauty when she was young. She used to be May queen, muse, had had quite her share of serenades, recited poetry, flowers, crowns, letters. They made her conscious of it, Mother said, men ogled when she passed. Once, she cried because just after communion, a wave of profound quiet washed over her soul, a man had knelt close by to nudge her. She had her first love affair when she had barely gotten over the shock of puberty. It was with a middle-aged zarzuelista who later turned out to be married and had a brood of children. She came home and had a stillbirth and the blood had not been washed from her drenched blankets when Grandfather almost brought his cane down on her but for the pallor of her small young face. Grandmother sank to the floor near the bed moaning she was a shameless wretch not to think of her younger sisters, God's miracle if any man would even look at them now. Tia Purificacion's eyes filled and just as quickly, Grandmother snatched her from the covers, kissed her repeatedly all over her sweaty face and begged for forgiveness.

The nurse came out of the screen partitioning the room. "Dr. Fernando will see you now," she said.

Mother got up first to support Tia Purificacion by the arm. The nurse adjusted her glasses and sprang to help them. I folded the *Life* on my lap and inserted it under the table.

Dr. Fernando, Tio Pablo, was wiping his hands with a white hand towel when we came in. He stood before a wash basin held up by a wrought iron stand, painted white, its three legs ringed together and worked out to the shape of an hourglass. Tio Pablo with white sideburns, smiling, whipped one end of the hand towel across the drier rack and waddled toward us, his swart face flushed with pleasure. He reached to crumple my hair, asked me how I was finding college, pinched me on the chin when I protested he was mussing my hairdo. He guffawed when I said he and Father always took for granted that we were always seven-year olds, grasped Inay and Tia Purificacion by the shoulders and called them "niñas." A younger brother calling them "niñas." It promptly dyed the top of their faded cheeks with vivid red and lit the soapy coat of their eyes. Hugging them close to his sides, crushing the stiff *pinokpok* of their butterfly sleeves and *panuelos,* Tio Pablo led all of us to the chairs grouped close to the window.

It was the coolest part of the room, the chairs were of tough, unpainted rattan with backs wearing half-oval cases of white denim tied with ribbons behind. The window was wide and low, almost opening the entire lower half of the wall. It carried cream-painted grills, four half-rolled spreads of reed blinds and a heavy load of clean robust ferns and mountain orchids. Across the room, the nurse went through quick very capable motions of fixing the place. She pulled the towel, folded it once and hanged it back neatly; sloshed the water from the basin, refilled it with fresh water from a pitcher. She halted before the enamelled steel cabinet, contemplated the skull on top of it, straightened its jaws, slammed a drawer here and there. Then she gave a quick pat to the cover of the examining table in the middle of the room, to shake the dust, and with a swift keen look that flashed her glasses, she left, her short rubber heels muted on the linoleum floor.

Of course, Tio Pablo, said, of course, her "niñas" were well. He never saw them looking as pretty. And young. Why, *Ate* Sioning looks hardly eighteen. On a flower-decked carroza, twirling a parasol, she can still be May queen, like—oh, not so long ago. Tia Purificacion's lips hinted a smile. Mother was impatient. "Sioning is sick, Pablito," she said.

Tio Pablo knew from the start. His eyes were at once professional, grave, anxious. "Something you ate, perhaps?" he said as his hand reached for Tia Purificacion's wrist, his eyes on the old woman's face as though the minute hand that kept his time slowly travelled across it. When he released her wrist, he held her face at arm's length, gently pried open her lower lids, squinted at the blood-red membrane, considered them for some time.

His questions were the usual chain of questions doctors ask. It was foolish to expect him to ask special ones just because Tia Purificacion was his sister. How was her sleep? he asked. Does she eat well? Does she have pains in the chest? In the head? In the belly? In the back? Does her hands and feet get cold? Does she have fevers in the afternoon? At nights? How are her bowel movements? Regular, huh? He half-tilted his head to catch Tia Purificacion's half-mumbled replies, his eyes alerted for signs while his fingers percussed on the flat back, dug into the hollow belly. Does it hurt here? How about here? Here?

Tio Pablo returned to his seat and did not say anything. His slender dark forefinger scratched at his sideburn, his bulk was hunched forward and his eyes shone with an intense look at thought. When he sat back on his chair and slapped his thigh, he was his jovial self again. "There is nothing wrong about you," he said. "All you've got to do is relax. You're tight as a golf ball."

He raised his arm and flexed it for all of us to see. Mother and Tia Purificacion watched with childlike concentration. "See what happens when I let go," Tio Pablo was saying. "Watch now," he said holding their gaze. "There. That's exactly what you should do. Loosen all knots of tension. They're bad. They're bad for the heart. They're poison."

"If it were as simple as uncurling a fist to free the flex," Tia Purificacion said pressing her palms together and resting her chin on the fingertips until she looked as though she was about to pray. "But this is different."

"Caramba, Sioning, I'd take you to play golf with me if you were a man. Great game," he exclaimed, his eyes glowing. "You're too dead serious but a bad swing, a good laugh will soon fix all that."

"Dead is right," Mother said settling back on the chair, "Sioning is like a half-dead fish thumping its tail on the bottom of a basket. No fight. Just complains. Complains. Complains. Not that I'm tired. But one must fight in life, show more grit. If there were mistakes in the past, the present is not space enough for apologizing. Not brooding—worst, constant brooding spreads a vapour that thickens so fast one can no longer see the forms of what had gone nor of what is to come." Mother's voice was soft and sad. Her small round face defined by the strands of white hair held a look of regret. She dubbed at her eyes when she finished as though tears had welled in them and she meant to dry them with her knuckles.

Tio Pablo traced the bushy growth of his brow with a slow finger. "If," he said, his finger making a slow descent from the hairy curve, "If I told you that Honesta is dead, would you go back to Julian and be at peace? You're still his wife, before God, you are."

Tia Purificacion's eyes were suddenly shot red. "When he laid a stick on my back, I ceased to be," she pulled her hands to her lap, balled them, "I swore!"

Mother laid her arm over Tia Purificacion's shoulder. "Sioning, Ate, you are tired," she said.

"I shall not be pulled away," the old woman declared with a determination I never saw her assume before. "Do you know, iha," she said drawing her face to me until it was so close I saw the stubs of her white lashes. "I had three lovers." She spread three wrinkled fingers before her face and repeated, "Three."

"Sion!" Mother gasped.

Tio Pablo slapped his thigh saying, "*Caramba,* Sioning, you didn't have to tell the child."

The horror they raised at the statement amused me. "Aw, Tio Pablo, please," I said, "I'm no longer a child." He met this with respectful silence, although his eyes, for the first time, regarded me seriously. "Besides," I added, "three isn't much."

Tio Pablo jumped from his chair as if shot: "You should not joke like that, *iha,* hey," he said with an uncertain laugh.

When I said I was dead serious, so cross my heart I was, he turned full on Mother, "*Santisima* Consuelo," he said, "what have you been teaching your child!" He faced the three of us with exaggerated sighs, looking as if for the moment he viewed the three women who have martyred him most. He turned on his heel, socked his fist into the hollow of his palm and kept at it while he paced the floor. "Liberal education, a girl at that, bah!" he spat. And with conviction, "Her mouth should be soaped."

"But really, some women who are by constitution promiscuous have more, crave more and are not in the slightest weighted down by the thought," I said brightly, "I read that in a place called..."

"*Silencio!*" Mother snapped.

Tio Pablo actually glared.

Tia Purificacion looked at me as though she was seeing me for the first time.

Ever since that day at Tio Pablo's clinic, Tia Purificacion would come to my room. She would come at the most awkward moments. When I have just about wrapped my legs with my checkered blanket, a book on my knees. When my fingers were gory with paints and poised over a new sketch waiting on the board. She would come in and sit on the bed, arresting me in my most private hours. She would start timidly, inquire after the book if I was reading. The sketch, if I happened to be working on one. Actually, it was a signal for me to drop my work and attend to her. Answer her questions. Tell her stories.

The story of the prostitute and Christ before the jeering crowd delighted her most. She never seemed to get tired of it. She would ask me to narrate it again and again. When I first brought up the story, it seemed I had hoisted a gem before her eyes and it must be remounted and anxiously re-examined for any undiscovered flaws. Most of the time, I would speak of the physiology of her being, the natural functions of the body, the secretions that rule it when the blood moves. She would listen in rapt attention, her old eyes excited with tears. I would speak in a matter-of-fact tone, careful with my terms and shades of meaning, I would keep my eyes carefully lowered, afraid to betray that I understood perfectly why she was anxious to hear all these from me. And she, for her part, would sit close, holding my arm as if to stay me, touch to her proving me as physically real as my voice. So quiet, she would gasp at the revelation of the ultimate charity of Christ as a child would at the most whimsical passage in a fairy tale.

More because she found Tia Purificacion quieter after such talks with me and perhaps because she always respected my judgment and was disposed to admit of any step that might help, Mother would let Tia Purificacion talk with me as much as the old woman wanted to. Once a week, in the mornings, Mother would take her to Tio Pablo's clinic where the three of them would proceed to Mandaluyong for Tia Purificacion's regular checkup and occasional electric shock treatments. Mother was discreet about it, she said, No, no, it wasn't anything more than to decrease her head pains. All perfectly natural.

One Friday evening, at six, Tia Purificacion entered my room. She had just been to church with Mother. She wanted to make the confession and Mother had been very enthusiastic before they left. Mother had made preparations two days ahead. Tia Purificacion wanted an open confession, a "heart-to-heart talk," she called it and she expressed strict preference for Father Guillermo, a gentle old priest whose sheer goodness of heart overflowed his features but who lisped at his Sunday sermons because he was so old and toothless. Tia Purificacion was gay and brightly talkative when they dressed for Church. Now, in the half-light of the room, where the dark slowly closed above the window framing her white head, she looked pale and tired and very old. Her lids were shadowed and when I peered into her face, it was thick and red with crying. On the lap of her *saya,* her hands rested with a death-like quiet.

I rose from my seat and stood before her. My nearness cracked her stance, jarred her. She turned her head and threw herself across the bed, covering her face with white trembling hands. "Nothing but a sinner," she muttered, "I'm nothing but a lowly, dirty sinner." Her whole body convulsed with sobs, her hair fell around her shoulders and whipped across her face. I waited for her to calm down; her sobs subsided slowly and drawing her hands from her face, she looked up at me with swollen lost eyes. She got up from the mattress and sat on the edge of the bed, visibly pulling herself together. She pressed her palms tightly on her temples, she did that whenever she had the head pains and without looking at me, whether in apology for her behaviour or sheer release, she said tautly, gravely, her words flowing as in a speech rehearsed in the mind many times:

"Nights on nights, I would imagine myself on Judgment Day, apart from my family, alone, God's finger pointing me to Hell, an Angel's flaming sword waving me in file with jostling sinners. An awful moment, my husband's eyes and those of my dead beautiful children would settle on me, mingled pity and questioning in them. Even when I turn to hide. Shame. Caught in a sea of moaning sinners bellowing wrath, spite! I would shriek, panting and cold and the scene would trail away from my eyes like a dream."

She was trapped in a whirl of words, her voice climbed in pitch and fell soft whenever her mouth opened and caught the wind. I sat down beside her and pulled her to me. She rested her head on my breast, tremblingly, heavily, tiredly, I started stroking her hair with great clumsiness. I did not know what to say, how to start. Words seemed suddenly stripped of power, useless. "A tear," Father Aubry had said to Atala, "a tear will suffice to God!" But Tia Purificacion's shoulders were still trembling, her flesh was sick and cold and you could see that she was not listening to me. I called to Mother, she would know what to do. She always knows. My eyeballs stung, they felt moistureless, rash with ache. You could not help but wish that whoever taught Tia Purificacion about God could have been kinder.

She changed since that day after Church. Mother did not want to talk about it but I gathered that the old Father Guillermo had shuddered in the damp and sunless sacristy and had vehemently refused to hear any further unless Tia Purificacion left Dalmacio and returned to her first husband. But his was not to set conditions, where was the absolution, I said, did he mark the sign of the cross over her head and thanked God for this lovely grace of another penitent? Mother looked tired of it all but patiently explained it to be, "Just another talk, *iha*, and Father Guillermo saw in it his chance to bring her back to whom the Church had bound her and he grabbed it. If Tia Purificacion needed the communion so much, it was not too high a price to pay."

"A price!" I said finding it ill-chosen and repelling, "Surely, Father Guillermo has not made a bargain counter out of God's own supper table?"

Mother refused to speak to me about it after that.

I talked to Tia Purificacion about meeting another priest. Each time I tried, she would break into a smile, shake her head. She was reticent, unmoved by any attempt to open her again. She talked with Mother a few times, but it was only to say that she would like very much to go back to Dalmacio.

I came home one day to find her gone. Mother said she had cajoled, pleaded to be brought back to Dalmacio. They lived in a three-roomed apartment that faced an alley and a stone wall in one of the smaller streets in Ermita. Dalmacio was an auto mechanic, a burly thick man with a mat of hair on the chest, about forty. I went there once when their only son, then fifteen, died and the pall bearers almost slipped on the oil-drenched floor in the alley. Dalmacio kicked at one of the spare-parts sticking like a leg in the way and broke open his toe; it was a bad cut by the way the blood oozed from the leather of his shoe. Mother said Dalmacio was a stableboy in the old house when Tia Purificacion came, half-crazy with misery and apprehension that her husband would come and take her back.

That night, Mother tossed in bed and fidgeted with the covers. When I kept saying, why, why, why, Mother, why, she broke her silence to blurt Dalmacio had a woman. He did not seem pleased to see Sioning back at all. The girl was a niece, he said, she had come to live in the house because she was to enter college the following month. Mother gritted her teeth, you could feel her seething hatred within the gauze net, "the brazen lying bull," she said, "the brazen lying son-of-a-whore!"

The last time I saw Tia Purificacion was at the National Mental Hospital in Mandaluyong. A month before, Mother and I visited her at Ermita. Dalmacio treated us fine, served crystal bowls of crushed pineapples and hot buttered cones. Mother insisted on taking Tia Purificacion with us but she refused to leave the house. Dalmacio's niece was in the porch reading some movie magazines; she did not as much as rise to greet us. Then like the whistle of the steel sides of a plunged knife, the news fell on us, Dalmacio had carted Tia Purificacion to Mandaluyong because she had grown "uncontrollable." Mother fainted promptly and after a flurry of smelling salts, face-slappings and give-her-more-air, she came to and demanded she be brought immediately to her sister. Tio Pablo brought us in his old gray Chevrolet and deposited us at a doctor-friend's office. Mother insisted on going to the wards herself but Tio Pablo refused strongly. The cells must be not very pleasant-looking; as we waited on the cold steel folding chairs in the office, Tio Pablo's friend kindly diverting our attention, cries and laughter cracked through the window over what looked like a beginning of a flower garden. It was a shock to even think they came from human throats, they stabbed the afternoon air like thin whines and the crazied snickers of snivelling animals trapped in a slaughterhouse. Mother sniffed at her handkerchief, I patted her on the arm. I was feeling sick myself, my stomach held what seemed to be a series of circus tumblers and I was sure that if I as much as bend over, I would throw up on the polished floor.

Tio Pablo came into the office followed by a nurse and Tia Purificacion. She was wearing a blue denim loose dress, faded at the shoulders and back, frayed at the hem, of minimum cuts for mass sewing. She looked clean and well-kept, she even wore felt slippers but thinner than when I last saw her. She eyed us indifferently, a dull, drugged look glistening her eye. Mother ran to her with a sob and before any of us could stop her, she had pulled Tia Purificacion to her and had locked the thin body in her arms. Tia Sion rubbed her face against Mother's shoulder like an affectionate kitten, ran her mouth the length of the shoulder and established it upon the slope of flesh above the crisp panuelo, held on until a sharp, surprised cry rang from Mother. Tia Purificacion then flung her head back and laughed. The nurse dragged her away. Tio Pablo ran after them and talked in low tones with the nurse, while he stood not eight meters from us and he held his hat by both hands before his tummy like an offering. Mother turned to the doctor and me, smiled bewilderedly and as her fingers pressed on her shoulder, it was with a tenderness a woman's hand would press upon the mark of a kiss.

(1955) First published in *The Literary Apprentice*, 1955, pp. 42-58.

marble. Under the roofed portico of the *Viuda's* mansion, the benches were lined on the granite floor, about eight long benches, each of which seated from eight to ten children, depending on how friendly they were at the time. In the center of the yard was a greenish fountain gushing brackish water into a round pool. To the children, the pool was an awe-inspiring symbol of sophistication and aristocracy; it had ceramic hand-painted and glazed bridges and tiny pagodas, here and there, a mauve toad or sea horse in moldy clay which the few surviving goldfish nibbled at or ignored. These, the children pampered and, when the *Maestra* was not looking, fed with finely-grated tobacco which the bigger boys unrolled from cigarette stubs picked from the streets outside. It was fun to watch the fins and golden tails wiggle drunkenly under the floating weeds and ferns.

To the children, it was not so much the profit to be gained from learning all about the Trinity in one person and one person in the Trinity (which was beyond them, anyway) or how the Holy Ghost descended on Saint John or how the cock crowed thrice when Peter denied his Lord. Clearly, to them it was the profit to be earned by collecting the little cards which were distributed after each cathechism lesson. *Asistencias,* the cards were called. The white cards merited double the points of the yellow ones—or ten points. Twice a year, at Easter and Christmas, *asistencias* clutched in one little hand, the children chose marked-up items like japanese cotton dolls, paper umbrellas, cardboard lanterns, tiny tin autos, blow pipes with match-boxes of peas rubberbanded to them, colored pencils with furry heads of toy animals stuck to one end, shiny trinkets, paste pearls, gaudy handkerchiefs, cheese cloths, rosaries and plaster figurines of numerous saints. The children realized the profit to be made from the barter and hoarded the *asistencias* like misers. On these two occasions, the stables in the *Viuda's* mansion would be cleared of horses and hay, and, at the smelly corners yellowed by manure, sprang colorful booths exhibiting the bright rag, paste and paper wares. Around each of them, the children milled and chattered happily. It was plain to see that learning all about the Lord was a profitable enterprise altogether and to the children, the profit was easy to come by, for the *Maestra* was a fat, languid woman who yawned while teaching them how to hook the fore and middle fingers and press them fervently against the forehead, chest and shoulders in the sign of a cross. And when they intoned the Apostles' Creed after her, she would roll her eyes heavenwards and then shut them, looking very pious, but the children could tell by the way her head jerked that she was merely trying to catch a few winks. On the rare afternoons when the *Viuda* stood in the balcony and looked down on the heads of the children, it was different. The *Maestra* waved her arms in a lively fashion and the voices of the children rose in singsong above the fountain and over the flowering pots where between the leaves, a smile showed on the old widow's face.

On Ash Wednesday the children marched off to Binondo church which was about four blocks away. They formed two lines, girls and boys, the smaller children at the head of the lines. The *Maestra* checked on their veils, rosaries and prayer books. The boys had sleeked down their hair with pomade and were solemn-faced; nonetheless, when the *Maestra* turned her back to check on the girls' veils, a pea-shot tore through the air into the left side of Ana Maria's eager face, barely an inch from her ear, as she held up a white square tulle for inspection.

The *Maestra* was livid with anger as Ana Maria cried, covering her moist face with the veil. The girls drew around to comfort her. The boys were solemn-faced as before; the little instrument of crime having been deftly passed from hand to hand and finally stuck behind a potted plant. When she realized what had happened, the *Maestra* turned on the boys; the circle of girls broke to give her room to pass for they saw that her puffy cheeks were purplish with rage, her eyes blacker than they had been between the pink slits of her eyelids. "Hands out for inspection!" she barked, "hands out, all of you— you—little swines."

She walked slowly down the line of the solemn-faced boys whose hands were stuck stiffly before them; she felt around their hips and pockets while muttering angrily, "On your first day of confession too! Oh, you little yellow-faced brutes who never sucked good manners from your mothers' breasts!" She was trembling with anger; Ana Maria was her favorite pupil.

"Was it you, Arsenio?" She had turned to the tallest boy in the line. Arsenio promptly turned yellower; he was perspiring under the furry beginnings of a mustache. He was about twelve; his hair like the rest of the boys had been plastered down with pomade but a tuft stood stubbornly where his cowlick was. "But I didn't, *Maestra!*" he whined flinging his grimy-rimmed fingers wide apart to show they were empty, "I didn't truly—why am I first to be suspected always— always!"

"Hep, hep!" the *Maestra* said puffing her purplish cheeks, "cut it out, enough, enough!" She threw down her hands, feeling helpless and tricked. She had reached the end of the line, empty-handed. "Now, all listen!" she snapped, "when we get to church, whoever the culprit—he must confess his sin and repent!" The boys smiled indulgently while the girls scowled on them. "Remember," she cried, her voice rising to a shrill pitch, "hellfireanddamnation!" She had spat them as one word, as though they burned her tongue. And further-more, she crossed herself quickly as if to ward off hellfire itself. She looked up and saw the children were quiet; slowly, as she turned to go, she imagined Arsenio snickering, heard him or some little boy suppress a laugh. She huffed to the head of the lines and patted the sniffling Ana Maria on the head and without looking back, out of her faded purse she drew out a long string of black beads from which dangled an enormous wooden cross. Pressing her dry thick lips on the cross, slowly at first, she began: "I believe in God—march, hep, hep—Father Almighty—keep in line, hep, hep. . ."

The veiled little girls' heads bobbed alternately in an uneven pattern; the pomade melted on the scalps of the little boys but they intoned the hail marys in a mechanical, dutiful singsong. Their mothers watched from their shutterless windows. The narrow street was deserted except by the intense yellow sun of Manila's hottest month. So they stayed close to the cool stone walls of the little shops, on the grey pavement close to the scent of frying oil of the empty *carinderias,* the odour of the pet shop where fat-breasted doves stuttered and balding monkeys snickered and so the children momentarily forgot the mysteries and listened instead to the excited calls of the little wire-caged world of flapping wings and shiny eyes. The *Maestra* clapped her hands and led them away from the pet shop. Past the noodle man and the little dusty shop where they baked crisp moon cakes, to the rows of squatting vendors now nodding in their siesta beside baskets of medicinal roots and leaves and gnarled twigs and water cans of flaming gladiolas and white drooping cups of lilies, to the heavy, hand-carved door with rusty hinges and into the musty caverns of the church. They stopped before the marble font and the *Maestra* watched the little fingers dip into the water and make the proper sign of the cross. The children moved to the pews beside the confessional, hushed in the dim interior of the church and awed by the bright eyes of the stained glass windows now afire against the afternoon sun. Awed by the statues whose heads wore jewel-encrusted crowns and whose enormous eyes seemed to pierce the very roof above. Awed by the doves with golden spread wings and rays and the floating heads of blue-eyed cherubs jutting out of plaster nimbus gathered under the slender feet of the Virgin which had crushed underneath a poised serpent with a glassy stare. Hushed under the heavy perfume of flowers and incense and melting tallow which filled the nostrils and made one feel heady. Hushed even now the pomaded heads as each took turns at the confessional and waited for the strange voice to murmur its blessings.

The *Maestra* fanned herself as she watched from the pew closest to the confessional. Once she had to reach out from her cramped position to motion to a child to return to his seat. He had refused to budge after the little window opened and closed on him three times. Except for this little incident, everything went on smoothly. When it was Arsenio's turn, she found herself paying strict attention; she had even tilted her head, in an effort it seemed, to catch a few of the things the boy had to say. But his murmurings were subdued and private and when he crossed himself and stood up to go, she was suddenly struck by the thought that the truth was lost to her, perhaps forever. She could ask the confessor, but what a foolish, daring thought, she mused, to even suggest it.

When they walked out into the sunlight again, the children squinting in the open brightness, the *Maestra* stood awhile, gathering them into some sense of order, getting the taller children at the end of the line. They were chatting and laughing happily as if relieved of some heavy task. She went about the routine of maintaining order in the lines as they marched back to Doña Leonora's mansion, but her mind was still on Arsenio and the truth. She felt somewhat depressed, as though the failure she suffered from Arsenio and the boys was reflective of the failure of her authority as a teacher. She, a teacher of fifteen years! No, there has to be a way, she urged herself. To the children, she said aloud, "Keep those lines straight, hep, hep...." They looked at her, startled from their animated conversations. "And cut out the talk and march!" she nagged them. The children kept in step, sullen and quiet, until they reached Benavides Street and made a turn to the portico of Doña Leonora's house.

Back on the benches, they sat and listened while she gave them the last instructions for their first communion. They were to wear white; long dresses for the girls and long pants and shirts for the boys. They were to gather by the portico on Easter Sunday where there was to be breakfast with the *Viuda* who had made all these catechism lessons possible. Then, there was to be the *asistencia* barter. This last announcement was greeted with scattered clappings as the children's faces brightened up at the prospect of converting their hoarded *asistencias* into various articles and goods.

When the clapping subsided, she smiled benignly on the children. "Listen all—because you've completed the lessons satisfactorily, this last meeting is worth not one card but. . . ." she paused dramatically, noting the eager faces and drinking in the growing excitement around her, "not one yellow card," she beamed, "but five—FIVE—WHITE cards." This unexpected magnanimity silenced the children into disbelief and it was a while before they realized what they heard was true. Fifty points! A wave of shouts rose from the whole congregation as the children jumped from their benches and swarmed around the *Maestra,* their eager hands reaching out for the cards.

"Order, order!" she commanded, sweating under the strain of warding off the jostling children "the little ones first—or all of you—nothing—do you hear me, NO CARDS!"

The threat worked; the children quieted down and the *Maestra* started to count out five cards for each child. When it came to Arsenio's turn; he was the last one in the line, she eyed him momentarily and then slowly counted out five cards. Arsenio looked on eagerly, his thin, yellow palm, upturned and waiting. She took time pulling out each card, her eyes on the young, expectant face. When she had pulled out all the five cards, she went over each to make sure they were singles, then she paused and opening them into a fan, as if commencing a game of *pangingge,* very quietly, she asked, "Tell me, Arsenio—it was you, wasn't it—who shot that pea?"

The smile on Arsenio's face froze. The children stopped their chatter and watched them. The fat woman looked at him intently. She noted with some degree of satisfaction that the little boy's face was beginning to break into a sweat again and that the thin lips twitched perceptibly. The boy raised his eyes to the five cards she had held out like a fan over his head. The children closed in on them in a tightening circle and he saw how their little hands clutched five *asistencias.* They stood mute, waiting for his reply.

"Well, admit it!" the *Maestra* said with a hint of triumph in her voice. "Say, I hurt Ana Maria and I'm sorry." Her eyes shone with a hard peculiar glint but she smiled as though to encourage him. He cleared his dry throat and his voice came feebly, "But *Maestra.* . . ."

"Admit it!" she said icily, anger welling up inside her again. Pride, pride!—he will not shame himself in front of the children and yet he was guilty as the devil, she thought. She snapped the fan of cards close; the sudden gesture made a cracked and final sound. Arsenio's face turned pale and his hand fell limply on his side. The children gasped. It was as if the game of tug they were watching had turned and snapped hard. The *Maestra* turned her back on him and the ring of children broke before her.

Arsenio found himself slowly being deserted as the children started to move away. With an effort, he found his voice—"Wait!" he cried, *"Maestra."* He took a few quick steps and stopped when she made an abrupt turn to face him. "The cards, *Maestra,* my *asistencias!"* He seemed about to cry and his eyes begged her.

"Well, I'm waiting, boy," she said evenly.

"I'm sorry," the boy said, his voice hardly audible.

"Aloud! And say, I'm guilty," the *Maestra* said.

"I'm guilty, I'm sorry," the boy repeated.

"Good!" she said, "that wasn't too hard to say, eh, boy?" Arsenio nodded as he reached out for the five cards she held out to him.

Easter Sunday was a bright clear day. Everything went on smoothly—the communicants were behaved equally well at God's and the *Viuda's* breakfast tables. And so it was with great contentment that the *Maestra* and Doña Leonora sat and watched from a square, slightly raised platform which has been built for them a short distance from the booths. The children gathered around the booths bartering their *asistencias* for some colorful little items. The sunlight filtered through the trees in the open patio and reflected on the fountain pool the happy faces of the children scurrying around with arms loaded with toys. Several times, the *Maestra* waved back greetings to the children and once or twice, she stood up to pull a child up on the platform and present him to the *Viuda.* When she spotted Ana Maria, she waved for her to come. The child came dutifully and kissed the hand of the *Viuda.*

The *Maestra* was helping Ana Maria down the steps of the platform when from the corner of her eye, she caught sight of a tall, lone figure whose back was turned to them. From where she was, she saw the frayed collar of the stiff and impeccably ironed shirt, a size too big for its wearer, and just below the shoulder, a patched square held by neat and repeated mendings. The boy was standing before a booth with folded dress materials and other gaudy, cheap apparels, apparently counting his too-few cards. As the boy turned, the *Maestra* got a glimpse of the stubborn cowlick on top of the familiar thin face. She moved back to her chair, struck by the realization that Arsenio was bartering for clothes while the rest of the children were scurrying about with toys and trinkets. As she sat back on her chair, she recalled how the boy looked up at the cards she held above his head and how his eyes begged. Fifty points—of course, he would admit anything!

As he came nearer the platform, for the first time in her long teaching career, the *Maestra* found herself unable to look and nod at one of her pupils. Why, he was just a boy, she told herself. But when Arsenio reached the front of the platform, the *Maestra* carefully diverted her gaze in the general direction of the mossy fountain until the boy disappeared into the huddle of colorful booths in the corner to mingle with the other children.

(1964) First published in *The Sunday Times Magazine*, January 9, 1965, pp. 37-38.

The Stairs

IT WAS A SHARP PAIN, a hard nut of pain which throbbed in the pit of her belly, different from any pain she had ever experienced before. Ligaya was jumping *piko* when she felt it and for a moment, she thought she would faint and fall on the hard ground marked with half-moon of the boxed patterns and the flat stones of their game.

Diwata and the other girl sat under the shade of the *ipil-ipil,* waiting for their turn. "Is something wrong?" they asked almost in unison.

"No, nothing—nothing's wrong," Ligaya said, the hard nut now seems to whirl, pulling every muscle of her stomach into a taut vortex until her belly felt rigid as a tin plate.

"Well, what are you waiting for then?" Diwata asked her quite sharply.

"It's nothing, stupid," Ligaya snapped back. "I'm just plotting my next move as you can see."

"You can't take all day, like a queen," the girl whose braids smelled of rancid coconut oil ventured, her thick Visayan accent prolonging the last word. To Ligaya, she was a no-name, a newcomer of their village where her family had come to settle as farmhands after a long sea voyage from the Visayas. She was a stranger and her words stung. The girl was squinting under the hot afternoon sun, toying with her braids as she regarded Ligaya at the center of the unevenly drawn half-moon.

Ligaya approached the girl with deliberate steps and hovered over her, her arms akimbo. "You can go back to where you came from if you don't like the way we play here!" No-name's hand fell from her braids to snatch her wooden clogs from the hard ground. She hugged them to her thin chest, the brightly-painted red clogs, raised her rear, as if set to race.

"Well, well," Diwata broke in, "it's just a game where some people must win and some people must lose. You've captured so many houses already, so why are you so greedy?"

Ligaya looked at the two, then walked away from the half-moon into the shade, slumping against the tree. "Well," she said, "well, if some people here can't wait, they can just go on without me. I'm tired of it anyway." The pain started to throb again, she pressed her palm against it to stop the ache.

"Suit yourself," Diwata said getting to her feet. "If some people think they can stop this game by quitting, ha!" By this time, she was in front of Ligaya, her dusty feet kicking up a clumsy dance to taunt her.

"You know what, you know what," she chanted, "some people here will see how we will split her houses! Split her houses!"

"That'll make mine four houses all in all," No-name said smiling up at Diwata.

"Now, all we do is decide who'll play first," Diwata said, extending her clenched fist to No-name. "Take three."

No-name spat into her palms and clenching one of them, offered it solemnly to Diwata. Their fists met on an imaginary line in the accepted preliminaries of the game. Twice they each swung their arms in abrupt gestures, intoning in sing-song,

"Jack and Poy, holi, holi hoy!"

And twice their arms rose and fell as they stomped their feet on the hard ground.

"My paper to wrap your stone," cried Diwata gaily, open palm against No-name's clenched fist.

Ligaya tore off the blades of grass growing around the base of the *ipil-ipil*. It was so hot even in the shade and there were the two of them in quiet concentration, fighting over her houses.

"Scissors will cut your paper," shouted No-name, "That's one for me!"

She chewed the tender shoots and spat out the bitter taste. Suddenly, she could no longer wait to see who was the winner. In an instant, Ligaya was up, running to the boxes marked "L" and before they could stop her, she was dragging her feet over her initials.

"You're both stupid," she cried. "You didn't even work for my houses, they're mine. Mine!" She dug her heels into the ground where a pointed stick had etched her initial. "Start all over again," she cried, making arch movements with her bare foot and raising a cloud of dust as she went on determined to erase all her houses.

"What did you do that for?" It was Diwata who broke away from No-name and was suddenly beside her. "You're no longer in the game!"

Ligaya shrugged her shoulder and continued with her task.

Diwata said evenly, "You'll stop that this instant!"

But Ligaya kept on swinging her leg. "Make me," she said.

"You're out of the game," cried Diwata. Before she could duck, Diwata had pounced on her and they fell on the hot dust. In a second, No-name jumped into the fight, the two of them pinning her down. Ligaya felt her hair being tugged at, by Diwata or No-name, she could not tell although she saw how their faces shone with sweat, their hard breathing drowning her own.

"Say, you give up!" No-name demanded, applying the full pressure of her palm against Ligaya's face on the hot dust. She felt Diwata twisting her leg. Ligaya lifted her head from under No-name's palm in order to answer when suddenly, she felt Diwata releasing her hold. No-name removed her palm also.

"Why, Gaya, your dress!" Diwata sounded greatly alarmed.

No-name started to whimper. "We didn't mean to kill you," she said leaving a streak of grime on her face as she wiped her nose with the back of her dusty hand. They both stood up, looking down on her.

"What's wrong?" Ligaya said jumping on her feet.

"We didn't mean to hit so hard," Diwata apologized.

"But you asked for it," No-name said, hiding behind Diwata.

"You can join the game again, if you want to. . ." Diwata offered.

"She'll have to see the doctor first," No-name suggested. "Meantime, let's split her houses until she comes back."

Ligaya paid no attention to them. She passed her hand over her forehead, examined her dusty arms and legs. Except for a few bruises, they looked all right.

"Look at your skirt," they said.

Ligaya twisted her cotton skirt and shrieked when she saw the blotted hem. Her first instinct was to run. She backed away from them, gathering up her skirt and twisting the soiled portion of it into a tight ball.

"Tell your mother we didn't do it or else. . .," No-name advised her.

Diwata looked at her quietly. Ligaya turned away from them and sped off, her hand still clutching the balled hem of her skirt. The trees and the thatched roofs floated above her and still higher, the blue strip of sky fled with her. She could feel the wind and the hot sun against her feverish face. From one or two windows, faces stuck out to look at her racing in the afternoon sun. As she turned the corner of the last hut before her house, a boy leading a carabao by a broken rope knotted through its nostrils shouted after her, "Hoy, *bata batuta,* where's the fire, hah!" Then he laughed derisively, his laughter following her to their backyard.

Ligaya slackened her pace when she reached their backyard. The backdoor was open. Her mother would be dozing off in her regular siesta on the bamboo *papag* in the kitchen, her greying hair loosened from its tight knot and spread over the heavily-starched, embroidered pillow. Ligaya held her breath as she entered the house on tiptoe. She was almost at the foot of the stairs when her mother's sleepy voice called out to her.

"Is it you, Gaya?"

"Yes, it's only me, *Inang,*" Ligaya answered.

"Come and lie down beside me, *anak,*" she said in the same sleepy voice.

"But I don't feel sleepy, *Inang,* not at all," Ligaya said.

"Then you can comb my hair and look for whites? They itch so."

"Later, *Inang,*" she said quickly climbing the bamboo stairs.

"Five whites for a centavo?" she coaxed.

Ligaya stopped. That was better than the seven she always insisted upon. But she said, "Later *na lang, Inang,* I'll be back..."

Ligaya ran up the stairs. Up where it was bright with the afternoon sunlight, the *sawale* windows have been pushed wide open and the sun spilled on the rocking chairs, the shiny tea table and the split bamboo floor. She ran to the little room where they kept the family's blankets, pillows, rolled mats and trunks of clothes. It was a small rectangular enclosed area which was dark because it did not have any windows. Just a tiny half-door. With a sigh of relief, she sat against the pillows and neatly stacked blankets reaching halfway to the slant of the low thatched roof. It was nice to hide there as she had done many times. The pillows smelled of starch and fragrant banana leaves which her *Inang* used to slide the hot iron on before pressing the clothes. She pulled a greenish woolen blanket and covered herself carefully, pulling the hem to her chin. There was the pain again. She was going to die, she thought. Somehow, her life was being drained away from her by some unknown and mysterious force. It happened many times before in the village. When one makes the mistake of insulting the *aswang* or *mangkukulam,* whether one did it willfully or not, they turn into malevolent spirits driven to revengeful rage so that there was no telling what they would be up to do. She thought hard on who she might have insulted. Last week, the neighbor's baby died for no apparent reason. She heard the woman next door whispering it was surely the *aswang* that did it with its long tongue which can take on the appearance of a thread innocently lying on the floor but in truth it was a tongue waiting out there to suck in an innocent human's liver! She shuddered and tried to shake it off her mind but her eyes sought the floor for any telltale piece of thread, she was happy to find none.

The sun was a red-orange ball which blinked at her through the slits of the thatched wall. In the center of the yard, she could see the *madre de cacao* in full bloom, its tiny soft lavender blossoms almost transparent against the afternoon sun. Gradually, the sun seemed to dip behind the hills and because she watched it for a long time, her eyes held its bright red ball against sky of gold even after it was gone. She closed her eyes and the red ball turned into a black circle which bobbed crazily above her teary vision. Then everything turned into a soft murkiness in the warmth of her green blanket cocoon.

Laughter broke the soft darkness, men laughing and water splashing as the rusty artesian pump was being cranked. "Whoa, big boy, whoa," it was her *Itang's* voice. She rubbed her eyes. They were home already, her brother's laughter drifted up to her hiding place. They were washing their plows, the carabaos and their muddy arms and legs. It must be suppertime and they would be looking for her!

But her sister Mely found her soon enough. She had just turned on the low-hanging bulb in the tiny room and was getting some towels from the trunk when she saw Ligaya.

"Hoy, what are doing there, little monkey?" she said.

Ligaya drew the blanket closer to her chin. "I like it here," she said.

"*Inang* is looking for you," Mely said draping two or three towels over her shoulder. She pressed down the lid of the trunk until the latch clicked close.

"She knows I'm here," Ligaya said.

"Gaya, come and help set the table or *Inang* will be angry...."

"I don't feel too well," Ligaya said.

"Are you sick?" With this, her sister's cool palm cupped over her brow. "Come for a bowl of hot soup then, *Inang* will give you some and then you'll feel much better."

"I'd rather stay here," Ligaya said.

"I had enough of your tricks, Gaya, you're not sick, you just don't want to help so why not just say so!" Mely yanked away her green blanket cocoon in one swift move. It was all too sudden, Ligaya shivered visibly, hid her face in her arms and started to cry.

Her sister replaced the blanket gently, turned off the light and left the room hastily. When Ligaya could wipe away her tears and bend over to peek through the slits of the bamboo floor, she saw her sister holding an excited conversation with *Inang* and *Tia* Waya, a spinster aunt. She saw her father being told while her brothers stood around rubbing the water from their hair with the towels Mely had handed out to them.

"But she's only a child," Ligaya heard *Itang* protest.

"Well, she's almost twelve," *Inang* told him quietly.

"There's no stopping these things," *Tia* Waya said shaking her head a bit too mournfully.

Itang walked to the bright stoves where supper was cooking. The flames flickered against the shape of his head. He drew out one of the burning pieces of wood from under the clay pot and lighted his cigar, drawing heavy puffs of smoke around them. *Inang* had followed and she stood behind him, waiting.

"Well," *Itang* said still sucking in some air, the tip of his cigar aglow, "well, it's your job, you know."

"Yes, of course, I suppose it is," *Inang* said.

Ligaya turned back to the pillows and hid her face. Strangely enough, she was still alive, considering it was evening already. And the pain seemed to have disappeared. She felt a little weak and somewhat depressed, otherwise everything seemed as it was before.

When she heard the bamboo stairs creak and she saw them enter the half-door, Ligaya pulled the blanket tightly about her. In the soft darkness, she could see *Inang's* bent figure, behind her was *Tia* Waya with some folded cotton napkins draped on her arm.

"Nothing's wrong, *anak,*" *Inang's* voice was gentle as she placed a basin of water near Ligaya. Ligaya looked up at her with frightened eyes, thankful it was dark in the room. *Inang* started to stroke her head tenderly, murmuring little endearments. Suddenly, Ligaya released her blanket cocoon and flung her arms about her *Inang's* neck, sobbing while she buried her face into the soft, sweet-smelling white blouse *Inang* wore. When her sobs subsided, they cleaned her, not bothering to turn on the light. Both of them were tender and they did not speak a word. Ligaya submitted herself meekly to their ministrations, permitting herself to be washed and bound, pinned up and clothed.

It was after all the supper things have been removed from the table and washed and the stoves have been brushed until only a thin bed of warm ashes remained for the cats to sleep on, after *Itang* and her brothers vanished off to the *municipio* to see their friends that *Inang* instructed them to sit around facing the stairs. Her sister Mely took the small black stool and sat near the stairs while *Tia* Waya sat on the bench, her back leaning against the dining table. *Inang* was busy setting up a clay pot filled to the brim with water on which a tin can floated.

Inang turned to Ligaya. "Now do as I tell you, *anak.*"

Ligaya hesitated but *Inang* held her by the hand and led her to the stairs. "Now, climb to the fourth rung, *anak,*" she said.

"So it'll last no more than four days," said her sister Mely, smiling knowingly.

"Some people here don't know when to remain quiet," said *Tia* Waya.

Ligaya climbed the stairs slowly and sat on the fourth rung, not knowing quite what to do. Her knees felt wobbly.

"Now, listen, *anak,*" *Inang* said slowly, "I'll count to three and then you jump about here," she was pointing to a spot near the jar.

The faces watching her below were indistinct under the single lamp hanging behind their back. Ligaya got up on her feet, wavered on the smooth curve of the bamboo step and then raised her arms as if getting ready to dive.

"Ready?" *Inang* had dipped the tin can into the jar and filled it full of water.

Ligaya nodded.

"One—two—," came *Inang's* slow count, "—three, JUMP!"

Ligaya jumped and was met with a splashful of water from the tin can and then another. Her clothes were drenched and she stood shivering as the three women surrounded and held her up, all three of them were talking at the same time. For a moment, Ligaya felt the water dripping around her legs, all cool and nice but inside she could feel the strange new warm flow and she did not quite know whether to laugh in relief or to cry in distress.

(1966)

When the Innocent is Found Guilty, Part of the Native Land is Exiled

WHEN YOU COME RIGHT DOWN TO IT, time is meaningless unless you mark it. You anchor it, so to speak, otherwise it floats like some gossamer ribbon on into infinity. Or if you do not go for my choice poetic image, let's say, it's just like punching computer tape, unless you punch, nothing comes out when you run it into that big IBM we call eternity. Like I don't care how educated you get, there's something to the old folks referring not to the calendar year but to the big event of each year. Usually disasters. Like the year of the big flood. Or the year of the big earthquake. Or the year the locusts came. Or something personal, like the year Father died. What I want to get at is now I find myself doing the same thing. Like I always remember 1965 as the year of the Grensville case. I would wave my hand and say, you know the year of the Grensville case and my husband would know I meant 1965.

1965. Grensville. Grensville, Wisconsin, USA, is dotted with muck farms, flowering in the summer months with huge heads of bright green iceberg lettuce, awaiting pickers. It is one of the many midwestern counties that migrant Mexican and Filipino farm workers head for during the summer months, unload their back packs onto hard bunks of the tiny gray shacks at the muddy edge of the farms, work the long summer hours, get paid by the week, then drive their dusty second-hand cars to some other farms, leaving the land to lay fallow for the autumn and winter months. It is said that Filipinos make good workers, agile because of their small size but I guess the main reason they get the job is because they are willing to live in very wretched quarters and for backbreaking work, accept modest wages. In a mechanistic age the lettuce pickers are an anachronism. But like asparagus, lettuce cannot be scooped up by machinery. They are fragile, almost, you might say, brittle as glass. So summer after summer, the pickers are induced to come to these midwestern towns. If they prove not only hard-working but well-behaved (mainly, they stay away from the white womenfolk) they are asked to come back the following summer. Which is why they keep mostly to themselves, the best insurance against trouble. At any rate, they don't come into much contact with the townfolks and if they wander into town for some beer or a movie, they are referred to as "one of those workers from the muck farms" and tolerated like poor relations, who are called to do menial jobs, are tolerated.

The first time we learned a county called Grensville existed was because a request was made to the Filipino graduate students at the UW campus in Madison for an interpreter. The Grensville County Court was sure that it could get a Tagalog interpreter for a Filipino migrant worker who murdered a young American boy. Murder! Now that was enough to jar you into the realities of living abroad. After all, there we were, isolated in the Madison campus, much like being in a summer vacation camp really, what with Lake Mendotta big as life and green as jade, flecked with sailboats in the summer and ice-boats in the winter and edged with fraternity and sorority piers. Well, when half of your life, like mine, has been lived in an academic sanctuary, so to speak, the rest of the world are fringes, blurred and distant. Now suddenly, here we were, ten thousand miles away from home, called to be interpreters for a murder case involving a country-man.

The prospect of going on a trip, all expenses paid, over and above a substantial interpreter's fee, quickly appealed to us. Oh, there was an altruistic side to it. After all, here was a rare time to come to the aid of your countryman. But there is one thing about living abroad on a government scholarship; in time you get very sick of chicken backs and wings no matter how charitable at 19 cents a pound it is to your budget. Well, you can fry, bake, roast, broil, boil and etcetera it but you can't kid yourself, it's still chicken backs and wings. But you don't write your family back home about these things. You write of crocuses in the spring, apple cider in the summer, red maple leaves in the autumn and the snow and toboggan rides of the winter and all about the racial riots and demonstrations, the assassinations and the strange new cities. Never, never your menus.

So we accepted. I mean, Manuel accepted the job. I merely tagged along. We took the Greyhound and were met in a tiny bus stop by the accused Filipino's lawyer, a balding, tall, somewhat heavy-set, middle-aged man. A Broderick Crawford to his bulging middle but minus a highway patrol car so familiar to Crawford's TV fans. We found out that he was a State Attorney before he went into private practice. He took us directly to his office, shoved some thick transcriptions of the previous court proceedings in long blue binders, advising us to read them carefully. Then he took us to a restaurant for some light supper and later drove us to a motel not far from the courthouse.

Transcriptions of court proceedings are extremely formal-looking documents, if you ask me. Enough to convince, I kid you not, the most cynical that the State is out to look after its constituents in the most systematic and proper way possible. The binders are prefaced by a title page which records the name of the State, the county court and the county, what it is a preliminary hearing of. This instance, the State of Wisconsin versus a named Defendant, the name of the honorable Judge on what *th* day of the month, the year and the hour, morning or afternoon. Then the *dramatis personae,* the lawyers appearing on behalf of either the plaintiff or defendant and in the order of their appearances, the ten or so witnesses, ranging from a 16-year old girl to the Coroner of Marquette County. The index page which follows will warm any librarian's heart; it shows at one glance, the names of the witnesses and how many times they were subjected to direct, cross, redirect and recross examinations. The second index page enumerates the exhibits, the Plaintiff's or the Defendant's and how many "for identification" and how many "in evidence" as numbered. After this initial impression, the rest of the pages can make anyone who takes pride in the noble profession of editing, break down and cry. You plod through words, words, words, squeezing substance from bulk, separating grain from chaff and as my favorite poetry teacher would put it, extracting a single fluid ounce of nectar from a million flowers abloom. Poetry teachers, as you very well know, have a predilection for things a-fire and a-blooming.

Substance, grain, or if you will, nectar, was that on the night of July 19, 1965, four Filipino muck farm workers were involved in the killing of a young man—18 years old, white Caucasian, model youth from the community's 4-H Club and his family's only son. The shooting took place on Highway 21, a police car ambulance reached the scene in time to find the youth lying alongside his car. Engine running, headlights on. There were some movements then but the youth was DOA when they got him to the county hospital, some miles away.

The receiving doctor of the emergency ward placed the young man's death at midnight. At that point, nothing could be done but to wait for the coroner for autopsy.

Magno Bayan, the prime suspect, scrawled as best as he could, the circumstances surrounding the killing:

"The four of us, Eddie, Richard and me and Freddy went down to Stubbe's bar about 5:00 P.M. in the month of July dated 16, 1965. That moment of enjoying ourselves drinking beer we didn't notice that the time passing very fast. And that moment the more we felt the enjoyment when our friends Carlos, Ricky, Mario and Jimmy went in the bar, so, I offered them to drink and join with us. Some of us played pool inside, after a short enjoyment, Carlos told me that they have to go home early because they have to work in the next morning. I told him, 'Yes, you go home now so that you can work after rest,' after I said that words but Eddie told him and he asked Carlos if they want to sleep with us in our cabin that we paid for $20 a month, so that after that we decided to go home, when we reached Frankie's Snack Bar, before we enter I saw some of my friends inside the snack bar, so Jimmy and I went inside but some of us remained outside the snack bar and what we did, we sat down near the counter and I ordered a cup of coffee.

"After a few seconds the rest of us went inside the snack bar and Mario sit beside me and Carlos was standing behind me, when I looked around and saw Richard playing the pinball and Eddie began to go around inside, and there he go back to the place where we were sitting and I heard him said to the waitress that 'Magno like's you very much.' I felt ashamed of what he did, I told him not to make that kind of joke and might she get mad at me. I don't know her, even her name, after that I told them let's go home we have to work tomorrow, but before we left they bought two cases of beer but I don't know who bought that beer, and who paid for it. Then the four of us went outside the snackbar (at the back) where the car was parked. The three of them Ricky, Eddie and Freddy were following me, and I go right away inside the car and laid my back a little in the sit so I can rest my eyes a little because I was very sleepy on that moment. But they remain outside the car, soon they go inside the car and I heard Eddie said let's go follow that car. I asked him what car? He said, 'that car just took off.' I asked him,

'Why? and what for?' So he told me Okay we will not follow that, when we reached the stop sign he gave a horn to Carlos, because Carlos doesn't know where the place we're going. I ask him again where are we going? He told me at the cabin, so we pass in the Highway 23, and I laid down my back again, a few minutes later, I heard Carlos's voice asking where is the place of our cabin. Then Ricky told him right away, follow that car. Carlos ask him why? Eddie answer him, 'Just follow that car.' Carlos ask him again 'That car?' Eddie said 'yes' so when I look outside the left side. I saw a white car passing by. So I told him again, 'What for you will follow that car?' and when Carlos pulling the car on the left side of Eddie's car, Eddie told him again stop that car, that time, I told Eddie not to stop his car, so that Carlos will not stop the white car. When Carlos pass the white car, I told Eddie again not to stop the car, 'you go ahead so that Carlos will not stop the white car.' When Eddie stop his car, Ricky went down the car right away and I don't know what happen on that moment because when I saw Freddy and Eddie went down to follow Ricky, I put my head down and I open the door and so I found myself beside them and I don't know why I shoot John Miller."

Phoof. This fractured letter goes phoof, I told my husband. Didn't know why he shot John Miller. But there it was, a young man, 18, was dead. There was nothing tentative about that. Certain, final, inexorable death. And the coroner's report was vivid and damaging while he marked the passages on an anatomical outline provided as Exhibit 8 in court. There were four gunshot wounds, he testified. Three entries and one exit. Bullet no. 1 entered the right cheek below the molar eminence striking the posterior pharynx, being deflected and exiting approximately one half inch below the left ear. Bullet no. 2 went through the ascending aorta and then through the pulmonary artery, across the mediastinum and just causing a slight contusion to the left lung and became spent. Bullet no. 3 entered between the tenth and eleventh dorsal vertebrae, grazed the left diaphragm and went through the inferior lobe of the left lung and became spent. Bullet no. 3 caused the boy's death, according to the coroner. All the bullets were removed, he further testified, in his presence and in the post mortem examination there was bleeding in the chest cavity, about 2 thousand cc's. "How much would that be in reference to the total blood of a human body?" he was asked. "In reference to the total

amount of blood in a person's body," he said, "it would be four-fifths."
Massive hemorrhage.

"Tough," Manuel said, "it's going to be tough."

We woke up to find the day was going to be one of those
strictly Seurat summer days, unbearably bright, all colors shining their
purest hues. The soft incline of grassy mound climbing to the courthouse was the clearest green you ever saw and I convinced Manuel
he should pose for a photograph. He stood rather stiffly in front of
the courthouse, the portfolio containing the court papers under his
arm, his pipe poised midair when the camera shutter clicked. "Well,
come on," he said, offering his hand for our climb toward the County
Prison. "Magno Bayan is waiting."

The County Prison was a thick concrete building below the
courthouse and it held several cells with iron bars. The sheriff stood
from his desk when he saw us enter. He knew about our coming,
that was obvious. But whether he approved or disapproved our coming,
he was careful not to show. He nodded at us and without saying a
word, unlocked the thick door leading to the prison cells.

Magno Bayan blinked at the bright sunlight as he walked out of
the row of prison cells. The sheriff led him to a corner by his office
where he set up three chairs. Magno Bayan kept his eyes to the ground
and looked up only when we walked to the chairs facing him. He
was shocked to see me, he was told that a male interpreter was coming.
He hesitated for a moment, then stood waiting for me to be seated,
his face breaking into a slow grin. My husband motioned him to sit
down, assuring him that we both came to help in whatever way we
can. Manuel said it in Tagalog which in itself sounded so soft and
reassuring that Magno Bayan sat down, mustering as much dignity
as the flappy folded sleeves and cuffs of the oversize orange prison
suit would permit.

Bushy-hair, wiry frame, little men. That was how a crime magazine account described the four Filipino farm workers. Magno Bayan,
who sat in front of us, trying to locate his hometown in the Philippines,
as if to establish his identity for us, was the prime suspect. He was
the alleged triggerman. His manner was diffident, punctuating his
phrases with the respectful and formal *po;* he knew that the gap
between us, aggravated by his present situation, was more than just
a matter of status or our civilian clothes and his bright orange prison
suit. But we were, at least, his countrymen and we talked his language.
When you are in a foreign country, that made a difference. As a
matter of fact, all the difference in the world.

"I pleaded *Guilty* to the murder," Magno Bayan said.

"You what?" my husband said as if fired at.

"*Guilty,*" Magno Bayan repeated, "I pleaded *Guilty* to the charge."

"But why?" my husband asked.

Magno Bayan waved his hands. "I would be deported, they told me," he smiled, "I would like to see my family again. Ten years ago, I left them."

"But," Manuel interrupted, "do you know the meaning of *Guilty* in a court of law?"

"*Akong may sala,*" he said quickly, eager to show us he understood what it was all about.

"No, no," Manuel said shaking his head vigorously. Whereupon, he proceeded to explain in as simple Tagalog as he could, the fine distinction between admission of guilt in our day-to-day world and in a court of law.

Magno Bayan listened quietly, straining to understand every word.

"What I'm trying to tell you is this, was John Miller your enemy?"

Magno Bayan was quiet.

"I mean," Manuel pursued, "did you plan to kill him?"

Magno Bayan looked at his shoes.

"Well, did you know him?" Manuel persisted.

Magno Bayan said, "Never saw the guy before."

"They will have to reconsider your case," I said.

"If you change your plea," Manuel said, "they will."

Magno Bayan said, "*Kayo po ang bahala.*" And he said it in the tone of one who had given up hope.

"*Aba, hindi ganyan,*" Manuel said. "Tell us what you think and I'll give the message to your lawyer."

"We can only say what you tell us," I said.

"If you say to change your plea from Guilty to Not Guilty, we'll tell him," Manuel said.

Magno Bayan scratched his head awhile. "*Sige,*" he said, "*gusto kong palitan.*"

As we stood to say goodbye, Manuel pointed to a scar on Magno's forehead and asked him where he got it. Must have been a deep cut, the scar itself where flesh had formed to close the wound, failed to cover the suture holes and the reddish lash seemed to turn redder whenever he strained to listen to us. It was a fall from a horse in

Sta. Ana, he said. He was a horse trainer during his early teens and the horse was a wild, buckling animal his master had wanted to break.

We shook hands with the sheriff and thanked him for letting us talk with the prisoner. As we sat on the bright lawn in front of the County Prison, Manuel told me that the scar would be very crucial in the case. The lawyer came to join us and so I failed to ask him if he meant that a plea of insanity would be entered instead. Almost at once, the two of them were in deep conversation about Magno Bayan's plea of Guilty.

The courthouse was slowly filling up with townspeople, they sat on the long, polished mahogany seats facing the raised dais of the Judge's bench and the witness chair. The high-ceiling hall shone with the warm yellowish-brown of old varnish, only the flags and framed photographs of Washington and Lincoln breaking the monotony of the place.

Manuel was sworn in as the principal witness of the day. He took his place at the witness stand and answered the questions of the Defense Attorney, speaking slowly and clearly as though straining to make sure that his every word is understood by everyone in the room. He explained his conversation with Magno Bayan and then pointed out that the most important revelation of this morning's exchange was the fact that the prisoner misunderstood the meaning of the plea of Guilty. There was a general murmur among the townspeople and the judge pounded his gavel and called for order several times before the noise subsided.

When the Prosecuting Attorneys, Father and Son, were asked if they had any questions to ask the Tagalog interpreter from the University of Wisconsin, the Father barely got up from his seat to say, "No questions." A general murmur shot through the audience and the Judge pounded for silence.

I told my husband when he joined me later that if there was some kind of popularity poll in that hall, he wouldn't make it even to the bottom of the list. He shrugged his shoulders. Before he made his statement, the Defense Attorney led us to the backroom of the courtroom of the courthouse to explain to the Judge and the Prosecuting Attorneys that there had been a misinterpretation of terms and his client would like to change his plea to Not Guilty instead. "Well," the Judge said, "Well, if this has been clarified, then we should accept the change. That's what we got an interpreter for."

He was an amiable old man who even pulled us aside to say how he enjoyed the few times he visited "the islands" and how well he remembered Quezon, Osmeña and the Polo Club.

It was midnight when we got back to the Madison campus and past 1 A.M. when we hit the sack.

"You know," I said, "what if Magno Bayan is not the killer?"

"What makes you say that?" Manuel asked.

"For one thing, there's that letter," I said, "that goes phoof?"

"Oh-ho," he said burying his head into a pilow "a phoof theory!"

"Listen," I said, very seriously, "has it occurred to you that the reason the letter goes phoof is because he had no details to supply when he got to the part about the killing?"

"And has it occurred to you," he said yawning in my face, "that it goes phoof because that is the part he would rather not remember?"

I must admit he had a good point there but I don't give up easy. Oh, no. "Well," I said, "with that scar and—and his inability to speak for himself, he could have been picked out as the fall guy."

"That's for his lawyer to find out," he said. "And will you please, Amelia Lapeña," underscoring my maiden name, as if he never married me, "quit this, I want to get some sleep, classes tomorrow."

"*When the innocent is found guilty,*" I said determinedly, "*part of his native land is exiled,* Publilius Syrus, circa 43 B.C." I love springing quotations for appropriate occasions, the more erudite and obscure, the better. And by God if ever there was an appropriate occasion, this was it.

"Publilius, hah! That's the last thing a wife should be," he said.

"Publilius?" I asked.

"Patriotic," he said, "at 1 A.M.!" On that, he turned his back on me.

Well, he did let a fellow countryman gain time, didn't he? And he earned the substantial interpreter's fee of $75 for a half day's work. What a relief, I thought, to go marketing tomorrow without having to skip the fresh fish and steak sections. And it felt good watching him on the witness stand, as he pointed out how the thin distinction of the technical meaning of a plea of "Guilty" would escape a layman and what it meant in Tagalog to say, *Ako ang may sala,* "I am guilty." So like a decent wife should, I shut up and let him sleep.

(1967)

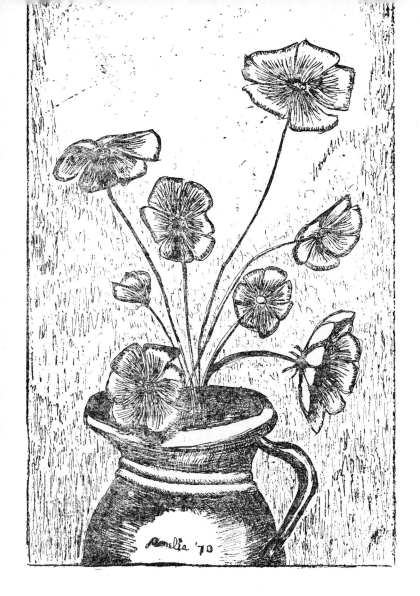

Tributes & Poems

Sepang Loca

T HEY FOUND SEPANG LOCA slumped over the mouth of a mud well,
dead. The townspeople who found her pulled her out and laid
her on the grass, discovered too her child, its tiny mouth and nostrils
choked up with mud and sand inside the slimy green of the well.
The townspeople who gathered that evening worked without talking
much, the menfolk especially. Gently they fished the child out of the
well, cradled it between Sepang Loca's breasts as if it was the most
natural thing in the world for them to do, and under the moonlight
the glistening naked body seemed to be as much part of the dead
woman as were her muddied arms, legs and quiet face.

Sepang Loca's womb was the town's tragic container really. It
grew the town's child whole at the end of every nine month's time
(only the slant of the eyes and the height of nose or crop of hair
giving away the identity of its father) and the town in turn held its
breath for her until the first shrill lifecry rose from the hut and Sepang
Loca emerged half-crawling from her bamboo door, dragged herself
through the tangles of cogon and vines in order to bathe her body
clean from the well.

The menfolk who smothered their lust in the *loca's* womb betrayed themselves at every lifecry and unmasked their own tragedy
and decay each time the *loca* half-dragged herself from the hut to
wash away from her body the blood and sweat of childbirth. For with
Sepa all was instinct. She was surprisingly strong, the gift of the feeble
of mind and at the end of every nine month's time, her mind ordered
and quieted for the occasion, she undergoes childbirth alone, whim-
perless through fresh blood and labor pains. Then like a mountain dog
that licks its teats clean for feeding, she half-drags herself to the well
for a bath. Lunacy would have numbed her against all rigors of social
disgrace as death at last spared her the humiliation of being stared
at. It was the menfolk who worked quietly that night, feeling and

with a mind moved as the many evenings with *loca* who shuddered for themselves alone most of all.

Between a number of our leaders and the menfolk of that town, there is not much difference. The first does as much choking up of its lust in the womb of the people as the other. With the menfolk of that town, desire is spent in one evening, or two, or three or four; Sepang Loca was a healthy woman and the maternal instinct with her was strong. With some of our leaders, desire feeds and with the years, inurement by force and practice here as strong as the other and like the menfolk to Sepang Loca, what matters if after nine month's time, out of the blood and the physical agony of an insane woman, there is a stillborn or a dwarf as long as lust is satiated for the night? The hellishness of a mad woman in the hands of a sane man ten times mad than she and the helplessness of the people in the arms of a cunning leader, Sepang Loca endured only the physical pains as a people can only suffer hunger for their bodies and those of their children; the menfolk must suffer the greater ache of mind and spirit as the leaders must. They suffer a greater death, if they are still capable of dying, at the sight of a hungering people as the menfolk died a greater death while gazing at Sepang Loca as she lay unmoving on the grass under the moon, a naked child glistening between her breasts.

(1953) First published in *The Philippine Collegian Little Review,* under the Literary Editor's column, "From The Subsoil, Upward," Graduation Issue, April, 1953, p. 7.

kills himself to deafen his ears forever to her cries of anguish. Flashes of colors, vivid and warm, against inky blackness of nights alive with all mysteries of rosy-cheeked and round-eyed goblins and elves who sing while they sew little pairs of high-buttoned shoes and red coats, of giant dogs that quietly stalk in many dark, sleeping towns to snatch erring children from their warm beds, of stoic-faced *capres* whose lighted cigartips glow in the darkness as big as red luminous plates while they sit smoking, their long legs crossed on rooftops—sometimes here in our own backyard, behind this very house, while we huddle closer still and even vie hotly for the pillow safest and closest to *Itay*. Of foolish and thrifty housewives who cut dangling threads to thread their needles with that they may sew little jackets for their unborn infants and find instead, too late, too late: blood dripping from that dangling thread's severed end which is in truth, a vampire's tongue!

Oh, nights of horror and beauty, of strangely-peopled darkness, of kingdoms of lovely princes and princesses and of interplays of evil and tragedy and goodness and victory all woven by a man who by mornings quietly sits behind a brown desk of an Accounting Division, in the Bureau of Internal Revenue and adds taxes, taxes, taxes amounting to millions: carefully, very carefully—not a centavo must be overlooked lest the red and blue lined sheets will never tally. Alive truly in those evenings with his little children for an audience and a cool, native mat lined with white linen-cased pillows for a night's theater! Who writes with a quiet voice and flaunts every changing scene with a great wave of veined hands. Who stages his strange worlds with backdrops smeared with live colors and rouges and masks each of his characters with artistry that can earn for him a job as make-up man in a theater or circus where all must be what the world believes them to be for at least the number of hours between curtain calls and curtain falls. Who with gleeful voice at every tale's end rewards all good and punishes all evil. (What if life could be reduced to that single level where the end is determined by what pound of good or what pound of evil one commits! Where one can say with as much preciseness as the butcher would on weighing meat: Thursday, it was a pound of good. Last Friday, a quarter of a pound of evil. Here you are, Ma'am or Mister, half pound of white and quarter pound of black, no more no less. Now, add! And without heat or hate, one adds or subtracts: what frustrations there will not be, nor recriminations, nor tears.) What world's great story-teller, tell me, has given a like nightly performance with so varied offerings, and with a free ride in his arms to each individual bed when each audience-member has fallen asleep and the night's tales have come to an end?

Night-worlds he shared with me on a piece of cool native mat—the time I understood *Itay* most—when apart from his ledgers and long account journals with eight others, he fed me full where the best of fish and rice can never satisfy. Lost to me forever—except in the mind, in the mind.

It is said that beside every deathbed, a white wisp of spirit rises to ask: Oh, speak! What wish have you before you die?

If beside mine, grant me one last feeble cry: Give me one night on that cool native mat with eight huddled little bodies beside my *Itay,* that with a child's believing mind, I shall once more have my strange worlds back: all mine! Give me back a night, one night with that hero-weaver of tales: *Itay.*

(1952) First published in *The Philippine Collegian Little Review* under the Literary Editor's column, "From the Subsoil, Upward," November, 1952, p. 7.

Vicente M. Hilario, 59

THERE WAS A FINE DRIZZLE at half-past four when the men propped the grayish coffin under the wet, black branches of the acacias. The lid which gleamed satin ruffles from underneath was opened and the people circled the coffin noiselessly, heavily. The white-bearded priest, brown garments trailing the wet blades of grass, raised a pinkish palm and traced a cross over the dead man once, twice. It was peace all around except for the thin noise the drizzle made on the leaves, the clear voice of the old priest in prayer and the drone of answering prayers from the bowed heads about him.

Then, it was time for the last look. Misty eyes and quiet tears. Through it all, the clear glass covering the white, immobile face inside the grayish coffin began to cloud from the cold of the rain.

It was an eternity before the satin-lined lid fell with a dull thud and the white, immobile face was no more.

The thud held the faces floating around it as in a spell. The figures stood rooted under the wet trees for some uncertain minutes, only the men in paint and cement-coated overalls, darted to the open mouth of the tomb to mix cement in their pails, the hollow sound of their spades defining circles in the watery gravel and cement joining the ceaseless noise the raindrops made on the leaves. A thick silence that kept space between the coffin and the tomb! One last quick silence before goodbye! They stood until the dead man's brother spoke gratitude and the spell broke under the voice. The sea of faces scattered like tuffy waves from the coffin to the lines of waiting cars.

Before the cemetery, there was the hospital. The white room before the gray tomb. The iron bed before the wooden coffin. Between the coma and the quiet peace was the bottle that dangled from a t-bar and fed the old man life by a tube and a needle. An old man back in swaddling clothes! The mighty professor, the "walking encyclopedia" prostrate in bed and accepting life without the slightest sign of protest from the trickling of liquid through needle taped to his arm-vein. No, no sound from the old man who spoke with biting sarcasm of life and its many irregularities in the classroom or out. The old man was too quiet.

I saw the old man through many still bright afternoons in the classrooms; once in the antiseptic white of a hospital room; under the dim covers of a parlor, the smell of crushed and wilted flowers rising from the carpeted floor and out at last under the dripping branches of the acacias over his tomb. The old man who used to scold me because he thought I could do better if I wanted to— because, because I neglected his class for writing.

I write for the old man now. My one last gesture of respect. My one little tribute to the old professor who hid his real feelings (to me, so crystal-clear) for all his students by sarcasm and sharp chidings. I write knowing he will not scold me now. The morning papers of June 2nd glared to me only too clearly:

Professor Vicente M. Hilario is dead.
Arteriosclerosis.
Age 59.

(1953) First published in *The Campus Life Magazine,* under the Literary Editor's column, "Clay Under My Thumb," June 1953, p. 3.

Faulkner Was Here

H E CAME INTO THE TIGHTLY PACKED THEATER, a small mild-looking man in powder grey suit, down through the ovation-stirred air, his white hair brave as a flag. Mr. William Faulkner. It was a rare experience, finely electric, to feel the presence of the man here, out of so much, so untouched by acclaim one is sure because he moved with ease and naturalness, without the air of defiance of the famed and so simple he was uncertain even whether to smile or raise a hand in greeting. The faculty and students on seats, jammed orchestra pit, aisles and clogged theater windows broke into thunderous applause when Mr. Faulkner walked up the stage.

Mr. Faulkner sat, folded his hands on his lap and one almost half-expected the stage to transform into a white farm house front porch; Mr. Faulkner to draw a pipe from the pocket of his coat and rock on his chair while surveying with keen quiet all that stood before the path of his eye. For all the time he was being introduced by Dean Tomas Fonacier, it was what Mr. Faulkner did—survey the audience. Applause arrested him from this preoccupation and rose him from his chair. And Mr. Faulkner bowed low, very low, twice, to acknowledge all these people who came.

It was June when the U.P. Writers' Club learned of Mr. Faulkner's trip to Japan. Immediately, a move to invite him to Diliman stirred the organization; the President's Committee on Culture and the College of Liberal Arts caught the spirit of the move and enthusiastically supported it. It was a heyday for the club-members as soon as the cable came that Mr. Faulkner had accepted to speak, they thought of greetings, welcome arches, yea, even cannon salute. But with the characteristic distrust for noise and trimmings, the sponsoring bodies settled for the usual run of posters and programs. The President pushed it up, declared eleven o'clock of August 25, 1955, no classes:

the sole proprietor of Yoknapatawpha county in Mississippi was to have the whole university for a noon audience.

One was to discover sharply that the mild-looking Mr. Faulkner spoke the way he wrote; he was oblivious to natural pauses, to inflection, to stresses, just as his prose run across the page comma-less, periodless; a sentence in his story, "The Bear," for instance, extending through the whole of six pages. Mr. Faulkner read his speech through twenty-five minutes, head bowed over his paper, and partly because of faulty acoustics, his voice barely audible through the first twenty-five rows of seats. But it was not without force, his unshakeable convictions stood planted squarely as he on the stage, and nothing in the world, one felt, could blow it out of his being.

To emerge scatheless out of so much decay and violence, to distill the pure out of so much impurities, to believe in love and honor even while witness to hate and greed—to Mr. Faulkner, it is a writer's duty to believe thus and in so doing to help man not only to endure but to prevail. As his novels are and his stories, his speech was a cantata on this one bright faith. Out of his black earth and derivered swamps and lurid women, out of killings and lusts and cowardices and betrayals, flowers straightforth love and temperance and compassion and honor.

Mr. Faulkner answered some questions after his speech; cocking an ear to catch each question and pausing only for barely a minute before replying. He was asked of Art and of Faith. He was asked of mechanization in our age, of Freedom, of Communism and of Democracy. He was asked of his novels; which of them he thought most highly of. To which he said, the novel that had caused him the most anguish, the most pain was *The Sound and the Fury*. He was asked to advise a young writer. He was even asked to explain why his writings were difficult to read. To each of them, Mr. Faulkner, with his low Southern drawl, answered wholeheartedly, freely, candidly.

Mr. Faulkner was whisked out of the theater by his companions before the students who flocked the stage stairs grew any bigger. Through it all Mr. Faulkner appeared unperturbed and mildly amused.

After a month, we still have the programs, the posters, the photographs. We even have Mr. Faulkner's voice on tape.

Yes, Mr. Faulkner was here.

(1955) First published in *The Philippine Collegian New Review*, September-October, 1955, p. 44.

A Tribute to
Gabriel A. Bernardo:
Mentor and Friend

DEAR FRIENDS OF PROFESSOR BERNARDO:

Those of us who work in the arts have more than our fair share of recognition in the community, in the media and elsewhere. Probably the very nature of our profession, the very public nature of our work, invites this public attention. It is so that even the most mediocre, given the proper PRO, can collect footage of media adulation that would fill volumes. However, there are those who in their quiet and private efforts have done enormously to influence a sizeable number of careers and lives, plus the direction of certain disciplines but who fail to elicit even half the recognition which most artists get.

The man to whom I shall pay my small tribute today, a dear departed mentor and friend, is one such man. Gabriel Adriano Bernardo, 86 years old were he alive to celebrate his birthday ten days from today, on March 14th. I understand as a matter of fact, these memorial lectures of which I am about to deliver the 4th in the series, is actually timed to commemorate his birthday. I cannot think of a more eloquent way of honoring a man than to remember him on his birthday, close to 14 years after his death, with a public lecture.

I said that Prof. B failed to elicit even half the recognition most artists get from the media. I should have said, a hundredth or a thousandth part, for only two tributes were paid to him, to fill a page of an album. One was entitled, "Our Dean of Librarians" by Alfredo Roces in "Light and Shadow" as published on Nov. 27, 1962 and another, an editorial from the same paper on December 7, 1962 entitled simply, "Professor Bernardo." It might be pertinent to point out that these two tributes were written within 10 days of each other;

the first while Prof. B wrestled with death after a crucial operation at the Ramon Magsaysay Memorial Hospital and the second, as he lay in state, a day after he died.

Those of us who have been privileged to work with him would realize that as he worked quietly, no noisy, drumbeating adulation should now disturb the quiet of his rest. But since, being mortals, we can only be at peace with ourselves after we arrange things in their right perspectives, we come together for this quiet, unassuming man, attempting to take a fresh look at him again, on the day of his birthday. And this we do, I dare say, with much affection and even more respect. I am sure you all must know the story of how several blind men approached an elephant and by means of touch, each tried to describe how the mammoth creature looked like. One feeling his way by the tail said it looked like a rope; another touching its trunk said how very much like a long hose it was; another its ear, how very much like a fan it was; another its leg, how very much like a post it was and another, its side, how very like a wall it was. I suppose, to a certain degree, we can all be likened to these blind men describing what their hands "saw" of a mammoth creature; each from his own vantage point, as many saw Prof. B, to be a biblio-grapher, another saw him as a folklorist, another saw him as a scholar, another a bibliophile, and so forth. I saw him as a mentor and friend and that is how I wish to talk about him today.

I met Prof. Bernardo at, you might say, the twilight of his years, in 1951 hardly 5 years before he was to retire, a little over ten years before his death. I was a young student then, given what was supposed to be one of the toughest assignment—to interview the University Librarian. I remember climbing the grayish unpainted building which is now the Gonzalez Hall in order to be on time for my appointment. To me, the whole meeting appeared to be one of confronting the lion in his lair. I went directly to his office on the second floor and this mighty lion looked up from under his bushy eyebrows, above the rim of his eyeglasses, chewing the end of his cigar as he looked me over. So, he said, you're Miss Lapeña. I think I know you, read a few of your works. Very good. At that magic moment, his image changed for me, to one of a lamb. At that moment, I thought to myself, well, a most promising beginning, he recognizes me as a writer. For I was told that Professor B held artists—writers, musicians and painters, as a special breed. This esteem springs from his sharing a common interest and common commitment. Aside from several highly per-ceptive reviews he wrote of literature and music, he had written a play called "Maria Kalabasa" and for many years he held the chairmanship of the U.P. President's Committee on Culture which has been instrumental in projecting so many artists on the U.P. campus.

He gave me some background information on how the library was destroyed during WWII by showing me first a small upright shelf containing some 50 volumes, the only remaining books of the old library, books which were out to borrowers during the bombings and were returned after the war. Then, he led me to what is now the Filipiniana Library, only at that time, it was a bare room full of crates and crates of wooden boxes marked: Joseph Ralston Hayden Memorial Library, crates reaching almost to the ceiling. But even before we reached that section, we passed through makeshift furniture, I surmised from lumber obtained from the empty crates. These rough shelves lined the windows and walls and if they formed divisions, they were carefully paneled with brown paper. These were the counters over which students reach out for their requested books.

Inside that huge 2nd floor where crates reached to the ceiling, Professor B told me how he spoke before various librarians' groups, telling them about the destruction of what took years to build, the jewel of a library in the midst of the Manila campus, scientific, humanistic, filipiniana collections, all gone. He said that getting to that part of his talk about the destruction, he found himself unable to go on, he would sit down, fighting off the strong urge to cry, his shoulders shaking. He said that then what he thought was his failure to complete his report turned out to be the most eloquent way of expressing the immense loss suffered by the University. It did not take very long after his return from the USA, when crates of books started to pour in. And there they are, he said, the beginning, of another library. But what can we do with all of these, he said with a helpless sweep of the hand, there must be a key to the treasure, or they are all useless as far as our students are concerned!

After the interview where I studiously took down notes from this man who poured out not mere words but his dedication to the cause of an institution which is rightfully the center of the university, Prof. B. expressed some doubts about my publishing the true plight of the University Library. Having been moved by the devotion of the man, I promised what no reporter should be bound to do—I promised to show him the draft of my story before it gets to my editor. It was a promise I kept. After Prof. B "approved" what I wrote, I typed a clean copy and submitted it to my editor who saw it important enough to merit the front page and the publication of the photograph of Prof. B standing in front of the crates and crates of books piled almost to the ceiling.

I cannot tell how my news story helped; judging from Prof. B's sincerity and devotion, I knew that he would not stop until he got the necessary funding for the mammoth project of cataloguing the hundreds of thousands of books and journals in order to provide "the key to the treasure." The next time I came to see him, the Library was buzzing with activity. My visit was occasioned by his letter asking me to come over for an interview, a formality really, because I found out that true to his word, he had recommended, and had received the approval of my appointment as Secretary of the University Librarian, a position vacant for so many years. Again, my getting the job was so characteristic of how quietly Prof. B worked. We met at the lobby of the Administration Building as I was delivering some papers to one of the offices on the first floor. He asked me what I was doing there. I said trying to earn a living so I can continue my graduate studies. I was then working as a clerk in the basement office of the Property Division where my job was to check on vouchers and order forms. He very quietly remarked that I was wasting my talents there and that he would try to do something about it. One Dean had made the same comment but nothing happened, so I didn't give it much thought. Then one day, I was told to come for an interview and then suddenly I found myself transferring from the windowless basement of the Administration Building to the 2nd floor office of the University Librarian, a day which opened so many windows for me, and I don't mean the many glass windows which lined all sides of that second floor.

My first days consisted of groping around. My typing assignment consisted of routine letters as there was *Mang* Ernesto who had been doing substantial typing for him. Prof. B's drafts of letters revealed his even, firm handwriting, the lines of which can best be compared to the standout signature in the American constitution—John Hancock's. How I wish I have kept even one such letter, all I have is a page in my file which I have kept these many years, a half-completed letter of recommendation of which he must have written hundreds for his many students.

Among my first tasks, was to put some semblance of order in his files and also, so I then thought, in his cluttered desk. That desk with a rollup top must be known to anyone who had met Prof. B. During my first day, I watched fascinated while our janitor, Pek, danced around it, dusting gently here and there, but doing nothing to touch the piles of papers and books with markers. I decided after a few days to make a more thorough job of it, so thorough it was discovered that there was a surface to that desk after all. I sat back and watched Prof. B's face when he returned. He took one look at his desk. I don't know whether it was joy or distress for he took it all quietly. It wasn't until after so many days that he brought up the matter. Very gently, he said, "Mely, *iha,* thank you for arranging my desk but please don't touch it. It took me all of these many days to find my things again." Needless to say, the desk went back to how it originally looked, the whole surface covered with papers and books, with but little space for writing. Now that my interest have expanded into many and diverse fields and my own working desk at home is beginning to look like his, I know what he meant by knowing just where things are and how desks are really quite sacred territories. My household has also learned to respect this important lesson.

I think the best teachers teach not by words but by deeds. But Prof. B did both, his devotion to research showed whether he intended to show it or not and because he believed in what he did, his devotion was unmistakable whenever he spoke of his work. From even before seven o'clock in the morning to six in the afternoon, he attended to his duties as University Librarian. It consisted of various tasks, aside from attending countless meetings of many university committees and honor societies. But from six in the afternoon, his time was his. I did not know what he did with it but for one day when I forgot something and decided to go back. The whole section was quiet, all windows shut, but in the middle of it all, way in the far end, under the light of a few flourescent lamps, was Prof. B bent over his index cards, oblivious to time and the need for oxygen. When I approached to say goodbye, he stopped long enough to explain what he was doing. It was the monumental bibliography that his colleagues were talking about in as much awe as one talks about the Taj Mahal, long boxes of index cards, worked over with neat notations, checked and re-checked for so many times with the patience and the endurance of a long distance runner. I was struck by the fact that here was a man, who was racing against time but who refused to be hurried. A lesser scholar would have published his work but not Prof. B. "Festina lente," was his credo. "Make haste slowly." After hurrying through my book, *The "Seditious" Tagalog Playwrights: Early American Occupation* in order to meet the required deadline, I knew what he meant. A printed book, irrevocable, permanent for all time, can be the best record in black and white, of a scholar's haste. After that evening, I told my friends hat I discovered what my boss thrives best on—the rarefied air exuded by books and index cards and the nicotine of his eternal cigar.

What are scholars made of? Certainly not sugar and spice and certainly not everything nice, stomach ulcers, for most of them, for forgetting that stomach muscles churn at fixed hours. When Mrs. Bernardo told me that her "Bembe" is suffering from it because he seldom finds time to eat the very substantial basket of lunch she sends him, I decided to fix him a glass of milk at our coffee break, mornings and afternoons. The first time I did that it brought an appreciative smile wide enough to shut his eyes. I remember being struck at how very Chinese he looked and of course he told me how in one of their trips abroad, he and Mrs. B were often mistaken for Chinese. One time, upon crossing the wide boulevard in some country, they spied a Chinese couple running straight toward them with outstretched arms and talking in very animated Chinese. He then expressed what every traveller knew at one time or another, the pangs of homesickness. "I felt sorry about disappointing them," he said, "you can imagine how I wish then that I knew how to speak Chinese."

When he found out that I painted and had exhibited as the only female member of the writer-painter group called Primitives, and how I was engaged in designing covers, programs and invitations for the U.P. Writers' Club, he made it a point to show me quality printing whenever he came across one. It was from Prof. B that I learned to appreciate the color, thickness, coarseness, darkness of the surface quality of bookpaper, how well it absorbed light and ink. While I could then recognize types because of my experience in editing, it was Prof. B who taught me the intricacies of the colophon of 15th and 16th centuries, how printing evolved. I guess you might say that I learned from his course on books and book design, another of his special knowledge, without having to enroll for it. Now that I have seen the publication of some of my books, I find myself applying some of the very basic principles of balance of design I learned from him. If some of them do not appear as I have been taught, I am the only one to blame plus perhaps my publisher who must, alas, also consider the cost of printing.

Any student looking back at a former mentor, begins to wonder just how much influence, consciously or unconsciously, has been transmitted to him. That would be a rather impossible task! For instance, because I have to make this tribute, I had to dig into my graveyard of memories, so to speak, and also, in order to help my memory along, I started reading on Prof. B. The Occasional Paper No. 5, published by the Bibliographical Society of the Philippines on "GAB: Librarian, Bibliographer and Scholar" as edited by Mr. Mauro Garcia, contained two very important items for me. These are: a reprint of *That Girl Has Wit* ("Maria Kalabasa"), from a 1940 edition of E. Fansler's *Nine Oriental Dramas* (Manila: 1940) and *Libraries in the Philippines* as reprinted from a 1949 Silver Jubilee Program of the Philippine Library Association. This is not to say that I did not read the others or that I did not find them important. On the contrary, I read this book from cover to cover, touched by all of the tributes made to this great man and humbled again by my reading of his very thorough and very scholarly essays, a feeling I first experienced when I read his paper on "Sungka," which, unfortunately for all of us, is not included in this collection.

A re-reading of "Maria Kalabasa" was important for me because it reminded me that I once directed this play for him, with all female cast (because we were short of male librarians) and that it must first have opened to me the possibility of the use of Philippine folktales as material for the theater. I think Prof. B was among the first to use this type of material for our theater. I did not even dream then that 18 years after, in 1974-75, when searching for materials for what I hoped to be the beginning of my work for Children's Theater, it was folklore I would turn to. Coincidence? Of the second item, "Libraries in the Philippines," I found reading it for the first time, that Prof. B pleaded, at the end of the essay for the creation of children's libraries, thus:

"For one thing, instead of attracting young children to the library, one of the condition for granting the privileges of borrowing is that the library borrower must be of legal age. This deplorable situation can be satisfactorily remedied only by throwing the portals of our public libraries wide open to our children, and by training them in the proper use of books and libraries when they are still very young. In some countries, this training starts with children of pre-school age."

Quite strictly by coincidence, I made the same plea for Children's Theater when I first started writing my children's plays. I mentioned also that training must start with children of pre-school age and that in Japan, children of kindergarten age are bused to the National Theater and that in Bali as in many parts of Southeast Asia, children are exposed to the educative process of theater from a very early age. However, it must be said that our only hope for the future is our children and in the final analysis, anyone engaged in any endeavour, would find the need to make the same plea if only to ensure the continuance of the enterprise. But that Prof. B made that plea for his institution—the library, and that I should make it for my concern which is the Theater, without my knowing he once made such a plea, is something rather meaningful to me.

As I look back, I must confess that the friendship and regard he showed me did not only extend to my development as a researcher, writer and designer. He was also concerned about me as a person, a human being. I did not realize that he was keeping track of the male writer-friends who came around during lunch time or after office hours. One day, after one such friend left, he commented to me with a smile, *"Mely, kung santo ang hanap mo, e nasa langit ang mga 'yon."* It was obvious then that he wanted me to make up my mind not to live the lonely life of an artist, alone.

I suppose I can wax poetic in remembering the many things Prof. B did for me during the two years I worked for him before I left for the University of Wisconsin on a scholarship obtained partly with the help of his letter of recommendation. But I am sure being the exact and exacting scholar that he was, he would rather that I tell it as closely to how it really happened. However, I cannot help but remember that the one lesson he taught me as mentor and friend was an unspoken lesson which I now conjecture he will accept even if I use somebody else's words in order to define it.

In Dr. Jose Rizal's *Noli Me Tangere,* the old *Pilosopong* Tasio in countering Ibarra's fear that he might fail in his enterprise of educating his countrymen, said:

"If that were to happen, if the enterprise should fail, you would be comforted by the thought that you had done everything in your power. In any case something would have been gained. The cornerstone would have been laid, the seed would have been sown. After the tempest some grain might perhaps sprout, survive the catastrophe, save the species from annihilation, and serve as grain seed for the children of the perished sower. The example of others can encourage those who only fear to begin."

For in so many ways, for me, as well as the many others like me, who have been privileged to have him as mentor and friend, Professor Bernardo is the perished sower whose example propelled us not to fear to begin!

March 4, 1977, 4th Bernardo Memorial Lecture Series
U.P. Law Center Auditorium, Diliman, Q.C.

Winter, 1964

The ground was white, iridescent
Where the snow fell last night
Turning to go, I saw a bird
A brown speck against white.

I felt it cold through the leather
Of my glove and for a moment I stood
Not quite knowing what to do
And feeling foolish for having
Picked a frozen bird up.

The doves which fed on the sidewalk
Looked silently, their inquiring
Heads cocked to one side
As if waiting for my decision.

I dug a little hole in the snow
And dropped the little bird there
Hoping the frozen tomb would shelter
It gently, at least, 'til Spring.

Lullaby to Renoir's "Little Boy with a Toy Soldier" at the Philadelphia Museum of Art, 1965

How soft
That mass of black hair
Must feel,
How warm
Those pink cheeks
How fragrant
That little red mouth;
Those blue eyes
Plucked from
    some molluscan bowels
Are pearls
New to the sun.

On Sunday visits
To the museum, my son
Thrice denied
My scarified womb, my son
Are you an old man now?
Or a corpse long gone?

Yet, your forehead
Shines here,
Forever feverless;
Mouth half open
In childish wonder,
One chubby hand

Smooth as candle
Clutching at a toy.
O my little son
O forever little boy.

On Seeing "Beclch" at the Theater of Living Arts in Philadelphia, 1967

Rained, pelted, enveloped
By stereophonic cacophony
Of native chants and monkey cries;
Flashes of jungle fauna and flora
Are blue blurs whirling
On all four walls.

Beclch tears with her teeth at a fresh liver
Scooped from a newly-slaughtered lamb,
While her husband drags a bloated
Purplish-green leg oozing elephantiasis;
Above them hang twisting torsos
And bleeding legs,
Negresses cavort while a human
On all four is a table whose
Head sticks out to stare
At a glass of wine.

When two bodies copulate on the aisle,
Or do a murky imitation of its rhythm,
People walk out of the theatre
While we sit still, untouched,
Feasting in carpeted comfort
On the madnesses, wildnesses, Oh
The extravagances of nature
Captured within these sheltering walls
In stereophonic, antiseptic
Synthetic, deodorized safety.

Why, it's only strings, wires, furs, lights,
Stuffed cotton and paints, tapes and slides;
And should copulation be real
Then that would, of course
Constitute the final act
Even in a theater.

The Twentieth Day in the Battle of Hue, 1968

I watched the twentieth day
In the battle of Hue
On a color television
Saw GIs in green fatigue
Vietnamese in black pajamas.

A reporter said the order came
(Just when the battle was stymied);
A museum blew up in grey smoke
Orange bricks strewn about it.
A spray of black earth
Touched the lens of the camera
As a man writhed on the dying grass;
The little people scurried
In all directions,
The faces of their children
Which floated in my livingroom
Were muddied
But the yellow skin shows
As does the white
Of their astonished eyes.

I watched the twentieth day
In the battle of Hue
On a color television
Saw GIs in green fatigue
Vietnamese in black pajamas.

Dreams, 1969

When Amihan smiles
In her sleep,
I say the baby
Must be dreaming;
My sociologist-husband
Laughs;
To dream, he says
You need symbols.

Well, the milk bottle
Is a symbol,
So is her pink, plastic
Pacifier
And her shiny, japanese
Rattle
And that dark, uterine
Existence
When lonely,
Afloat,
   Agile,
Astronaut
She.

And, do not forget
Perhaps, sometimes,
She dreams
Of me.

The Irreverent Gallery-Keeper at 42nd Street, 1970

Cancer eating away his nose
He whittles at the doorstep.

Dem paintings bin der but no body comes no more
Hundreds of places like dis in Philly
Bigger ones, who cares.
Did ya see da one wid scissors and buttons,
Three hundred dollars?
And dat hunk of metal
Eleven hundred.

Look dem works bin to eight other
Places 'fore dey put em in dis place here
Dem is known guys,
Painters, see.

Look, lady
I always thought I wuz crazy
But now I know, see?
His ash-blue eyes focussed on me.

Oh, if ya wanna go up
Tis all da same wid me,
Just step over da threshold
I painted it dis mornin.

Plays

Sepang Loca

(A PLAY IN ONE ACT)

PREMIER PRESENTATION

On May 22, 1957 at 8:00 p.m. and the following day at 3:00 and 8:00 p.m., *Sepang Loca* was presented by the Wisconsin Players of the University of Wisconsin in Madison at the Play Circle together with two other prize-winning plays: David Starkweather's *Excuse Me, Pardon Me* and Milton Polsky's *Night of Mourning*. It was directed by John Morrow, assisted by Judilee Tash; sets were designed and executed by the author; choreography by Thais Robertson and guitarists were Vic Llames and Emy Layague. The original cast consisted of: SON, Bob McElya; SEPANG LOCA, Thais Robertson; DANCING WOMEN, Leigh Dean, Laura Foreman, Jacqueline Goland, Peggy Post; MOTHER, Elaine Sulka; FATHER, Don Castelo; ELENA, Leigh Dean; PEDRO, William Smith; CARDO, Tony Roemer; NICOLAS, Stan Samber; JUAN, Dick Brooks and VILLAGE WOMEN, Laura Foreman, Jacqueline Goland, Sharon Hayden, Peggy Post and Judilee Tash.

CHARACTERS:
(In the order of appearance)

        SON
        SEPANG LOCA
        Two fishermen
        Five dancing women
        MOTHER
        FATHER
        Townsfolks: ELENA, PEDRO, CARDO, NICOLAS

SCENES:

    1—Village dustroad before Sepang Loca's garden
    2—Village church yard
    3—A kitchen
    4—Same as 1, this time the whole scene revealed

There will be need for only three settings: Scenes 1 and 4, middle stage; Scene 2, left side of middle stage; Scene 3, right side—each to be spotted while SON *narrates story. In all flashbacks while narration is going on, movements are pantomimic and dance-like. Dimming and blackout, as indicated each time throughout text, should hold the characters transfixed—like figures in a painting.*

SON *(spotlighted, stage right)*: By the time my men get done with this part of the old hometown, it will be crusted clear through with a foot deep of cement. Think on't—a thick crust of cement on every stone, every inch of dirt, every living thing lodged within the heart of this yellow earth. A highway glaring white under the intense yellow sun. And yet, now *(sitting and picking up stick to point with),* this you see was once the village *(dimming on Son, gradual lighting on road, Scene 1, characters coming to life slowly as narration gathers details)* dustroad. It was a busy little dustroad. Brown fishermen with slimy green nets slung over their shoulders, village women balancing deep baskets of silver-bodied fish on their heads—they would walk on this dustroad, down to the sea or up to the marketplace, dark seaweeds entwined around their bare legs, their mouth white with seasalt, their head bands fluttering in the hot air, their happy chatter breaking through the heavy yellow dust clear as the animated gobble of fowls. I used to watch them. They were simple-hearted really. Brown and strong. They heave the heavy burden of fish from the sea their women sell or barter their catch for rice. They lead a simple life, marvel secretly at the strength of their women *(gradual dimming),* humbled at the coming of each child. They die old, their lungs clogged with salt and their skin toughened like leather by seawater *(complete blackout).* There used to be a grass hut *(slow spotting)* here beside which stood a stone well. We had to cut through this land. My men bulldozed the place and swept everything away as though they were matchsticks. As they were uprooted and rolled aside before the mouth of the machine, I remembered. My men knew nothing at all about this place. They came with me from the city. We have been sent by the Government. But I, I remembered. Ten, or was it nine years ago? Perhaps, it did not even happen at all? Sepang Loca *(flash on a brightly-costumed woman walking down the dustroad, a meeting between her and two brown fishermen who each brush against her arm. She flees from them to one side of the stage and cowers. The two fishermen walk on, throwing their faces up in laughter.)* they used to call her. They say that each town has one of them *(spot dimming on Sepang Loca, in cowering position.)* Yes, one of them *(complete blackout.)* in every town.

One of them in every town—a toddling idiot with a perpetual grin, a town's clown. We, we had this bright speck of a foreign bird it seemed, buxom and brown, her hair pulled back and shining with coconut oil. Ah, but she had firm breasts and thighs, this Sepang Loca. Once, during the Feastday of Santa Clara *(flash on Scene 2— a church yard festooned and bright with paper buntings and lighted lanterns. On one side, stands a huge statue, the only visible part of it being the hem of its heavy velvet gown resting on a flower and candle-decked carriage. It has stopped in the center of the church yard after the procession and before it, five women are dancing.)*, I saw her dance. The women come here when they are infertile, they come to dance and chant their prayers. They come wearing their brightest dresses and straw hats covered with flowers. It was into this circle that Sepang Loca entered dancing. She was wearing a red skirt and a crown of red flowers. Giant gumamelas— they were bobbing wildly while she danced and threw her skirt high and stomped the ground. The women tried to stop her, danced around her to cover her from our view. But Sepang Loca would snake her way out of their circle each time and danced impetuously, her supple body thrown in full abandon to the dance, her arms beating the air like wild wings, her crown of flowers quivering like red tentacles. The women grew more and more horrified. Heavens, how would Santa Clara take all of this—this vulgarity! Sepang Loca's thighs gleaming under the lanterns and the men cheering! They all, in an unmistakable wave *(dimming),* swooped on her like a cloud of hawks until the crown of red flowers was no more *(complete blackout).*

My old man died when the war was about to end in the Philippines. The Americans landed in Leyte and town after town was being liberated. The Japanese army was retreating to the North; in its wake, across the land there was burning, looting and killing. Some Japanese soldiers stuck sticks of dynamite and blew up the bridge before they left town. A shrapnel, big as an axehead, flew and struck Father down on the nape. Almost severed his head. We brought him home and Mother sank moaning at the sight of so much blood. She wasn't strong after that. Just like a shadow. She doted on Father, Mother did. I guess that's why she died shortly after. She never got up from bed after she fainted. But that evening—

Flash on Scene 3, a huge white-washed kitchen. A cool, old kitchen with high half-oval windows lined in threes across its thick adobe

*walls so that without the massive stone stove filling one corner, a
big iron funnel forming an inverted "Y" over its red flaming mouths,
the low pantry and immediately above it a row of bronze pots and
pans gleaming alternately in the darkness, one might think that he
had stepped into one of those roomy Spanish conventos. There is a
small flight of steps peeping on the deep end of the stage. On the
opposite side is a half-open door from which now the orange glow
of the setting sun has streamed in. The orange path is caught on the
cobbled floor and between the legs of a round table. There are three
chairs around it, quiet and waiting. The linen is white and spotless.
The table is set.*

MOTHER *(coming down the steps and turning her head to call)*:
Be sure to mop the floor, Mauricio, mop it up *por Dios y por Santo.*
One would think I have a household of mayors by the way you
people behave. What a lot falls on a woman the day she bursts from
the womb. Ah... *(going around the kitchen stove to table, fixing
supper)...* a woman has to do this, a woman has to do that and
then pooh *(swinging a wooden ladle)* life comes...

SON *(taking the ladle and putting it in to his mouth)*: ... to an end.
Hummm, *arroz caldo!* I'm famished.

MOTHER: You always are. Go on there *(taking the ladle and shooing
him off with it)* and wash. Go.

SON: But first *(ceremoniously kissing her hand and then her cheek)*
there! *Buenas,* Mama, *buenas.* And now your blessings.

MOTHER *(making a big sign of the cross over his bowed head)*: The
Lord's bountiful blessings on you, Son.

SON: Thank you, Mama.

MOTHER: How's work, Son?

SON *(walking to the kitchen sink while rolling up his sleeves)*: We
have macadamized the road to the Camino Real. Tomorrow, the
men have made a pact on't, at the sight of the Camino Real, at no
less than ten feet they swore, they will throw up their shovels and
drink *tuba.* Pedro that sly fellow, has three bamboo tubes full ready—
the reddest to burn our throats.

MOTHER: Ten feet? Oh, you little children! Touch the Camino Real
and then rejoice. Bah, men are such fools, they grovel with joy at
the sight of a door. You'll drink with them?

SON: You ask me if I can stand near a spray and not get sprinkled with water! Where's Father?

MOTHER: In the bathroom. Poor man, he must have gone to sleep again. It comes so easily when one is old. I have caught myself dozing off a number of times too. I would sit here darning a sock, here by the fire and then my stitches begin to blur, my thread and sock, they roll to the floor and my chin falls on my chest and I wake up in a jolt. Ay, me, we are getting older and older each day. We know, yet we can not do anything about it. First, it was the cradle's here and the grave's there. Then, it comes to be the grave's here and the cradle's there and how we crossed the line is really beyond a poor old woman's thinking. Ah, but it happens, it happens. And then it is all over. Son I beg of you *(putting a bowl on the table)*, stay away.

SON *(wiping his hands with a towel)*: Huh?

MOTHER: Stay away from wine! It's an evil spirit. I remember Ronaldo once, I remember it distinctly. He was swaying on the road, his shirt front drenched with blood, his eyes....

SON: Aw, Mama!

MOTHER: Son, I tell you. Let me tell you—Ronaldo once....

SON: We take a few glasses, Mama, but after what? After days and days of digging up the shape of a road, under the sun, the stones are live coals, the shovels like lead. Mama, I tell you, we throw all of these down and free our bodies. Wine is the wind.

FATHER *(coming down the stairs)*: Who speaks of wine, heh?

MOTHER: Your son. He speaks of wine and the wind—and, and liberation!

FATHER: Wine and wind! You should see the men who are brought to my office, *hijo,* they roll in the dust like swine imploring, Have mercy, *Señor Alcalde,* my family would starve. Bah, I don't see any liberation. And the wind, it brings no fouler smell than wine and sweat combined.

SON *(weakly)*: I speak of drinking until you feel a few feathers floating in your head.

FATHER: Aha, the very feathers that should go to the nest. The very feathers! Their families starve because they *want* the feathers *(pointing to his head)*, here!

MOTHER: Tee-dum. It is getting dark. Ay, these windows are for birds. Bring in the lantern, Son. Let's have supper. Aha, I have the meatiest mutton and broth, ay, the bones are dripping with clear golden marrow. I went to the slaughterhouse myself and picked them. You both shall be warmed to your bones. Oh, button your collar, Mauricio, you'll catch cold. Looks out at me like an eye! First time I saw it, Son, like a big black teardrop it was, Father pulled himself up proudly this way. And he said, Paz, he said, my Father gave me this and he pointed to his chest, and I'll give it to my son! It was the first sign I sought when I nursed you for the first time. Well, come now and say grace, Father. Put the lamp there and take your seat, Son. The soup is getting cold and I detest a rim of fat around my bowl.

FATHER: Lord, we thank Thee for this blessing of a full table. Always look with grace, we pray, upon this house and all its tenants.

MOTHER: Amen.

SON: Amen.

FATHER: Hummm, soup's good, Mother. Yes, very good; reminds me, we are to bring a jar of coffee to boil for the folks at the Aplaya. Quite a confusion going on in the place. I had to send a squad down there late this afternoon. The town's full of curious people. Something happens, a brawl starts in one of the streets and they flock to the spot like flies. The Camino Real had to be cleared off for the traffic. The cars tooted their horns and the *calesas* jingled their bells until the place sounded like a mess of a marketplace. It took my men two hours to clear that noisy tangle, the motors and horses on one side and the people on the other. I promised we'll be there tonight.

MOTHER: What's all this? Not having left the house, this is all very strange to me. Start where you should, Father. Start from the beginning. Oh, something has happened and I did not even know. Oh, this is terrible. Why, it seems that I'm not part of this town at all!

FATHER: First, another bowl of soup, Mother. This is very good. Wouldn't you like to have some more, Son? Mother *(calling out to her while she stands before the stove)*, put more, some more for Danilo. By the way, Son *(lowering his voice)*, I did not mean to be so hard. I drink too, you know. Like I always say, Son, a man's entitled to a vice—if he has the pocket for it! Heh!

MOTHER: A ladleful for each of you, no more. You must have room for the meat. Now, Mauricio, from the beginning.

FATHER: When I left the Aplaya, the place had quieted down, a few of the men stayed. They built a bonfire in the yard and a bamboo crane over the stone well.

MOTHER (collecting the soup bowls): A bonfire! A bamboo crane! What are all these for? Oh, something exciting has happened, ay, truly and I did not even know.

FATHER: Oh, Mother, I'll tell you everything if you just give me time! Pass the sauce, Son. As I was saying, the men built a bonfire in the yard and a crane over the stone well in Sepang Loca's garden. This morning, it was almost noon I think, old Elena said she heard a baby crying. From Sepang Loca's hut, that is. Old Elena was gathering some camote tops and she said that she sat up and listened. She ran back to her house and cooked some soup to bring to Sepang Loca. You know how it is with that woman, being alone and as old Elena says, she snarls at anyone who tries to go up to her hut and help her at those times. I should say this Sepang Loca's strong and remarkably well-ordered when her time comes.

MOTHER: Such shame! Ay Santísima Madré, ay, such shame!

FATHER: So old Elena goes there limping, the bowl of soup to stir, as old Elena puts it, to stir Sepang Loca's milk. For the child, you know. But the mother and the child are not in the house. Old Elena said that she looked and looked and they were not in the house. She was alarmed to say the least, she flew out of the hut shrieking that Sepang Loca and her child have vanished. The people came and they started looking all over the place, inside the house and in the garden. Until finally, finally, someone remembered how Sepang Loca goes straight to the well after her child is born. She bathes herself clean, as you know, and the baby too.

MOTHER: Oh, it is a miracle each time—how her babies manage to stay alive. And she too, how she lives on and on. The fire of blood and the ice of water from the well! She's as strong as a carabao, surely, or the devil keeps her. I see no other explanation. Women die of less. No, it can't be true. And yet it is, she lives on while her babies grow transplanted in some other houses, each home fearfully waiting for that streak to show. Ay, it is terrible. Ay, such shame, such shame!

FATHER: They were right. They came upon her after clearing the bushes. She was slumped over the mouth of the stone well, her arms dangling down the slimy inside of the stone wall.

MOTHER: *Santísima,* and the child!

FATHER: She must have dropped it. That is what the men are trying to find out.

MOTHER: It is taking them so long!

FATHER: They're almost sure. Sepang Loca must have had a spell of dizziness. She isn't as young as she used to be.

MOTHER: And she's dead!

FATHER: She was cold and dead when they found her. Must be too much loss of blood.

MOTHER: *Madre mia,* cold and dead!

FATHER: She isn't as young as she used to be. She isn't as strong. You didn't know about this, Son?

SON: We have moved away from the place more than a month ago. I heard the confusion and saw the crowd from a distance. Guess I wasn't too interested. We worked hard so we could finish much before it got dark. You know, we were afraid it would get dark.

MOTHER *(reaching out for his hand)*: Oh, he works hard. Someday, you'll be building bridges and highways, Son. That will be the day, I may be in the grave by that time or still alive, a blabbering old woman, but even now as I think on it, I'm proud of you. Joining town to town, why, even God will be proud!

FATHER: I'm ready for my coffee now, Mother. Then we can rest a little while and go to the Aplaya. They must be waiting for me. I would not be surprised if someone should come for us now.

MOTHER: This coffee is hot, be careful. Pass the cream and sugar to Father, Son. Push your plate away, here, let me have it. Your coffee. Oh, it's very hot. I shall not have mine, I think. I'll clear the table and stack the dishes in the sink. I can do them when we come home tonight. Do you suppose it is going to take them long, Maurico?

FATHER: The well is deep and quite narrow. The men were still tying up the bamboos when I left them. They have to look for a small fellow to do the diving. Then we'll know if the child is inside the well.

SON: Can it be in any other place? If the woman, if Sepang Loca, is slumped over the mouth of the well as you said?

MOTHER: There can be no other place. Ay, such shame, such shame!

FATHER: We'll find out. Mother, take a wrap. It is cold out there with the sea close by. Better put on a sweater, Son.

SON: I don't think I'll go. I'd rather stay here and read.

MOTHER: Read!

FATHER: How can you say such a thing!

MOTHER: Not come! The whole town's there.

SON: I shall not be missed.

FATHER: You die, the whole town misses you. You are not there, everyone asks about you. You are alive, you are there and nobody pays you mind. We are a funny lot. You should be there, *hijo*, the men are taking turns at the well while the women watch and keep the coffee warm on the fire. Mother, the coffee jar.

MOTHER: I'm refilling it, Mauricio. Go up there and get my wrap, Son. It's in the top drawer of the bureau. You won't miss it—it's my old blue wrap with little black puffy balls.

FATHER: I think we'd better take the lantern too.

(Gradual lighting of the middle stage for Scene 4, while Scene 3 slowly dims out on the MOTHER who is refilling the coffee jar, the FATHER in the act of taking the lantern from the table and the SON coming down the stairs with his sweater on and the blue wrap in one hand. They all stand transfixed until complete blackout in Scene 3 and the full lighting of Scene 4 are attained simultaneously. One side has a tall bamboo crane with a few men around it. They are unrolling the rope into the well and pulling it out at intervals. They work in heave-hos, the end of the rope apparently holds a man as they call down into the well a few times. On the other side, before a small bonfire over which a kettle hangs, sit a few huddled figures. Except for this fire and the torch held above the well, the scene is totally a play in these three predominant colors; purple, blue and gray to

black. The FATHER, MOTHER *and* SON *walk into the scene, the* FATHER *holding his lantern aloft to discern the faces which call greetings to them.)*

FATHER: Good evening. Good evening to all of you. I kiss your hand, Old Mother Elena. Hoy, Pedro, Nicolas, Cardo! So good to see you all here.

ELENA: The Lord's blessings on you, *Señor Alcalde,* and to the *Señora.* There is room around the fire, right here. Unless you want to see how they are doing at the well?

MOTHER *(sitting down):* The men can go there. I shall sit here where it is nice and warm. I brought some coffee, Old Mother Elena.

PEDRO *(yawning):* Ho-hum, that's good. Coffee warms the stomach.

ELENA: That's all you have been doing—warming your stomach.

PEDRO: Here's space for you, Danilo. Fresh coffee is poured this way first and then down the line.

ELENA *(sharply):* Can't you think of something better?

PEDRO: Oh, sure. I should have brought *tuba,* it warms the blood too *(nudging the Son),* eh, Danilo? If I didn't promise you those three tubes full?

ELENA *(throwing up her hands in despair):* He is beyond hope! What is a mother to do? One can only try so hard! Ay *Señora,* what monsters we raise!

MOTHER: Sometimes, we can only pray.

ELENA: I have grown callouses on my knees, *Señora.* Ay! I make devotions to the Holy Virgin. I have lighted, oh heaven knows how many tapers! How many trips have I made, ay, on my knees to all the holy and immaculate saints in the church. I beat my chest, tears run down my cheeks like twin-rivers. I implore the heavens to hear me, ay, I'm hoarse with begging. Does it do any good? Ay, *Señora,* *(sweeping a hand to her Son),* as you can very well see.

MOTHER: You should join your Father, Son; they need strong men. Yes, Old Mother Elena, I should think it is a mystery what our wombs bring to the world.

PEDRO: You should see Sepang Loca now, she's all *(passing a hand quickly across the front of his shirt),* and dead. Out there, on the grass. She looks so dark, Danilo, oh, so dark.

MOTHER: Son?

SON (*rubbing his eyes*): No, I think I'll stay here. I'll go maybe later.

NICOLAS: I should like to have some coffee, Old Mother Elena. One gets cold easily when one is old, kind old mother. But indeed, it is a cold night. The air is cold and still like Sepang Loca there.

DANCING WOMAN 1: Yes, like Sepang Loca.

DANCING WOMAN 2: Do the gods watch or the devils?

DANCING WOMAN 3: How you speak! Have care! It is her first night. Her spirit still hovers over her body. It listens.

DANCING WOMAN 2: Your words creep into my bones. Ay, now I tremble with fear.

DANCING WOMAN 3: It's the solemn truth. Sepang Loca's spirit (*pointing emphatically in the direction of the well*) floats there, unable to move away too far. Suddenly it finds itself free and it is bewildered.

DANCING WOMAN 4: Oh, by the third night, it should have pulled itself away, the corpse would be well-covered with earth by then and so it would fly away free as the air.

DANCING WOMAN 5 (*very solemnly*): It makes a nine-day journey to the higher regions, away from all these impure elements and for its safety, we pray for nine nights. On the thirtieth night, my mother used to tell me, it comes back to visit briefly the people and the objects its owner loved intensely or hated intensely. Then, away it goes again.

DANCING WOMAN 2: We should not have come. Now, the night is dark, there is a wide field on the way to my house and over a wall at one end of it is an old mossy cemetery. Ay, I shall stay here all night I think and wait for the morning.

CARDO: This can go on and on. Bah, such foolish women!

PEDRO: May it go on and on. Ah, such sweet little women!

DANCING WOMAN 1: Stay with me, Felisa. Ay, I hope my husband comes to take me home. But he comes home so tired. I give him his supper, he finishes it and straight off falls asleep with his cheek on the table. Before we were married, he used to fold his napkins under his plate like a gentleman. Now, he falls asleep. Ay! He does not even know that I'm here.

CARDO: Now they tremble with fear. Bah!

PEDRO: When they get so frightened, we can quiet them down, heh?

DANCING WOMAN 3: My husband comes and at once they tie a rope around his waist and lower him into the well because he is small and light and he can stay under water like a fish. They have been dipping him and pulling him out, I shall not be surprised if he is blue all over with the cold.

DANCING WOMAN 2: Will we stay all night? A child lies somewhere, in the black heart of that well. Maybe it is not there at all? And the men keep working. Ay, they are all silent while they work. As if their faces are made of stone!

DANCING WOMAN 3: It is a deep well. Truly, a deep well. Weeds— weeds choke its bottom. A net of weeds! A net to hold him under. They will find it hard to pull him up. When they do, he'll be dead! Uuuh! Oh!

ELENA: *Silencio,* Felisa. Stop your sobbing this very instant!

MOTHER *(pulling the woman to her)*: We search for a child, woman. It is difficult to search for a child. Think, if it were your own.

DANCING WOMAN 3: Mine! (*She sobs louder.*)

DANCING WOMAN 1: Felisa and I, we all, we danced and prayed to the blessed and most holy Santa Clara for a child.

DANCING WOMAN 2: A seed in our dry wombs.

DANCING WOMAN 5: To sprout in a season of growing.

DANCING WOMAN 4: And it is given to that woman out there!

DANCING WOMAN 5: It could be a boy.

DANCING WOMAN 1 *(with wonder)*: Yes, it could be a boy!

DANCING WOMAN 4: It could be anything. Ay, but for the grace of having a child.

NICOLAS: I have grown old, not a single hair on this head can now hide the dark but have I known what a woman is? There is a war, a famine comes over the land, somewhere the angry mouth of a volcano cracks open and spits mud and fire but a woman, she thinks of nothing but to have a child. My dear dead Bestra, God rest her soul *(crossing himself quickly)*, my little sweet wife, when she spoke of a child, tears stood in her eyes and her lips trembled. When our son was born and she lay dying, with my own hands, I bring to her lips the face of the child and she kissed it and she died smiling. *(Unable to control himself, sobs)* Ay, a woman! What power has she through a thing so small? Why with a thumb I can press those tiny nostrils! And yet—yes, it is life! My little Bestra, she smiled. So clear, her face shone. From that coffin, through the mud, that smile was a shout, I gave the world a child! It is all *(shaking his head sadly)* confusing to me.

ELENA *(turning to the Mother)*: I came this afternoon. To her house I go with a bowl of hot broth. To stir her milk, I say to myself. To stir her milk for the baby you know.

MOTHER: Mauricio told us.

ELENA: And is she there? No! And the child, is it there? No! And so I walk around the house calling to her. Sepa, Sepa, I call out to her. Does anybody answer? You ask me, *Señora.*

CARDO: I thought all at once of the well.

MOTHER: And did you get an answer?

ELENA: No one. No one answers. I look into her small room, *Señora,* there is her mat spread upon the floor and a crumpled blanket. They have vanished, I say to myself and I run out of the house calling the neighbors. They have disappeared, I say to them, Sepang Loca gave birth to a child but they have both disappeared. How do you know, they ask me. I heard a baby cry, I say to them. I'm old, I'm a little deaf, but I heard a cry!

DANCING WOMAN 3 *(lifting her head)*: She heard it with—her heart!

DANCING WOMAN 1: Her face was white when I saw her. She was like a ghost and could hardly speak.

DANCING WOMAN 4: I said to Felisa it was impossible that they should vanish. There is an explanation for everything, I say.

CARDO: I thought all at once of the well.

NICOLAS: Eh, eh? Did you mention the well? Of course, I told them about the well. Why, out before that very road, I said to them, To the well! Go look there and you will find her and the child.

DANCING WOMAN 5: How is a man to know all these things. I ran to the well myself, *Señora,* while they were having a fine chat out there. I ran out there. I ran. I cleared the bushes myself and saw the well. And I shrieked, *Santisima,* I shall never forget it. How she hanged over the mouth of the well like a limp sack of rice. And they all came running and they saw me on my knees.

DANCING WOMAN 1: She was trembling all over.

DANCING WOMAN 5: I could hardly stand. How could I tell if I was cold or hot? I could hardly get up on my feet.

DANCING WOMAN 1: We had to pull her up. Her hands were cold. She was trembling all over and could not speak.

DANCING WOMAN 4 *(sharply)*: A curse be upon its unknown father!

ALL THE WOMEN: Ah!

ELENA *(crossing herself)*: Such things could not be said. Oh, all you dear and lovely saints, close your ears. It was a mistake.

DANCING WOMAN 4: It was no mistake.

PEDRO *(aside to the Son)*: She deplores the waste. Watch that woman.

SON: I shall go there *(he stands up)* and see what I can do to help.

PEDRO *(meaningfully)*: Sepang Loca lies over there before the well, but there is room to pass on either side.

SON *(softly but firmly)*: I can find my way. I have eyes.

ELENA: Ay, what we say at times. But when a mother has a son, she thinks before she speaks.

MOTHER: When a woman has a son, sometimes, she does not speak. To all other sons she is a mother. Ay, I have a son who is a builder and I am proud to say it.

NICOLAS *(slapping his leg)*: It is cold and the mosquitoes are beginning to come. You can hear them coming like the waves.

CARDO: Now, if the body is found, that is another matter. Think of it, old Nicolas, two drowned bodies.

NICOLAS: Heh, Sepang Loca did not drown. I tell you, young man, she was on the well but hardly in it. In order to drown, doesn't one need water? Well, she was reaching for water but hardly because she wanted to drown.

CARDO: Oho! Now, let me tell you about foul air, old Nicolas. There are two *(spreading two fingers),* I repeat, two plain ways of dying of foul air. One, you breathe it in. And two *(triumphantly putting up his fingers before the old man's face)* you stop breathing so you do not get it into your system. I ask you, is this right?

NICOLAS *(admitting the logic but knowing a trick is up somewhere):* Yah, but... I mean....

CARDO *(blandly, quick to grasp the confusion):* And so, you die whether it is in or out of your system! In like manner, old Nicolas, Sepang Loca drowned whether the foul water of that well yonder got into her system or not. *(Old* NICOLAS *tries to protest.)* Now, I grant you that the situation may not be entirely similar but, old Nicolas, but! water is one of the more powerful elements, and this you may not know—it has fury and sound and smell and some weak soul upon absorbing any of these into its system is forced to swoon. And the creature soon falls *(sweeping his fingers along the ground, old* NICOLAS *following the gesture with fully fascinated eyes)* dead! And if such a creature died because of water, what manner of dying is it but drowning?

PEDRO *(clapping his hands while old* NICOLAS *sits utterly speechless):* The very font of wisdom! The very master! *(Declaiming)* Crawl back to ancient Delphi with tails between your legs, oh you oracles, for shame! Ricardo Sanprocopio, the great master has come!

CARDO: Now, you shut up there, man!

NICOLAS *(peering across them):* I think it is the *Señor Alcalde* himself coming. Quiet you two!

FATHER *(approaching the group):* It won't take too long now, I should say. Juan thinks he has touched the body of the child. *(A murmur of awe is heard from the women.)* They have to pull Juan out once in a while. That's what is taking it so long. He gets tired, Felisa. The last time they let him down, they threw in about thirty feet of rope. Juan said he'll give a real strong tug as soon as he gets the child.

ELENA: You should have some coffee, *Señor Alcalde.* And you, *Señora,* let me fill your cup.

MOTHER: I had enough, Old Mother Elena, it was good coffee, thank you.

FATHER *(extending his hand for a cup)*: Thank you, Old Mother Elena. Ah, it is so good to sit down by the fire. My feet are dead. The place's too damp.

NICOLAS *(ruefully)*: Too damp. I'm afraid I'll have an attack of rheumatism when I reach home. I can feel my muscles tightening. It is a sure sign.

FATHER: Juan said the well is clogged with weeds and vines and the sides are slippery with moss. It is an old well. He has to work in the dark. We wanted to tie the lantern to the rope but the jigging might spill the kerosene on Juan and burn his clothes.

CARDO: The jigging will certainly spill the kerosene on Juan and burn him.

DANCING WOMAN 3 *(as if in great pain)*: Ay, no, no!

NICOLAS: He is a good fisherman, that Juan. I remember I threw him out of the boat the first time he came fishing with me. Your baptism, I shouted after him. He bobbed up and down and sank before I caught him. Son of thunder! How was I to know that he didn't know how to swim? After that he stayed in the sea, I tell you, a playmate to the fish!

DANCING WOMAN 3: When he comes home, his mouth is gray and his eyes are bloodshot. I sometimes think his hair will turn to seaweeds and he will grow scales and fins.

CARDO: He has the eyes of a fish, it won't take long.

DANCING WOMAN 3 *(turning full on him)*: With that nose, if you had a mane, you could pass for a horse!

DANCING WOMAN 5: Take your claws off my husband, bury them somewhere. Besides, he is right, your husband does have the eyes of a fish.

DANCING WOMAN 3: Watch out, you go too far. What are you being so haughty for, may I ask? Just wait till a snail spots that snout of yours and it will come crawling and claim you as a relative.

DANCING WOMAN 5: Santa Barbara!

PEDRO *(looking at the two women hopefully)*: This should develop into something exciting.

ELENA: Keep quiet, you two.

DANCING WOMAN 4: Suddenly they seem excited at the well.

MOTHER: They're pulling the rope up. Son *(calling out),* Son, did Juan find it? Son, did he?

SON *(walking very slowly toward the group):* He tugged at the rope. They're pulling him up.

CARDO: *Señor Alcalde,* in accordance with the law, they are, one might say, the responsibility of the state? What I mean, *Señor Alcalde....*

FATHER: Oh, yes, yes, the treasury will provide for everything, the burial rites, the coffins—everything!

CARDO *(grasping the Father by the sleeve):* Ay, *Señor Alcalde,* you are God-sent. Without you, what do we do? We're lost!

FATHER *(pulling the hand on his sleeve):* Tush, tush, it was nothing. I try to do my job the best I can in the best way I see it.

NICOLAS: I nailed a coffin for my wife, my little Bestra, my kind, quiet woman. With my own hands I built for her a sturdy box. Why, for Sepang Loca I will be willing to nail together the coffins. She was a poor harmless creature, God rest her soul.

ELENA *(crossing herself):* And that of her child, Amen.

DANCING WOMAN 1 *(rising):* That's Juan's head!

DANCING WOMAN 3 *(rising):* He is green with moss all over his shoulders.

DANCING WOMAN 4 *(rising):* And he holds....

DANCING WOMAN 2 *(rising):* The child!

(At this point the whole group has risen to its feet and is hushed with awe. They all walk slowly toward the well, the FATHER leading the way. The SON walks slowly behind the rest. They all watch as JUAN comes out of the well into full view and holds high the body of the child as though it were a trophy. Some of the women fall on their knees, the sight is too much for them. The rest of the surrounding has grown dim, the spot where the well is now the only bright spot. The FATHER takes the body of the child quietly. The rest of the group are silent.)

FATHER: It is a boy!

WOMEN *(echoing incredulously):* It is a boy!

DANCING WOMAN 1: Ay, he has black hair and a good chest.

DANCING WOMAN 5: Such long full legs!

DANCING WOMAN 4 *(approaching and peering at the body)*: Let me take a look at him. His little mouth is choked with sand and moss.

ELENA *(crossing herself)*: God help us. Ay, the poor little thing! And to think that I heard it cry.

JUAN: He was lodged between stones in the bottom of the well. I had to clear the weeds and it was dark. Then, I eased the stones. His little body was soft and it floated awhile when freed.

DANCING WOMAN 3 *(pulling her shawl off)*: Take this, you're shivering like a wet mouse.

JUAN *(letting his wife wrap her shawl around his shoulders)*: For a while it floated until I caught it.

(The SON *turns his back to the group and walks slowly away into the shadows. He hesitates, halts, looks back.)*

DANCING WOMAN 4: I thought at first it might be mud, but look, it is a mole, here on his chest. A big black mole shaped almost like— a, a black drop!

FATHER *(snatching the child and investigating, then weakly)*: A big black tear!

PEDRO *(sneeringly)*: Sure a black tear!

MOTHER *(her glistening eyes search the group until they fall on her Son whose back is turned to her; suddenly everything is clear to her, she bites the back of her hand to keep from crying out)*: It is a son! All of you *(with a controlled sob)*, behold, it is a son! *(Blackout)*

SON *(back to his original position at the opening of the play, his head is bowed)*: There was no rebuke in her voice, only a great sadness. They laid the child between Sepang Loca's breasts as though it was the most natural thing in the world to do. Under the moonlight, the boy seemed almost a part of Sepang Loca as were her muddied arms. I have built so many highways and some bridges. She said, my Mother said, that even God will be proud. Oh, but tomorrow *(breaking the sticks in his hands and throwing the pieces away)*—tomorrow my men will pour the cement. *(Complete blackout)*

[END OF THE PLAY]

(1957) First published in *The Literary Apprentice,* 1958, pp. 592-611.

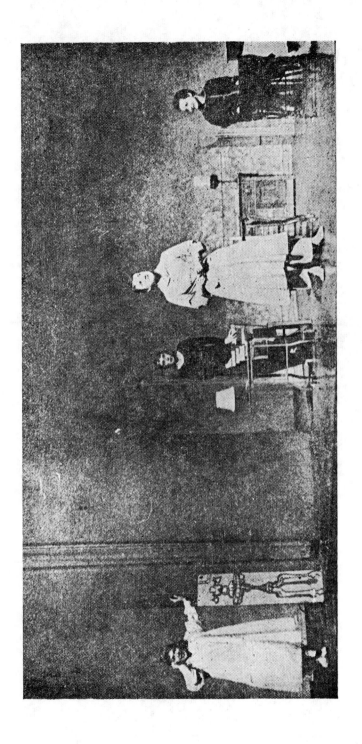

Rooms
(A Play in One Act)

A NOTE TO THE READER

Rarely does Row-Peterson's Division of Drama publish a play that is as boldly "advanced," as frankly "sophisticated," as *ROOMS,* by Miss Amelia Lapeña. The life-problems which the major characters—especially Dora and Ada—have to confront are starkly and realistically dramatic. "No punches have been pulled," as the saying goes—nothing glossed over, diluted, or romanticized. *ROOMS* is an adult play, involving adult characters compelled to meet adult crises. Directors, actors, and audiences accustomed to "lighter" fare will find Miss Lapeña's play a different—perhaps even a stunning—experience. As Publishers, however, we nonetheless feel that here is a memorable drama honestly conceived, ably executed, and motivated with the utmost skill and sincerity. We are, therefore, proud to add this unusual theatre-piece to our repertory.

STORY SYNOPSIS

ROOMS is a dormitory, one wall removed to provide a private glimpse into the lives of eight girls—intimately into the lives of four. In the two rooms and the personalities thus exposed, we come to know the painfully shy bookworm, Lizza, and her poised, sophisticated roommate, Martha, who is determined to be a dancer. In the adjoining room, practical Ada, with a headful of common sense, bends over a letter she is writing home; but she is soon to be interrupted by her desperately overwrought friend, Dora—Dora with a dark secret too awesome to carry alone and too awful to share with others.

While an unseen musician practices hesitant, fumbling finger exercises on her piano and as various young women cross to answer the telephone, to make a trip to the bathroom, or wait in the living room for their dates, all the small but meaningful clashes between pleasure and pride, dreams and realities, hopes and despairs are brought incisively—and sometimes decisively—into focus.

"How does a girl start being—brave?" queries the naive introspective Lizza. "I've never done anything foolish or childish in my whole life." (But before the night is much older, she *will*.) ..."Go slow, Lizza," cautions the worldly-wise Martha. "If a boy really loves you, he'll help you not to be frightened. Go slow—you'll get there fine."

And over in the other room, tragedy stalks the terrified Dora. "I—I can't tell Gary," she protests. "And I can't tell my folks. Marvin isn't really a bad sort, Ada. He was—kind to me that evening. Help me, Ada! I want so desperately to be free! *Free!* If you'll only lend me fifty dollars... the doctor said two hundred, but I'm sure if you'd lend me fifty, he'd...." And loyal, compassionate, steadfast Ada— shall she write the check and be cruel, or shall she hold it back and be kind? A life—perhaps two lives—are in her hands.

Through the eventual conquests of their doubts, their dreads, the girls gain insight into themselves and into the sardonic twists of fate which have caught them up. And through it all, their youth, their despair, and their faith are so touchingly human, so exquisitely painful to behold. ... A frank but tastefully sophisticated play, *ROOMS* is sure to lay a powerful and haunting hold on the mind and heart of the beholder.

CHARACTERS:
(In the order of appearance)

MARTHA, *who hopes to be a dancer; knowing, essentially kind*
LIZZA, *who understands books—but not men*
ADA, *reliable, firm, but compassionate*
DORA, *who hungers for love—and a way out of her dilemma*
*GIRL AT THE PHONE
*GIRL IN A TERRY-CLOTH ROBE
FIRST GIRL STEPPING OUT
SECOND GIRL STEPPING OUT

SCENE: A girls' boarding house.
TIME: Seven o'clock in the evening. Any weekday.

The scene is a three-dimensional "portrait" of the interior of a girls' dormitory or boardinghouse. The essential elements of the setting consist of a cyclorama, columns, and four tables—each with a chair and lamp—arranged across the stage from Right to Left and facing imaginary windows which look out over the audience.

A wall, imaginary or profile, extends from Upstage Center (UC) to Downstage Center (DC), cutting the playing area in half. As a result there are basically two rooms here, the one on the Right (R) half of the stage belonging to Lizza and Martha, and the one on the Left (L) to Ada and Dora; and they are lighted or dimmed in accordance with the shifting focus of the action. At extreme Downstage Right (DR), against a column, hangs an imaginary wall telephone. At far Downstage Left (DL), the side of a column is an imaginary door to the bathroom. Both areas may be spotlighted on cue. A doorway Up

(*Note*: The arrangement of the furnishings and doorways may, of course, be varied at the discretion of the individual director; and additional furniture, realistic or stylized, may be added as desired. The semi-stylized profile or "cutdown" setting shown in the photograph was used in a production by The Wisconsin Players at the Play Circle, University of Wisconsin. The Floor Plan Diagram (see p. 156) was evolved by Professor Kirk Denmark, Chairman of the Department of Drama, Beloit College; and the action and movement suggested in the ensuing playscript are integrally related to it.

In substance, the present arrangement calls for the desks or tables belonging to Martha and Ada to face inward toward the imaginary or profile wall, near Center (C), rather than toward the audience. There is a pouf or hassock near the center of the room at Right and slightly downstage; and near Left Center (LC), in the opposite room, an armchair has been substituted for Dora's desk. Some of the action described by the playwright would necessitate the inclusion of a dresser for Dora's belongings at far Up Left Center (ULC) and, in the opposite corner, a cabinet or a small table with a drawer.)

---

* GIRL AT THE PHONE *and* GIRL IN A TERRY-CLOTH ROBE *may be played by the same actress.*

Right (UR) gives access to the room occupied by Lizza and Martha, and another—at Upstage Left (UL)—opens into Ada's and Dora's room.

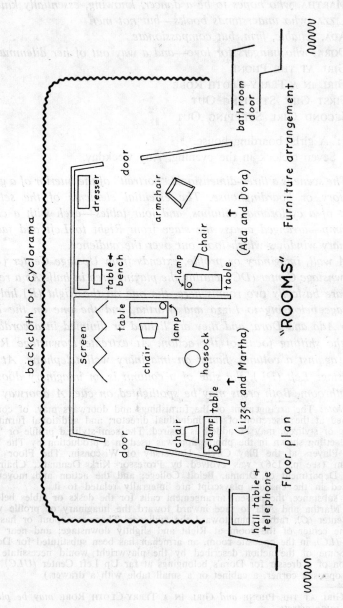

"ROOMS"

Floor plan   Furniture arrangement

backcloth or cyclorama

dresser

table + bench

door

armchair

chair

lamp

table

(Ada and Dora)

screen

table

chair

lamp

hassock

(Lizza and Martha)

door

chair

lamp

table

bathroom door

hall table + telephone

The curtains open, and the scene is slowly illuminated. Revealed in frozen, statuelike positions are three girls. MARTHA, *in black ballet tights and with arms arched over her head, stands at Right Center (RC). Her roommate,* LIZZA, *in pajamas and housecoat, is seated at her desk or table near Downstage Right, peering studiously through her dark-rimmed glasses at a book. Over in the adjoining room,* ADA, *also in housecoat and pajamas, is seated at her table or desk near Center (C), writing a letter.*

Faintly at first, finger exercises on a piano are to be heard from another room somewhere in the house. They are repetitive and—sometimes—hesitant, painful. Soon the table lamps are turned on, and the rooms bloom under full lighting. The finger exercises on the piano and the GIRLS *come to life simultaneously.* MARTHA *tilts her head back and begins to dance.*

MARTHA: One-two-three. She makes me mad. One-two-three. "Higher!" "Faster!" "Can't you get the music into your souls—or are you cows?" One-two-three. "Why, I do swear, you've got *hooves* there!"

(At this barrage—excited by the remembrance—she dances faster, almost angrily, and then slows down again. The telephone rings. Pulling a funny nightcap over her curlers and dressed in pajamas, the GIRL AT THE PHONE *runs in from DR and picks up the receiver of the imaginary telephone as a spotlight brightens on that area.)*

GIRL AT THE PHONE: Hello. ... Who? Virginia who?... Virginia Glow? Oh, yeah—yeah, this is her. I mean, this is she—her! *(After a pause; in angry surprise.)* Well, *Jonathan!*

MARTHA: One-two-three. If she weren't one of the best—! *(Groans faintly.)* Insults every damn single day. One-two-three. Listen to her teach, and you'll think you're in a slaughterhouse. Pigs. Cows. Hides. Hooves. One-two-three. One time, a girl cried because she was told she danced like a goat with its tail pegged to the ground. One-two-three.

GIRL AT THE PHONE *(icily)*: Okay, okay. Now, about Saturday. Let's talk about Saturday. What happened to you? We waited until nine o'clock!

MARTHA: One-two-three. All my savings. Left the folks in Alberta—just to come to this place. *(Determinedly.)* Gotta show her some day. One-two-three. Must say she uses colorful language.

GIRL AT THE PHONE: What do you mean—the east clock? We stood under the *west* clock!

(MARTHA stops her exercises, squares her shoulders, lifts her nose haughtily, balances an imaginary pince-nez on it, and then speaks mimickingly.)

MARTHA: "I must declare, Miss Springfield, by the shade of the great Natalia, you dance like a goat with eetz tail pegged to the ground!" Ha-ha-ha!

(She whirls back into her exercises, apparently accustomed to the stony silence of her roommate, Lizza.)

One-two-three.

GIRL AT THE PHONE *(shifts position)*: And you expect me to believe *that,* of course.

(MARTHA again stops her exercise routine, glances at Lizza, then walks DRC, and peers out the imaginary window—over the heads of the audience.)

MARTHA *(to Lizza)*: Any luck, kid?

GIRL AT THE PHONE: Well, I'll be darned!

(LIZZA lifts her eyes from her book for the first time.)

LIZZA: Whatever do you mean?

(MARTHA cocks her head toward Lizza's window and nods toward the unseen house across the alley.)

MARTHA: Our handsome young friend, Mr. Stoneface.

LIZZA: Oh—him. No, he hasn't looked up from his notes and his—slide rule and pencils and ink bottles. *(Sighs.)* Not once.

GIRL AT THE PHONE: That sounds exciting, Jonathan. . . . Oh? All the kids are coming, huh? You're an absolute genius at parties. Oh, of course I'd love to come!

MARTHA: Hmmm. *(To Lizza; getting an idea.)* Say, why don't you try blinking your table lamp at him?

GIRL AT THE PHONE: Friday is okay by me.

LIZZA *(horrified)*: Martha! I'll do no such thing!

GIRL AT THE PHONE: So now let's get this straight. The east clock?

(MARTHA turns her back on Lizza, returns to her original position at RC, and resumes her exercise.)

MARTHA: One-two-three. *(To Lizza.)* You make it sound like—like high crime. Girl told me... one-two-three... they do it at Miriam Hall.

GIRL AT THE PHONE: Okay. The east clock, then.... What?

(LIZZA thinks about Martha's suggestion, then dismisses it.)

LIZZA: They're a bunch of juveniles at Miriam Hall.

GIRL AT THE PHONE *(angrily)*: What do you mean—the bank? You said Marshall Field's last time, didn'tya?

MARTHA: One-two-three "A bunch of juveniles," she says. One-two *(Changing her routine.)* Oh, Lizza, you sound so ancient I could turn you over to the Archeo Department. One-two.

GIRL AT THE PHONE *(very angrily)*: J. Jonathan Warrenblob! "At Marshall Field's," you says. And that's where we waited—and waited— *and waited!*

MARTHA *(stops suddenly, turns to Lizza.)*: Lizza, were you ever young?

LIZZA *(very coldly)*: There's a distinct difference, Martha, between youth and juvenility.

GIRL AT THE PHONE *(tugs angrily at her funny nightcap and shouts)*: Oh, for crying out loud!

MARTHA: Oh, pooh!

(She runs to extreme URC, stands with her back toward Lizza, makes a huge gesture of turning the pages of an imaginary giant dictionary, exaggerates the pantomime of running her forefinger down a page, turns to Lizza, and declaims with much affectation.)

Aha, my dear woman! *"Juvenility* is the quality or state of being juvenile." And youth... *"Youth,* my dear..."

(She turns back to the imaginary dictionary, thumbs through the pages, runs her forefinger down a page, and again faces Lizza.)

"... is the state or quality of being young." *(Clearing her throat and cupping her hands before her.)* Harrumph, therein lies the difference!

GIRL AT THE PHONE: Oh, so okay. So now we get it straight, huh?

LIZZA *(putting her book down and facing Martha)*: Will you please stop pestering me?

GIRL AT THE PHONE: You better be there by seven-thirty.

LIZZA *(turning back to her book)*: And stop acting so childish.

GIRL AT THE PHONE: I'll not be caught standing under no silly clock for two hours. . . . What? . . . Sure, it's the east clock. *(Chuckling demurely.)* Oh, I just said *silly* clock, you silly man!

MARTHA *(quietly, sincerely; walking toward Lizza.)*: That's just it, Lizza. . . you've never done a childish thing in all your life.

GIRL AT THE PHONE: Aw, okay, so we waited for only an hour. *(Warningly.)* But let me tell you. . .

LIZZA *(turns to face Martha squarely)*: Oh, Martha! Oh, the things you say sometimes.

(The lights begin to dim on Lizza's and Martha's room in the Right half of the stage. Simultaneously, ADA, in the room in the Left half of the stage, lifts her head, listens for a moment, and then calls out toward off L.)

ADA: Is that you, Dora?

DORA'S VOICE *(off UL)*: Yes, Ada.

(MARTHA, in the meantime, grasps Lizza's shoulder, gives it a friendly squeeze, and then—under the slowly dimming lights in the Right half of the stage—walks upstage to her table near C. LIZZA looks after her thoughtfully and then turns back to her book, but somehow we know that her mind won't really be on her reading again—not completely. MARTHA gradually resumes her dance exercises, counting in a low voice as the lights brighten somewhat on Ada's room at Left.)

GIRL AT THE PHONE *(outraged)*: J. Jonathan Augustus Warrenblob! That's no way to talk to your girl!

(ADA turns and looks up as DORA enters at UL. Looking tired and dishevelled in street clothes and a sloppy beige raincoat and hat, DORA is carrying a suitcase; and her walk is vaguely unsteady. ADA, quickly sensing that something is amiss, rises, goes to Dora, and helps her with the case.)

ADA: Dora! You don't look well. Is there anything wrong?

(DORA *releases the suitcase to Ada, walks wearily to the chair at LC, pulls her hat off, and runs her fingers nervously through her hair. Her voice is faintly blurred, but she is trying valiantly to keep it under control.*)

DORA: I . . . I'm tired.

(*She sinks into the armchair LC and lets her rain hat slip from her fingers to the floor nearby.* ADA *takes the suitcase UL and puts it down near the table or dresser there. Then, eyeing Dora narrowly, uneasily, she walks back down to her desk near C.*)

ADA: Gee, it's good to see you again, Dory. I missed you all week.

GIRL AT THE PHONE: Oh, Joey! (*All saccharine now.*) Oh, you sweet, sweet man!

DORA (*very quietly*): Just came to get my things, Ada.

ADA (*surprised*): Oh, Dora, why? (*As* DORA *hesitates.*) Something *is* wrong! What is it, Dora?

GIRL AT THE PHONE: Speak louder. Nothing under your breath, J. Jonathan Augustus . . .

DORA: Things are . . . not well . . . at home.

ADA: Oh.

GIRL AT THE PHONE (*shifting position*): Oh.

DORA: I came tonight b'cause I wanted to find you home. All the way, I kept saying, "What if she isn't home?" You see . . . I gotta *talk* to you, Ada, like. . . like we *used* to talk.

GIRL AT THE PHONE: Okay, I hear you, honey.

ADA (*with a reassuring smile*): Sure, Dora. We'll talk.

(DORA *rises and walks listlessly about the room.* ADA *watches her uneasily.*)

DORA: Can't find anybody to talk with. At home, everybody's running off somewhere. You've got to have someone to talk with. Quiet-like. You know. . . .

GIRL AT THE PHONE (*very affectedly*): Au revoir, mon bon ami! . . . Ha-ha-ha, that's French, you silly man! (*After a pause.*) Naw—never mind!

DORA (*near DL*): Because you can't keep everything to yourself. (*Oddly strained.*) It's one thing on top of the other—so heavy you could choke! *(Turns, looks pleadingly at Ada.)* You *gotta* talk. Somebody's gotta *listen!*

ADA *(soothingly)*: Sure, Dory, sure.

GIRL AT THE PHONE: Sure, hon, see you Friday.

ADA *(leaning against the chair near her table)*: Was writing my folks a letter before you walked in.

GIRL AT THE PHONE: East clock. Marshall Field. *(Giggles.)* Oh, you killer!

DORA: Can I talk with you, Ada? *(Pacing eagerly to front of chair LC.)* Please, can't you write the letter tomorrow? I want to talk very badly tonight.

ADA: Sure. *(Crossing to Dora.)* Better take your coat off, dear.

GIRL AT THE PHONE: I must be off, hon. Yep, seven-thirty. 'Bye, sweet.

(The spotlight fades on the telephone area, as the GIRL AT THE PHONE hangs up the receiver and exits DR.)

DORA: No, I'll keep it on. *(Draws her raincoat closer about her shoulders.)* I don't know, Ada. I feel sorta cold tonight. *(Shivers slightly.)* Cold in a summer night. Ha-ha-ha. Mom should hear that. Me—cold in a summer night. She always says—she always says to the neighbors, "Dora's forever saying she feels hot. She'd love to go around with nothing on."

(She shivers again, sinks wearily down into the chair at LC, gazes vacantly out over the audience, and grows reminiscent.)

One afternoon.... Gary and me were in the backyard, having fun. Monkeying around. I was wearing my old blue swimsuit, and we were out for a suntan. And then Gary—he started getting sleepy, and I tried pushing him and blowing in his ear and all that fooling around, you know. Then Mom came out the back door to hang up her wash, and she saw us kissing. *(Shakes her head, faintly disgusted.)* Next day, she was shooting her fool head off: "A pack of lazybodies doing nothing but sunning and romping in the grass and trying to have a baby right in the yard where all the neighbors can see." *(Sighs heavily.)* Mom is that way.

ADA *(gently)*: Can I get you some coffee, Dora?

(She stoops and picks up Dora's rain hat. The lights begin to brighten

on the room at Right. MARTHA, *who has been dancing near RC, stops and takes a long, deep breath.)*

MARTHA: I'm all worn out—whew!

ADA *(her hand on* DORA'S *shoulder):* It'll keep you warm.

She starts to move upstage, but DORA *rises and tries to restrain her.)*

DORA: Don't go, Ada!

ADA: Don't be silly, Dora. It'll only take a minute.

She puts the rain hat on the dresser ULC and then hurries out UL. Alone, DORA *walks away from her chair, tries to take off her raincoat, has difficulty, and decides to keep it on. Then she strolls aimlessly about again as the lights fade on the room at Left. The piano music grows louder.)*

MARTHA *(irked by the music):* Wish she'd stop playing that stupid fugue.

LIZZA *(absently):* House rules say eight.

MARTHA: Well, for God's sake, what time is it, anyway?

LIZZA *(consulting her watch):* It's only twenty of.

With a mock groan, MARTHA *rests her forehead against the imaginary wall URC.)*

MARTHA: Don't tell me we have to listen to Mrs. Beethoven for twenty minutes more. It's murder!

LIZZA *(quietly):* Martha?

MARTHA: Yes, Lizzie?

LIZZA: I've been thinking about what you said.

MARTHA *(lifting her head from the wall):* I'm sorry, Liz. *(Turns, looks at Lizza.)* That was mean. Forget it.

LIZZA *puts her book down and turns to face Martha.)*

LIZZA: No, Martha, you're right. It hurts, because what you said was true.

MARTHA *moves to the center of the room at Right and resumes her exercises.)*

MARTHA: Should learn to keep my big mouth shut... one-two-three... sometimes. For God's sake, Liz, just because I got excited....

LIZZA: I said you're *right*. You're right—I've never done anything foolish or childish all my life.

MARTHA (*stopping her exercises completely*): Oh, Lizzie, surely...

LIZZA (*adjusting her eyeglasses*): Childhood was a brief period for me, Martha. Sometimes I wonder if I ever had one—actually.

MARTHA (*sinking on pouf or hassock, opposite Lizza's table*): Don't be ridiculous, Liz. Forget it. I tell you I didn't mean what I said.

(LIZZA *takes off her eyeglasses; they are bothering her.*)

LIZZA: So you didn't mean it, Martha. (*Rises.*) But all the same—it's true.

MARTHA: Now look here, Lizzie....

LIZZA: Let me explain, Martha. Just let me explain. (*Remembering.*) Mom died when I was seven. She was lots of fun. If Mom had lived, perhaps—perhaps it would have been different. But she died when I was seven. I was seven, and Bob was nine when Dad took over.

(*She walks slowly, pensively, below Martha and across toward the imaginary wall near DC.*)

He treated us like grownups, Dad always did. Books and concerts. Dad beaming with pride when we joined discussions with ease. Bach and Freud and Nietzsche and Tolstoy—spouted them off like little monsters with full-grown heads. At first, we did it for Dad. Then it went on and on. You grow a reputation; people expect it of you, and so you keep on.

(*She turns to Martha and continues in a less reminiscent tone.*)

Now as I look at it, Martha, I—I think I kept on because I was too frightened to stop. I kept discussing and arguing, 'cause I felt if I stopped, I'd be lost. (*Toying with her glasses.*) Talk became a wall you built around you. You are brave; everything's under your control as long as you are able to shine in a discussion. (*With a shrug and an odd, mirthless chuckle.*) But boys are able to stand it for a time only—then they start avoiding you.

(*She begins walking back toward her table DR.*)

And then one day ... one day you discover ... you discover you're growing up, and you feel your body has suddenly become a stranger to you. All your readings can't help you when you feel funny at a boy's side.

MARTHA *(affected by Lizza's words)*: I felt funny too once, Lizzie. I felt so awkward. Honest, I'd feel so funny I used to giggle! A lot. Why—all a boy had to do was to say something—*anything*—and I'd break into giggles all over the place. It was so messy.

LIZZA: But *I* never went through a—giggling stage, Martha, like most girls. *(Shrugs again, turns to her roommate.)* I'm different, Martha.

MARTHA: Oh, shoo! *(Rises, holds up her hands.)* See my hands? I used to think they were the largest and ugliest things in the whole world. I didn't know where to put them and keep them hid. *(Shrugs.)* Now I've accepted them, and they don't seem terrible any more. They're mine now *(dropping them to her hips)*. . . and I've forgotten about them. We all felt funny one time, Lizzie, each of us—in our own ways. Growing up is a confusing business.

LIZZA *(sadly)*: Sometimes, Martha *(slowly sitting at her table again)* . . . sometimes I wish I had been allowed to grow like. . . like a child.

(The lights begin to fade on Lizza and Martha and grow brighter on the room at Left as ADA enters from UL, carrying a saucer and a cup. DORA now stands in front of the armchair LC, her fingertips pressing against her forehead.)

ADA *(cheerfully)*: Here's your coffee, Dora. *(Crossing to Dora.)* How do you feel?

DORA: Headache.

ADA *(giving Dora the cup and saucer)*: Aspirin?

DORA: Yes, please.

MARTHA *(yawning)*: Well, I guess I'll have me a short nap. *(Lying down on the floor at RC.)* Hard board for a strong back, they say.

(LIZZA puts her glasses on, picks up her book, and stares moodily out the window in front of her table. ADA walks upstage to a small cabinet near UC, takes out a bottle of aspirin, brings it downstage, and opens it. The piano music grows louder for a moment, then it recedes.)

ADA *(at Dora's right; casually)*: Been drinking again, Dora?

(She hands Dora an aspirin, recaps the bottle, and slips it into the pocket of her housecoat. DORA swallows the aspirin and takes a drink of coffee. The piano music swells again for a moment then recedes again.)

MARTHA *(yawning again)*: Ho-hum. Mrs. Beethoven's sure got ambition.

DORA *(to Ada)*: Yes.

ADA *(unhappily)*: Oh, Dora, you promised!

DORA: Now, don't be angry, Ada. Pa gave me a ride back, like I told you. And we stopped at three bars on the way and—

ADA *(shocked)*: Three bars!

(Exasperated, she paces upstage.)

DORA: Yeah, you see, driving makes him thirsty, Pop says. He loves to drink. Helps his liver.

ADA *(turns front)*: Well, I . . . now I've heard everything! *(Sternly, coming down to Dora.)* Take off your coat.

(She takes the cup of coffee from Dora, carries it across to the desk near C, puts it down, returns to Dora, helps her to remove her raincoat, lays it across the arm of the chair, returns to her desk, picks up the cup of coffee, goes back to Dora, and hands it to her.)

Now, sit down and drink your coffee, Dora. Thirsty, indeed! Three bars on the way!

(She gathers up Dora's raincoat and begins to fold it neatly. Off L, there are sounds of footsteps coming downstairs; then two girls stepping out enter from upstage of the column at DL. They are wearing party dresses, with coats draped over their shoulders or thrown over their arms. Both girls look very eager and very pretty.)

FIRST GIRL *(as she enters)*: Well, they said to be ready before eight *(Starting across toward DR, in front of the two rooms.)* Let's wait in the living room.

SECOND GIRL *(following the First Girl)*: Now, are you sure this Randy Potter's gonna like me?

FIRST GIRL: Sure. Now—now, all you have to do is to relax, Cathy.

SECOND GIRL *(hesitating briefly near DC)*: Oh? Relax?

FIRST GIRL *(hesitates and turns to the Second Girl)*: Yeah, 'cause everything's wrong with you, Cathy. You don't drink. You don't smoke. *(Crossing on toward DR.)* Why, you're so damn healthy you make all the guys sick!

SECOND GIRL *(startled, as she hastens after the First Girl)*: Huh? Whatta y'mean—healthy?

(THE TWO GIRLS STEPPING OUT exit behind the column DR. ADA, meanwhile, has taken Dora's coat upstage and laid it neatly on the dresser ULC.)

ADA *(to Dora)*: A good soaking in the tub might help some.

DORA *(emphatically; sitting in armchair LC)*: I'll soak in no tub, Ada!

ADA *(crossing toward DL)*: Keep quiet. And finish your coffee.

(The lights begin to brighten on the bathroom door DL.)

DORA *(plaintively)*: I just want to *talk*, Ada.

ADA *(going out through the imaginary door to the bathroom)*: Sure. We'll talk after you have your bath.

DORA: Aw, Ada.

(She shrugs helplessly, gives her attention to her cup of coffee, and starts sipping the hot liquid. MARTHA, in the room at Right, lifts her head from the floor.)

MARTHA: Say, is it eight?

LIZZA *(checking her watch)*: Well, almost.

MARTHA *(shouting off toward the unseen piano player)*: Hey, eight o'clock! Ho-ho, eight o'clock!

(The finger exercises on the piano come to an abrupt halt; the "practicer" bangs on the keys angrily and then slams down the cover of the piano. MARTHA settles back with a laugh.)

Mrs. Beethoven—our own dear Mrs. Beethoven—off in a huff, ho-humm!

(ADA re-enters through the imaginary bathroom door DL.)

ADA: Well—the tub's all yours, Dora. *(Crossing to Dora.)* Your towels and an extra robe are on the chair.

DORA: Aw, Ada, I tell you I'm all right. Now that I had the aspirin—and—and this coffee, I'm all right, really!

ADA *(taking Dora by the arm)*: Sure, I know you're all right. *(Nodding toward DL.)* Now, go in there and show me—before I dump you in myself!

DORA (*meekly*): You said you'd let me finish my coffee.

ADA: Oh, for Pete's sake! One tiny cup and you act as though it was a demijohn! (*Insistently.*) Okay—now, up you go. Come on. (*Urging Dora to her feet.*) Up!

DORA: I just want to talk with you, Ada. Like we used to talk, Ada.

ADA (*firmly guiding Dora toward DL*): Sure, sure. We'll talk all you want, Dora—after the bath.

DORA: Aw, all right, all right. (*As she exits through the imaginary bathroom doorway.*) My, but you're a little tyrant!

ADA (*calling after Dora*): Just yell when you need anything.

(*She walks back to her table, sits, thinks for a moment, then decides to continue writing her letter. The lights fade on Ada's room and gradually come up on Lizza and Martha.*)

LIZZA: Martha... you asleep?

MARTHA: Nope.

LIZZA: Martha...?

MARTHA: Yes, Lizzie?

LIZZA: How does one start being brave?

MARTHA (*getting up on her knees*): What's that?

LIZZA: Well, *you* look so brave and sure when you're with boys. How does one start being brave, Martha?

MARTHA (*settling on floor, crossing her legs like a Buddha*): Oh... yeah. Well, I guess you start like everyone else. You just... let go.

LIZZA: Yes? Well, how do you "let go," Martha?

MARTHA (*bending her torso forward over her crossed legs*): Oh, Lizza, you sound like a babe-in-the-woods.

LIZZA: I wish you wouldn't laugh, Martha. I'm serious.

MARTHA: I wasn't laughing at you, honey.

(*A GIRL IN A TERRY-CLOTH ROBE enters at far DR and crosses toward DL. She has a toothbrush and a glass in one hand and is swinging a towel in the other. She sings as she crosses.*)

GIRL IN A TERRY-CLOTH ROBE *(singing)*:
"He said he'd treat her right
    When he held her tight;
If might is right—then he
    Treated her so-o-o right. . ."

(She opens the imaginary door to the bathroom DL, then shuts it quickly.)

Ooops—sorry! Just wanted to make sure.

(She sits before the door, her back against the column.)

LIZZA: Well, I'm afraid, Martha. . . that's what's wrong with me. I get so tight and tense inside, I just can't let go.

GIRL IN A TERRY-CLOTH ROBE *(in front of bathroom door)*: Sure, take your time. Take your time.

LIZZA: Now, a *boy* can make the hurdle easier. I guess it's simpler with boys. At least it was simpler with Bob. One night, Bob came home real late. Dad was waiting for him in the living room. I held onto the banister and listened. Dad was very angry; he was shouting. But from that night on. . .Bob walked around with a kind of knowing smile. He seemed to have suddenly grown up. He was more gentle with me. . .more thoughtful.

GIRL IN A TERRY-CLOTH ROBE *(half-singing; very sweetly)*: Oh, shoo—take your time. Take your own sweet time. I'm in no hurry.

LIZZA: Martha?

MARTHA: I'm listening, honey.

LIZZA *(timidly)*: Martha. . .were you. . .were you ever. . .intimate with a boy?

MARTHA *(getting up and turning her back to Lizza)*: Why, Liz! I. . . .

LIZZA *(quietly)*: Were you frightened much, Martha?

MARTHA: I. . .I guess I was, Lizzie.

GIRL IN A TERRY-CLOTH ROBE *(brushing her teeth)*: In case you're interested, I've started on my bath. I just love to eat Pepsodent.

MARTHA: Howard and I were very young then, Liz. I guess if a boy really loves you, he'd help you not to be frightened much. *(Shrugs, faces Lizza.)* But Howard was very young—barely out of high school.

(Sighs, sinks down onto the hassock.) And I was just a silly girl who thought she was madly in love.

(The lights begin to fade slowly on Lizza's and Martha's room at right and begin to grow brighter on Ada's room at left.)

ADA *(tilting her chair back and calling toward DL)*: Everything all right, Dora?

DORA'S VOICE *(off DL)*: Yeah...fine.

ADA: Need any help?

DORA'S VOICE: No. *(Calling out to the Girl in a Terry-Cloth Robe.* Okay, it's all yours.

(The GIRL IN A TERRY-CLOTH ROBE rises, pulls the toothbrush out of her mouth, and speaks almost incoherently.)

GIRL IN A TERRY-CLOTH ROBE: Gee, I can hardly believe it!

(She gathers her glass and towel and exits through the door to the bathroom DL; and the spotlight goes out with her.)

MARTHA *(on the hassock near RC)*: But you—you'll be all right, Liz. Don't worry.

LIZZA: Oh, I hope so, Martha! 'Cause I'm such a scaredy-cat.

MARTHA *(earnestly)*: Go slow, Lizzie. You're a fine kid. Go slow—you'll get there fine.

LIZZA: You make everything seem right, Martha.

MARTHA: Do I, Lizzie?

(Embarrassed, she rises goes back to her RC position, and renews her dance exercises.)

One-two-three. I'm glad I do. One-two....

(Her voice fades out. DORA enters from the imaginary door to the bathroom DL. Looking somewhat refreshed, she is wearing the pajamas and the robe Ada has presumably laid out for her, and is carrying a towel.)

DORA *(as she appears)*: That tub almost scalded me.

ADA: Well, how do you feel?

DORA (*drying behind her ears*): Oh—all right, I guess.

ADA (*rising and turning to Dora*): Want a glass of milk and a cold sandwich, Dory?

DORA: No, I'm not hungry.

ADA (*with an encouraging smile*): You look much better already.

DORA: Well, I don't feel much better.

ADA: Maybe you should have some sleep, Dora. (*with a step toward Dora.*) Look—I'll fix your bed. All you have to do is slip in. How does that sound?

DORA (*folding her towel*): Don't put me off again, Ada. (*Quietly; draping towel over back of chair LC.*) Can we talk now? Please, can I talk with you now?

ADA: Oh, all right, Dora.

(*She turns her chair to face Dora and sits.* DORA *sits in the armchair LC. There is a slight pause.*)

DORA: I...I don't know how to start, Ada. (*Tensely.*) Now I don't know how to start.

ADA: Don't sound so grim, Dora.

DORA: That's funny. (*Shakes her head, runs a hand across her brow.*) All the way here, I knew how I'd say it—how I'd start—how I'd tell you.

ADA: Oh, Dora—it can't be that hard!

DORA: I—I want to tell you, Ada. Ada, I...I'm going to have a baby.

ADA: *Dora!*

DORA (*rising*): Don't look at me that way, Ada, please!

(ADA *is silent, and* DORA *paces around her chair and upstage.*)

I had to tell you before I told anybody else. Ma wouldn't understand. I'm afraid to tell Pa. Besides, he was too drunk to listen, anyway. I had to drive half the way here before he sobered up.

ADA (*rises*): Are you sure, Dora, about the—about the baby?

DORA (*turning to look at Ada*): Yeah, I'm sure. (*Pacing back down to the armchair.*) The doctor confirmed it for me this morning. I drove thirty miles out of town to see him. I was ashamed to see old Doctor Peters. Besides, he'd tell the family, and I'm not ready for that just yet. (*Distractedly; sitting on arm of chair LC.*) Oh, Ada, I don't know what to do!

(*She suddenly buries her face in her hands. ADA crosses to her, holds out her hand, but is uncertain whether to touch her. She decides against it, lowers her hand, turns, and walks away toward C.*)

ADA: You should tell Gary, Dora. You should tell him about... about everything. If he has any....

DORA: I can't tell Gary, Ada. I can't!

ADA (*turns*): But you must! (*Crosses to Dora.*) Look—for the baby's sake and yours—

DORA: You don't understand, Ada. (*Stands.*) It's not Gary's.

ADA: Good heavens, Dora!

DORA: Oh, I wish it *were*, Ada! You don't know how much I wish it were! (*Turns, paces distractedly DL.*) He'll hate me, Ada. I know he'll hate me. I'll never see him again. (*Suddenly turning toward Ada; fearfully.*) Ada! I'll kill it! That's what I've been thinking all day.

ADA (*trying to keep her voice down*): Now, look here, Dora—!

(*She hastens toward Dora.*)

DORA: I—I tried pills, Ada. (*Pacing below Ada, toward C.*) Can you imagine it—I tried pills? (*Laughs thinly, nervously.*) At night, I'd be alone and feel it, and I'd think of ways of pressing against it to make it stop. (*Piteously; turning to Ada.*) But it keeps beating there—so safe, Ada, so safe!

ADA (*hurrying across to Dora*): Stop it, Dora! Do you hear me?

DORA (*near hysteria*): I'll kill myself, Ada—that's what I'll do!

ADA: Stop it, I say! (*Slapping Dora.*) Stop! (*Suddenly puts her arm about Dora's shoulder and pulls her close.*) I—I'm sorry, Dora, I'm sorry....

DORA (*burying her face in Ada's bosom*): Oh, Ada, I don't know what to do. (*Weeping uncontrollably.*) I just don't know what to do!

ADA: Hush, Dora, hush.

(The spotlight comes up on the bathroom door DL, as the GIRL IN A TERRY-CLOTH ROBE re-enters there. Her towel is wound like a turban around her head; she carries her glass and toothbrush; and as she crosses blithely toward DR, she sings.)

GIRL IN A TERRY-CLOTH ROBE *(singing):*
"Te-dum, hummmm-dum...
    He said he'd treat her right.
But the moon was bright...
    And...oh what a night!
What a *night! What* a night!

(The spotlight fades on the bathroom door as the GIRL IN A TERRY-CLOTH ROBE exits DR. ADA, her arm still about Dora's shoulders, eases her down into the desk chair near C, and speaks comfortingly, reassuringly.)

ADA: Here, Dora, you sit down, and I'll get you a glass of water.

(She crosses to UL and exits. The lights fade on the room at left and comes up on Lizza and Martha.)

LIZZA *(putting her book down):* If I do anything foolish, would you laugh, Martha?

MARTHA *(busy with her dance exercises):* Now what are you up to, Lizzie?

LIZZA: Well, I was just thinking...see? I was thinking I've never done anything foolish. So what would seem...just cute, you know... just cute to *some* girls would seem ridiculous if I were the one to do it. You know—quite unthinkable?

MARTHA: Oh, do it, Liz! *Be* ridiculous, what the hell!

LIZZA *(turning to her book again):* Still... oh, I don't know....

(MARTHA stops exercising, crosses to her table near C, and picks up a hairbrush. The lights begin to fade very slowly on Lizza and Martha. MARTHA yawns and stretches.)

MARTHA: Ho-hummm. Make mistakes like the rest of us—what the hell!

(She brushes her hair vigorously and—during the ensuing scene— starts to set it up in pin curls. ADA enters from UL with a glass of water

and some capsules, crosses to Dora, and hands the glass to her. DORA
takes it meekly and sips the water.)

DORA: I thought it would be simple, Ada, going to a drugstore...
'cause lots of girls have done it. And nobody need know. *(Excitedly.)*
Why, I know how Cynthia—now, you know how Cynthia—why, Ada,
she—!

ADA: Hush, now, Dora. *(Holds out capsules.)* Here. Take these.

DORA: What's that?

ADA: Something to relax you, Dory. They'll do you some good. Now,
take them.

DORA: No, no—none of those pills for me.

ADA *(firmly; as if persuading a child)*: Now, Dora, take these—like
I tell you. *(Insistently.)* Here, *(As* DORA *reluctantly takes them.)* That's
the girl!

LIZZA *(tapping her fingers and peering out window DR)*: You'd think
that he'd look up *sometime.* I mean—at least *once.*

MARTHA: He must be blind, peeping and peeping all day through that
(pulling her fingers apart to shape a cylinder) ...peeping and computing all day long!

*(*DORA *gulps down the capsules with a drink of water. She then hands
the glass to Ada.)*

DORA: I—I've thought about it, Ada. I'll tell Gary. I want to tell him
badly.

ADA: Sure, tell Gary. *(Leans across behind Dora, puts glass on her
table, and pats her roommate's back.)* And then tell your *family,* Dora.
They must know. They will know.

DORA: I can't tell my folks, Ada. *(Shaking her head forlornly.)* Never
could tell them anything. They don't understand at all how—

ADA *(cutting her short)*: Now, see here, Dora. Nothing like this has
ever happened before. How do you know they wouldn't understand?

DORA: I know them, Ada, I know. *(Rising.)* Marvin offered to marry
me, Ada. But I won't have him. We—we need just a little kindness,
Ada. *(Walking slowly, thoughtfully, toward LC and slightly upstage.)*
He was kind to me that evening. It was one of those evenings when

Ma was shooting her fool head off, and Pop just sat there too drunk to care. And so I left the house, just to be away. Because you can stand only so much nagging and picking and fighting.

(She pauses for a moment, grasps the back of the armchair LC, and peers out over the audience—remembering, justifying.)

Marvin was in high school with me. He has always been nice, but he drinks quite a lot. He saw me on the road, and he sort of walked a little way with me and listened to me talk. Then he asked me to have a drink with him. And then he...he started being so nice. He isn't a bad sort, really, Ada. *(Suddenly burying her face in her hands.)* I—I can't tell my folks all this! They won't understand at all!

ADA *(crossing to Dora)*: Listen to me, Dora. The baby will come—it will come unless something happens to it.

DORA *(weeping; turns her face away)*: I wish something *would* happen, Ada! I wish something would—'cause I don't want it at all.

ADA *(laying a comforting hand on Dora's arm)*: Look, Dora—you tried. You said you tried hard to get rid of it.

(DORA lowers her hands, turns eagerly to Ada, and speaks softly, confidingly, almost in a whisper.)

DORA: Not *everything*, Ada. Not....

ADA *(very firmly)*: You said you tried, Dora. *(Turns from Dora, walks away a step or two.)* And now it's too late for anything to happen.

DORA *(almost tearfully; with desperate eagerness)*: No! *No! (As* ADA *stands with her back toward Dora.)* Not too late, Ada, not too late! *(Grasps Ada by the shoulders.)* You—you'd help me, Ada—you can help me. *(As* ADA *tries to protest and moves away another step.)* No, let me finish, Ada. There's a doctor—he'd be willing to do it. It wouldn't hurt much. I don't care if it hurts, Ada—the knife. Then it will be as if nothing had happened at all!

ADA *(gently; turning to face Dora)*: Dora, listen to me—

DORA *(desperately)*: I'd be *free!* Just think! Oh, I want so much to be free! *(Turns, paces to front of armchair.)* I'm sick of thinking and listening and being afraid. Waiting for it to stop beating so I'd be sure it's dead. I want to be free. *(Turn to Ada; imploringly.) Help* me to be free, Ada—like a new person. *(Trying to regain control of her emotions.)* Look, Ada—I've saved one hundred dollars from the camp last summer. *(Pacing back to Ada.)* The doctor said *two,* but I'm sure if you'd lend me fifty, he—he'd settle for that.

ADA *(softly; shaking her head)*: No, Dora.

DORA *(clinging to Ada's sleeve)*: Fifty, Ada. Only fifty? I'd pay you back later.

ADA *(decisively)*: No, Dora, no.

(DORA stares at Ada for a moment, uncomprehending; then, obviously hurt and bewildered, she releases her hold on Ada.)

DORA: Fifty would set me free, Ada. I promise to work hard and pay you every single cent.

ADA: I'd give you fifty, Dora *(as DORA's face lights up hopefully)*... I'd give it to you... as a gift, Dory...if I could be sure it would set you free.

DORA *(desperately)*: It would, Ada! Oh, it *would!*

ADA: Listen, Dora. *(Earnestly; her hand on Dora's arm.)* I'll let no doctor butcher you. *(As DORA pulls away.)* Can't you see it's too much of a risk, Dory?

DORA *(breaking down)*: I'd take the risk, Ada. *(Striding away to armchair again.)* I'd take all the risks. Do you think I care, Ada? Do you think I *care?*

ADA *(gently)*: Then I won't let you, Dora. *(Crosses, stands at right of Dora.)* I won't let you.

(DORA turns and stares at her.)

DORA *(savagely)*: You're a nice one to stand there and be so smug and cool about it. *(Acidly.)* You won't let me—you won't let me! *(Shrilly.)* Stand there like a judge. You won't let me! *(Her voice heavy with scorn.)* My, my! Like an immaculate judge—you won't let me. *(Drops into armchair and sobs.)* Afraid you'd get dirty!

ADA: With blood, yes! *(Compassionately; looking down at Dora.)* Dory...understand me, Dory...you are asking me to do something that I....

DORA *(weeping)*: I told you everything, Ada. If I had just come here and just borrowed fifty, you—you wouldn't know that I—

ADA: But you told me, Dora. *(Pleadingly.)* Can't you see that makes a difference? You *told* me!

DORA *(frantically; looking up at Ada)*: Then give me fifty and forget I told you! I'd go away, Ada, like you've never known me. What do you care? Before we met in this room we were strangers.

ADA: But we've lived together here, Dory. We've shared so many things. We're *not* strangers. *(Dropping to one knee and looking up at Dora.)* Can't you see it won't work? *(Taking Dora's hands in hers.)* Look, Dora, you—you can get a job—work somewhere. We'll look for a place where you can work until it comes. You'll have to leave school—earn some money somehow—so you can save a little for the hospital bill and clothes and things.

DORA: No, Ada, *no!* They'd wonder why I left school and the job at the store. Gary would be wanting to know why, and Ma would be asking why. She'd get hysterical, and Pop would be staring and staring, and—

ADA *(kindly, persuasively)*: It will be a big blow, but you've got to tell them and then go away somewhere. Everything will settle down quietly after a while.

DORA *(wearily)*: Please, Ada. Give me fifty. It would be simpler.

(ADA *stands, looks at Dora for a long moment, then goes to her desk, pulls open the drawer, takes out her checkbook, writes a check, tears it from the book, and walks back to Dora.)*

ADA: There! *(Thrusts the check in front of Dora.)* Now, go, Dora. Get out!

(DORA *takes the check eagerly, scans it, folds it quietly, slips it into her pocket, looks up at Ada, and then guiltily withdraws her hand from her pocket.)*

DORA: Don't look at me that way, Ada!

ADA *(quietly)*: Pack all your things, Dora. (DORA *rises.)* Get out of this room!

(DORA *turns, walks upstage to her suitcase, puts it on the dresser ULC, opens the drawers, takes out some folded clothing, and starts piling it into the case.* ADA *returns to her table near C, folds her arms, and stands staring out the imaginary window.)*

DORA: Ada?

(ADA *does not answer.*)

Can't you see I've got to take the chance, Ada? I've got to start all over again—like—like a new person. I've got to take the chance while there's still time to be—to be free, Ada!

ADA *(scornfully)*: Free! *You* speak of being free! You want to be free!

DORA *(slams down the cover of the suitcase)*: Don't scoff, Ada. I don't want you to scoff at me.

ADA: What do you care if I scoff, Dora—if I scoff, if I laugh? You've got the fifty. Hurry before it's too late. Go! Be free!

(DORA *comes down to the armchair LC, picks up her towel, glances uncertainly, hopefully toward Ada, and then suddenly crosses to her.)*

DORA: If you only knew how it is to want to be free, Ada. I....

(*She takes Ada by the arm, but* ADA *impatiently shakes her off.*)

ADA *(quietly, coldly)*: Go away. Stay away from me.

DORA: Ada, no!

ADA: I said *get out of this place*, Dora!

(DORA *releases Ada's arm; her face is hard.*)

DORA: All right, Ada... *all right.* I'll go and get dressed.

(*She turns away, then stops and looks briefly, hopefully back at* ADA, *who is standing beside her desk, staring stonily out the window. Then* DORA *bows her head, walks sadly DL, and exits through the imaginary door to the bathroom. The lights fade on Ada's room at left and come up on Lizza and Martha at right.*)

LIZZA *(looking out her window)*: He has such a nice, quiet face.

MARTHA *(inserting a clip into a pin curl)*: It always starts out that way: He has a nice face. He has a quiet face. He has a *nice, quiet* face.

(LIZZA *leans back on her chair and sighs.* MARTHA, *finished with her pin curls, picks up her comb and adds a few finishing touches to her hairdo.*)

LIZZA: He must be blind—or dead!

(MARTHA, *comb in hand, gets up and walks to the door UR; something—or someone—has caught her attention. She gazes off UR.*)

MARTHA *(to Lizza)*: Well, what do you expect? Peering and computing—peering and computing. . . .

*(*LIZZA *sits up suddenly, as if she remembered something good. She smiles, steals a glance at Martha, and sees that her back is turned.* LIZZA *then gazes excitedly out the window, very timidly reaches under her lampshade, and turns her lamp on and off in a few quick flashes. She peers out the imaginary window cautiously, shading her eyes from the glare of the lamp. Her expression is eager, hopeful. After a moment, her face falls; she sits back, looking very disappointed.* MARTHA, *who has been glancing off through the doorway UR, gives an exaggerated gasp and calls mockingly off to an unseen friend.)*

Look out there! *(pointing; for Lizza's benefit.)* It's the Lady of the Camellias—out for her scented bath—with nary an aspen leaf!

(She walks out through the doorway UR, calling off goodnaturedly.)

Hi, Lil! How's Jack?

*(*DORA *re-enters from the bathroom DL; she has changed into her street clothes. She walks uncertainly to Ada, makes a move as if to touch her on the shoulder, decides against it, and crosses upstage to her desk. She puts on her raincoat and cap, snaps the hasps of her suitcase, and pulls it off the dresser. She turns to go, stops abruptly, puts down her suitcase, runs quickly to Ada, and lays a hand lightly on her shoulder.)*

DORA: Ada, I want to say good-bye. I want *us* to say good-bye, Ada.

*(*ADA *twists her shoulder away from Dora's restraining hand and says nothing.)*

I would like you to know—I—I believe in what you said, Ada. I believe that—that everything's going to be all right. Because—because when you come to think of it, there's nothing—nothing one can do but *believe* in someone.

*(*ADA *turns slowly to look at her.)*

You've always been the stronger one. It—it's terrible to have to leave. *(Softly, in almost a whisper.)* I'd like you to know. . .I'm afraid. I'm so afraid.

(She digs into her pocket, pulls out the check, kisses Ada on the cheek, puts the check into Ada's hand, then quickly turns, runs upstage,

grabs her suitcase, and hurries out UL. ADA, as if shaken out of a stupor, raises the check, stares at it, suddenly realizes, runs UL, and calls through the doorway after the departing Dora.)

ADA *(calling off)*: Dora! Dora!

(Across in the room at Right, LIZZA steals a glance UR, makes sure that Martha hasn't come back into the room, furtively reaches under her lampshade again, and turns the lamp on and off in another series of quick flashes. Then she sits back and waits. Suddenly, she leaps forward, stares out the imaginary window, gasps, jumps up, and covers her mouth with her hand.)

LIZZA: Martha! *Marrrtha!*

(ADA walks slowly, dejectedly, back to the center of her room at Left, hesitates, glances over her shoulder toward the doorway UL, goes to her desk near C, holds the check up again, gazes at it wonderingly, crumples it, sinks into her chair, drops her head onto her desk, and sobs softly. The lights start to dim on the room at left. MARTHA, mildly alarmed, runs in from UR and crosses toward the hassock.)

MARTHA: Yes, Lizzie? What—what happened?

(LIZZA, unable to control her excitement, points at the imaginary window and stammers.)

LIZZA: Ooh, Martha! He—he *winked!*

(MARTHA stops, realizes what Lizza has done, laughs, throws her comb into the air, and executes a gay pirouette. The lights—with one exception—begin to dim on the room at right. As LIZZA takes off her glasses and clasps her hands ecstatically to her throat, the only bright spotlight on the stage lights up her face. Then the lights in both rooms, including the solitary spotlight, slowly dim to a blackout as the curtains close.)

[END OF THE PLAY]

(1958) First published as Acting Edition, New York: Row, Peterson and Company, 1961, 38p.

Walking Canes and Fans
(A PLAY IN THREE ACTS)

PREMIER PRESENTATION

On September 14, 15 and 16, 1962 at 7:00 p.m., *Walking Canes and Fans* was presented by the Speech Association of the University of the Philippines in Diliman, Quezon City, at the Arts and Sciences Theater (now the Wilfrido Maria Guerrero Theater). It was directed by Benjamin H. Cervantes; Set Design by Bibs Lesaca and Dennis Nagtalon; Lights by Isnani Mohamad and Eric de Guia; and Sound and Music by Voltaire Gungab. The original cast consisted of: MOTHER, Terry Montelibano; ISABELITA, Barbara Gordon; JUANING, Joji Feraren; FIDELA, Sonia Valenciano; ANGGE, Essie Reyes; COSME, Mauro Baltazar; DON CARLOS, Ding Guevara; DON AGUSTIN, Roger Birosel; DOÑA CARLOTA, Victory Orara; DOÑA REMIGIA, Beverly Villar; PADRE CARMELO, Greg Cadhit; TINO, Arturo Morales; WEDDING GUESTS, Mary Ann Leyden, Isabelita Barnachea; Citizen & Soldier, Ramon Calces.

CHARACTERS:
(In Order of Appearance)

ANGGE	ISABELITA
COSME	DON CARLOS
DOÑA CLEOTILDE	DON REMIGIO
FIDELA	THE CITIZEN
PADRE CARMELO	FIRST SOLDIER
DON AGUSTIN	SECOND SOLDIER
DOÑA CARLOTA	LUCIO
WEDDING GUESTS	TINO
JUANING	

TIME AND PLACE OF ACTION:

Act I The House of Doña Cleotilde in Tondo, Manila
 Scene 1: 1895, Six in the morning, early part of the year
 Scene 2: Afternoon of the same day.

Act II The same house, 1896, 20th of August, early morning.

Act III The same house.
 Scene 1: 1897, 9th of May, early morning
 Scene 2: Early evening of the same day.

THE SETTING:

The living room of the huge, concrete house of Doña Cleotilde in Tondo, Manila. It is the ornately-furnished home of the established rich; a huge, cavernous shelter with arched doorways and mahogany panels.

There is a wedding, apparently—from the bronze-necked lamps with prisms cascade satin ribbons and lilies, all pure white. Just about the center is a window, richly draped and beneath it is an antique sofa flanked by matching straight-backed chairs. To one side is an arched doorway leading to the vestibule and the wide stairway below; to the left is a smaller arched doorway which leads to the rest of the rooms in the house.

There are vases without flowers on the low, tea tables and on the floor are scattered some cuttings from the lilies, evidently the decoration isn't quite done. A reading table at one end of the room, some more chairs and at the edges of the arched doorways, beribboned pots of palmettoes.

ACT I

SCENE ONE

ANGGE *(entering, a feather duster in one hand and table cloths draped over her arm)*: Hurry up! Tidy up! More flowers there! Here! These covers on the tables. Red for the round. White for the square. Scrub the floor! *(Turns to see Cosme has not moved from the doorway, a mop on his shoulder and flowers cradled in one arm. He is yawning.)* Oy, I'm talking to you!

COSME: To me? *(Looking behind him.)* Why I thought there was an army here, hah!

ANGGE *(takes a swing at Cosme who ducks with much agility)*: There are only the two of us, *torpe,* so you better move like the army. Put those flowers on that table.

COSME: Flowers on the table! Out with the vases in the pantry! More flowers! This place looks and smells like a *few-ne-rar-ia!*

ANGGE *(creeps from behind Cosme and pokes him with the feather duster)*: Oy, what are you mumbling about? Move! Move! Go on, move!

COSME: Yes, Sir, heh, yes, Ma'am! Oh Angging, how cruel you are to me. Oh how you mock me! *(Punctuates each plea with a full swing of the mop on the floor.)* How you order me about! How you shout at me! How you beat me! *(Exaggerated solemnity)* Yet, God is my witness, I still feel the same about you!

ANGGE: *Oy,* this is not the time for that kind of talk. There's so much to do! The *Señorito* is coming home with a bride. *(Picks up her Señora's fan and fans herself)* Imagine! A bride in this house. *(Dreamily)* A lovely bride in white lace, white shoes, white stockings! Lilies and ribbons! *(Ecstatic)* Oh!

COSME: You can be like her, Angging, if you'll just say you'll be mine.

ANGGE (*overwhelmed by the image of herself as a bride*): Oh, Cosme....

COSME (*eagerly*): Oh, say it, Angging. I've waited for fifteen years! Surely, you can't say you're still too young.

ANGGE: *Que terible!* What are you standing there for? Didn't I say move!

COSME: But your answer, Angging?

ANGGE: Wait another fifteen years! *Consumecion!* There, I can hear the señora coming. Hurry!

COSME: But Angging....

MOTHER (*calling, offstage*): Angge, I can't find my fan, the lace one with beads.

ANGGE: Yes, Señora, it is here by the window. (*Puts the fan down.*) Go!

COSME: Your answer now, Angging....

ANGGE: Pick up all those stems.

(COSME *sticks the stems and leaves to his ears, makes a final protesting growl but sees the Mother, exits dragging the mop behind him.*)

MOTHER: Everything looks beautiful!

ANGGE: You're...you're beautiful, Señora, like a queen!

MOTHER: My son—he'll be proud?

ANGGE: And your new daughter.

MOTHER: Daughter—what a strange word! My daughter. To have a daughter at last! Twenty years ago when the doctor said there'll be no more children and your *Cabesang* Leonardo died, this house echoed only Juaning's voice. How strange! Now the walls seem to smile, a daughter is coming!

ANGGE: And pretty soon, Señora, with God's blessing, the grand-children!

MOTHER: Why, yes—many of them! His father was a strong man.

ANGGE: I remember him when he first took you home. He was a tall man, but that day he seemed even taller. He said, Angge, he said to me, this is your Señora. Serve her well.

MOTHER: And you came, timidly, to kiss my hand. How small you seemed and how frightened. How long ago was that, Angge?

ANGGE: Thirty years, Señora.

MOTHER *(walks around the room with wonder)*: Thirty years! Still the room was like this, Angge, there were flowers, white roses—dozens of them. They sprang from every corner of the room like luminous fireworks. White ribbons and roses, they filled the house with a perfume which has stayed in my mind these many years. Then you took my wedding bouquet and asked if you may lead me to my room. It seemed such a big house.... It has grown smaller now, crowded with so much memories. *(Comes to the table.)* Oh, here's my fan. Has Fidela come?

ANGGE: She'll come directly, Señora. It's only a little past seven.

MOTHER: Seven's the hour of the mass. How I wish I didn't miss the ceremony.

ANGGE: But it was the *Señorito's* wish that you rest, after such a long illness... anyway so you can welcome them home, Señora.

MOTHER: Oh, but I shouldn't have listened to him. *(Looks out the window.)* I think that's Fidela's carriage. Go, meet her at the door.

ANGGE: At once, Señora. *(Exits.)*

MOTHER: Soon they'll be home from church, smelling of incense and candles and flowers! My little children! Ah, I can hardly wait! *(Turns.)* Fidela! *(They kiss.)*

FIDELA: Grumblings? An old woman's grumblings? On your son's wedding day too!

MOTHER: What took you so long? Oh, Fidela, this is the day! How does it look?

FIDELA: Your house's a cathedral of flowers!

MOTHER: My son, would you believe it—he's married at last!

FIDELA: Should it be a surprise! I know how many *novenas* on your knees for a daughter-in-law, you sly old woman.

MOTHER *(laughing)*: And you too went down on your knees with me. And don't forget, you implored louder!

FIDELA: Oh, implored we both did! Oh, I wanted to see the wedding but Juaning insists that I stay here with you. They're almost home. Oh, I'm so excited, I feel giddy!

MOTHER *(walks around)*: Only half-filled with water.... *(Calls out.)* Cosme! Isabelita says she would like to offer her bouquet at the *Cabesa's* tomb.

COSME: You called, Señora?

MOTHER: Yes—fill the vases with more water, ice water from the pitcher, the flowers will droop.

COSME: At once, Señora. *(Runs off.)*

FIDELA: And from the cemetery...?

MOTHER: They'll drive home. By then the guests have arrived.

FIDELA: With the guests here, it will be a big, happy welcome. And the musicians?

MOTHER: Oh, yes, they're coming, coming. Wine bottles have been chilled. See the mountain of grapes, oranges and lemon blossoms on the wedding table?

FIDELA: Hah! And the *lechon de leche!* So tiny on the platter!

(COSME enters with a pitcher, goes about filling the vases and then exits.)

MOTHER: Do you think Isabelita will like me?

FIDELA: She'll love you like her real mother.

MOTHER: I'm afraid, Fidela. I do want her to be happy here with my son and sometimes, for a few hours with me. The young seem fearsome when they're happy. I got the terrible feeling when I look at them—They're saying, old woman, go away! Don't you see we want to be alone?

FIDELA: But we had better leave them alone, Cleotilde. The first few days, we can chat, *(mock seriousness)*...two, old, forgotten, outcasts —we'll wait until they remember us again.

MOTHER: Oh, Fidela, for how long?

FIDELA: Oh, you make me laugh! A week, a month, who knows? We've both been married!

MOTHER: All the talk about the revolution is what worries me, Fidela. My children don't have enough time! Marriage laws are explicit about how marriage is for a lifetime—but if the war comes?

FIDELA: Padre Carmelo told me last week that the Spanish Armada is invincible and Spain's cause has God's sanction from the very beginning.

MOTHER: The people are hungry! And hunger, Fidela, is the mother of a revolution!

(The musicians are heard playing gaily offstage.)

Hah, the musicians!

FIDELA *(goes excitedly to the window)*: And the wedding guests, Cleotilde, their carriages are filling the driveway!

MOTHER: Come, Fidela, we must meet them.

FIDELA: How do I look?

MOTHER: Like a scarecrow!

(Both exit; laughter and indistinguishable chatter offstage.)

FIDELA *(re-enters, with guests and musicians)*: Sit down, everyone, I shall have the drinks brought in.

MOTHER: Come and sit with us, Padre Carmelo, by the window. It's cooler here.

PADRE CARMELO: This is nice, *hija mia.*

FIDELA: Padre, do you wish a small drink?

PADRE CARMELO: A glass of orange or fruit juice will do, Fidela. The tropical heat is killing. *Pero,* in Spain, the heat, *que terrible tambien....*

MOTHER: I don't suppose you've met some old friends here. Padre, may I present, Señor Don Agustin Tarceles from Negros. He's an old friend of my husband and looks at Juaning as a son. And this is his wife, Doña Carlota.

PADRE CARMELO: God's blessings on you both.

DON AGUSTIN: We've heard so much about you and your parish, Padre Carmelo.

PADRE CARMELO: In Negros? San Simeon! News really travels. *Bueno, diga me,* what have you heard?

DOÑA CARLOTA: That you've done so much to change the way your parishioners live—no illicit relationships, no child born out of wedlock. . . .

PADRE CARMELO: *Es verdad,* all of them are living under God's grace and protection. I do my duty—to see to it that each man lives properly and within God's laws, never to stray from the flock. If anyone strays—to do the proper penance for, *gaudium est Angelis Dei super uno peccatore poenitentian agente.*

FIDELA *(re-enters with Angge who holds a tray of drinks)*: It's grape, Padre. *(To Angge.)* Angge, see that the guests are served.

(The orchestra strikes up the wedding march.)

MOTHER *(stands up, all the guests are up, general excitement)*: Oh, they've come home. It's Juaning!

PADRE CARMELO: *Que graciosa! Muy simpatica!*

DON AGUSTIN: It's as if our own son's gotten married!

DOÑA CARLOTA: Yes, oh yes!

FIDELA: Oh, I feel giddy! I'm going to faint!

(The pair enters in full view.)

A GUEST: *Mabuhay,* Juaning and Isabelita!

ALL *(raising their glasses)*: *Mabuhay!*

ANOTHER GUEST: May all sicknesses and misfortunes keep away!

ANOTHER GUEST: And only happiness and children come!

ALL: Yes, yes! Happiness and many children.
And the devil sickness keep away!

JUANING *(raises his hand to quiet the guests)*: Thank you, my friends. Isabelita and I, we thank you all for your good wishes.

A GUEST *(singing)*: Later he would be warmed
Not only by our wishes,
And never more alarmed
By lack of love and kisses!

(Brings the glass to his lips with a resounding smack, then bows to the guests who clap and cheer the pair.)

JUANING: Here, Isabelita, you sit beside Mother. *(The ladies kiss the young bride.)* Tio Agustin, I was so happy when I saw you and Tia Carlota. I was afraid you won't be able to make it. You sounded so uncertain in your letter.

DON AGUSTIN: Trips from Negros are so irregular, my son. But as you can see, we wouldn't miss your wedding for anything. Your Tia Carlota could hardly wait to meet Isabelita. She said, the loveliest for her dear Juaning.

DOÑA CARLOTA *(approvingly)*: She's lovely.

ISABELITA *(tries to cover her embarrassment)*: Juaning talks a lot about you, Tia Carlota, next to Mother, of course. I'm happy to meet you at last. And you too, Padre Carmelo, Juaning told me so much about you.

PADRE CARMELO: All the good things, I hope. Yes, only the good things.

ISABELITA: Oh, here come my parents. They're eager to meet you all.

DOÑA REMIGIA: Oh, we're sorry to be late *(fanning herself vigorously)*, the driver couldn't find this street. I told him to follow the others. He was following the wrong carriage!

DON CARLOS: It led us...ha, ha...to the cemetery. The stupid fellow was following a funeral procession. And me, determined to live to a hundred like my father!

MOTHER: Oh, yes, Don Carlos and Doña Remigia, let me introduce to you Padre Carmelo, our parish priest. And this is Don Agustin and Doña Carlota Tarceles from Negros.

JUANING: And this is Tia Fidela, Mama's constant companion. Tia Fidela used to chase me around when I was a boy.

FIDELA: He was an active boy, always getting into mischiefs. He loved to taunt me.

JUANING: I loved the way you turned red in the face...how you'd chase me around the house, into the garden.

FIDELA: Oh, he was a little devil, Isabelita!

MOTHER: Fidela dotes on your husband and he knows it. So, poor Fidela!

DOÑA CARLOTA: He's been spoiled by so many women, Isabelita.

DON AGUSTIN: Yes, we're worried.

DOÑA REMIGIA: Well, Isabelita can control her Papa and I tell you, Carlos is the most spoiled, the most uncontrollable. . . .

DON CARLOS: Tush—don't believe my wife, don't ever! I'm a martyr actually. I'm a silent suffering saint waiting to be canonized!

PADRE CARMELO: I'm sure that Isabelita can handle him.

FIDELA *(lightly)*: Yes, give him the *garrote* once in a while. . .then, don't feed him. . . .

JUANING: Yes, the tactics of the Spaniards on the *Indios!*

FIDELA *(chidingly)*: Juaning. . . .

PADRE CARMELO: Whatever made you say that, Juaning, *porque?*

DOÑA REMIGIA: I'm sure Juaning didn't mean to offend. . . .

DON AGUSTIN: The *garrote* and starvation are but two of the many instruments of torture being used by the authorities, Doña Remigia. And you must admit yourself, Padre Carmelo, that the conditions in the islands is getting from bad to worse.

PADRE CARMELO: The *garrote* and starvation are good for the body as well as the soul. The authorities are only doing their job and if they must adopt these measures, it is because the *Indios* abuse the freedom given to them.

JUANING: Freedom?

DON AGUSTIN: Yes, Padre Carmelo, abuse what freedom? Among the small and the weak, what freedom is there to abuse?

JUANING: You're right, Tio Agustin—In our midst is tyranny which feeds on our indifference. Why do we sit by and watch it, rotting, bloated beyond proportion, beyond recognition. . .why? Because it is the more comfortable thing to do. The poor fight back because they have nothing to lose.

PADRE CARMELO: *Nada. . .que nada?* And their lives? Their families? You call these nothing?

JUANING *(evenly)*: To be a slave is to be nothing, Padre Carmelo, we who have not tasted how it is to be kicked and eat the dust, we shall never know why men must fight back!

DON CARLOS: I understand, Padre Carmelo, the city is the seedbed of *insurrectos*. There's a man, they say he's quite a leader of the poor, being a poor man himself.

PADRE CARMELO: A maker of walking canes and fans, *caramba,* what a leader he makes!

FIDELA: A maker of walking canes and fans?

DON AGUSTIN: We've heard about him from as far as the Visayas. He might be tougher than you think.

DOÑA CARLOTA: We heard that his temper's as quick as his tongue. And he's willing to die for the cause of the country if necessary.

PADRE CARMELO: He's an unschooled adventurer, a speculator who'd risk the lives of his followers to satisfy his violent ideas. A roustabout! The Spanish authorities will know what to do with him when the time comes.

DOÑA REMIGIA *(fanning herself vigorously)*: Oh, I hope that time never comes. The revolution will impoverish us all!

MOTHER: Imagine the killings!

FIDELA: Yes, they're always bloody.

DOÑA CARLOTA: And our houses razed to the ground, the fire will eat us all!

JUANING: Blood and fire! That's a revolution. What a pity, Padre Carmelo, if a poor maker of walking canes and fans would someday upset the old order and give the country its revolution, or shall we call it, a baptism of blood and fire?

PADRE CARMELO: Your maker of walking canes and fans has more sense than to start a revolution. He and his *insurrectos* will remain underground where they belong. You don't fight a revolution with sticks and spittle. Unless they can outnumber and outarm the superior Spanish Militia, they are wise to remain underground.

DON AGUSTIN: If the government could smoke them out as early as possible.... I know how power gathers and grows underground. Someday, like the angry volcano, its mouth cracks open and inferno let loose, *caramba!*

PADRE CARMELO: Then God will protect us and the Spanish cause! For our cause is God's cause. We came to teach you God's word—

and our reward? Oh, well, *Qui fecerit et decuerit, hic magnus voca-bitur in regno caelorum!*

JUANING: You should strive first to be called great on earth, Padre, then to be called great in Heaven follows.

PADRE CARMELO: *Bien, muy bien!* Not only do you remember your Latin, my son, you're as much of the philosopher you were when you were a student. He was a great dissenter in our classes in Logic. Always arguing....

MOTHER (*snatching this lighter turn of the conversation*): The long table is waiting. Come, everyone...to the dining room before the soup gets too cold and the wine too warm. And Isabelita must be famished. Come, come, everyone! (*They exit.*)

(*Lights dim while* COSME *walks in to rearrange the chairs while general murmurs of approval and sounds of dishes and silvers are heard. Then the lights brighten up and the guests return giving comments about the food, etc. A program of songs, two guests, a male and female render a song each, then a duet. A rigodon led by the newlyweds follow. A toast is proposed and while the glasses are raised and shouts of "Buenas!" are made, the curtain falls.*)

SCENE TWO

It is a few hours later: the wedding guests have departed. Against the curtain, COSME *crosses the stage apron, loaded with wedding presents. He's mumbling:* "I tell you it's only the rich who have fun in life. The poor do nothing but scrub and carry!" *Before he disappears, the curtain rises to reveal* ANGGE *sweeping the remains of the party under the chairs. She looks up and sees* COSME *enter.* "Oy, who told you to bring those boxes here?" COSME *places the boxes down on the sofa, mops his brow,* "The Señora, why?" ANGGE *embarrassed,* "Ah, the Señora ba?" "The Señora said, clear the carriage, the Señorito and Señorita will use it for their trip to Tarlac," *lowering his voice,* "for their honeymoon."

ANGGE *straightens up and throws the broom to Cosme who catches it deftly.* "Finish up sweeping, take away all the glasses. And hurry up, there's much to do..." COSME *goes to her eagerly. She blurts out to his face,* "...in the kitchen!" *She leaves.* COSME *stands shaking his head. He surveys the room and decides to put away the glasses first. Picks up the tray and whistling the wedding march, goes about the tables. Picks a half-filled glass, places it on the tray, removes his hand slowly, gazes at the glass thoughtfully, steals a glance at the door, takes up the glasses and downs its contents in one big gulp. His face breaks into a slow smile. Does the same with the rest of the glasses; this pantomime lasts for sometime until the whistling, the tray and the steps start to waver. He suppresses a hiccup and the tray almost drops. He walks to the door bumping against Juaning and Isabelita; he is profuse with apologies.*

JUANING *(pats Cosme on the shoulders)*: It's alright, Cosme, you must be tired. Go get some rest.

COSME: Thank you, Sir, a long, happy marriage to you...hic... and the Señorita! *(Exits.)*

JUANING: Quite a fellow, he's been with Mother since he was five, I think.

ISABELITA: Is he and Angge—are they married?

JUANING: He's been after her since I can remember but... ha, ha... that Angge's hard as rock. Look Isabelita, our presents. *(He walks to the sofa and picks a card at random.)* Here's a nice wish, "To Juaning and Isabelita:

> May the children be many
> And the quarrels few;
> May life be like honey
> And love always new!—Cora"

ISABELITA *(crosses to look at the card)*: Oh, that's my friend, Cora Reyes, she loves to write verses. Class poet.

JUANING: I know the Navarros won't forget. My, this is a big box. Now, let me see...

ISABELITA: Juaning, there's something I wanted to ask you, something important....

JUANING: This can be a set of good wine glasses and a decanter. I've always wanted a good set and I mentioned it to them once, I believe...

ISABELITA *(takes the box away, quite firmly)*: Juaning, tell me please! This morning...you were very vehement about the Spanish *garrote*...

JUANING: This looks like a box of silver. Don't you want to take a look at the design?

ISABELITA: Juaning, you were severe with Padre Carmelo many times. This revolution, this maker of walking canes and fans, do you know him? Are you...do you have anything to do with...the revolution?

JUANING: Oh, Isabelita, that's all men's talk!

ISABELITA: If you'll only say a definite no!....then I'd believe you and be at peace.

JUANING (*takes her by the shoulders*): It's not what one talks about just after a wedding. Look, dearest, you better get your wrap, we've got a long trip ahead of us.

ISABELITA: Oh, Juaning, I'm so afraid. Tell me now, before we go that you're not in this...this trouble. Swear to me, Juaning!

JUANING: Of course, don't be silly! That's all men's talk.

MOTHER (*offstage*): Well, that's the last of the guests. They all seemed to have enjoyed the party.

(JUANING *and* ISABELITA *break from their embrace.* MOTHER *and* FIDELA *enter;* MOTHER *catches the sad look on Isabelita's face.*)

FIDELA: Well, so you two have been looking at the presents? Those came from your carriage. There are many more in the dining room.

ISABELITA: I was just going to get my wrap. Mother, Tia Fidela, please excuse me. (*Exits.*)

MOTHER: Juaning, is something wrong with Isabelita? Something upset her?

JUANING: No, Mother, she's just tired. She wasn't able to sleep last night. She told me three of her friends slept in her room, teased her until three in the morning. I better help her with the suitcases.

FIDELA: See that you have enough warm clothes, it gets cold evenings in that farm.

MOTHER: Cosme has the carriage ready. I'll tell him to carry the suitcases down for you.

JUANING: It's all right, Mother. I can manage. (*He goes off hurriedly.*)

MOTHER: Well, Fidela, it looks like our work is done...all the guests are gone and pretty soon, Juaning and Isabelita.

FIDELA: Well, don't talk that way...you make it sound like this is after a funeral instead of a wedding.

MOTHER: I'm sorry, Fidela, but the house seems so empty after all the noise and the music.

FIDELA: You're just tired. You've been up since early this morning. And you've not taken your siesta...remember what your doctor says?

MOTHER: Well, I guess I can help the children sort out the boxes and make a list of their well-wishers.

FIDELA: Aren't you coming in for your siesta?

MOTHER: In a few minutes...let's wait until the children have gone.

(JUANING *and* ISABELITA *re-enter.*)

JUANING: Well, goodbye, Mother, Tia Fidela. Isabelita and I will be back in a week.

MOTHER: Take care of each other, my children. And God's blessings.

FIDELA: Soon as you get to the farm, give our regards to *Mang* Destro and his wife. I'm sure that they'll take care that you two have everything you'll need. (JUANING *and* ISABELITA *exit.*)

MOTHER *(goes to the window to watch the departure)*: Juaning, tell Sixto to drive carefully! *(Hears the sound of the carriage driving away, turns to Fidela.)* Oh, I wonder if they heard me at all?

CURTAIN

ACT II

SCENE ONE

SCENE: The same House
TIME: Early morning of August 20, 1896

(COSME *and* ANGGE *cross on stage apron;* COSME *carries a straw bag full of vegetables and balanced on Angge's head is a wide basket of fruits.*)

ANGGE: Oy, Cosme, are you counting lamp posts? Hurry you! They might be home now from the baptism.

COSME: Yours isn't half as heavy as this. Go on! Those fruits have to be washed.

ANGGE *(stops center)*: And those vegetables are to be washed and cooked. Come on, this is no moonlight night, *por Diyos!* I hope there aren't too many guests.

COSME *(stops and mops his brow)*: One or two maybe.

ANGGE: What do you mean, one or two?!

COSME *(looks cautiously around)*: The Spaniards are getting suspicious of wedding parties, baptisms and funerals. When people gather, they think there's something *sob...re...sobresibe* about it.

ANGGE: Subversive, *torpe!*

COSME: Yeah, that's the word! *Mang* Sixto said, *sobresibe!*

ANGGE: Well, I must say these must be dangerous times if the Spanish army won't even permit weddings and funerals. How are the people to live?

COSME *(the gravity of the situation slowly dawning on him)*: Yeah, *(slowly)* why...that means we can't get married anymore, Angging. We should've, a year ago. A year ago, they were two. Now three, a son at that. Aren't you envious?

ANGGE: *Tse!* Why should I be? I'm comfortable as it is. Husbands are a headache especially if they insist on having their way.

COSME: But you kept me hanging all these years!

ANGGE: Well, if it will please you...hang yourself!

COSME: You're cruel, oh Angging...you're heartless. Well this is goodbye... *(starts off.)*

ANGGE *(with new interest)*: Are you going to kill yourself?

COSME: Yes, in a revolution! No one will say I killed myself because of unrequited love—for that would be such a waste...but everyone will say I died for my country!

ANGGE: Ha-ha...for the country!

COSME: What...why are you laughing?

ANGGE: Ha-ha...they won't take you in...they need brave men!

COSME: Then, Angging, I pity you. You don't know the real Cosme... *(Lowers his voice)* I've been attending their meetings every night. Where do you think I've been going...the *pintakasi?*

ANGGE: Naw, you haven't!

COSME: To dedicate my life to you...you refused me...now, I'll dedicate it to a bigger cause, my country's. (*Closes his eyes and pounds on his chest with exaggerated gestures.*) So help me God, I've seen the light!

ANGGE: Oh, Cosme (*with evident and growing admiration, tugs at his trousers*) a revolution is dangerous!

COSME (*pulls his trousers up and recites at random*): Marble white and flashy outside, inside they crawl with worms and rot! Oh, let me not be content with the skin, for it is not eaten, it only covers... a bitter meat!

ANGGE: That's lovely, Cosme. I didn't know you love poetry!

COSME: Poetry...*bah!* It's pure gold! It's Emilio Jacinto's *Liwanag at Dilim*. And do you know who belongs up there with the leaders? (ANGGE *shakes her head, mystified*)...Señorito Juaning, that's who!

ANGGE (*quite shaken*): Señorito Juaning! This can't be, you're mistaken! Oh, the Señora will have an attack. (*Makes move to go.*)

COSME (*grabs Angge's wrist, pushes her backwards, his face pressed against hers, threateningly*): No one must know—not his mother—or wife, understand?

ANGGE (*bent awkwardly, but manages to raise her hand*): No one—I promise, Cosme. My lips are sealed.

COSME (*releases her suddenly*): Good! (*Continues reciting*) "For even so, majority of the people are dragging behind them the heavy chain of slavery and shame! (A SPANISH SOLDIER *appears at stage right. He eyes them suspiciously.* ANGGE *sees him but not* COSME *who has now taken the center position his arms outspread.*) The multitudes are subjugated by the powerful selected few. Oh, Sons of the People, despoiled of the fruits of your own labor, ARISE! (ANGGE *tugs at his shirt urgently.*) All men are created equal (*The* SPANISH SOLDIER *is almost directly in front of Cosme.*) for their being is one!

ANGGE (*tries to smile and waves an uncertain goodbye at the soldier*): Well, so you know (*nudges* COSME *who sees soldier for the first time*) your lines, Cosme, (*aloud, carefully and distinctly*) oh, ha-ha—won't the prompter at the *zarzuela* be surprised!

COSME (*petrified, salutes the soldier and quickly picks up the vegetables*): Yeah—ha-ha (*catching on*)—won't they die of surprise. *Buenas tardes, Tardes noches! Ehe, noche buena!* (*Jumps while lifting his hat.*) *Hasta la vista!*

(*Both exit running to stage right; the* SOLDIER *is left on the stage, scratching his head and looking after them. With a chuckle, he too goes—the opposite direction.*)

(*Meanwhile, the curtain rises to reveal the same living room. The mother enters holding a child dressed in long baptismal clothes. She is followed by Doña Remigia, Isabelita, Juaning and Don Carlos.*)

MOTHER: Well, my dear *Christian* son, I must say you behaved well in the church.

JUANING: Slept through it all as though it was the most boring thing in the world!

ISABELITA: Ha-ha, except when the water was poured, he shrieked.

DOÑA REMIGIA: Yes, what lungs!

MOTHER: Well, he's getting restless, the bonnet's too tight, Isabelita. There—there....

ISABELITA: Give him to me, Mother, I'll get him into something more comfortable.

MOTHER: Better yet let's give him his bath. Come, Remigia, let's watch how our grandson slaps the water and overturns the powder box.

DOÑA REMIGIA: Now—now, he'll spoil your new gown!

(*Exit the three women.*)

JUANING (*selects two cigars and hands one to Don Carlos. They smoke for a while*): That child will be smothered with love! He's well surrounded.

DON CARLOS: By all the women—and we're quite forgotten. Well, we had our day....

JUANING: You sound morbid today, Papa.

DON CARLOS: The world is no place for laughter. And these have been strange days—people going hungry—dying. And the *guardias civiles* are getting more brutal each day. Look at me, Juaning, I'm an old man, an old fool who's sixty but who wants to be a hundred.

But I smell a war coming, the signs are all over the country. I tell you, the sky is ominous with the coming death and pestilence. Why don't you and Isabelita, the whole family come home with us? The city is no place for a new family. Let's give the young a chance in life, I always say, a fair chance!

JUANING: Better times are coming, Papa, if we'll just be patient. We suffer these, these discomforts for a just cause.

DON CARLOS: When a *Guardia Civil* comes and takes you away, it will be no little discomfort. The women are unaware of what's happening. It's our duty to keep them where it's safe.

JUANING: I've nothing to do with the revolution, Papa...why should they come here?

DON CARLOS: Isabelita told me you've nothing to do with the revolution...now you tell me! All right, all right, I believe you, *iho*. But one doesn't have to be a member to be judged guilty.

JUANING: What do you mean?

DON CARLOS: The leaders approached some of the rich and prominent citizens and begged us to join the revolution...most of us refused to have anything to do with it. We were told we have to... our names have been forged on documents saying we're contributing heavily to the Katipunan and that we're in sympathy with the plans and principles of the movement. We're implicated...all of us!

JUANING: Implicated! Who told you this?

DON CARLOS: They've arrested Don Francisco Roxas for an execution...the rest are bribing the Spanish officials to save their necks.

JUANING: But this is madness! Look, Papa, the idea was to get the rich to contribute some money...a revolution costs money. The list was drawn up and we thought if the rich were to be involved... We...it was the farthest thing....

DON CARLOS: We? You, Juaning? An...an *insurrecto?* You've joined these bandits who'll have our women killed, our children butchered, our homes burned!

JUANING (*angrily*): THEY'RE NO BANDITS! They're upright men and women who live and swear to an iron code of honesty, simplicity and loyalty. To a life that is free and decent for everyone, Papa.

DON CARLOS: Bought at the price of innocent lives!

JUANING: The innocents are always the first to pay...cite to me any war, any revolution, any catyclysm that brought violent changes, reforms...its roads are strewn with bodies of the innocents. The very foundation of your Church, Papa, is smeared with their blood!

DON CARLOS: Then it is with the blood of Isabelita and your son you'd smear the foundation of this....this edifice of freedom you're building? *(JUANING is quiet.)* Come away from the city, my son, your duty as a father is to save your own family!

JUANING: No, no, Papa. I've sworn... with my blood!

DON CARLOS: Your family's your blood, Juaning! While there's time, come away! The Spaniards are making mass arrests, the whole city will not sleep tonight. It's madness to stay in this holocaust of arrests and killings!

JUANING: Papa, there isn't time!

DON CARLOS: But there is...the carriage is ready!

JUANING: No, Papa, I'm sorry. I have to go...to Pugad-Lawin... to warn my comrades. Take care of Isabelita and my son, swear it! *(There is a loud knocking at the front door.)*

DON CARLOS: The *Guardias!* Hide, Juaning!

FIDELA *(rushes into the room before the men have time to move)*: Where's Cleotilde? Oh, I've done something terrible!

JUANING: Tia Fidela! *(Leads her to a chair.)* Here, rest awhile, I'll get Mother. *(He runs off.)*

DON CARLOS: I'll get a glass of water. *(Exits.)*

MOTHER *(comes running into the room with Juaning and Doña Remigia)*: You're pale, Fidela! What happened?

DON CARLOS: Here, drink first, Fidela...that's it....

FIDELA: Oh—it was terrible, Cleotilde and I didn't know...understand, I didn't know!

MOTHER: Tell us slowly, Fidela.

FIDELA: It was a confession...understand, a sacred, private confession...in the holy church!

JUANING: You're not making any sense, Tia Fidela....

MOTHER: Hush, Juaning! It's all right, Fidela, start from the beginning.

FIDELA: A confession, Cleotilde...I...I confessed to Padre Carmelo all about the revolution...

DON CARLOS: Still...'twas a confession, a holy act!

DOÑA REMIGIA: To be sealed until death...with the holy priest.

JUANING: The revolution! What else...what happened!

FIDELA: My brother Teodoro told me all about the *insurrectos,* their plan to overthrow the government.

JUANING: Why Teodoro?

FIDELA: I don't know until later...they had a fight, Apolonio and he. My brother wanted revenge. And me...I was so frightened I had to tell someone...my Father Confessor...

MOTHER: And he kept it? *(Everyone hushed, expectant.)* It's a confession, a holy one! (FIDELA *shakes her head and breaks down with sobs.)*

JUANING: *(grabs her by the shoulder, forces her to look at him):* Did they get proofs? DID THEY GET PROOFS? ANSWER ME! PROOFS!

FIDELA: The Padre got excited...called some soldiers...forced me to lead them to the printing shop...of *Diario de Manila.* We found copies of Katipunan letters....

JUANING *(lets her go, slowly):* The whole organization is doomed!

FIDELA: Late last night they forced open...locker of Policarpio Turla... Signature was found in the receipts...the Spanish officials found a dagger, the rules of the society and many documents. Oh Cleotilde, then they started making mass arrests! Before tonight, they say, the jails will be full and also Fort Santiago. Then the executions...

JUANING: I must go! At once!

DON CARLOS *(tries to stop him at the door):* NO, JUANING! We can all go...the carriage!

MOTHER *(with great calmness):* Go, my son, we'll take care of everything here.

JUANING *(runs back to embrace her)*: Goodbye, Mother. Take care of Isabelita and my son. I'll... I'll try to be back.

MOTHER: God's blessings! We'll all wait. *(JUANING exits.)*

DON CARLOS: NO, JUANING, WAIT! But... but Cleotilde....

MOTHER: COSME! COSME, COME QUICKLY!

COSME *(enters running)*: You called, Señora?

MOTHER: QUICK, follow your Señorito! See that he's safe, hurry! And Cosme....

COSME *(turns back)*: Yes, Señora!

MOTHER: Cosme... *(her voice breaks)* guard him with your life!

COSME: I promise, Señora! *(Runs off.)*

DON CARLOS: We could have gone away, all of us to the farm, the carriage is ready!

MOTHER *(softly, gently, as if speaking to a child)*: Then, we'll never be able to look at each other, my son and I. We'll be safe in the farm but we can never look into each other's eyes without remembering this morning and the betrayal said here.

FIDELA: I've sent him to his death and how I loved him!

DOÑA REMIGIA: You knew all along and never told us?

MOTHER: It was only last night that I was sure. He left the key to one of the drawers in that desk, I was looking for some writing paper. Before I saw the documents, I knew Juaning must have something to do with the revolution. My son's impulsive, like his father....

DON CARLOS: Your son is a true believer, Cleotilde.

DOÑA REMIGIA: I must go at once, to my daughter....

DON CARLOS: No, Remigia, she must not know!

ISABELITA *(offstage)*: Be sure and watch him, Angge. And call me when he wakes up. *(Enters gaily.)* Oh, I thought he won't go to sleep, ever! Such temper! Must be because he's now a Christian? Ha-ha... *(Notices for the first time that everyone is quiet.)* Something's happened? To Juaning? Where's he?

MOTHER: Nothing happened, child. Your Tia Fidela came bringing bad news about Juaning's friend... he had to leave at once and see him.

ISABELITA: He must have been in a hurry...he didn't even say goodbye.

DON CARLOS: His friend's in great danger, *iha*...

MOTHER: He said to tell you he's sorry and that he'll come home as soon as he can.

ISABELITA: In time for lunch, I hope. I've prepared his favorite soup.

FIDELA *(starts weeping again)*: Oh, it's terrible!

ISABELITA *(goes to comfort her)*: Don't worry, Tia Fidela, everything will be all right. Please don't cry.

MOTHER: Yes, of course, Fidela. Listen to Isabelita—everything will be all right. *(There's a loud knocking at the front door; all freeze— then, MOTHER makes a move to go.)*

DON CARLOS *(restrains her)*: Stop!

MOTHER: Must be Juaning! He's come back!

ISABELITA: Let me open the door, Mother—to surprise him!

DON CARLOS: I said stop all of you! It might not be Juaning.

DOÑA REMIGIA: Might not be Juaning! Carlos, DON'T GO!

(DON CARLOS frees himself from his wife, goes to the door. All the women watch, apprehensively. He re-enters with two Spanish soldiers and a citizen in a white suit.)

SECOND SOLDIER: Have no fear, ladies. We've come on a special mission. It won't take long if you all cooperate!

MOTHER: How, cooperate?

THE CITIZEN *(waves an envelope)*: We have orders for this house.

DON CARLOS: What orders, gentlemen?

THE CITIZEN: For the arrest of Don Carlos Sandoval, are you Don Sandoval?

DOÑA REMIGIA: You can't arrest an innocent man!

FIRST SOLDIER: That's to be proved. Anyway, it's merely routine investigation.

THE CITIZEN: The order: *(Reads)* "This is an order for the arrest of the person of Don Carlos Sandoval, now, in Manila, for aiding the revolution through financial and/or material donations."

FIDELA: But—he's a peace-loving gentleman!

MOTHER: Let's be sane! Young man, this is my house and Don Carlos is my guest. I've to see that nothing happens to him.

THE CITIZEN: Oh, nothing will—if he comes with us peacefully.

FIRST SOLDIER: Otherwise, this is not intended to frighten you, ladies— but this house is surrounded!

DON CARLOS *(calmly)*: Get my cane and hat, Isabelita.

(ISABELITA goes.)

DOÑA REMIGIA: No, Carlos, don't go! It's...it's a...a trap!

DON CARLOS: It's merely routine investigation, my dear. I'll be back when they find out their mistake.

MOTHER *(suggestingly)*: I've some jewels, Carlos...quite a few pieces ...very attractive...

DON CARLOS: That won't be necessary, Cleotilde...but thank you for offering them.

(ISABELITA comes back with hat and cane; hands them to her father and then embraces him.)

ISABELITA: We'll tell Juaning, Papa, as soon as he comes back.

DON CARLOS: Yes, *(Absently)*...yes, of course, child. Take care of yourself and your mother. I'll be back. *(DOÑA REMIGIA breaks into tears, he embraces her.)* No tears, Remigia, you know I can't stand them.

DOÑA REMIGIA: Bring your lunch...or...or a...blanket at least, Carlos.

MOTHER *(exits)*: I'll get one.

FIDELA: It's all my fault! I'm to be blamed!

DON CARLOS: All of us are to be blamed, Fidela, all of us, together.

MOTHER *(comes back with a rolled woolen blanket; hands it to Don Carlos)*: This'll keep you warm.

SECOND SOLDIER *(snatches the blanket from Don Carlos)*: Espera! *(Inspects the blanket by unrolling it, folds it and throws it back to Don Carlos.)*

DON CARLOS: Goodbye, Cleotilde...take care of my family.

MOTHER: They'll be safe with me, Carlos.

THE CITIZEN *(takes Don Carlos by the arm)*: If you're ready, Sir!

DON CARLOS: *(shakes off from the hold)*: I need no help from *your kind! (Quietly puts on his hat and marches ahead to the door.)* I'm not that old...yet. *(All exit, following at some distance.)*

DOÑA REMIGIA: Hush, child, remember what he said, no tears!

(Offstage, shots—the women turn up their faces to the door, all visibly shaken.)

ISABELITA: Papa!

MOTHER: No, child—just a signal.

FIDELA: Yes, yes—a signal for a capture!

(The soldiers and the civilian re-enter and face the women who now watch their movement without saying a word.)

ISABELITA *(with a sob)*: Papa?

THE CITIZEN: We regret very much! But he was...he was arrogant....

FIRST SOLDIER: He insisted on walking ahead, won't follow orders....

SECOND SOLDIER: He tried to escape....

DOÑA REMIGIA *(her eyes are dry as she tears away from ISABELITA who tries to stop her, she faces the men, her fists are clenched as she raises them to strike at the soldier's chest)*: Mentirosos! Traidores!

(She falls on her knees, her shoulders shaking with uncontrollable sobs.)

CURTAIN

ACT III

SCENE ONE

SCENE: The same house
TIME: May 9, 1897, early morning

The curtain is down; ANGGE and COSME cross on stage apron, weighted down with all sorts of articles. COSME carries a sack bulging with goods, his shoulders draped with stripes of brightly-coloured cloth, from his neck dangles a bronze lamp and perhaps a pair of shoes tied

together by the laces. He also carries a blue antique-looking vase.
ANGGE *who follows him is holding a wrapped bundle of various things,
a yellow parasol with frills sticking out from one end. Both are smeared
with soot, very grimy-looking and very happy.*

COSME *(stops center, lays down sack and wipes his face)*: Ha-ha
Angging, sometimes a war has its good points...now, look at us,
the poor—loaded with the goods of the whole world!

ANGGE: *Ay,* truly—you look like a Japanese bazaar!

COSME: But was I fast! Grab! Grab, grab! Fight your way, Cosme,
into that store before the flames lick these God's graces away!

ANGGE: *Oy*—listen to that talk! This morning you refused to move
from your mat. Yew, I'm still sleepy, you said, leave me alone! And
there Tekla was yelling, Fire! They're looting the stores. Bah, you
men! We have to think of everything!

COSME: Naw—it isn't such a bad haul. But look at all the useless
things you grabbed.

ANGGE: Useless! *Oy,* Cosme, look at that vase! Can you cook rice
in that?

COSME *(holds up the vase)*: Cook rice in this, she says! Why, Angging, this is for our room to put flowers in. It'll be for us to look
at, for our children to admire!

ANGGE: In this war! There were pans and pots in the corner...and
you reach out for...that vase!

COSME: Aha! A yellow parasol, and what did you take that for?

ANGGE *(opens and twirls the parasol on her shoulder)*: Well, I've always wanted one since I was a young girl. Anyway, since we got
married, I've got only two pans for cooking. Two pans! And one of
them leaks!

COSME: Well, considering the elaborate dishes we always...ah par-
take! *(Counts with fingers.) Adobo, pansit, lechon, chopsuey, morcon....*

ANGGE: Naw, you're hopeless, simply hopeless! I don't know why I
decided to marry you after all, you're nothing but a dreamer, a clown!

COSME: It's the only way to survive a war, *loka!* To dream, to laugh,
and when the grabbing is good—to grab! Dissenters like *Señorito*

Juaning don't last. Where's he? Hiding in the woods, up those hills...
while his family starves. But look at us, we know how to dance the
tempo, so here we are enjoying the loot!

ANGGE: Well, the pantry in the house is almost empty and the Señora
doesn't know how close we are to starving. Ay, the rich are so helpless! And we have to take care of them, Cosme, since they're so proud
and helpless.

COSME: Yeah! And this revolution might last longer than we think...
(Shakes his jute bag.) that's why I grabbed a few things to eat!

ANGGE: And what do you think *(Pats her bundle.)* these are? People
who die of starvation die with their eyes open...now I don't want
that to happen to us! But people are dying of hunger everywhere!

COSME: If they're not being stuffed into those iron cages! If it's not
hunger, it's suffocation. And it's all a matter of whether you want to
die with your eyes open...or your mouth!

ANGGE: The *Guardias* are getting violent! In the market yesterday,
they hanged a man by his wrists and the people looked and saw his
fingernails turn blue!

COSME: The closer they are to defeat, the more violent they get.
That's how men fight, Angging. *(Looks around cautiously.)* The tide
is turning! We're winning, I heard. But you wait...when the time
comes, I'd take my bolo and *(Whishing an imaginary blade.)* cut off
the heads of these Spaniards myself. After collecting forty heads in a
heap, I'd plant our glorious banner over it and shout, *"Mabuhay!*
Long live freedom!" Then, I'll kill myself!

ANGGE *(aghast)*: You wouldn't!

COSME *(with much bravado)*: You still don't know the real Cosme, eh!
Well—come on, let's go home...we'll have to go back for more!

*(He exits, dragging the strips of cloth behind him, the lamp jigging.
ANGGE follows meekly. And as they leave, the curtain slowly goes up
to reveal the half-darkened living room, the draperies have been drawn
across the windows. The MOTHER is seated before the writing desk,
sorting out some papers. On the desk are two piles of paper, on the
floor is an empty box.)*

MOTHER *(reading aloud)*:

"VIII Insofar as it is within your power, share your means with the poor and the unfortunate.

IX Diligence in the work that gives sustenance to you is the true basis of love—love for your own self, for your children, and for your brothers and countrymen.

X Punish a scoundrel and traitor and praise all good work. Believe likewise that the aims of the K.K.K. are God-given...."

(There is a shuffling noise outside the door; the MOTHER *hides the papers hastily and without moving from her seat nor turning her head, she calls out.)*

Who's there?

ANGGE: It's us, Señora. *(Signals* COSME *to the kitchen; he tiptoes to the door.)*

MOTHER: Oh? *(Turns and sees the bundle.)* Well, I see you took the baby out for a walk. That's good for him! (ANGGE *is about to correct this mistaken impression when the* MOTHER *turns back to take the papers out of the drawer where she shoved them.)* And Angge, as soon as you put him down to sleep, tell Cosme to come here. I've an urgent job for him.

ANGGE: At once, Señora *(Exits.)*

MOTHER: These should be burned. *(Puts the papers into box on the floor.)* I should have done this long ago but Juaning says not to touch his things.

COSME *(enters)*: You called, Señora?

MOTHER *(covering the box)*: Now listen carefully, Cosme. All the papers in this box must be destroyed, understand? Go to the backyard, cover this with leaves and burn the whole heap, you understand?

COSME: Yes, Señora.

MOTHER: Watch it burn, poke into the ashes—see that nothing remains.

COSME: I'll watch it burn, Señora.

(Offstage, there's knocking on the front door; COSME *freezes but the* MOTHER *signals him to leave through the back door. He exits.)*

MOTHER *(calls out)*: Who's there?

PADRE CARMELO: It's me, Padre Carmelo. May I see you for a few minutes?

MOTHER: The door's open, Padre Carmelo, come in.

PADRE CARMELO (*enters*): *Buenas,* Cleotilde...I'm not intruding?

MOTHER: Good morning, Padre, what ill wind brings you to the house of an *Indio?*

PADRE CARMELO: Come, my child, sarcasm and vile? I've come to help you and Juaning....

MOTHER (*sharply*): Juaning isn't here! Perhaps, he's dead... somewhere in the hills...while we wait like fools for him to come home.

PADRE CARMELO: Listen to me, Cleotilde, why do you suppose they've spared this house? All these months I've kept them from your door. I know Juaning steals home whenever he can! The *Guardias* are insistent...they want to come and ransack this house but I've been firm. Now, I can't keep them away much longer, they came directly from the *Gobernador-General,* they're official orders!

MOTHER (*coldly*): That he can come home to us...in fear...we owe to you. That we live uneasy in a house unmolested while all our neighbors have been carted away, we owe to you. Thank you, Padre Carmelo, but tell them...they can come and turn the house upside down, there'll be not a sheet of document, not a trace of my Juaning's hair!

PADRE CARMELO: But I've come to warn you....

MOTHER: You betrayed him and many young like him a year ago, Padre. What can you possibly tell us now that's so important?

PADRE CARMELO: What you call a betrayal...was a moral duty to me!

MOTHER: It was a holy confession, private, in good faith...in the house of God!

PADRE CARMELO: My government was to be overthrown!

MOTHER: Deceit and cunning, you used your holy office!

PADRE CARMELO: Everything we've done was to be wiped away! Listen to me, Cleotilde, this house is scheduled to be searched tonight, at nine.

MOTHER: It doesn't matter! It'll be a waste of time!

PADRE CARMELO: I shall try to come with them.

MOTHER: You belong *with* them, Padre...but you need not bother!

PADRE CARMELO: It was never a bother to come to your house, Cleotilde. *(He stops at the door thoughtfully.)* Not even a war can change that. *(Exits.)*

*(*MOTHER *looks after him without moving from where she stands.* ISABELITA *enters with a letter; she stops when she sees the Mother.)*

ISABELITA: I've a letter from Mama...you were talking to someone, Mother?

MOTHER: Yes...He had some important news to tell.

ISABELITA: About Juaning, Mother? Is he coming home? Is he caught? Where's he, Mother? Can we go and see him?

MOTHER: Not about Juaning, poor child, But as important! This house is to be searched tonight! The *Guardias* will ransack every corner, we've to be prepared! I've cleared his desk...if there are any papers in his room?

ISABELITA: He works at that desk all the time, but I'll check....

MOTHER: Yes, call Cosme...he'll know how to dispose of them. Oh yes, is everything all right with your mother?

ISABELITA: Yes, the letter...Mama says they're quite safe. They've been harassed by investigations, but Mama managed to silence the officials with a few pieces of her old jewelry. Mama says she can't take it anymore with Papa dead and us so far away...but she's safe, thank God, although she still insists that we join them since it's safer out of the city, she says. She sends her love to little Pepito and to you.

MOTHER: I think your Mama is right, Isabelita, you and the baby will be safer out of the city.

ISABELITA: We can't leave you, Mother. And Juaning when he comes home?

MOTHER: He'll be happy if he knows you're safe, Angge and Cosme can stay with me....

ISABELITA: No, Mother, leaving this house is out of the question. *(She goes to the door.)* I'll see about the documents. The baby must be awake. *(Offers her hand.)* Care to come, Mother?

MOTHER: I'll... *(Smiles.)* ...I'll be happy to, dear child!

CURTAIN

SCENE TWO

SCENE: The same house
TIME: The same day, early evening

As the curtain goes up, the MOTHER *is watching Angge knotting the corners of a squarish piece of cloth over a heap of clothes.* COSME *comes in and puts down a suitcase. He exits to the dining room.* ISABELITA *is peeping through the drawn curtains; she appears terribly upset.*

ISABELITA *(walks to the Mother)*: Oh, Mother, you can't change your mind so quickly! It isn't fair! You've agreed that we're all to stay here. Besides the trip'll be cold for Pepito. And the *Guardias* are coming, Mother...let us stay and see that nothing happens to you. Oh now, please, Mother?

MOTHER *(gently but firmly)*: No, Isabelita, you'll cover many miles tonight. Pepito can sleep in the carriage, Cosme will drive and Angge can watch over the child while you catch a few winks. In the morning, you'll wake up in the bosom of your dear parent!

ISABELITA: Then come with us, Mother! All of us must leave the house! All of us must leave the city!

MOTHER: No, child, the *Guardias* are coming tonight, quite late... I must be here to meet them. *(Sees the sad expression on Isabelita's face, goes and embraces her.)* Oh, I'll be all right. Look, you can send Cosme back for me after two or three days. I'll follow as soon as Juaning comes home. Someone has to tell him where we are—eh?—don't forget that, child!

ISABELITA: I'll see if Pepito's asleep, get him ready....

MOTHER: Yes, yes, wrap him well—plenty of blankets! *(Her voice falters.)* His little head...a bonnet...remember, the draft! (ISABELITA *exits.)*

ANGGE: Everything's packed, Señora.

MOTHER: Very good, Angge. You and Cosme load them in the carriage. Tell Cosme to bring enough water and hay for the horses....

ANGGE *(heaving the bundle on her shoulder)*: I'll tell Cosme to come for the suitcase, Señora, then—we'll be on our way.

MOTHER: Take care of them, Angge—I'm entrusting to you—the wealth of my house!

ANGGE: I'm to leave you—and you are—my greater jewel, Señora! *(Seizes the hand of the Mother and kisses it.)* God keep you! *(Runs off.)*

(The MOTHER remains rooted on the spot, she makes an effort to follow, deeply touched. A loud rapping offstage, front door.)

MOTHER: Yes, who's it? (FIDELA *bursts into the room, slippers clasped to her breast, her hair streaming.)* Fidela! *(Shocked at her appearance, but cold.)* Are you hurt?

FIDELA: Ah—I ran all the way....

MOTHER: You came running!

FIDELA: Imp—important news!

MOTHER: More important than *that* news—that betrayal you told us *that* night. *(Bitterly.)*

FIDELA: I'd give my life to undo that night, Cleotilde! I've given my money, my jewels to the cause, nursed the soldiers—my house's a hospital where all day a kettle of boiling water awaits to wash wounds. I've spied, I've carried messages—oh, if they'd only give me a rifle!

(She buries her face in her hands, sobs. The MOTHER runs to her, ISABELITA rushes in.)

ISABELITA: I heard someone—why—it's Tia Fidela—some hot tea?

MOTHER: Yes, child, Tia Fidela is quite sick.... (ISABELITA *exits.)*

FIDELA: I'll be all right, Cleotilde—not sick—just tired—running—travel all day....

MOTHER: Don't talk—wait for the hot tea, Isabelita has some on the stove....

FIDELA: No, Cleotilde—listen to me—carefully!

MOTHER: Here's some pillows, rest!

ISABELITA *(re-enters with cup of tea)*: Here's the tea, Tia Fidela.

MOTHER: Good! Now, drink, Fidela! All of it. . . .

FIDELA: Thank you, Isabelita. We've to move fast—I've been from Naic—some trouble, split among the two factions of rebels, the *Supremo* walked out of the meeting, mad!

MOTHER: There was shooting. . . ?

ISABELITA: Juaning? What happened to him?

FIDELA: He's alive. . .

ISABELITA: Thank God!

MOTHER: Alive? How did you know, Fidela? Is he coming?

FIDELA: Tonight! With a companion—they've deployed their forces— the other faction, Magdalo, it's called—is after them. The Supremo's been captured with his brother—Juaning's distraught!

MOTHER: Pursued by his own countrymen!

ISABELITA: Coming tonight! *(Suddenly, very frightened.)* Oh—the *Guardias!*

FIDELA: Eh, eh? What *Guardias?*

MOTHER: They're coming tonight—to ransack the house—orders from the *Gobernador-General!*

FIDELA: Oh—oh! He told me himself—he plans to come home tonight!

ISABELITA: Oh, we must stop him! Mother—I'll wait at the corner— to warn him. . . .

MOTHER: That will be dangerous—besides we don't know what time he's coming—but we know that the *Guardias* are coming at nine. . . .

ISABELITA: If the Spaniards take him away—I'm sure—we'll never see him again—oh! *(They are quiet for a while.)*

FIDELA: I know! A beggar!

MOTHER: Huh? Who?

FIDELA: Me! I can beg in the streets, wait till they come...the Spaniards won't suspect anything when they see me.....

MOTHER: Yes, of course—that's clever, Fidela!

FIDELA: I've learned a few tricks.

MOTHER: Quickly, dear friend—ask them to come by the small door—the backyard. Knock three times—Cosme will be at the door. (FIDELA *exits.*)

ISABELITA: You'll let us wait for Juaning, Mother? Now that he's almost at our door!

MOTHER: The danger is great....

FIDELA (*rushes back into the room*): They've come, Cleotilde! Juaning had a huge bundle of twigs and branches on his head—like a wood-cutter! They're in the backyard, getting rid of their loads.

ISABELITA: He's back!

MOTHER: Quick, Fidela—tell Cosme to stand guard at the gate—a long whistle if anyone comes! (FIDELA *exits;* JUANING *comes in with his companion, unshaven, dirty and unrecognizable. The taller one runs to kiss the Mother and upon seeing Isabelita, goes and embraces her.*)

JUANING: Mother, Isabelita, this is my friend, Tino. Didn't think we could make it here, eh, Tino?

TINO: Yes, ma'am—most of the time we walked apart.

JUANING: I carried a bundle of wood—Tino carried a paddle.

TINO: The Spaniards think that all *Indios* are fishermen—never been to the sea all my life—my first time to handle a paddle (*laughing*)—and I walked on land! (*All laugh heartily.*)

MOTHER: Wash up and get a good meal before the *Guardias* arrive.

JUANING: *Guardias?*

MOTHER: They're coming at nine—orders from the *Gobernador-General!*

JUANING: We'll eat on the way—no time to lose....

MOTHER: The carriage is loaded with food and clothes....

ISABELITA: Mother wanted us to leave the city—stay with Mama until the war's over!

MOTHER: Why, yes... *(Her face breaks into a big smile.)* you two can go instead of Cosme and Angge. Isabelita, tell Angge to give them clothes—quick, everyone! *(They exit.)*

FIDELA *(re-enters)*: I told Cosme to watch the gate and whistle loud and clear if anyone comes. Where's everybody?

MOTHER: They'll be back in a short while. *(Mysteriously.)* Remember your plan—to beg?

FIDELA: Oh, well—yes?

MOTHER *(smiling)*: Well—I've picked up a few tricks at deception myself—I hope it'll work.

FIDELA: I tell you, Cleotilde—most of these *Guardias* are actually dumb—if they win the war, it would be out of sheer number and force!

ISABELITA *(enters carrying her son who's wrapped heavily in blankets)*: Juaning says we wait in the carriage—they won't take long. Mother, your blessings. . . .

MOTHER *(kisses the child and Isabelita)*: The Lord's blessings, my children.

ISABELITA: Come away with us, Mother!

MOTHER: Angge and Cosme—and Fidela—we'll follow you later. Go now, quickly.

ISABELITA: Goodbye, Tia Fidela.

FIDELA: Goodbye, child, you'll be safe—at last! (ISABELITA *exits. Looks out of the window;* JUANING *enters wearing Cosme's clothes, he wears a tattered straw hat.)* Well, we have three hours before the *Guardias* come. . . .*(Sees Juaning.)* Oy, Cosme! I told you to wait at the gate, remember—to signal.

JUANING *(turns to her and whistles)*: Like this?

FIDELA: Why, it's Juaning! *(Laughingly, they embrace each other.)* Why, you rascal, I thought all the time. . . .

MOTHER *(laughs, fully satisfied at the success of her little deception)*: I have something to give you, Juaning—won't take me long. *(She goes.)*

JUANING: Promise me, Tia Fidela, you'll stay with Mother.

FIDELA: Of course, son, I'll stay with her until the war ends. *(Exits.)*

MOTHER *(re-enters holding a tiny velvet box)*: Here, Juaning, take this—it'll see you there safely.

JUANING *(takes the box and opens it)*: Why, Mother—it's your jewels! *(Snaps the lid close and hands it back.)* No, Mother—keep it—when the war's over. . . .

MOTHER *(refuses to take it, firmly)*: . . .when the war's over—it won't do as much good! Look, Juaning, pay your way through—if anyone stops the carriage—a jewel here, a jewel there! If there are any left at the end of the trip—give them to your comrades in the revolution. Every pearl—every diamond will buy sacks of rice to feed the hungry army. It's too little to give them when so many are giving away their lives!

JUANING *(places the jewel box on the table)*: I'm not sure about the revolution anymore—our *Supremo,* yes—that poor maker of walking canes and fans was arrested by his countrymen—insulted because he's unschooled. Arrested like a common thief—he and his brother, after a meeting with the Magdalo faction—he—he walked out, you see. . . . The other faction says they're a danger to the revolution, dividing ranks when what's needed is unity. They've taken him to the mountains—to be shot. I wanted to follow—with my men—but he ordered us back. So you see—the Revolution will never be the same. . . .

MOTHER: Remember, Son—you said it once, a revolution is a baptism of blood and fire!

JUANING: I don't know what to believe anymore. With innocent men like Father killed and tomorrow—the *Supremo.* All over the fields there must be hundreds like me who don't know what to believe— who fight perhaps because there isn't anything else to do!

MOTHER: War exacts a high price—it must be paid!

JUANING: But all the innocent people killed, Mother—and now, brother against brother!

MOTHER: Then brother against brother it shall be! Will you weaken now, Son, with so many killed?

JUANING: But I do weaken, Mother, many times—out there in the fields, I keep seeing Isabelita's face—her quiet rebuke for her Papa's death and each time I come home—her eyes—they belong to all the women who've lost a son, a husband, a father or a sweetheart!

MOTHER *(evenly)*: Then take that look with you to battle and fight hard!

JUANING: But I dare not, Mother—the revolution is dying—the *Supremo's* gone!

MOTHER: The *Supremo* started the war—you believed in him and if you but partly believe in everything you fought for, the revolution will not die. Fight the war to the finish! Your father will say that if he were alive tonight. *(Points to the jewel box.)* There, my Son, use them to fight this war.

JUANING *(reaches out for the jewel box)*: Yet—it might work. Yes, of course *(rather thoughtfully)*—it will! We must continue the struggle until the freedom we all long for is attained!

(TINO walks into the room, rather awkwardly—in Angge's clothes, a bandana is tied close to his face. They all try to keep from laughing.)

TINO: I'm not sure I'd like this idea at all!

JUANING *(goes after him, stops him)*: Hu-ops! Come along, my pretty-pretty—a pumpkin carriage awaits us! *(Takes a few exaggerated waltz steps, extends his arm with much ceremony and guides TINO who shakes a fist at him, the Mother and Fidela behind them, doubled up in laughter.)*

MOTHER: Pull your hat close to your face, Juaning—be careful when you drive! (JUANING *kisses his Mother and Tia Fidela; they both exit. Offstage, the sound of a carriage driving away while the two women watch from the window.* FIDELA *sits down, apparently exhausted.)* Perhaps you should fix yourself up a little, Fidela? Our guests must not suspect anything.

FIDELA *(sees the Mother trying to hide her tears, gets up from the sofa)*: Yes—a good idea. *(Exits.)*

MOTHER *(wiping her tears, then she straightens up, remembering something)*: Angge! Cosme! Come quickly!

COSME *(enters)*: They've driven off, Señora.

ANGGE *(enters)*: You called, Señora?

MOTHER: Yes, both of you, listen carefully—in a little while, the *Guardias* will be coming—go and see that all the rooms are in order.

The clothes Juaning and Tino discarded, bury them under the dung heap in the stable, Cosme. And you Angge, see that the bathroom is clean—the men shaved and washed—go and scrub all the marks away! Go quickly, both of you! *(Both exit.)*

FIDELA *(re-enters)*: Well, I feel much better.

MOTHER: You look much better—hungry, I suppose?

FIDELA: Well, yes—but I can wait until after the *Guardias* inspect the house. I don't think I can get anything down—everything's in knots.

MOTHER: Be cheerful, Fidela—the war's about to end. I know it because I've never seen my son look so happy. He's changed a lot—yes, the war has tempered him. He has that—that gift—that drive to grasp the moment as it comes and enjoy it. It is a quality among the old and the wise only—or those who have seen Death....

FIDELA: You read your son like the mariners steer their ships by the stars—but you're his mother—maybe you're right. I've seen a lot of dying and killing, Cleotilde, I need someone to tell me everything will be all right. To hope—to look forward to a day....

MOTHER *(with sadness in her voice)*: ...Not far away—when this room will echo again the music, the laughter and the sound of people's voice? Not fear or searching or deception! Yes, we must hope for that time, Fidela—otherwise with everything so bleak, we can only slit our throats 'cause there's no meaning to living anymore!

FIDELA: You really believe, Cleotilde, that a time will come when laughter will be all over the land again—and we, the old, can watch the young at play and be blessed with the sound of their happy voices?

MOTHER *(takes Fidela's hand, seriously)*: But I do believe it, Fidela—I don't think I'll stop believing it until the day I stretch my toes out and close my eyes to die.

(FIDELA *sighs gratefully. There's a knock at the door.* COSME *and* ANGGE *rush into the room, "The Guardias," they warn.)*

MOTHER *(stands up and walks slowly to the door)*: In a few years Fidela, it would all seem like a bad dream.

COSME *(runs to the door)*: Let me meet them, Señora.

MOTHER: That won't be necessary, Cosme *(She motions him aside.)*

Offstage the soldiers can be heard shouting, "Abre la puerta!" And while FIDELA, COSME *and* ANGGE *watch with much apprehension, the* MOTHER *goes as the lights fade out slowly in the huge room around them, darkening the tall, softly-flowing draperies, the slender stems of the bronze wall lamps, the inscrutable ancestral faces, the ornate chairs. The knocking gets insistent and louder—only a spot remains on the figure of the Mother whose shoulders are erect, whose white hair are now silver under the light—as she opens the door of her house to the Guardias Civiles.*

FINAL CURTAIN

NOTE: The first draft of this play had a different ending. I have decided to include it in this book, for those who want a brighter ending.

FIDELA *(earnestly)*: You really believe, Cleotilde, that a time will come when laughter will be all over the land again—that we, the old, can watch the young at play and be blessed with the sound of their happy voices? You do not say it merely to quiet my fears?

MOTHER *(takes Fidela's hand, seriously)*: I believe it, Fidela! I don't think I'll stop believing it until the day I stretch my toes out and close my eyes to die.

*(*FIDELA *sighs gratefully, her eyes shining. There is a knock at the door. They both stand up and wait expectantly.* PADRE CARMELO *enters followed by three Spanish soldiers.* PADRE CARMELO *stands aside as one of them goes to the Mother and holds out a rolled sheet of paper.)*

THE SPANISH SOLDIER: *La orden Señora, del Governador General!*

MOTHER *(unrolls the document, reads it briefly and hands it back)*: *Si, mi casa es para ustedes. Pero, Señores, no vale la pena!*

THE SPANISH SOLDIER *(rolls up the document and sticks it under his arm)*: *Si, lo creo, Señora, pero es la orden! Con su permiso! (He turns snappily to his companions and orders them to search the house. The two soldiers leave to do his biddings. He stays in the living room and orders the* MOTHER *to open the drawers of the writing desk. The* MOTHER *obliges and watches the soldier as he goes over the papers. The two soldiers return empty-handed. He pushes the drawer shut and faces the soldiers. They shrug their shoulders.) Bueno, Señora, gracias! (He bows.) Todo hombre debe cumplir con su deber!*

MOTHER *(smiling)*: Ya lo creo!

PADRE CARMELO *(circles the sofa, looking at* FIDELA *as if he sees her for the first time)*: Well, Fidela, I see you've come to visit Cleotilde? *(Lowers his voice.)* Anything new, my child, anything important which you think we should know?

(The MOTHER *waits at the door, her hands clenched, a breathless moment, straining to hear Fidela's reply to the Padre's query.)*

FIDELA *(waving her hand and getting up from the sofa to see them to the door)*: Oh, nothing new, Padre Carmelo. We're just two old, foolish women and we love to chat and chat!

*(*PADRE CARMELO *follows the Spanish soldiers, pausing briefly in front of the Mother to say goodbye.)*

PADRE CARMELO *(lamely)*: It is the war that makes us so suspicious, Cleotilde, while our real selves look on from somewhere.

MOTHER *(smiling)*: I believe you, Padre, goodbye!

*(*PADRE CARMELO *leaves with the soldiers. The* MOTHER *runs to the window, parts the drapes and peers down the yard.* FIDELA *goes back to the sofa and sits down rather thoughtfully.)*

FIDELA: They're gone. I can't believe it!

MOTHER *(still at the window)*: There are about ten of them in the yard—Cosme showed them around properly, I hope.

FIDELA: Isn't the war terrible? All the killings and dying—the deception!

MOTHER *(crosses to the sofa and leans on the ornately-curved back)*: Deception—in order to save lives! In a few years, Fidela, it would all seem like a bad dream.

FIDELA *(sadly)*: Oh yes, I hope, I hope. . . .

MOTHER *(sits beside her)*: Oh just think, Fidela, in a few years, Pepito will be going to school!

FIDELA *(dreamily)*: Why, yes, but of course, Pepito. . .

MOTHER *(takes Fidela's hand and pats it)*: We can spend our time sewing clothes for him, we can plan for them when the war's over. . . .

(FIDELA *looks up slowly at the Mother; their eyes meet briefly and then they start laughing softly as the lights slowly fade in the huge room around them, darkening the tall, soft-flowing draperies, the slender stems of the bronze wall lamps gleaming yellowly, the inscrutable ancestral faces, the heavily carved backs of the chairs until only their faces remain, framed by white hair, now silver under the light.*)

[END OF THE PLAY]

(1960-61) First published in the *Aurelio Tolentino Drama Workshop Workbook*, 1975, pp. 101-34. (Preliminary Edition.)

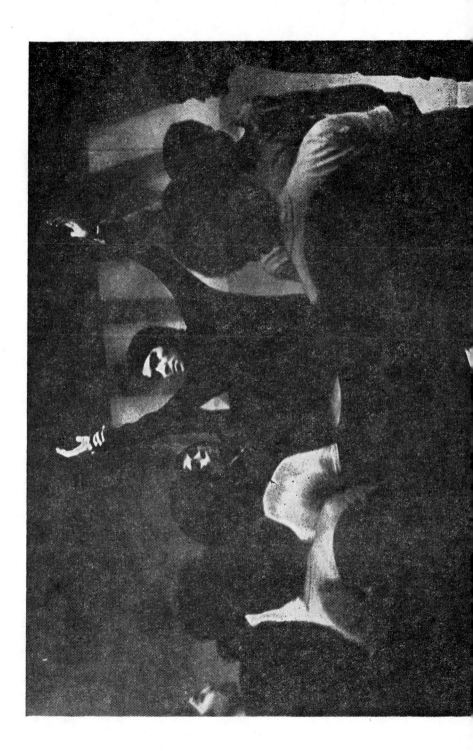

The Short, Short Life of Citizen Juan

(A PLAY IN THREE ACTS)

PREMIER PRESENTATION

On November 25, 26, 27, 1971 at 7:00 p.m., *The Short, Short Life of Citizen Juan* was presented by the Sigma Delta Phi Sorority of the University of the Philippines in Diliman, Quezon City, at the Abelardo Hall of the College of Music, together with the launching of the book as published by the U.P. Press. It was directed by Behn Cervantes, assisted by Lena Lubi and Evelyn Pangilinan; Music Director was Jose Maceda; Sounds director was Lyca Benitez; Choreographer was Ester Rimpos, Art Director was Lynette Advincula and Lighting Director was Peping Generoso. The original cast consisted of: FEMALE DANCER, Esther Gomez; CIDRA, Winnie Collas-Monsod; ALBULARIO, Joonee Gamboa; SIMA, Ruby Umali; JUAN, Nestor Torre, Jr.; PEDRO, Tony Cervantes; ARSENIO, Bing Pabalan; DON MUNDO, Rudy Francisco; ASKAD, Bert Asuque; TOWNSFOLK 1, Gilet Marco; TOWNSFOLK 2, Danny Sandejas; TOWNSFOLK 3, Bert Asuque; LADY 1, Nenette Tiongco-Puyat; LADY 2, Geline Hernandez; LADY 3, Cota Deles-Yabut; LADY 4, Cecille Crisostomo; GENTLEMAN 1, Tom Porillo; GENTLEMAN 2, Bonggoy Vernao; GENTLEMAN 3, Ernie Zarate; GENTLEMAN 4, Vic Puyat; SANCHO, Gilet Marco; TOWNSPEOPLE I, Eddie Abad, Jojo Almaan, Rene Fernandez, Edwin Gidaya, Esther Gomez, Mon Jante, Lanette Javier, Alvin Manacsa, Tess Mejia, Evie Menez, Joe Narciso, Veedo Pena, Edwin del Rosario, Manny Tuazon, Danny Villarante; TOWNSPEOPLE II, Bobby Aguila, Ricky Barreiro, Sandra Chavez, Ester Du, Boy Esteves, Hudi Favila, Jasmin Gaite, Lorna de Guia, Ben Madridejos, Temy Pascual, Walter Quintos, Inez Sandejas, Louie Sison; TOWNSPEOPLE III, Deng Abad Santos, Roni Coquia, Vic Escobar, Joji Fruto, Noli Gerona, Ora Guarin, Ling

Laqui, Evelyn Lee, Clem Luciano, Liza Morales, Merci Padilla, Jorge
Reyes, Bobby Roco, Danny Sandejas, Phoebe Torres, Wheelie Valerio,
George Yang.

CHARACTERS:

(In Order of Appearance)

FEMALE DANCER	TOWNSFOLK 1
MALE DANCER	TOWNSFOLK 2
A VOICE	TOWNSFOLK 3
CIDRA	MAHJONG PLAYER 1
ALBULARIO	MAHJONG PLAYER 2
SIMA	MAHJONG PLAYER 3
JUAN	MAHJONG PLAYER 4
ARSENIO	GENTLEMAN 1
PEDRO	GENTLEMAN 2
TOWNSPEOPLE	GENTLEMAN 3
WOMAN	GENTLEMAN 4
MAN	SANCHO
DON MUNDO	A MAID
ASKAD	MOURNERS

SYNOPSIS:

ACT ONE

SCENE ONE. Juan's home. Early afternoon.
SCENE TWO. The town's meeting place. Early evening.
SCENE THREE. Juan's home. Late evening.

ACT TWO

SCENE ONE. Juan's home. Afternoon, one month later.
SCENE TWO. The Albulario's home. Morning, the following day.
SCENE THREE. Don Mundo's office. Evening, several days later.

ACT THREE

SCENE ONE. Juan's campaign headquarters. Afternoon, one month
later.
SCENE TWO. The town's speak-easy. Same day, a few hours later.
SCENE THREE. Juan's home. Same day, early evening.
SCENE FOUR. Don Mundo's home. Same day, late evening.
SCENE FIVE. Juan's home. Same day, midnight.

The set may be changed with the use of flat arches and varied lighting effects. I have visualized a multi-levelled set with a ramp running across the entire background. Center stage serves as space for Juan's home, the town's meeting place and Don Mundo's home; stage left serves as space for the Albulario's home, the town's speak-easy and stage right serves as space for Don Mundo's office and Juan's campaign headquarters. The set should remain simple, almost bare, except perhaps for the props and overhead lamps which may be lowered for set changes; that is, chandeliers for Don Mundo's home and electric bulbs or oil lanterns for the town's speak-easy, the town's meeting place, Juan's campaign headquarters and the homes of the Albulario and Juan. At the center is a screen for film projection and two square screens hitched together stand on either side of the stage for four alternating slide projections. These are merely suggestions, of course, because while the action of the play dictates the set, ultimately, the responsibility for the set design rests squarely on the shoulders of the designer.

Two flanks of dancers run down the aisles clicking their bamboo clappers in unison. A female dancer joins them in the middle aisle and climbs the stage apron. Then imitating the deaf-mute language, she dances an accompaniment to an offstage voice which says: "The play which you are about to see is called, THE SHORT, SHORT LIFE OF CITIZEN JUAN, *a play in three acts by Amelia Lapeña-Bonifacio. It was started in 1968 in Philadelphia and was completed in the summer of 1970, at the Eugene O'Neill Theater Center in Waterford, Connecticut. There, ten thousand miles away, under the heat of the August sun, the author imagined she could smell the Pacific rather than the ever-present Atlantic ocean and could feel the heat of the Philippine rather than the North American sun. (Aside) But we know how mixed up some of them are! Now—let me see, she told me to tell you that the setting of her play is* any Philippine town. *And, oh yes, the time is* now *and the characters are actually all of us— yes,* you *and* I.*"*

The dancers exit.

ACT I

SCENE ONE

Juan's home. It is early afternoon. At rise, CIDRA *enters with the Albulario following her somewhat reluctantly.*

CIDRA: Aling Sima! Aling Sima!

ALBULARIO: She isn't home, maybe?

CIDRA: She's always home, *Apo.* Aling Sima!

ALBULARIO: Let's go back. I have many...there are many people waiting to see me. You cannot imagine...cases of broken bones *(touching the parts of his body),* headaches, toothaches, armaches, stomachaches....

SIMA *(calling offstage):* Come right in, please. I'll be out in a few minutes.

CIDRA: I told you so, *Apo*. She's been expecting us since this morning.

ALBULARIO *(straining)*: Heh, Moning? Moning? I thought you said this is Sima's house?

CIDRA *(shouting)*: Not Moning, m-o-r-n-i-n-g, mor-ni-iinng. She's been waiting since this morning.

ALBULARIO: Oh, well, that's good.

SIMA: Oh, please sit down. I'm sorry to take so long. In my condition, it is harder to get up in the morning, my feet go numb all the time.

ALBULARIO: Lime? Did she say lime? I have some in my pouch here for chewing. Aren't you a bit too young to indulge. . .? But you can have some, I don't care.

CIDRA *(gesturing)*: His hearing is bad but he's the best albulario in town.

SIMA: I know. *(Aloud to the Albulario.)* I'm due a few months from now, so I asked you to come, *Apo*.

ALBULARIO: I know. You have not asked me but let me tell you— I've brought into this world no less than five hundred, *five hundred,* babies. You have but three more months to go, more or less.

SIMA: Time of the harvest. That will be a good time. Juan can stay home for the day.

ALBULARIO: Huh? In what way? (SIMA *tries to correct him but the old man has turned away.)* Oh, yes, there are two ways. One is by the shape of the womb. If it is a little plateau, sort of roundish on the sides and a wee, mind you, just a wee bit flat on the top, it's a girl. They take up, the girls I mean, more room, you know. If it's a sharp incline, a hard little peak on the top, it's a boy. The hardier of the human race are positioned in a peculiar spartan knot. Now, the second way is by the mother's face. If it is a madonna's, a face full of grief, *dolorosa,* then it's going to be a boy, they bring suffering. A happy, jubilant face such as yours means a girl, they bring joy to this world. With twins, merely add, you know, the womb is bigger. . . . Yes, yes, it never fails. You're going to have a girl.

SIMA *(loudly)*: Would you like to examine me in the room, *Apo?*

ALBULARIO: No, Ineng, just sit here. All I want to feel is if the child is in position.

SIMA: I've always wanted a girl.

CIDRA: Oh, but boys are always fun—all those muscles, ummh. *(Somewhat embarrassed.)* What I mean is they can do so much work. And don't forget, you lose a daughter when she marries but through a son, you gain a daughter-in-law.

ALBULARIO: Heh, heh, low? (CIDRA *tries to explain but the man does not listen.)* Hah, low! What do you know about these things. *(*CIDRA *gives up.)* Nah, it's just the height for her time. After nine months, you'll see how they settle in the womb, all ready to burst forth, squealing in protest and thrashing about and pink, pink like a new-born piglet. For did he ask to be born anyway? When it's been so comfortable, warm, enclosed, moist, safe, secure, sanitary, soft, silent where he was. I ask you, why come out at all?

CIDRA *(to Sima): Apo* has some very funny ideas. He thinks a lot.

ALBULARIO: And hot. Yes, why come out in this heat? You're in fine shape, Ineng.

SIMA: I'm glad. Would you care for a drink, *Apo? (She remembers she must speak louder to be heard.)* Would you care for a drink, *Apo?* I've prepared these for you.

ALBULARIO: Oh yes, Ineng. It's been a long hot walk.

CIDRA: Delicious rice cakes.

SIMA: Yes, have some more. Here.

CIDRA: This is plenty enough. Thank you.

SIMA: There's plenty. Here let me wrap up the rest for you.

CIDRA: Don't bother, please.

SIMA: It's no bother. I insist. *(She gives each of them a wrapped portion of rice cakes; they thank her.)*

ALBULARIO: Now remember to call me as soon as you feel it coming.

SIMA *(loudly):* How will I know that it's really time, *Apo?*

ALBULARIO: It will come like sea waves. Up and down. Up and down. Up and down. Just breathe with it, mind you, with, not against, do you understand?

SIMA: With, not against.

ALBULARIO: Never, never against, otherwise the pain will break all over you like a shattered crest. Never against, remember that.

SIMA: I'll remember, I mean, *(loudly)* I'll remember, *Apo*.

CIDRA *(gesturing)*: He really knows his business.

ALBULARIO *(at the door)*: Ines? Oh yes, tell Ines, my wife, if I'm not home. And lastly, Ineng, remember you are a container, a big earthen jar. Be strong, walk softly, be steady. Until at last it is time to split the jar.

(Lights fade.)

CURTAIN

SCENE TWO

Town's meeting place. It is early evening. At rise, JUAN *enters with Arsenio, Pedro and some other townspeople. Some are carrying torches, they spill all over the place, a few positioning themselves on the ramp.*

JUAN: But it's out of the question. You know I can't do it.

ARSENIO: We know you, Juan. You can do it.

JUAN: Why me? There are so many more powerful men.

PEDRO: They are not one of us. But you are. We will never forget how you stood up and spoke for Arsenio when no one would dare to face Don Mundo.

ARSENIO: You saved me from being thrown into prison for a crime I did not commit. Yes, Juan, you go up there and we will all go up with you.

PEDRO: You will be our eyes.

ARSENIO: Our voice.

JUAN: No, I can't consider the idea now. It's impossible.

ARSENIO: Nothing's impossible when you have the workers behind you. Right, *mga kasama?*

PEOPLE *(starting to lend their pressure)*: Yes, yes, nothing's impossible. Nothing, nothing, nothing... *(On and softly under.)*

PEDRO: Yes, nothing's impossible when you have the workers behind you. *Kasama kami!*

PEOPLE: *Kasama! Kasama! Kasama! Kasama!... (On and softly under.)*

JUAN: No, No! We have to be stronger than that!

ARSENIO: Stronger? We are the rocks that hold mountains up.

PEDRO: Our sinews are iron! Our hearts, lumps of lead! Why, if we move as one, the ground will tremble!

PEOPLE (*stop chanting "Kasama" to take up the next phrase*): Move as one! Move as one! Move as one!... *(On and softly under.)*

JUAN: Elections are serious business. Listen to me! I've seen so many fail because all they had was sheer numbers. I have had no education, as you all know.

PEDRO: A diploma is just a sheet of paper.

PEOPLE: Paper, paper, paper... *(On and softly under.)*

JUAN: And no name.

ARSENIO: We will repeat your name until there is nothing in our mouths but the sound of it.

PEOPLE: Juan! Juan! Juan... *(On and softly under.)*

JUAN: And no money!

PEDRO: We will gather eggs from the nests, get grains from our bodegas, pull off the very clothing from our backs....

ARSENIO: We will be poor for you.

PEOPLE: Poor, poor, poor, poor... *(On and softly under.)*

JUAN: No! No! I shall have no one impoverished on my account!

(Voices stop abruptly.)

ARSENIO: Impoverished? *(Laughingly, to the people.)* IMPOVERISHED! What a word! *(Pauses, drops his voice almost to a whisper.)* What we are asking for is—HOPE!

PEOPLE: Hope. Hope. Hope.... *(On and softly under. JUAN is silent.)*

PEDRO: Look, Juan, what we are asking for is what a tree seeks from the sky, what it sucks from the earth.

ARSENIO: As sea to the fishes.

PEDRO: Sky to the birds.

ARSENIO: Forest to the beasts.

PEDRO: EXISTENCE!

ARSENIO: LIFE!

PEOPLE: Life. Life. Life.... *(On and softly under.)*

PEDRO: You will give it to us, Juan.

ARSENIO: You must give it to us, Juan.

JUAN: Look, when I came to this meeting... all the way to this place, you talked of nothing but my candidacy, but I must ask you....

PEDRO: You are our only salvation.

PEOPLE: Salvation. Salvation. Salvation.... *(On and softly under.)*

ARSENIO: Our only hope!

PEOPLE: Hope. Hope. Hope.... *(On and softly under.)*

JUAN *(feeling himself trapped)*: My friends, I beg you to remember... beg you to reconsider... but you know my position from the beginning....

PEDRO: Our life!

PEOPLE: Life. Life. Life.... *(On and softly under.)*

JUAN: *Mga kasama,* I implore you, try to see the problems....

ARSENIO: Our brother! *Kapatid!*

PEOPLE: *Kapatid! Kapatid! Kapatid!...* *(On and softly under.)*

JUAN *(pleading now)*: Try to understand me, see my position.... You who are my childhood companions, my friends....

PEDRO: Our APO!

PEOPLE: *Apo. Apo. Apo...* *(On and softly under.)*

JUAN *(faltering, about to give up)*: My people, I...

PEDRO *(knows they have won)*: OUR LEADER!

PEOPLE (*softly, gradually growing louder*): Leader! Leader! LEADER! LEADER! LEADER!

(They wave their torches and continue chanting as the lights fade.)

CURTAIN

SCENE THREE

Juan's home. It is late evening. At rise, SIMA *is seated, busy sewing some baby clothes. She holds them up against the light, singing a lullaby as she does.* JUAN *enters. He kisses his wife.*

SIMA: The *Apo* was here, Juan. I asked him to come.

JUAN: Oh! And is everything all right?

SIMA: Yes, he said the child is due in three months, more or less.

JUAN: Three months.

SIMA: He said the pain will come like the sea waves and I'll know when it's time.

JUAN: Three months. Time of the harvest. A good time.

SIMA: I fear the pain.

JUAN: Three months. I will be home for the day. The harvest will be over by then.

SIMA: He said I must try to breathe with it, not against it and yet... I'm frightened, Juan!

JUAN (*he goes to her*): You must not be frightened. I'll hold your hand and the pain will pass on from you to me.

SIMA: Do you know what he said?

JUAN: No, tell me.

SIMA: He said... he said it will be... a girl!

JUAN (*he lifts and swings her around*): A girl! My girl will give me a girl! Scent of papaya blossoms in my house! A girl!

SIMA: Oh, put me down, Juan. Uuh, that made me dizzy.

JUAN: Careful, now, *Nanay*.

SIMA: I'm all right. *(Picks up her sewing.)* You know, I didn't realize that one so small could need so many things.

JUAN: Well look at this! Aren't the sleeves a bit too tiny?

SIMA: Oh, you. She'll probably wear this until she's ready to walk.

JUAN: Well, I suppose they come in one size. And those, will she use up all that?

SIMA: Cidra said three dozens, that's only two.

JUAN: All right, now what am I supposed to do? I mean, what can I do? Remember I was partly responsible too!

SIMA *(laughingly)*: You wait like all proper fathers do—patiently.

JUAN: Well, I can't just sit around, let you do all the work. Of course, I'll build her a crib. Yes, that's it, a crib.

SIMA: Good idea. Make it a cradle, Juan. *Nanay* said that babies reared in cradles turn out to be well-mannered children.

JUAN: A cradle it is. *(He sits by her and holds her close.)* Happy?

SIMA: I'm happy we met.

JUAN: Yes, just think. . .if we didn't.

SIMA: Oh, but we had to meet.

JUAN: I watched you from a distance, under that old ipil tree where the road turns to the river. I watched weeks, months, I think. Then one day, you walked by, so close, I said, good morning. You looked at me, frightened, shy, your eyes.

SIMA: You looked at me so hard, I was frightened.

JUAN: Frightened?

SIMA: I think. . .I sensed. . .I felt. . .how is a girl to know about these things?

(Flashback. MAN and WOMAN meet on the ramp. They act out this scene pantomimically, their movements dancelike and slow. Very much like a silent movie flickering in bluish light against a screen. JUAN and SIMA remain in their seats, their eyes riveted to a certain point above the audience as though the pantomime was being played out front. They speak the lines.)

JUAN: May I help carry your wash, *Ading?*

SIMA: I have a strong head, *Manong,* and used to carrying my wash.

JUAN: At least let me lift it up for you? *(WOMAN nods and the MAN lifts the tub of wash and balances it on the Woman's head.)*

SIMA: Thank you, *Manong.*

JUAN: My name is Juan. You are Sima, daughter of the blacksmith, *Mang* Justo?

SIMA: Yes, I am. *(WOMAN starts to go.)*

JUAN: I know you. *(MAN falls into step with WOMAN. JUAN gets up from his seat and calls after her.)* I've been watching you everyday. My father is a farmer. I am...I am a farmer, too.

(WOMAN continues to walk. MAN follows.)

JUAN: We work the farm, the big hacienda across the river.

(WOMAN continues to walk. MAN follows.)

JUAN: I felt, well...I just had to talk to you. You are not angry, I hope?

(WOMAN continues to walk. MAN follows.)

JUAN: Well, may I come again tomorrow?

(WOMAN stops. MAN waits.)

JUAN: I will not talk if you don't want me to. And if you say so, I will stay under that tree, that distance away.

(WOMAN does not say anything.)

JUAN: Well, may I come?

SIMA: It is not for me to say what you can and cannot do. *(WOMAN smiles at man and walks away. MAN waits until WOMAN is gone, then jumps and shouts with joy.)*

JUAN *(goes back to Sima)*: Sima?

SIMA *(resumes her sewing)*: Yes?

JUAN: We had *that* meeting.

SIMA: Yes?

JUAN: Something important turned up.

SIMA: Yes?

JUAN: They want me to run.

SIMA: Yes?

JUAN: Is that all you can say, Yes? Look, did you hear what I just said, they asked me to run.

SIMA: And you accepted.

JUAN: Yes.

SIMA: I see.

JUAN: They were very persuasive.

SIMA: I see.

JUAN: They pleaded. They begged.

SIMA: I see.

JUAN *(turns away angrily)*: Don't *I see* me! The whole town practically outshouted me!

SIMA: You know best, Juan.

JUAN: In other words, you disapprove?

SIMA: You know I always go by your decisions, Juan. Only. . . .

JUAN: Well, only. . .what?

SIMA: Juan, you know. . .politics. . .well, we're not rich.

JUAN: Don't I know that! But they need me, Sima.

SIMA: Then, they will stand by us.

JUAN: They'll stand by us. It's about time we unite. Yes, about time we work together. They promised. . . .

(Lights fade out as they reach out to each other.)

CURTAIN

ACT II

SCENE ONE

(Projection of superimposed slides and newsreel bits of what is apparently a hectic and noisy political campaign of two grinning, fist-shaking candidates. Crowds cheering. Buntings and banners waving. Sounds of bands and fireworks. Slowly the images and glare fade.)

Juan's home. It is early afternoon, one month later. At rise, JUAN *is seen going to the door to see who is knocking. It is* DON MUNDO *and his bodyguard.* JUAN *invites them in.*

JUAN: We are honored by this visit, Don Mundo.

DON MUNDO: Heh, oh, this visit. *(He has some kind of nervous laugh.)* Yes, heh, this visit. Well, I was around the neighborhood so I told Askad here, my bodyguard, say hello to *Mang* Juan there, Askad.

ASKAD: Good afternoon, *Mang* Juan.

JUAN: Good afternoon, please be seated.

DON MUNDO: Thank you. Heh, as I was saying. I told Askad here, well if that isn't Mang Juan's house. Heh, Askad, I said to him, let's drop in for a visit heh, a short five, ten minute visit. After all, we're both candidates for the same position.

JUAN: So we are.

DON MUNDO: It's all a friendly fight, heh, you fight clean. Heh, I fight clean.

JUAN: We do not know of any other way to fight.

DON MUNDO: Heh, did you hear that, Askad? That's the kind of talk I like to hear, heh, heh. Heh, listen and you learn something.

ASKAD: Sure, Boss.

*(*SIMA *comes in with a tray.)*

JUAN: I think my wife would like you to have some tea. She prepared some rice cakes too.

*(*SIMA *goes about quietly serving the guests.)*

DON MUNDO: Well, Sima, heh, what do you think about being the wife of a politico?

SIMA: I try not to think about it, Don Mundo.

DON MUNDO: You have a lovely wife, *Mang* Juan. Her father used to work for us. She was the prettiest girl around. Heh, heh, don't think I didn't notice. She'll look good in the municipio for a change, heh.

JUAN: The elections are a long way off, Don Mundo, and we do not presume victory until we see the results.

DON MUNDO: A very practical attitude. Heh, did you hear, Askad, do not presume. Do not presume, heh, heh. So many things can happen.

(SIMA exits.)

ASKAD: Sure, Boss.

JUAN: You still have not told me why you came.

DON MUNDO: Oh but I did, heh, heh. I was around your neighborhood. . . .

JUAN: I should be the last person you would like to see in this neighborhood.

DON MUNDO: Heh, heh, now that's not true. There might be some things we disagree about on the platform, heh, but you're a neighbor and I hope a friend, heh, heh.

JUAN: I can only speak in the simple manner we have grown to know. I think you've come to ask me to stop attacking you and your record as a public official.

DON MUNDO: Ask you to stop? I am a government official, heh, and therefore, therefore must protect that right. Heh, heh you keep on saying what you please, I know ways to protect my reputation.

JUAN: I'm glad to know that you have ways to protect your reputation. You'll need them these coming months.

DON MUNDO: But you're right, heh. I came here for a reason.

JUAN: Well?

DON MUNDO: Heh, it's something very important.

JUAN: If it is, I'll call my wife. . . . I'm sure she would like to hear it.

DON MUNDO: No, heh, this is between you and me. Wait for me, heh, downstairs, Askad.

(ASKAD exits.)

JUAN: I cannot see what is important for both of us that must be said in secret but go ahead, I'm listening.

DON MUNDO: Your wife is about to have a child. Your first, heh?

JUAN: You know very well it is.

DON MUNDO: All right, all right. What I'm getting at is, things being the way they are. What I mean is it's getting to be very expensive just managing to stay alive these days, heh?

JUAN: Well?

DON MUNDO: Look, elections cost money, heh. I know how low in funds....

JUAN: We're doing just fine.

DON MUNDO: Heh, not that it's any business of mine....

JUAN *(emphatically)*: It isn't.

DON MUNDO: What I'm driving at...heh...let's face it, Juan, you're a poor man and your wife is going to have a baby. Heh, so many more months to go before the actual voting.

JUAN: Well?

DON MUNDO: You know that I have money to spend even if these elections were to run, heh, for years.

JUAN: So you've come to offer a proposition.

DON MUNDO: Heh, heh, it's simple....I can deposit a certain amount of money, heh, in your name, or if you choose, your wife's....

JUAN: I think I know what you mean, Don Mundo.

DON MUNDO: No, let me finish. Heh, I can deposit a certain amount, a big amount, mind you, heh....

JUAN: In my name or my wife's.

DON MUNDO: In your name or your wife's, heh....

JUAN: If I pull out.

DON MUNDO: If you pull out. *(Pauses, then lamely, almost apologetically.)* I could have put it differently.

JUAN: But it all boils down to that, doesn't it?

DON MUNDO: All right, heh, your answer?

JUAN *(evenly)*: I think you better leave.

DON MUNDO: Wouldn't you like to know how much?

JUAN: I'm not interested.

DON MUNDO: But you must be, ₱100,000 is a lot of money.

(JUAN is silent.)

DON MUNDO: Think on it, heh?

JUAN: There's nothing to think about.

DON MUNDO: Oh yes, there is, heh. After all, friend, it might be the most important decision you'll make in your life.

JUAN: I think you better leave, Don Mundo....

DON MUNDO: You know where to find me.

JUAN: Don't wait for me.

DON MUNDO: A check for ₱100,000 will be waiting for you.

JUAN: You and your check can wait in hell!

(Lights fade.)

CURTAIN

SCENE TWO

The Albulario's home. It is morning, the following day. At rise, the ALBULARIO is busy stirring some potion in a pot. CIDRA is seated in front of him, fanning herself vigorously.

CIDRA: Me? I don't have any problems.

ALBULARIO: Huh, emblems? Oh, emblems. The Katipuneros are old but their emblems, *Ineng*, are kept in the moo-seh-oms.

CIDRA: I said *(shouting)* I don't have any problems. Prob-le-eeems! I came here for *Aling* Sima. She's been having pains but she still has two months to go.

ALBULARIO: *Lintik!* Even corpses have problems, *Ineng*. (Stirs the potion.) There...inside the caverns of their tombs, they ask, how long before the worms get to us?

CIDRA: Well, of course, there's Tonio. He can't seem to make up his mind when to marry me.

ALBULARIO *(crushes some herbs and drops them into the pot)*: Sssh!

CIDRA: You do a lot of mixing, *Apo.*

ALBULARIO: Heh? Heh? *(Whispers over the pot.)*

CIDRA *(loudly)*: I said you do a lot of mixing. Mix-iiing. Not an appealing smell, if you ask me. *(Pinches her nose.)*

ALBULARIO: Mixing, ah yes! Chemistry is the secret of my trade—a lizard's tail, a 'roach's leg, silk squeezed from a spider's womb! These tiny herbs, hmmm, a twig of this, a root of that, a leaf of this, a sprig, a bud! Then a prayer breathed gently, sssh gently, ever gently over the steam. *(Close his eyes and spreads his arms ceremoniously.)*

CIDRA: *Santisima,* he's a magician.

ALBULARIO: Sssh, ssh, now whist, whist! Moon, whist, moon, I call you to hasten a ray into each bubble. Come skim, come glide over this magic mixture and fill each quivering dome with your image before they burst into liquid. Oaah come oooh moooon!

CIDRA: I don't like how he looks but I promised to fetch him. Let's hurry, *Apo.*

ALBULARIO *(his voice has grown strange, hoarse)*: Ala-ala AH! Bigha-bigha NI! Tupad-tupad DA! ZOOOM Bum BA! *(Shivers then covers his eyes quickly.)*

CIDRA: My mother told me that tides and madnesses rise with the moon. I shouldn't come here when the moon is full.

ALBULARIO *(tastes the mixture from a ladle, his face contorts, he falls twisting to the floor.)*: A-aaaaa. Ah Ah Hah!

CIDRA: *Susmaria,* he's dying! *Apo! Apo!*

ALBULARIO *(straightens up, smiling)*: *Lintik!* It's a success!

CIDRA: It is?

ALBULARIO: Success! Success! *(Resumes stirring the pot.)* Now, then, tell me the sickness—a baby who refuses to suck...or a baby who refuses to be weaned.... A boy with cramps...or loose joints.... A grandfather with ague...or a grandmother with rheumatism.... A husband who lacks ardor...or has too much....A woman who can't have a child...or a woman who can't stop.... A jilted lover... a philandering uncle....

CIDRA *(very impressed)*: All those diseases?

ALBULARIO: Yes, even *bursitis!* Who has it?

CIDRA: Oh, he's hopeless.

ALBULARIO: Did you say Don Lopes? But he didn't complain when I last visited him.

CIDRA *(gesturing)*: He should pour some into his ears.

ALBULARIO: Four years? Tsk, tsk, that's a long time to suffer. I'll go to him.

CIDRA *(aloud)*: Well, are you ready, *Apo?*

ALBULARIO: Yes, yes...in a minute...there are bottles here, some place...in the corner, I think. You should have some too, Cidra.

(Finds the bottles and starts pouring the mixture.)

CIDRA: *Susmaria,* no!

ALBULARIO: Yes, for Tonio. Come here and have a taste.

CIDRA *(shudders)*: No. Thank you, *Apo.*

ALBULARIO: Come on! Here! (CIDRA *obeys hesitantly)* Lick the spoon. (CIDRA *sticks out her tongue, a good distance away, her eyes closed.)* Well, what are you waiting for?

CIDRA: Please, *Apo,* I'm too young to die.

ALBULARIO: *Diyasking ire!* What are you saying! Come closer here. (CIDRA *obeys taking a few tiny steps.)* Closer! *(She hardly moves.)* Stick out your tongue! *(She obeys.)* This is very good for you. *(Goes to her and presses the ladle on her tongue.)* There!

CIDRA *(grimaces)*: Uuuuuh! My throat is burning! Aaaaah!

ALBULARIO: That's how you know when a medicine is good, *tonta!* The more they sear and snick the throat. The sweet, wishy-washy kind never heals. Now here's for Tonio, so he'll make up his mind. Pour some in his coffee, rub a whiff behind your ears and a spot on your bodice.

CIDRA: But, *Apo,* I want him alive.

ALBULARIO: Five? Five drops and he'll marry you on the spot.

CIDRA: Oh, what's the use. Come on, *Apo.*

ALBULARIO: Coming, coming.

CIDRA: I'm sure *Aling* Sima must be tired of waiting.

ALBULARIO *(to audience)*: Inting? Did she say Inting? I thought it was Tonio. These women! You can't trust them anymore!

(Lights fade.)

CURTAIN

SCENE THREE

(Projection of superimposed slides and newsreel bits of crowds and candidates; dominating are flashes of bigger and more enthusiastic crowds for Juan. Slowly the images and glare fade.)

Don Mundo's office. It is evening, several days later. At rise, DON MUNDO *is pacing the floor; he appears somewhat agitated.*

DON MUNDO: I told you to be very, very careful.

ASKAD: I was, Boss.

DON MUNDO: Heh, he did not see you?

ASKAD: He did not see me.

DON MUNDO: Not even your shadow?

ASKAD: Not even my shadow, I swear, Boss.

DON MUNDO *(still suspicious)*: He did not hear your voice, heh?

ASKAD: Not my voice.

DON MUNDO: We cannot be too careful. He cannot be corrupted, as you know. Heh, he has a special immunity, a special vaccination against all temptations.

ASKAD: He will prove to be a fish like all of us.

DON MUNDO: I tried to lure him. He had eluded, heh, all my traps.

ASKAD: There's always a spear to pierce the toughest hide.

DON MUNDO: What he has, heh, is an armor of scales.

ASKAD: Then we must find the hole in the armor, turn the fish over and you'll find its soft underside, a throbbing spot close to the gills, its life center, the source of its being.

DON MUNDO: I trust that's what you're doing, heh?

ASKAD: Yes, Boss.

DON MUNDO: And so?

ASKAD: Have you seen a fish washed ashore?

DON MUNDO: Yes?

ASKAD: A beached fish flapping its fins and tail is a sight to see. Without water, it is lost as you know, its sense of direction becomes faulty, it loses balance and crazed by the dryness it feels, it squirms, it flaps, it contorts, until at last it flips on its backside. Then the sun will do the job of drying its soft belly and scorching its guts.

DON MUNDO: Heh, heh, don't speak to me in riddles, Askad! There's that impending disaster in these elections. Heh, I feel it! I know it!

ASKAD: You must trust my plans. When did I ever fail you?

DON MUNDO: I do trust you, heh.

ASKAD: You will see results in a few weeks.

DON MUNDO: In a few weeks!

ASKAD: *Hinay-hinay,* Boss, the tentacles of this scheme will move out gradually, quietly, secretly....

DON MUNDO: *Puñeta,* words, words, heh. What I need is action.

ASKAD: Action, Boss, in a few weeks. *Konting pasensiya lamang.*

DON MUNDO: My hand will not show?

ASKAD: Not even a hair, not a shadow of a hair!

DON MUNDO: Askad.

ASKAD: Yes, Boss?

DON MUNDO: You're sure, heh, everything will be all right?

ASKAD: Everything.

DON MUNDO: Yes, heh, of course.

ASKAD: Well, I better go now, Boss. *(Turns to leave.)*

DON MUNDO: Heh, Askad?

ASKAD: Yes, Boss?

DON MUNDO *(makes a cutting gesture under his chin)*: None of that, heh?

ASKAD: Yes, Boss.

DON MUNDO: So long as that is clear.

ASKAD: Yes, Boss.

DON MUNDO: You know I can't stand the sight of blood, heh.

ASKAD: I know that, Boss.

DON MUNDO: So! Heh, everything is clear between us.

ASKAD: Everything, Boss.

DON MUNDO: It's best to spell things out, heh.

ASKAD: Sure, Boss.

DON MUNDO: So there won't be any misunderstanding later, heh, Askad?

ASKAD: Sure, Boss. Will that be all?

DON MUNDO: Yes, that will be all, heh.

ASKAD *(turns to go)*: I'll be back this evening.

DON MUNDO: Yes, keep me posted, heh, always?

ASKAD: I'll let you know everything that happens.

DON MUNDO: Oh yes, Askad, heh, tell me... what if the fish refuses to leave the water?

ASKAD: The fish, Boss?

DON MUNDO: You know, heh, the fish on the beach....

ASKAD: Oh yes, the fish. If the fish refuses to leave the water for the beach, we know what to do.

DON MUNDO: Well, tell me, heh.

ASKAD: The strategy, Boss, is very simple. We dam the water source, dry the lake. Hah, Boss, can you see it?

DON MUNDO: Go on, heh.

ASKAD: Then not only he but all the other fish will lie exposed on the dry bed. All of them, Boss, flapping and squirming on the dry bottom.

(ASKAD'S *laughter is almost hysterical and as* DON MUNDO *joins him laughing, the lights fade.)*

CURTAIN

ACT III

SCENE ONE

(*A montage of film strips and slides showing the campaign. Speech-making in full swing; Juan and Don Mundo and their alternate crowds. However, discordant music and slides for Juan. Meetings breaking up, people dispersing, etc.)*

Juan's campaign headquarters. It is afternoon, one month later. At rise, PEDRO, startled at the sound of someone approaching, leaves a paper bag on the desk and heads for the door.

PEDRO: Ha, *Ka* Juan, good evening. I thought you were not coming. Arsenio was here a while ago.

JUAN: Good evening, Pedro. He left without waiting for me?

PEDRO: He was in some kind of a hurry, he said.

JUAN: That's strange. Did he say when he's coming back?

PEDRO: He didn't say.

JUAN: But that's very unlike Arsenio.

PEDRO: Yes, very.

JUAN: We are going to talk about finances today. The elections can't wait. As our treasurer...he...did he say where he was going?

PEDRO: He didn't say, *Ka* Juan.

JUAN: Well, we can wait a while more. How about the others?

PEDRO: Here. (*Hands him some notes.*) Most of them asked to be excused.

JUAN *(reads the notes)*: But they don't say when they can come again for another meeting.

PEDRO: They didn't tell me anything, *Ka* Juan.

JUAN: What is this...some kind of a joke?

(PEDRO *is silent.*)

JUAN: Well, is this some kind of a joke? A conspiracy? Tell me, Pedro.

PEDRO: Just a coincidence, maybe.

JUAN: That everyone is suddenly taken ill on this one particular day?

PEDRO: I don't know, *Ka* Juan.

JUAN: On the very day of an important meeting...everyone sick! There must be some kind of illness that's catching. A plague? An epidemic? Well?

PEDRO: I don't know, *Ka* Juan.

JUAN: Speak up and tell me, Pedro. *Tell me!*

PEDRO: I can't, *Ka* Juan.

JUAN: *You can't?* But why not?

PEDRO: Because....

JUAN: Because...what?

PEDRO: I gave my word.

JUAN *(quietly)*: Gave what word? What word?

PEDRO: I told you already...I promised...isn't that enough?

JUAN: No, that's not enough. Look, let me get to the bottom of this. You were about to leave when I got here.

PEDRO: No, no, I was waiting for you, *Ka* Juan.

JUAN *(approaches him)*: No, you were not.

PEDRO *(retreats)*: But I was, believe me, *Ka* Juan.

JUAN: You were about to.... *(Continues to approach him.)*

(PEDRO *snatches the paper bag from the desk and heads for the door.)*

JUAN *(grabs him)*: Nobody is going anywhere. (PEDRO *tries to struggle, flailing his arms.* JUAN *hits him and knocks him down on the floor. He drops the paper bag and money is spilled on the floor.)* Well, what is this?

PEDRO: Please, *Ka* Juan, I can explain everything.

JUAN: You better. *Well,* Pedro?

PEDRO: I was asked...to...to deposit the money in the bank. Last night...there were prowlers, you see and....

JUAN: So you've been chosen as our safekeeper?

PEDRO *(eagerly)*: Yes, yes.

JUAN: So you're going to the bank with our money.

PEDRO: Yes, *Ka* Juan.

JUAN: So you're going to the bank with our money...*in a paper bag.*

PEDRO *(backing up)*: You must believe me, *Ka* Juan.

JUAN *(evenly)*: That's the people's money you're stepping on, Pedro. Get down on your knees and pick them up, one by one.

PEDRO *(kneeling to pick the bills)*: You can ask them, please, *Ka* Juan. They will tell you the same story.

JUAN *(unlocks the desk drawers)*: Did you clear out the desk? There should be more money than that. *(Slams them shut.)* DEMONYO! EMPTY! EMPTY! EMPTY! (PEDRO *turns to go.*) You stay where you are. *Putang ina,* Pedro, how long have you been stealing from us? *(Shakes him by the collar.)* FOR HOW LONG?

PEDRO: I took only...what's...what's left. Please, *Ka* Juan, you're hurting me!

JUAN *(tightens his hold)*: What do you mean, "Only what's left"?

PEDRO: The rest of the money's gone.

JUAN: Gone? *(Pushes him away.)* Gone! Who took the money?

PEDRO *(crying)*: I don't know, *Ka* Juan. My family is hungry. They told me the campaign is dying. After what's being whispered in town, it's everyone for himself.

JUAN: *Being whispered in town?* Everyone keeps quiet when I appear. *(Fiercely.)* What's being whispered, tell me, Pedro or I swear....

PEDRO: Please, *Ka* Juan. I'll tell. Arsenio...the others...they said Don Mundo has deposited an amount of money, big...big money... in your name...so....

JUAN: So I'll withdraw from the elections. Do you believe that lie? *Do you? Well, do you?*

PEDRO: No, no, not to withdraw....

JUAN: Not to withdraw...what do you mean?

PEDRO: Please *Ka* Juan, let me go. Here's all the money. I beg your forgiveness. Just let me go.

JUAN: You are not going anywhere until you tell me.

PEDRO: Please, *Ka* Juan, here's the money. Things are better left unsaid...we understand...something beyond your control...no hard feelings...among us....

JUAN: What's all this nonsense? *(Grabs him by the arm.)* You are going to spare nothing or I'll kill you!

PEDRO: *Ka* Juan...*Ka* Juan...We...we...heard the money is for....

JUAN: Yes, yes?

PEDRO: For...to keep you...uh...quiet...about...about...

JUAN *(sharply)*: Quiet about what?

PEDRO: Quiet about..about...Don Mundo's child.

JUAN: Don Mundo's child? What Don Mundo's child?

PEDRO: The one...the one...your wife carries.

JUAN *(in a shocked voice)*: THE ONE MY WIFE CARRIES! *(Flings him away.)* My God! Oh, my God!

(Lights fade.)

CURTAIN

SCENE TWO

The town's speak-easy. It is the same afternoon, a few hours later. At rise, as JUAN *approaches, a few of the townsfolk turn their backs on his greetings. A few walk away, ignoring him completely.* JUAN *is puzzled but he goes on to order his drink.*

TOWNSFOLK 1: The usual, *Ka* Juan?

JUAN: No, *doble, Mang* Ambo. *Marka Demonyo.*

TOWNSFOLK 1: *Walang biro ito. (Pours drinks.)* What are you celebrating?

TOWNSFOLK 2: Yes, tell, so we can join you, *Ka* Juan.

TOWNSFOLK 3: Yes, not much fun celebrating alone. We're all here to drink with you. *Mang* Ambo, bring out your best wine.

JUAN *(gulps down drink)*: So you'll all join me in one big celebration?

TOWNSFOLK 3: If you tell us what it is all about.

TOWNSFOLK 2: Some more glasses here. And the strongest *lambanog!*

TOWNSFOLK 3: Yes, yes, after all, it isn't everyday that our Mister Candidato honors us with his presence.

JUAN: Another *doble.* Same.

TOWNSFOLK 2: Well, we're waiting.

JUAN: So I see. All very eager.

TOWNSFOLK 3: All very eager....

JUAN: All very interested.

TOWNSFOLK 3: All very interested....

JUAN *(gulps down drink)*: If you must know...you are all welcome in celebrating it...understand...I'm celebrating my deathday.

TOWNSFOLK 1 *(crossing himself)*: *Susmariahusep!* You don't joke about such things.

JUAN: Why not? We celebrate birthdays, why not deathdays?

TOWNSFOLK 1: It's no laughing matter.

TOWNSFOLK 2: You don't joke about death.

JUAN *(slowly, perhaps a little tipsy now)*: I'll-joke-about-anything-when-it-pleases-me-to-joke-about-anything-which-pleases-me-to. Understand? ANOTHER DOBLE HERE! *(He grabs the bottle and pours drink.)*

TOWNSFOLK 3: Nah! Nothing's sacred anymore....

TOWNSFOLK 1: To some people....

TOWNSFOLK 2: I'll say....

TOWNSFOLK 1: Everything's a big joke....

TOWNSFOLK 3: Nothing really matters anymore....

TOWNSFOLK 1: Not their country....

TOWNSFOLK 2: Nor their town....

TOWNSFOLK 3: Nor their homes....

TOWNSFOLK 2: Nor their wives....

JUAN (slowly): Just now, what did you say?

TOWNSFOLK 2: What?

JUAN (slowly): Just now, what did you say?

TOWNSFOLK 2 (evenly): Nor their wives!

JUAN: What do you mean by that?

TOWNSFOLK 2 (evenly): You know very well *what* we mean, Mister Candidato.

(The others laugh.)

JUAN: Why, you! *(Lunges at* TOWNSFOLK 2 *but is held back. He tries to free himself.)* SINUNGALING! BAYAAN NINYO AKO!

(While JUAN *is being dragged away,* TOWNSFOLK 2 *shakes a fist at him. The others regroup, singing and drinking as the lights fade.)*

CURTAIN

SCENE THREE

Juan's home. It is the same day, early evening. At rise, the ALBULARIO is pounding some leaves while CIDRA is preparing some hot drink.

JUAN (rushes into the room): Where's she?

CIDRA: Juan!

JUAN: Well, where is she? *(Close to Cidra's face.)* My God-fearing, my innocent little wife?

CIDRA: Juan, you're drunk!

JUAN *(swaying)*: I'm never more sober in my whole, entire and in-in-incredible life! Now, show me where my wife is or you get the whole, the entire and the in-in-incredible back of my hand. Understand?

CIDRA: *Apo* is with her. *(Tries to stop him.)* No, Juan, she's not well. Your wife is a very, very sick woman...so much blood she lost... we tried to look for you...everywhere....

JUAN: So the *Apo* is with her.

CIDRA: I don't know what you mean.

JUAN *(mimicking)*: "I don't know what you mean." Well, he's a man, isn't he? In other words, he's the possessor *(Gesturing.)* of a little something....

CIDRA: *Susmariahusep!*

JUAN: And my dear wife is a woman...why she is...is that clear enough to you or do you want me to draw you a picture?

CIDRA: I will not stay here a minute longer except your wife is too sick to be left alone, you fool!

JUAN *(makes as if to strike her)*: Nah! *(He goes into the bedroom, sees his wife in bed and seems momentarily stunned by the sight.)*

ALBULARIO *(touches his arm)*: Your wife is very sick, Juan.

JUAN: Leave us alone.

ALBULARIO: She must have all the rest she can get.

JUAN *(shouting)*: Leave us alone.

(The ALBULARIO exits.)

SIMA: Juan? Is that you?

JUAN *(walks to her bed)*: Yes.

SIMA: There's nothing to worry about. *Apo* wants me to rest, that's all.

JUAN: Yes, yes, rest.

SIMA: The pains started again this morning so I asked Cidra to call the *Apo*. You remember how it was last month...when we called the *Apo*.

JUAN: Yes, I remember.

SIMA: I had the chills, then the bleeding stopped. My legs are numb but all the pain's gone.

JUAN: I saw a good friend of yours today.

SIMA: A good friend?

JUAN: Yes, and this good friend said that Don Mundo sends a message of love and goodwill specially to you.

SIMA: Juan...I....

JUAN: This friend said that Don Mundo said, my love and goodwill to your lovely and goodwilled wife.

SIMA: Juan? Is something wrong, Juan? Is anything wrong, Juan?

JUAN *(ignoring her questions)*: Hah! Now, that's something coming from the richest man in town. Do you know that richest men in towns generally don't have time to send messages of love and goodwill... except...except...to women who are themselves...you see...love-ly and goodwill-ed!

SIMA: Juan, you're...you've been drinking!

JUAN: Hah! My love-ly and goodwill-ed wife, I've been drinking!

SIMA: Juan!

JUAN: Yes...I've been drinking...and walking...and thinking. And do you know...today what I experienced is the liberation of the spirit. My spirit, woman, was gagged...hogtied...nailed down...and so now...we both broke loose...swiftly and simultaneously...my spirit and me!

SIMA: Juan, listen to me, please!

JUAN *(turns away)*: Funny thing...about the spirit...once it is liberated. It tells a man many wild stories...it taunts...it tempts... it pricks...it goads...it mocks! Oh, how it rides a man! Through forests and fields...and deserts and caves...through water...through air...through fire...through ice! As I am now driven! *(He falls on his knees.)* Oh, my little wife.

SIMA *(half-rises to embrace him; he rests his head on her as if exhausted)*: My poor husband, I cannot understand half of what you said.

JUAN *(pulls himself away)*: All those who take must...in the end... pay!

SIMA: What are you saying? Oh, what are you talking about?

JUAN: The debt! The debt must be paid...then everything will level off...the waters will be stilled...the air quiet again...and this mad ride...will end!

SIMA: Ssssh, Juan, rest, my husband. I promise to tell you all you want to know though I have no secrets hidden from you.

JUAN *(turns to go)*: No, I must go...there's nothing to talk about... nothing here...nothing to hope for.

SIMA: There's us...the child. That's everything.

JUAN: That's nothing! *(Wildly.)* Nothing, nothing nothing to me!

SIMA: Juan!

JUAN *(grabs her arm)*: Look, woman, as soon as he is born...just as soon as he is released from your whoring hole...give him to his rightful and almighty father!

SIMA: Have you gone mad? *Susmariahusep,* what are you saying!

JUAN *(evenly)*: And the richest man in this town, woman, the richest man will smile his nicest smile! Because...because...by then...he owns us all! All! Every goddamned man! Every goddamned woman!

SIMA: No, Juan, no!

JUAN: Every goddamned child!

(He runs to the door.)

SIMA *(runs after him)*: No, no, Juan! *(Holds on to him.)*

JUAN: Let go! Whore! *(He strikes her.)* *Puta!* *(Exits.)*

SIMA *(tries to get up)*: Juan!

CIDRA *(rushing in with the ALBULARIO)*: *Aling* Sima!

SIMA: Stop him! Ask my husband to come back!

(They help her back to bed. She is writhing in pain.)

(Lights fade.)

CURTAIN

SCENE FOUR

Don Mundo's house. It is the same day, late evening. At rise, the LADIES *are playing mahjong while the* GENTLEMEN *are holding a caucus and drinking in the adjacent room. For the moment, Don Mundo's office, stage right, is vacant.*

LADY 1: The way I see it, it won't last long. You know how he goes for the slender type.

LADY 2: All the munching she does in front of the TV. No wonder she's grown fat. Chocolate, candy bars, chicharon, peanuts...stuffs everything into her fat mouth. Yes, I think I'll get rid of...let me see...this? No, no, this. *(Throws down a tile.)*

GENTLEMAN 1: Yes, I think it will be best to go down the list. Take my own hometown, for instance.

LADY 3: Just what I need. *(Reaching out for the tile.)* Thanks, Clara. Well, the only exercise she gets is what she gets in bed. *(They laugh.)* And...and she's not getting much of that lately, considering how long he stays away campaigning.

GENTLEMAN 1: My men tell me that we'll get no more than 60 per cent of the votes there.

LADY 1: She should try one of those reducing saloons, the steam baths and the massager belt may be pure torture but you can see results.

GENTLEMAN 2: That's too narrow a margin. You must do something about it.

LADY 4: Yes, Alma, I can see you're back to size 10. Well now, looks like somebody is holding up the game here.

DON MUNDO: Look, we, heh, can't go on forever telling them what to do.

LADY 3: Namely you, Lilia. It's your turn.

LADY 4: Ay, *que lastima!* So sorry.

GENTLEMAN 2: We tell them while we still can. It's the most expedient way unless you have some other ideas.

LADY 4: Here we go. *(Throws down a tile.)*

GENTLEMAN 3: Don't make me laugh, Augusto...these are men who will do as they're told, don't give them any ideas about us reasoning with them.

GENTLEMAN 2: And it just might complicate things, you know.

LADY 2: Looks like we might be leaving for another trip. Narciso got word from his office. One of those survey trips.

GENTLEMAN 2: How about your ward?

LADY 3: Tell him to try for Brussels or London next time, Clara. PUNG! Finally got what I've been waiting for. Europe—that's where all the action is.

LADY 4: The in-thing is Peking...or didn't you know?

GENTLEMAN 3 *(reading from a notebook)*: Ninety per cent as usual although I look forward to the day when I can say 99 or even 100 per cent clean through, no dissension.

LADY 3: Well, Hong Kong's still a shopper's paradise but the water's brown as tea and Tokyo's smog can give you bronchitis. Well...what do you know...girls—MAHJONG! *(She collects bets, they turn the tiles over and begin mixing them up again.)*

GENTLEMAN 3: As our records show, we're spreading our good graces thicker and wider this year, so who knows, one of these days I'll surprise you all and report 100 per cent.

LADY 1: Are you getting all the dollars you need? New York can be exasperating when you don't have the dollars to spend, Clara. All those gorgeous shops on Fifth.

GENTLEMAN 2: And your ward?

DON MUNDO: Eighty-five per cent or less. It's hard to tell, heh, at this point.

GENTLEMAN 2: And why is that?

GENTLEMAN 3: Juan seems to be campaigning more forcefully and reaching more people, isn't he?

LADY 2: Well, the same bets. Here's mine.

(Others say "Mine" and bets are placed, etc.)

DON MUNDO: He's a born speaker. . .for one who never went beyond the high school.

LADY 2: Narciso's getting all the allowance he needs. . .the maximum per diem. . .you know. . .and I'm buying some dollars off the black market.

LADY 4: If you need more. . .I know a friend who has a friend who has a friend.

GENTLEMAN 3: Yeah, you can learn a few tricks from him, Mundo. If you ask me, you should go to one of his campaign talks instead of sending your men all the time.

LADY 2: At what rate?

LADY 4: ₱7 to $1 flat, I heard.

DON MUNDO: I know how to handle the man. Let me do it my way, heh.

GENTLEMAN 2: I hope you know what you're talking about because we have barely a month before election day.

LADY 3: Clara, get me. . .no, no I have enough tiles here, I think, *(Counting.)* get me one of those Lady Clairol Shampoo-In hair color, will you? Light brown.

DON MUNDO: We have exactly one month and twelve days. I know what I'm talking about and you'll see what I mean when election day comes.

LADY 4: I can use some of those Avon pink eye-shadow, just in case they happen to ring you in your hotelroom. You know, my daughter who was in college there say they ding-dong your doorbell and sing out, "AV-OON calling!"

LADY 2: It's Aaaa-VON CALL-iing! Lilia. *(Picks up a tile.)* Just what I need, thanks a lot. I saw the advertisement on TV in Frisco when we were there in '67.

GENTLEMAN 3: Well, that covers that. We'll take up the matter of expenses before we adjourn. I trust that everyone is adequately supplied?

(General agreement.)

LADY 3: Go to 42nd Street when you get to New York City, Clara, it's like going to Hamburg, Germany.

LADY 4: Sex and smut. Smut and sex. When will it end?

DON MUNDO: Here, Sancho, see that their glasses are always filled.

SANCHO: Yes, Sir, right away *po*. *(Goes around filling glasses.)*

LADY 3: Don't be so Victorian, Lilia, it's the new age of freedom. . . we're still in the middle ages here it seems.

GENTLEMAN 3: Well, next in our agenda *(Consulting his notebook.)* is this problem of rising demand for land ownership among the tenants.

(General murmurs.)

LADY 4: For my children's sake, I wish we'd remain in the middle ages. Too much license can corrupt, you know.

LADY 2: Too many restrictions can lead to tragic endings too. If you ask me the world is getting too crowded, less and less good food, less and less jobs. What we're getting plenty of are drugs, pollution and violence!

GENTLEMAN 1: It's amazing how they now have the nerve to even suggest it.

(General murmurs.)

LADY 4: Why, they say in America, they're so free, boys and girls stay in one dormitory. And according to my daughter, they kiss right on the streets while waiting for the traffic lights to change. *Que horror!*

LADY 3: Oh, to be young and in love! Or would you rather they're shooting each other down on street corners?

GENTLEMAN 3: I suggest you all consider what this confidential report says, gentlemen. *(Distributes folders.)* Direct from no less than the *Apo*.

LADY 4: Privacy, Perfecta, is the cardinal rule in love-making. My little terrier is more discreet. He waits for night time.

LADY 2: You're an incorrigible teacher, Lilia, how did you get him to learn such restraint?

(All laugh.)

LADY 4: You can laugh all of you but don't forget the senses must be held in check...it's like being in complete control of the horses or they fly off in different directions and split the carriage apart.

LADY 2 *(very amused)*: Split the carriage; Horses! Even your analogy, Lilia, belongs to an age long gone. *Panahon pa ni Methusalem!*

DON MUNDO *(reading)*: *Caramba!* This sounds serious, heh.

GENTLEMAN 1 *(reading)*: It's those communists again, I tell you.

GENTLEMAN 2 *(reading)*: Oh, come on, you've not even finished reading yet.

GENTLEMAN 1: Just the same, it's those communists, I tell you.

LADY 1: Just what I need. KANG! Looks like I smell some money coming to me. Itchy palms. Never fails.

GENTLEMAN 3: Well, gentlemen, it need not come if we can do something to stop the tide. The "seemingly inevitable tide" as this report says, quote, unquote.

GENTLEMAN 1: Like you build a dam....

GENTLEMAN 2: To re-direct power—right!

LADY 3: Wonder when I will win. Looks like it's only Lilia and Alma that the gods are smiling on.

LADY 2 *(throws down a tile)*: Oh, be patient, Perfecta.

GENTLEMAN 3: Well, the *Apo* asked us to put on our thinking caps, so to speak. Consider page 4, gentlemen.

LADY 1: MAHJONG! Didn't I tell you!

LADY 3: There she goes again. Here, you might as well take my purse too.

LADY 2: Oh, Perfecta, we didn't come to win anyway.

LADY 3: Awright, where's the goody foody then?

LADY 2: Oh Perfecta!

LADY 3: Well, might as well get something for coming.

LADY 1: I did ask the maids to prepare something for our *media noche*.

GENTLEMAN 3: Doesn't that look like your hacienda, Mundo?

DON MUNDO: *Caramba,* it is!

LADY 2: Something light, I hope. You remember how it was when Alma here had a whole *comida china* last time? I had heartburn and nightmares.

LADY 1: So let me check. *(Exits.)*

DON MUNDO: And this is your sugar plantation, I swear, heh. Sancho, here, fill the glasses.

(SANCHO goes around filling the glasses.)

LADY 3: What have you heard about Carmen lately?

LADY 4: The same stories but you can't believe them all.

LADY 2: I believe my unquestionable sources.

LADY 4: Meaning?

LADY 2: Meaning, they were within seeing and hearing distances.

LADY 3 *(archly):* Oh, do you have them on the payroll too?

(They laugh.)

LADY 2: *Santisima,* Perfecta, certainly not! But you know how Carmen, poor thing, gets around and tells everyone, absolutely anyone who'll listen.

LADY 4: That's what I mean...I think she's gone out of her mind ...spinning those awful, fantastic lies!

GENTLEMAN 2: A few more ice cubes would do it. Fine, thanks, Sancho.

GENTLEMAN 4: Do you still get your liquor at the U.S. base?

DON MUNDO: Yes, some. Most of those are gifts though.

LADY 2: *Santisima,* I must admit she leads quite a swinging life. When you can cut through as thick a swath of men as she has.

LADY 3: Let's face it, some women don't exactly go for stability of marriage like you and I, Lilia. They're forever children after the merry-go-round.

LADY 1 *(entering)*: Did I hear merry-go-round? Well, girls, here comes the goodies, ready or not.

(A MAID *follows, pushing a serving cart around, the women surround her. General exclamations and comments of appreciation.)*

DON MUNDO: Good thing we're beginning to accept that the problem exists. Some of us here seem to think that if we ignore the problem long enough, it will go away.

GENTLEMAN 3: *Caramba,* I hate insinuations.

DON MUNDO: I'm making a general statement...first, we must be aware that the problem exists.

LADY 1: Did I miss a lot? What's with the merry-go-round?

LADY 2 *(between bites)*: The subject, Alma, is poor Carmen.

GENTLEMAN 2: Next, we look for solutions. Suggestions, *pares,* ways to solve this growing threat.

LADY 1: Yes, the latest is Adolfo, have you heard?

LADY 4: But he has not started to shave yet!

DON MUNDO: It seems that the first step to take would be to make a list of all the tenants and consider their individual merits and length of service, heh, heh.

GENTLEMAN 2: Second. Second. Sounds all right to me for a first step. *(Lowers his voice.)* If what I do next is left entirely to me.

(General agreement.)

LADY 3: Poor Carmen is no poor Carmen at all.

LADY 4: But why?

LADY 3: She has, Lilia, what us decrepit old ladies no longer have —a lot of desire matched by a lot of stamina.

LADY 4: *Que terrible,* Perfecta...50-year-old woman with a 16-year-old boy. It's absolutely gross!

GENTLEMAN 4: If you ask me, bold new steps must be taken. A few strong-armed tactics here and there and we clear this threat in a hurry.

ASKAD *(enters and whispers something to* DON MUNDO*)*: He's waiting in your office, Sir.

DON MUNDO: Excuse me, gentlemen. Please take over, Augusto *(Goes off with Askad.)*

LADY 2: Here, I can't eat too many of these, can I? *(But she fills her plate.)*

LADY 1: Do you know what the men are discussing now? Land for the landless.

LADY 3: About time.

DON MUNDO *(entering his office)*: Well, Juan, heh, this is a pleasant surprise. Do sit down, heh, sit down.

LADY 2: What do you mean, about time?

LADY 3: I mean they deserve the titles to the land they've worked their hands to the bones these many hundred years.

DON MUNDO: It's time you came, Juan.

GENTLEMAN 3: Does anyone have the time?

JUAN: I want to talk to you alone.

GENTLEMAN 1: It's half an hour to midnight.

DON MUNDO: All right, heh, Askad, leave us alone. Nobody must disturb us, for any reason, understand?

ASKAD: Sure, Boss. *(Exits.)*

LADY 4: You know, Perfecta, the more I think about it, the more I'm convinced that as you grow older, you sound more and more like a communist.

DON MUNDO *(holding out a box)*: Have some cigars, Juan. Relax, heh.

LADY 4: You all know very well when the time comes and we can no longer control our properties the way we do now, there'll be chaos, absolute chaos!

LADY 3: Speak for yourself, Lilia, our tenants look perfectly capable to me.

GENTLEMAN 3: Well, next in the agenda is finances, I think, if we're all agreed on presenting our suggestion on making a list of all our tenants. In the meantime, you can be thinking of some other possible ways and means.

LADY 4: You can give away your lands, Perfecta. With all the money you've stashed away in Swiss banks, you don't need them.

DON MUNDO: How about a drink?

JUAN: No, thank you.

LADY 3: Money in Swiss banks! Where do you get your information —*Time* magazine?

DON MUNDO: You don't seem to be well.

LADY 1: Well, shall we go back to mahjong, ladies? Take your plates with you, there's enough room on the table.

(They all return to their seats.)

JUAN: Oh, I'm all right considering. . . .

DON MUNDO: You mean considering how we're beating you from all sides, heh?

JUAN: Meaning, how you're stabbing me from all sides.

DON MUNDO: Heh? Now, Juan, that's no way to talk. We're still friends and after this election and things start to settle down, I'll be the first to see that we do something for you.

JUAN: That's very magnanimous.

LADY 4: Mix them well, ladies.

GENTLEMAN 3: One thousand pesos sounds impressive enough to me, we're getting results, there's no need to change a good thing.

LADY 1: Get your tiles, everyone.

DON MUNDO: Shall I write out the check, heh, heh?

GENTLEMAN 1: Let us say, ₱1,000 is the base, you can go higher depending upon the circumstances.

GENTLEMAN 2: That may be but don't let on you'll go higher or they'll all abuse your generosity.

JUAN *(absent-mindedly)*: The check?

DON MUNDO: That's why you came, isn't it?

JUAN: Oh, yes, the check. That can mean a lot to my wife and the child, of course.

DON MUNDO *(expansively)*: Of course, heh, glad to help, glad to help. *(Opens his desk drawer to get his checkbook.)*

GENTLEMAN 1: Do we need to make an accounting for the ₱200,000 each of us got?

JUAN *(approaching Don Mundo)*: It's really very generous of you.

GENTLEMAN 3: Let's see what the records say.

LADY 4: Just what I need. *(Picks up a tile.)* KANG!

DON MUNDO: It's a small amount really. *(Hands the check to Juan.)*

JUAN *(looking at the check)*: It's the biggest I've ever seen.

GENTLEMAN 1: We can ask Mundo.

GENTLEMAN 3: No need, I'll find it here.

DON MUNDO *(smiling)*: Your wife will be happy, I'm sure.

JUAN *(smiling)*: She'll be delirious.

DON MUNDO: Heh, I knew you'll come to your senses. . . .

GENTLEMAN 3: Here, I said I'll find it—all we account for is. . . victory!

JUAN *(slowly)*: Why did you do it?

DON MUNDO *(lighting a cigar)*: Do what?

GENTLEMAN 3: Here pass it around.

LADY 3: Wonder how much longer it will take them to wind up things?

LADY 4: Who knows. . .these talks can last until morning.

LADY 1: Let's have some coffee then, strong coffee.
(The MAID goes around serving the ladies.)

JUAN: Why did you do it to my wife? My child?

DON MUNDO: I warned you, heh, from the very beginning, I warned you.

JUAN: All part of your smear campaign?

DON MUNDO: We move on a well-coordinated plan, my men and I....

GENTLEMAN 1: *Caramba,* this is the way to talk. No accounting! ₱200,000!

JUAN: To eliminate the opposition...to kill... to plunder! I never thought you can sink that low....

GENTLEMAN 2: Let's drink to this, everybody!

DON MUNDO: Don't be a child, Juan, I never lose an election as you know.

JUAN: So you spare no violence!

DON MUNDO: You, Juan, happened to stand in my way, heh, you don't expect me to welcome you...to embrace you....

GENTLEMEN *(raising their glasses)*: TO VICTORY!

JUAN: ANIMAL! *(He lunges at Don Mundo, stabbing him repeatedly on the chest.) Ulupong! Kamatayan, ahas!*

GENTLEMEN *(raising their glasses)*: TO VICTORY!

LADY 1: Did you hear a moan?

LADY 3 *(throwing down a tile)*: Must be my husband...when it comes to talk about giving up part of his wealth, he moans.

(They all laugh.)

(While JUAN escapes, the MEN continue their toasting and drinking and singing, the LADIES their mahjong game. The lights slowly fade.)

CURTAIN

SCENE FIVE

Juan's house. It is past midnight.

Townswomen are beginning to gather, some with lighted candles around the living room of Juan's home. Center lies SIMA, covered with a sheet. They surround her, starting their prayers for the dead.

JUAN *enters the house and sees what is happening. He runs to his wife, hesitates, uncovers her face and kisses her. Then he dashes to his room.*

270 : SEPANG LOCA AND OTHERS

While the women continue their prayers, JUAN *pulls a dark sweater over his head, momentarily, he stops, his shoulders shaking visibly, then he reaches for a gun, tucks it under his belt, puts on a straw hat and escapes from the house.*

While the women continue their prayers, there is a slow blackout until the lighted candles remain flickering on the scene. Then the sounds of clappers join the prayers while the curtains fall.

[END OF THE PLAY]

(1968-71) First published in paper back edition, Quezon City: University of the Philippines Press, 1971, 82 p. [out of print].

White Holocaust or A Pacific Playwright's Protest against the Bomb

White Holocaust or A Pacific Playwright's Protest Against The Bomb

(A PLAY IN ONE ACT)

CHARACTERS:
(In the order of appearance)

Character 1	Character 7
Character 2	Character 8
Character 3	Character 9
Character 4	Character 10
Character 5	Character 11
Character 6	

SCENES:

1 — Mammoth Projection of the Human Face, Center, on the Cyclorama.
2 — Projection of the Human Skull, same size, Left.
3 — Projection of the Human Face, Neural Network, same size, Right.
4 — Left and Right Projections Move to Center, fuse for a few seconds, then disintegrate.

The Characters are assembled in a triangular arrangement; they are wearing various colorful half-masks and when about to speak their lines, they move DS to face the audience. Behind them is a mammoth projection of the human face.

Music, consisting of bells, begin to play. Two Characters in workman's clothes walk gingerly, very much like clowns would on high wires, to the apron of the stage. The music stops.

CHARACTER 1: Just line up dat splice and I'm in business.

CHARACTER 2: OK, Boss. Now I got it.

CHARACTER 1: Yeah, but ya got it through my able assistance.

CHARACTER 3 *(steps forward)*: My only philosophy is it could be worse, you know?

CHARACTER 4 *(follows)*: Yeah, whatever you do, it's a problem.

CHARACTER 2: Right, Chief. I gotta give ya E for dat.

CHARACTER 1: How are ya comin' wid da white?

CHARACTER 2: 'Old your 'orses. Just a sec.

CHARACTER 1: I see only da red. Sure yar pullin' it right?

(They pause.)

CHARACTER 2: Whaddahells 'oldingit?

CHARACTER 3: Some parents ya'd think all they want would be to have children with their manners all arranged.

CHARACTER 4: Right—right you are.

CHARACTER 3: You know, they just want their children neat and clean.

CHARACTER 4: Yep, noses clean, bottoms dry.

CHARACTER 2: Ya got one of dem pulleys?

CHARACTER 1: Is it still going?

CHARACTER 2: Sure, it's still going. Wear your glasses in front of where yar eyes is. Da nose don't see.

CHARACTER 4: Neat and clean, how right you are.

CHARACTER 3: Well-mannered—it's the word she always uses. God, I only wish she'd see how her daughter talks. 'Cause her daughter doesn't. Her daughter's so well-mannered, she won't even talk!

CHARACTER 4: You don't say!

CHARACTER 5 *(steps forward, raises a lecturing finger)*: As you must remember, Weber says every choice implies rejection. Now take the very simple act of choosing which sandwich you want for lunch. When you pick a tuna, you have automatically rejected ham, egg, cheese, beef, pastrami, lettuce, etc., etc.

CHARACTER 6 *(steps forward, folds hands together, piously)*: At every heart, every human being has the infidelity of the Apostle Thomas hidden in some shadowy recesses where it whispers to itself, 'I'll not believe what I do not see or touch.' So says the Connecticut Yankee. How many amongst you today would believe me if I say the Lord is descended in our midst. That He is with us, watching our every move, witnessing all our infidelities, our corporate disloyalties, the treachery we perpetuate, the numerous lies, lies LIES!

CHARACTER 2: Three more feet to go.

CHARACTER 1: How many?

CHARACTER 2: Would ya believe, two?

CHARACTER 1: Well, let 'er go another good foot and a half.

CHARACTER 2: Foot and a half coming up.

CHARACTER 4: How right you are—but she's such an elegant person. Neat as a pin. Coiffured always and manicured always. Faultless, I tell you faultless.

CHARACTER 2: Plenty of it here.

CHARACTER 1: What's making it so tough then?

CHARACTER 2: Ya gotta pull 'arder. What's wrong wid ya, boy?

CHARACTER 3: Yeah, faultless, every strand of hair in place and her house—so neat, you feel like screaming. She goes around like this *(gesturing)* scrub, dust, sweep, dust, sweep. I saw her husband, you know what? He comes in, sits in a corner and covers his face with evening papers so he doesn't have to look at her.

CHARACTER 4 *(gasps exaggeratedly)*: Is that right?

CHARACTER 5 *(raises a lecturing finger, again)*: Kenneth Burke called poetry "Equipment for Living"—may we not then look upon its inevitability in our lives as much as good paintings on our walls and the well-made furniture and the well-made rugs in our rooms? Surely when the Greeks made drama and poetry part of their religion and tied these to nature like when an actor says look at that setting sun, the sun really, at that precise moment, is setting in the west and coloring all the actors on the stage with brilliant light. . . .

CHARACTER 1: Whadiysay?

CHARACTER 2: More, do ya want more?

CHARACTER 1: Nah! Let me try.

CHARACTER 6 *(crossing arms over chest)*: If we were to find what is hidden in our hearts, to bear our very souls to ourselves and start all over again. There is still time and God is willing. God is patient. He is waiting. He is waiting! Repent now, my dear brethrens.

CHARACTER 5 *(raises a lecturing finger again)*: And—and now look at this impressionistic painting, for example. Can you imagine looking at another picnic again without invoking in your mind's eye, the image of this afternoon, this quality of sunlight, this park, these people. Or can you look at another woman descending a stairway without thinking....

(His voice fades as he walks away.)

CHARACTER 3: Yep, how right you are. She's a lovely person, a lovely person. Faultless and all that. But let's face it—to have two daughters with broken marriages both!

CHARACTER 4 *(gasps exaggeratedly)*: Is that a fact! Two daughters!

CHARACTER 2: Put dat down right here and drop it.

CHARACTER 1: Look it can't even put dat one.

CHARACTER 2: Ya know I can't get the box in until I 'ave all the wires in. Dammit!

CHARACTER 7 *(steps forward and crosses stage apron)*: It's a wengo.

CHARACTER 8 *(runs after the child)*: You mean, a *mango,* dearest.

CHARACTER 7: But it looks like a wengo, Mommy. It don't look like no mango.

(They cross back to the group.)

CHARACTER 6 *(smilingly)*: Surely—surely you must be thinking there must be a fine technique involved in naming things. Aha! Have you thought of who ever named a rose a rose? Or a horse a horse? Why not a horse or a rose or a rose for a horse. What is that you say? They don't smell the same? Animal, Mineral, Vegetable, Animal....

(Walks away.)

CHARACTER 4: Right, how right you are. One day she came to me to ask what it was I fed her daughter that made her rave so. And you know, there's nothing I cook that she doesn't cook herself but the difference is I let the kid eat and don't watch none that she eat this and eat that. I feed her ice cream and if she wants another piece of pie, another piece of pie she gets.

CHARACTER 5 *(steps forward)*: As—*(raises a lecturing finger)* as Webster defines it, Metaphysics is that branch of science which treats of first principles, including the science of being which is Ontology and of the —*(faltering)* of the origin and structure of the universe which is Cosmology which is always intimately linked with the theory of knowledge which is Epistemology. *(He walks back to the group. Arms linked, they step forward to walk leisurely across stage apron, each ringing a handbell.)*

CHARACTER 3: It's time. It's time. It's time.... *(They walk back to the group.)*

CHARACTER 7 *(running forward)*: I want another wengo, Mommy!

CHARACTER 8: Mango, dearest, here. And wipe your face please.

CHARACTER 7 *(gesturing)*: Wipe, wipe, please, please.

CHARACTER 8: Oh, thank you Mommy.

CHARACTER 7: Thank you Mommy.

CHARACTER 8: Welcome, sweetheart.

CHARACTER 7: Welcome, sweetheart.

(Child runs back, mother follows.)

CHARACTER 3: Well, after all, she's just seven. You don't tell her to worry about her figure that early.

CHARACTER 4: How right you are. She'll have a lot of worrying to do—then. *(They both look down at their figures and burst out laughing.)*

CHARACTER 1 *(crosses downstage)*: Put it down over there.

CHARACTER 2 *(follows)*: Watch it, watch your hands. Ya don't want no lady fingers for dinner.

CHARACTER 1: Oops, steady to the right. Dat's it!

CHARACTER 3: Yeah, right. Let her enjoy it while she can, I always say.

CHARACTER 4: Right.

CHARACTER 3: Hey, you should see my cats. Darlings, darlings. . . .

CHARACTER 4: Oh, how many you got?

CHARACTER 3: Two—they're the cutest you ever saw.

CHARACTER 4: Well, we must get our cats together sometime.

CHARACTER 3: You got cats?

CHARACTER 4: A cat.

CHARACTER 3: Oh.

CHARACTER 4: Our apartment is very small.

CHARACTER 3: Oh, I see.

(They walk back.)

CHARACTER 5 *(steps forward, raises a lecturing finger)*: In other words, in other words, as Aaron writes, if we are to make an analysis of Marx, it is impossible to define the political regime simply by the class supposedly exercising the power. The political regime of capitalism cannot be defined by the power of the monopolists any more than the political regime of the socialist can be defined by the power of the proletarist. In the capitalist system, it is not the monopolist who personally exercises power; and in the socialist regime, it is not the proletariat which personally exercises power. *(Walks back.)*

CHARACTER 6 *(walks forward, spreading his arms)*: It is the essence. The essence! When a Chinese painter paints a duck, for instance, it is not a duck, it is not a *particular* duck, it is *all* the ducks he had ever seen flying, swimming, waddling around. In short, when he feels he is ready to paint, the duck he paints is the *essence* of *all* ducks.

CHARACTER 1 *(steps forward)*: Is it over there? I don't wanna tap it in.

CHARACTER 2: How's dat? Solid?

CHARACTER 1: Yeah, solid, man.

CHARACTER 9 *(crosses the stage apron on roller skates, a mike boom in one hand and a TV script in the other. His face is lit up with a wide*

TV *smile)*: DID YOU SAY YOU'RE LONELY? YOUR BOYFRIEND OR YOUR GIRLFRIEND IS DRIFTING AWAY? WELL LISTEN, USE NO-WORRY MOUTH-WASH. INSOLENT NO-WORRY MOUTHWASH. HURRY, HURRY, SO YOU CAN FORGET TO WORRY!

(He skates back.)

CHARACTER 7 *(running)*: Mommy, Mommy, Mommy!

CHARACTER 8: Oh, do stop running around in circles! And what is it this time?

CHARACTER 7 *(stops SC)*: I wanna pee!

CHARACTER 8: Hold it sweetie, we're almost there.

CHARACTER 7: I wanna pee, pee.

CHARACTER 8: Hold it, OK, that's Mommy's good baby. OK, Mommy?

CHARACTER 7: OK, Mommy.

(They walk away.)

CHARACTER 4: We didn't plan on getting one except one afternoon close to quitting time, two secretaries from downstairs came up with this kitten, see. They were going to throw it out of the building. Would I like to have it? I said I'll take it home for the meantime. So we got an empty box, cut a hole on the side. There I was on the bus with this meowing box on my lap and everyone looking for where the sound was coming from. My husband took one look at it then gave me a look that said are you nuts? Then the kitten curled around his foot and went to sleep. All right, my dear husband says, you can keep her until Christmas. That was three Christmases ago.

CHARACTER 3: Well, you know how it goes, you don't own a cat. . . .

CHARACTER 4: Yap, a cat owns you.

(They walk away.)

CHARACTER 5 *(steps forward, raises a lecturing finger)*: Walinowski wrote, "The outlook of the individual folklorist inheres in his pro-fessional habits. Students of literature generally conceive of folklore as the literature of the non-literate people and treat recorded folk-lore analytic techniques that are in vogue in literary circles. Compa-rative linguists discover raw materials for the study of exotic languages in the text of folktales that have been recorded in the original language.

Cultural anthropologists envision folklore as the embodiment of popular traditions, the symbolic representation of social organization and a key to the mentality of the people from whom specific folk material are obtained. Psychoanalysts ransack folklore and emerge convinced that the symbolizing activities of the human psycho are everywhere the same."

(He departs.)

CHARACTER 6 *(steps forward)*: Changes, changes. Why even languages change. Did you know, for instance, that the word stink began as a respectable member of the English language? It was a compliment then to say that your perfume stinks. Yes, beware the changes, changes....

(He moves away.)

CHARACTER 1 *(tapping an imaginary surface)*: Yeah, solid as rock.

CHARACTER 2 *(looking around)*: Ya know, it won't be so bad if we didn't have this damn library here.

CHARACTER 1: Can't ya push them?

CHARACTER 2: Whadda ya mean push? There must be millions of these gadamn books here.

CHARACTER 1 *(scratching his head)*: Yeah, we'd have room without this hell's whole stack of books I won't confoose my only God-given mind with.

CHARACTER 2: Ya said it, Junior.

(They move away.)

CHARACTER 3 *(waving some photographs)*: Here, here, I just got some photos. Here they are, the darlings. They're really lovely.

CHARACTER 4: Say, look at all that color!

CHARACTER 3: And look at this. Will you look at this one.

CHARACTER 4: But they're absolutely lovely!

CHARACTER 3: See this one, that's Busie. She was reaching out for the camera.

CHARACTER 4: Now, isn't that sweet.

CHARACTER 3: I took all 36 shots, would you believe it? Finished up the whole roll.

(They start to go.)

CHARACTER 4: You don't say. Lovely cats, lovely, lovely.

CHARACTER 3: Yep. Just shoot, shoot, shoot. Must get all these tricks in living color.

CHARACTER 4: Well, you must. Cats are even cuter than babies!

CHARACTER 2 *(passing both hands on an imaginary wall)*: Yep. Here. Drive it through here, I think.

CHARACTER 1: Are ya crazy? Dat's thin wall. *(Tapping)* Hear dat?

CHARACTER 2: Yeah, whaddaya know. Sounds hollow.

CHARACTER 1: Like what's on top of your shoulders.

CHARACTER 2: Look who's talking—Mr. Einstein.

(Both move away.)

CHARACTER 7 *(about to cry)*: I feel cold, Mommy.

CHARACTER 8: Didn't I tell you to hold it?

CHARACTER 7: Feel cold, Mommy.

CHARACTER 8: You should be. Oh whattamess.

CHARACTER 7 *(they start to move away)*: Carry, Mommy?

CHARACTER 8: Oh, sweet, walk please. We don't want to spoil Mommy's pretty dress, do we? Oh whattamess!

CHARACTER 7: Sticky, sticky, Mommy.

CHARACTER 8: Oh, whattamess!

CHARACTER 1 *(tapping)*: This is it. *(Pointing at imaginary wall.)*

CHARACTER 2: What?

CHARACTER 1: The spot, the very spot, the very exact spot, stoopid! *(Tapping again.)* Hear that?

CHARACTER 2: Yeah, man, yeah, Solid!

CHARACTER 10: Yahoo, brother, and wow! What a drag?

CHARACTER 11 *(close behind)*: What?

CHARACTER 10: Whee, man, I said wanna drag?

CHARACTER 11: It's not *the* thing?

CHARACTER 10: Can you believe, *it is?*

CHARACTER 11: OHBOYOHBOYOHBOYOHBOY!

3 CHARACTERS *(ringing bells in unison, leisurely)*: It's time. It's time. It's time. It's time.

CHARACTER 10: OK, it's your turn.

(They both turn and solemnly face the audience, their mouths turn up into big smiles. Behind them a mammoth projection of a human skull, appears on the left side of the head.)

CHARACTER 5 *(steps forward)*: In music, these may be groupings of instruments belonging to the same family, such as the string quartet, or those of different families like the flute, cello and harp. To mention only a few customary combinations: trios, made of violin, cello and piano; the woodwind quintet, a combination of flute, oboe, clarinet and bassoon trio, etc., etc.. . ..

CHARACTER 6 *(follows)*: And what is love. Ah! As Keats wrote once,
They may talk of love in a cottage,
And bowers of trellised vine—
Of nature bewitchingly simple,
And milkmaids half divine. . .
But give me a sly flirtation,
By the light of a chandelier—
With music to play in the pauses,
And nobody very near.

(Both move away.)

CHARACTER 4 *(walks forward)*: He said he's coming. He said he'd love to come but.. . ..

CHARACTER 3: But what?

CHARACTER 4: He is worried about the cuisine. Can you imagine, that's how he said—he's worried about the cuisine.

CHARACTER 3 *(mimicking)*: Oh, Edna, you know I'd love to come but I'm worried about your cuisine, my dear. Well, what did you say?

CHARACTER 4: Well, I told him I'd prepare something really elegant— you know, spare ribs with oriental sauce, honey and all. Then fried rice and so on?

CHARACTER 3: I tell you! What you have to do these days to get them to come! For all that, I'd love to come myself.

(They start to move away.)

CHARACTER 4: Well, that's what you'll get anytime you decide to come.

CHARACTER 3: Thanks, Edna, you're so good to me.

CHARACTER 1 *(steps forward)*: Hand me the wires, willya?

CHARACTER 2: Oh-oh, here's dat damn problem all over again.

CHARACTER 1: As dat fellow T. S. Eliot says, "It's one noosance for another!" Right, Junior?

CHARACTER 2: Right, Professor.

CHARACTER 1: Hey, hey! Willya look at dat.

CHARACTER 2 *(looking at an imaginary object)*: What is it?

3 CHARACTERS *(cross stage apron, ringing handbells, a little less leisurely this time but still unhurried)*: It's time. It's time. It's time. It's time.

CHARACTER 1: It's a pretty pitchur.

CHARACTER 2: Yeah. I know dat is a pitchur. But whatsit?

CHARACTER 1: Saay, dat's somethin' ain't it?

CHARACTER 2: Yeah, dat's somethin' awright. But whatsit?

CHARACTER 1 *(straining to read)*: It says right here, Still Life, A Vase of Flowers by 'enri Ma—Ma—tis—si. Say?

CHARACTER 2: Ah well, if it says so. . . .

CHARACTER 5 *(steps forward, raises a lecturing finger)*: On freeing man his illusions, Freud in *The Future of an Illusion* said, "Perhaps those who do not suffer from the neurosis will need no intoxicant to deaden it. They will have to admit insignificance in the machinery of the universe, they can no longer be the center of creation, no longer the object of tender care on the part of a beneficent Providence. They will be in the same position as a child who has left the parental house where he was so warm and comfortable. But surely infantalism is destined to be surmounted. Men cannot remain children forever; they must in the end go out into *hostile life.* We may call this *education to reality."*

(He moves away.)

CHARACTER 1: Well, I see da flow'rs.

CHARACTER 2: Yeah, man, I see da vase.

CHARACTER 1: But what's dat paper 'anging on top?

CHARACTER 2: Where? Oh yeah, must be the Daily Noose. Can't be the Inquirer on account of its size.

CHARACTER 1: Yeah. *(Thoughtfully.)* Yeah.

(They both leave.)

CHARACTER 6 *(steps forward)*: What, you ask, is Paradise? In 1481, William Caxton, a translator of *Reynart the Foxe,* wrote that as developed by Christian fancy, the earthly Paradise (as distinguished from celestial Paradise) is the old garden of Eden, which lay in the Far East beyond the stream of Ocean. Mohammed said that Paradise is a dwelling place promised the faithful. And furthermore, Lord Byron observed that the Koran allots at least a third of Paradise to well-behaved women." *(Leaves.)*

CHARACTER 9 *(crosses the stage apron on roller skates, a mike boom in one hand and a TV script in the other. His face as usual, is lit up with a wide TV smile)*: NOTE ANYTHING LATELY? DO YOUR WIFE AND OFFICE MATES TURN AWAY WHEN YOU GO NEAR THEM? COULD IT BE THAT YOU NEED THIS NEW AND POWERFUL DEODORANT, NO WORRY. SEE HERE, IT LASTS HOUR AFTER HOUR AFTER HOUR. IT'S NEW! IT'S FORTIFIED! HURRY, COME AND SEE, NO WORRY.

(Skates away.)

CHARACTER 10: *(walks to SC)*: "War is the father of all things." Thucydides, circa 400 BC.

CHARACTER 11: *"Pax hominum genetrix, pax es custodia rerum. Pax regna ligat, pax congregat urbam."* Peace, creator of man, peace is the protector of everything. Peace binds kingdoms together, peace assembles the city." Pontanne, circa 1778.

CHARACTER 10: "The fate of nations is still decided by their wars." Frank Black, Chicago speech nominating Theodore Roosevelt as Republican candidate, June 22, 1904.

CHARACTER 11: "Peace in our time. First principle of the official mind." H. C. Bailey, *The Bishop's Crime.* Circa 1941.

CHARACTER 10: "God is always on the side of the biggest battalions." Voltaire, circa 1770.

CHARACTER 11: "It is the province of kings to cause wars, and of God to end it." Cardinal Reginald Pole to Henry VIII, circa 1540.

CHARACTER 10: "To wars, my boy, to wars!
He wears his honour in a box unseen,
That hugs his kicky-wicky here at home."
Shakespeare, *All's Well that Ends Well,* circa 1602.

CHARACTER 11: "Peace,
Dear Nurse of art, plenties and joyful births."
Shakespeare, *Henry V,* circa 1599.

CHARACTER 10: "War must be for the sake of peace." Aristotle, *Politics,* circa 330 BC.

CHARACTER 11: "Wars are not fought to change anything. They are fought to preserve the *status quo.*" Pierre van Paassen, *The Day Alone,* 1941.

CHARACTER 10: "War is a singular art, I have fought sixty battles and I learned nothing but what I know when I fought the first," Napoleon I, circa 1812.

(They start to move away.)

CHARACTER 11 *(stops as if he remembers something)*: Oh, yes. "I wish it cud be fixed up *(lowering his voice)* so's the man that starts the war could do the fighting." F. P. Dumne, *War and the War Makers,* circa 1899.

(Slowly the lights change and a third projection of the same mammoth size as the human head and human skull is projected on the background. It is also a human head, only this time it is the neural network.)

CHARACTER 3: Opening?

CHARACTER 4: The bargain sale. The once-in-a-year.

CHARACTER 3: Almost forgot, OK, let's go.

(They leave.)

CHARACTER 5 *(crosses to SC)*: We shall also need to assume that the standard deviation of the Y's for each X are the same regardless of the value X. This assumption will be discussed in connection with the topic of correlation since correlation is essentially a measure of spread about the regression line.

CHARACTER 6 *(follows)*: According to a book on Zen Buddhism, a master was asked by one of his disciples to define what Zen Buddhism is. The master said, turn to the next page and there you will find the definition. The pupil did as told and found a white, blank page there. What are we to interpret from this? Ah, could we say, may we say, because it contained nothing, it could be anything or everything? Or perhaps, a futile nothingness?

CHARACTER 7: And what's the ending. Mommy?

CHARACTER 8 *(reading)*: Well, it says here, And so they caught the bad witch, poured the boiling, molten lead into her ear, got the pitchfork and caught her in one sweep and while Gretel held the door of the oven open, Hansel threw the screaming witch into the red roaring flames. Ohhh.

CHARACTER 7: Why, Mommy?

CHARACTER 8: Nothing, sweet, Mommy's just getting a little sick in stomick.

CHARACTER 7: Why, Mommy?

CHARACTER 8: On account of the ending, sweetheart.

CHARACTER 7: Very pretty ending, Mommy, why?

CHARACTER 8: Sweetheart, will you please stop asking Mommy so many questions?

CHARACTER 7: Why, Mommy?

CHARACTER 8: Because life would be so simple if you stop asking so many questions. Just stay quiet, listen and obey, and no questions please.

CHARACTER 7: Why, Mommy?

CHARACTER 8: Oh, I give up. *(Goes.)*

CHARACTER 7: Why, Mommy, but why? *(Follows.)*

3 CHARACTERS *(cross stage apron, ringing bells in unison)*: It's time, It's time! It's time!

CHARACTER 1 *(crosses to SC)*: If I gotta listen, I gotta listen. OK, shoot....

CHARACTER 2: OK, now my wife's a librarian as ya know?

CHARACTER 1: And so?

CHARACTER 2: Well, do ya or dontcha want to hear it?

CHARACTER: 1: OK, OK, I'm listening.

CHARACTER 2: Well, one day a priest came over to her desk and asked for a book called, *The Sex Life of a Parish Priest.* My wife says if der's such a one, she shoulda see it first. She opens all da packages, see.

CHARACTER 1: There's a problem, da pump lost its prime. Gotta be sure there's no air in da system. How come is it dat ya 'ave all da time to shoot da breeze when there's so much scraps waiting to be picked around here?

CHARACTER 2: OK, OK, quit biggie bossie. Want me to take a boat to Shanghai, OK? I stay away from Peking.

CHARACTER 1: Willya cut it out. Jesus I wish I've da time.

(They start to go.)

CHARACTER 2: OK, pick, pick *(bending to pick up imaginary objects)* pick.

CHARACTER 5 *(steps forward)*: On June 16, 1945, the Scientific Panel working on the Atomic Project, made the following conclusion, "With regard to these general aspects of the use of atomic energy, it is clear that we, as scientific men, have no proprietary rights. It is true that we are among the few citizens who have had occasion to give thoughtful consideration to these problems during the past few years. We have however, no claim to special competence in solving the political, social and military problems which are presented by the advent of atomic power."

CHARACTER 9 *(crosses on roller skates, equipped as before, his face lit up with the usual wide* TV *smile):* LADIES AND GENTLEMEN, ARE YOU TIRED OF NOISES FROM CARS? JET PLANES? BABIES? THEN HURRY, GET NO-WORRY EARPLUGS AND PUT SILENCE IN YOUR EARS. AH, PEACE! USE NO-WORRY EARPLUGS AND AT LAST, AT LONG LAST, HEAR YOURSELF THINK! REMEMBER OUR BRAND, N-O W-O-R-R-Y!

CHARACTER 6 *(steps forward):* Remember the opening lines of the *Iliad?* "Sing the wrath, O Goddess, the baleful wrath of Achilles son of Peleus, that laid on the Achaean ten thousand sorrows, and sent away goodly souls of heroes to Hades, and themselves it gave to dogs and all the birds; and the counsel of Zeus was fulfilled, from the day when first Atreides, king of men, and the divine Achilles quarrelled and stood apart. Who among the gods set them twain to fight." *(Shouts.)* Who set them twain to fight?

CHARACTER 3 *(steps forward):* Was that a sale!

CHARACTER 4: Was it ever! Did you see me fighting with that lady? It was fun!

CHARACTER 3: I got some lovely chains for my cats.

CHARACTER 4: They're all you think about.

CHARACTER 3: Well, look who's talking.

CHARACTER 4: Me, I sometimes detest them.

CHARACTER 3: But all this time—you never told me. But why?

CHARACTER 4: Can't stand them sometimes.

CHARACTER 3: Oh?

CHARACTER 4: I find them kinda indiscreet.

CHARACTER 3: Indiscreet?

CHARACTER 4: Yeah, on account of they clean their parts in front of company, you know.

CHARACTER 1: Will you stop clowning and pick all those loose wires. Jesus Christ!

CHARACTER 2: Righto, Professor, here goes.

CHARACTER 1: And the equipment too, hear? And lock up the box. I don't want no missing screwdriver in the morning.

CHARACTER 2: Screwdriver, he says. Was more'n dat last time.

CHARACTER 1: Whadda ya say?

CHARACTER 2: I said it was more 'n dat last time. Somebody stole my transistor radio.

CHARACTER 1: OK, SO OK. Sure you locked da box?

CHARACTER 2: Sure, locked da box, locked da storeroom, wanna lock up da building too?

CHARACTER 1: Don't be funny. And remember to come on time tomorrow.

CHARACTER 2: Yep, Boss. I'll put the alarm clock right under my pillow.

CHARACTER 1: Ya do dat and let's see what happens.

CHARACTER 2 *(beating with his fingers)*: Ya'll see awright. Tick-tock-tick-tock-tick all night long!

CHARACTER 7 *(crosses to SC)*: Another story, Mommy?

CHARACTER 8: Mommy had enough stories for one night, love. Now go to sleep. Goodnight, Mommy.

CHARACTER 7: Goodnight, Mommy.

CHARACTER 8: Goodnight, love.

CHARACTER 10: Repent, repent! Repent now and avoid the rush later! Repent now! Hurry, hurry!

CHARACTER 11: Well, hurry up so we don't miss the first show.

CHARACTER 10: Repent! Repent! Look, man, they paid me an hour to wear this sign. So an hour it is. Repent now and avoid the rush later, folks!

CHARACTER 11: Can't you cut it down to half, man? The show's starting in fifteen minutes!

CHARACTER 10: You know I can't do that when I sign my name on a contract. Repent! Repent! They won't hire me again, man!

CHARACTER 11: OK, but you're going to miss all the chicks!

CHARACTER 10 *(agitated)*: OK, go ahead, willya. Repent! Repent!

CHARACTER 9 *(crosses the stage apron on roller skates, equipped as before. His face is lit up with a wide TV smile)*: THE WEATHER'S GOING TO BE HOTTER AND HOTTER, AND HOTTER! HA-HA-HA! THERE'S A THICK SMOG FLOATING OVER THE PACIFIC AREA. AND ANOTHER'S RISING OVER THE CHINA SEA. AND FOR A FAST ROUNDUP ON THE WEATHER, HERE GOES:

> CHICAGO'S BEARABLE
> MOSCOW'S TOLERABLE
> PARIS' MISERABLE
> NEW YORK'S DISGUSTING
> LONDON HAS DISAPPEARED!

WEAR YOUR MASKS, WEAR YOUR MASKS IS MY ADVICE. BUY THE N-O W-O-R-R-Y MASKS! HURRY! HURRY!

3 CHARACTERS *(rush to SC, start ringing handbells sharply, insistently)*: TIME'S NOW! TIME'S NOW! TIME'S NOW!

CHARACTER 1 *(sharply)*: What did dey say?

CHARACTER 2: TIME'S NOW?

CHARACTER 3: Did you hear what they said?

CHARACTER 4: TIME'S NOW?

(Lines are said in rapid fire fashion, each line punctuated by the ringing of handbells.)

CHARACTER 5: They said what?

CHARACTER 6: TIME'S NOW?

CHARACTER 7: What did they say, Mommy?

CHARACTER 8: TIME'S NOW?

(Lines are said in rapid fire fashion, each line punctuated by the ringing of handbells.)

3 CHARACTERS *(keep on ringing handbells)*: TIME'S NOW! TIME'S NOW! TIME'S NOW!

(There is a flash of white light.)

CHARACTER 3: What's that?

CHARACTER 4: Just a bit of lightning, I guess....

CHARACTER 5: Did you see that bright flash?

CHARACTER 6: Blinding, wasn't it?

CHARACTER 5: Came from the east, I think.

(Flashes of white light, then a deafening explosion and the whole stage becomes immersed in red. Pause. The Characters raise their arms, remove their masks simultaneously and place them under their armpits as fencers do. Underneath there are no features except for the eye sockets and their gaping mouths. Half of their faces are covered with white stockings pulled taut over their hair. They all look alike. Their movements are slow, somnolent but precisely executed as though a fencing master is directing, counting out for them. The handbells continue ringing.)

CHARACTER 1: Well, see you tomorrow, Junior.

CHARACTER 2: So long, Senior! Now where did I park da car?

CHARACTER 3: See you for coffee?

CHARACTER 4: In the same place, OK?

CHARACTER 5: Now, take Monet....

CHARACTER 6: Consider the Spirit, dear people....

CHARACTER 7: Goodnight, Mommy.

CHARACTER 8: Goodnight, love.

CHARACTER 9: Remember NO WORRY! HURRY! HURRY!

(Blue light pervades the stage now. The three images projected on the background move toward each other, fuse for a few seconds and disintegrate. All characters in shadow except for characters 10 and 11.)

CHARACTER 10: Actually it gets cooler as it rises.

CHARACTER 11: Yeah, man, can you beat that. That's really beautiful!

(The handbells stop ringing.)

(Blackout)

[END OF PLAY]

(1969-72)

Glossary

"*Aba hindi ganyan...*" "Don't take it that way..."

Acacia, n. (bot.) Any *mimosaceous* tree of the genus *Acacia*, cultivated for its fine wood and spreading branches for shade.

Adobo, n. A popular or national Philippine dish of pork and chicken cooked in vinegar, pepper corns, crushed garlic and often with soy sauce.

"*Ako ang may sala.*" "I bear (the burden of) the guilt" or "I am guilty."

Aling, n. Aunt. Tagalog for woman.

Anak, n. Offspring, son or daughter.

Andas, n. Spanish term for a stand for statues of saints, set on wheels for processions.

Apo, n. Honorific patriarch, lord or superior.

Arbulario, n. (var. *Herbulario*) Herb doctor.

Arroz Caldo, n. (var. *aroskaldo*) Rice porridge with pieces of chicken sauteed in garlic onion and ginger.

Aswang, n. (var. *asuwang*) Folkloric evil creature, said to be capable of assuming diverse forms, specially human form with horse hooves and tail.

Ate, n. Honorific for an elder sister. (var. *Manang, Kaka, Manay, Atsi, Achi, Manding*)

Balut, n. Boiled duck's eggs with embryo, considered a delicacy and popular with beer drinkers.

Banaba, n. (bot.) Timber producing deciduous tree also cultivated for its medicinal and beautiful light purple flowers.

"*Bata Batuta,*" "*Hoy, bata batuta...*" An expression used to taunt, literally, "Hey, boy with a stick..."

Buri, n. Straw used for basketry and hat-making from the buri palm tree.

Cabesa, n. (var. *Kabesa*) Sp. for head; honorific for leader or chieftain of tribe or community.

Carinderia, n. (var. *karinderia*) A native restaurant serving hot viands and rice, usually over a counter.

Chopsuey, n. A Chinese dish featuring a mixture of meat and seafood with slightly cooked green vegetables and cauliflower.

"*Diyasking ire . . . ,*" Roughly equivalent to, "Darn you . . ."

Few-ne-rar-ia, n. Actually, *funeraria* or funeral parlor.

Garrote, n. Strangling apparatus for capital punishment.

Gumamela, n. (bot.) *Hibiscus rosasinensis,* hibiscus China rose, cultivated for its beautiful flowers and used as hedge or fence.

"*Gusto kong palitan.*" "I would like to change (my plea)."

"*Hinay-hinay . . . ,*" "Slowly, very slowly . . ."

Inay, n. (var. *Nanay, Inang, Ima*) Mother.

Ineng, n. (var. *Nene, Inday, Nini, Ining, Ading*) Appelation for young girl.

Ipil-ipil, n. (bot.) *Leucaena glauca,* a slender tree with thin leaves and broom seeds, used for reforestation work. The bark produces brown dye, the seeds are roasted and substituted for coffee and making bags and the leaves provide good feed for goats.

Itay, n. (var. *Tatay, Itang, Tata*) Father.

Ka, pron. (var. *Ikaw*) You.

Kadena de Amor, Sp. name for flowering vine with white or pink blossoms.

Kaing, n. Bushel basket of woven bamboo with wide open mouth and two opposite handles.

Kalesa, n. (var. *Calesa, Carromata, Caretela, Kalesin, Karumata, Tiburin*) Horse-drawn chaise.

Kapatid, n. (var. *Atid, Utol, Kaputol, Manong, Manang*) Brother or Sister. Literally cut from the same material.

Kapre, n. Sp. for a folkloric giant who appears at night seated on rooftops and smoking giant cigars. The Philippine *kapre* is said to originate from the giant soldiers known as Kaffirs from Kaffraria, a province of Persia.

Kasama, n. Companion, comrade, a person with whom one keeps company often.

"Kayo po ang bahala..." "You make the decision for me..."

"Konteng pasensiya lamang." "Have a little patience" or "Be patient."

"Kung hanap mo ay santo, nasa langit ang mga 'yon." "If it's saints you're looking for, (you won't find them on earth) they're in heaven."

Kuya, n. (var. *Koyang, Kaka, Manong, Manoy*) Appelation for an elder brother.

Lambanog, n. Palm wine.

Lechon de leche, n. Roast suckling pig.

Lintik, n. Lightning. Has very strong emotional connotation when used as an expletive in " Anak ng lintik!" or "Son of lightning!"

Liwanag at Dilim, Light and Darkness by Emilio Jacinto, the Boy General of the Philippine Revolution of 1898.

Lola, n. (var. *Lelang, Impo*) Grandmother.

"Mabuhay!" "Long live!"

Mahjong, n. A Chinese game consisting of cube ivories with symbols of sticks, balls, flowers and Chinese characters incised on them.

Mang, Honorific for Sir. A title of respect when used before one's first name.

Mangkukulam, n. Witchdoctor.

Manong, n. Sp. for *Hermano,* meaning brother. In the Philippines, it could also mean a male devotee.

Media noche, Midnight.

Morcon, n. Meat sliced and rolled with hard boiled eggs, sausage and strips of pork and stewed in tomato sauce and potatoes.

"Na lang..." "To this point only..."

Nanay, n. Tagalog address for Mother.

Novena, n. Prayer offering for favor asked.

"Panahon pa ni Methusalem." Meaning, it is obsolete. It happened during the time (or within the lifetime) of Methuselah, a patriarch said to have lived 969 years.

Pansit, n. A Chinese dish of noodles mixed with small cuts of pork, sausage, chicken, shrimps and vegetables.

Papag, n. Bamboo bed.

Piko, n. Hopscotch; a native game of skip and jump while kicking a flat stone without touching the lines.

Pintakasi, n. A popular Philippine game involving trained game cocks, usually accompanied by betting.

Po, The more formal form; *Ho* being the more familiar form used to express respect to elders and superiors.

"Putang ina..." "Your mother is a bitch."

Sawali, n. Woven bamboo splits used for walling partitions.

"Sige..." intrj. "Go on" or "Go ahead (do it)."

"Sinungaling, bayaan ninyo ako." "Liar, let me go."

Susmaria, (var. *Susmariahusep, Santisima*) Jesus Mary.

Tamarind, n. (bot.) tamarind (tree and fruit).

Tia, n. (var. *Tiya, Ale*) Aunt.

Tonta, Stupid.

Tuba, n. Wine made from the juice of palms.

"Ulupong, kamatayan ahas..." "Cobra, death to a snake."

Viuda, n. Sp. Widow.

"Walang biro ito." "This is no joking matter" or "This is serious."